**Techno thieves. Virtual vandals.
Cyber sleuths.
But even in the future,
crime doesn't always pay. . . .**

"Pein Bek Longpela Telimpon"—Waghi knew how to bargain—after all, he had dealt in pigs many times. But the Papua New Guinea tribesman wasn't too familiar with paper money. He knew that the briefcase he stole from some Europeans must be worth something, and when a voice came from one of the tiny, mysterious devices inside, he fell under the influence of that most universal of human emotions . . . greed.

"The Mojave Two-Step"—In Vegas of the future, life is glittering but dangerous. Crossing the wrong person could get you tied to the back of a slot machine walking into the deadly, burning desert. But Coker knew Lady Luck was smiling on him, even after he met the one-armed bandit walking down the highway. . . .

"The White City"—The serial killer is a thing of the past, a lurid historical oddity, since the authorities now have the ability to catch a murderer before he disposes of his very first victim. Unless an assiduous student of history can find a way of circumventing the process. . . .

FUTURE CRIMES

EDITED BY

*Martin H. Greenberg
and John Helfers*

DAW BOOKS, INC.

DONALD A. WOLLHEIM, FOUNDER

375 Hudson Street, New York, NY 10014

ELIZABETH R. WOLLHEIM
SHEILA E. GILBERT
PUBLISHERS

First Printing, October 1999
1   2   3   4   5   6   7   8   9   10

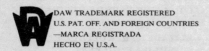

ACKNOWLEDGMENTS

Introduction © 1999 by John Helfers

Pein Bek Longpela Telimpon © 1999 by Alan Dean Foster

The Mojave Two-Step © 1999 by Norman Partridge

Shakespeare Minus One © 1999 by Barbara Paul

Good Repair © 1999 by Craig Shaw Gardner

The Kidnapping of Roni Tahr © 1999 by Alan Rodgers

In Memoriam © 1999 by Mike Stotter

Sleep that Burns © 1999 by Jerry Sykes

The Death of Winston Foster © 1999 by R. Davis

Glory Hand in the Soft City © 1999 by Jay Bonansinga

The Crime of Transfiguration © 1999 by Will Murray

Pia and the King of Siam © 1999 by Janet Berliner

The Serpent Was More Subtle © 1999 by Tom Piccirilli

Tinker's Last Case © 1999 by Ron Goulart

All the Unlived Moments © 1999 by Gary Braunbeck

The White City © 1999 by Alan Brennert

Setting Free the Daughters of Earth © 1999 by Peter Crowther

CONTENTS

INTRODUCTION

by John Helfers

Warning: the following introduction is not for the faint of heart.

Having said that, let's talk about crime.

If one looks up the definition of crime in any dictionary, a variation of the following will often be found: "An act or omission of a forbidden act or omission of a duty governed by law which makes the offender liable to be punished by that law." Even that specific language cannot even begin to cover the gamut of crimes that man is capable of committing against his fellow man. Ever since Cain picked up a rock or piece of wood or clenched his fist, and with malice aforethought, struck down his brother Abel (for those who prefer to uphold the evolutionary side of history, just imagine a caveman coveting his neighbor's mate or dwelling, and picking up his club before going to pay that neighbor a visit, with the same result), humans have been plotting to commit crimes against nature, against humanity, and, in several cases, crimes against our very souls.

For it is the invasive nature of most crimes that shock us, an assault of our homes, of our privacy, of our very bodies, shattering the peaceful, tranquil world that we once knew. Even if we just witness a crime, there is an overwhelming feeling of having been invaded, that nothing is safe anymore, that there is nowhere to run, nowhere to hide. And when the crime is senseless, such as the occasional rash of mass public shootings that seem to crop up at least once a year (and repeating at an alarmingly rapid rate), then the crime is even more horrifying, because we stop to look around us and wonder: *who's going to snap next, and will I be in the same room with him or her when they go?*

Of course, with the advance of technology, crime has become easier to commit. Clubs and rocks have given way to pistols and hunting rifles, and nowadays, who's going to argue with a bullet? Complicated con games are being replaced by computers, with which it is possible to rob thousands of people without ever seeing their faces. As life grows more complicated with each day, it will be easier to let things, information and such, slip through the cracks. And there will always be enterprising people who will use those found things for their own benefit.

When we first came up with the idea for this book, we were curious as to the types of stories we would receive, whether they would be full of high-tech gadgetry and victimless crimes, or if the writers we asked to contribute still thought that crimes would be committed face-to-face, one person against another. We were pleasantly (or perhaps unpleasantly would be a better choice) surprised to discover an intriguing mix of both the high tech and low tech, from the thieves who score an unusual haul in Norman Partridge's story to a deadly culture clash as envisioned by Alan Dean Foster. No matter how futuristic the society, and how technologically advanced the law enforcement, somewhere, sometime, someone will always be committing a crime.

PEIN BEK LONGPELA TELIMPON

by Alan Dean Foster

Alan Dean Foster was born in New York City and raised in Los Angeles. He has a bachelor's degree in Political Science and a Master of Fine Arts in Cinema from UCLA. He has traveled extensively around the world, from Australia to Papua New Guinea. He has also written fiction in just about every genre, and is known for his excellent movie novelizations. Currently, he lives in Prescott, Arizona, with his wife, assorted dogs, cats, fish, javelina, and other animals, where he is working on several new novels and media projects.

WAHGI first heard the muffled screams and angry curses as he was rummaging through the dumpster. Not that this was unusual. Late at night in Boroko there were frequent fights between men who had blown their weekly paycheck on cheap beer staggering drunkenly out of illegal pubs, between tired whores and their customers, between predatory taxi drivers battling over fares with irate passengers unable to pay—even the chickens that clucked and pecked their way across the central square around which the rundown shops were situated were usually in rotten mood.

But this encounter was different.

Instead of trade pidgin, the combatants were spewing an inarticulate mush of proper English, Strine, and several foreign tongues Wahgi did not recognize. That was notable. After four PM, the few tourists who braved the square in search of artifacts, Sepik River wood carvings, and illegal bird-of-paradise plumes were usually gone. After five, when the last European-owned stores padlocked their security screens for the night, only local people were left. To hear European tongues this late at night suggested goings-on that were far from normal.

Like everyone he knew, Wahgi was intensely curious about the wonderful things white people carried around with them. He was among the first of his tribe to come down from the Highlands into the capital in search of work to help support his family. Highland people learned quickly, and it did not take a village Big Man to realize that these wonderful objects could only be obtained with a pocketful of money. Yams were not accepted currency in the stores, and only rarely would a sympathetic checker, perhaps not long down from the Highlands himself, accept a pig. If anyone had told Wahgi a year ago that it was better to possess a fistful of brightly colored paper than a stockade full of pigs, he would have scratched at his arse-grass and looked upon them as if they had taken leave of their senses.

But the fact that the Highland people had only made contact with western civilization in the 1930s did not mean that they were irredeemably ignorant. Only isolated.

What bad thing could possibly happen to him if he just went to see what was going on? Certainly he wasn't having much luck rifling the contents of the smelly dumpster. Stretching himself to his full five foot five, he boosted himself up and out and followed the sounds of dissension. Scattered among the shouts and curses like corn seeds between rows of sweet potatoes was much grunting and snorting. It reminded him of rutting pigs crammed into a pen too small for them.

There were four men fighting in the dark covered accessway that ran between the Ha Chin dry goods store and the *niuspepa* shop. Even though he couldn't read, Wahgi liked to go into the *niuspepa* shop to look at the pictures in the glossy magazines, especially the ones that showed women of all colors in skimpy clothing. That is, he did until the shop manager chased him out, realizing that the hick Highlander had no money.

Concealing himself in a corner near the back alley that intersected the accessway, he watched the fight in silence. Even though he could see no *longpela naips,* or machetes as they were called in the Aussie stores, he could tell that the fight was serious. Though he couldn't see which of the four men was wounded, fresh blood, black and wet, was running on the cracked concrete, mixing with the betel nut juice stains. He wondered what they were fighting about, here too late at night in an unlit passage in a poor shopping area like Boroko.

Then he saw the suitcase. It was much smaller than the ones the ground crews unloaded from the planes at the airport. Too small to hold much of anything in the way of clothing, which is what he knew white people usually carried in their baggage. The small suitcase lay off to one side, propped against the grill of iron bars that protected the *niuspepa* store. Was it worth four men fighting over? If so, it might be full of something valuable. Maybe, he thought excitedly, money paper.

He gauged his chances. The men were wholly occupied with one another. In the village he had been a good hunter, bringing back tree kangaroos, monitor lizards, rats, hornbills, and crowned pigeons. Like all Huli Highlanders he was small and stocky. If they saw him, would they forget about their own fight and come

after him? Though new to Port Moresby, he was confident he knew the hidden places of Boroko better
than any European.

Besides, he hadn't eaten since yesterday.

Waiting until he thought the moment just right, he
slid out of the shadows and along the wall, keeping
low. Providentially, the suitcase had a handle fastened
to the top. He was a little surprised to find that the
case was made of metal instead of the soft fabrics and
leathers he was used to seeing at the airport, but it
was not particularly heavy. Small in stature the Huli
might be, but every man had muscle as dense as the
stump of a mahogany tree.

Gripping the suitcase in a fist of iron, he slipped
back the way he had come, keeping the black iron
security bars against his spine. None of the comban-
tants noticed him. As soon as he reached the alley, he
turned and ran. That was something else Highlanders
were good at.

He did not stop until he was halfway to the suburb
of Koki, where he shared a shack of salvaged wood
and tin with two other young men from the village.
Like all the buildings in Koki, it was built on stilts out
over the water. It was not a bad place for poor people
to live. No one could sneak up on you unless they had
a good, quiet boat, and the tide provided the services
the nonexistent sewage system could not.

Pausing on the Ela Beach road beneath the harsh
yellow lights of a British Petroleum station, he settled
down beneath a hibiscus bush to inspect his prize.
Even to his country eyes the case looked expensive.
Though small, the lock proved resistant to his probing.
But only momentarily.

One of the night attendants at the station was another Huli, not from Wahgi's village but a man he
knew casually. Though suspicious, the attendant lent
him the hammer and heavy screwdriver his fellow clan
member requested. He knew Wahgi wouldn't run off
with them. That would have put the attendant in deep

trouble with the station's owners, which would have turned into a payback situation against Wahgi's village. Every Highlander treated the ancient tradition of payback with extreme respect, and Wahgi was no exception.

Modern as it was, the lock eventually yielded to Wahgi's strength, persistence, and single-minded determination. After returning the tools, he went back into the bush to examine the case's contents. In these he was both disappointed and puzzled.

The case contained a number of small electronic devices that were as alien to Wahgi as if they had fallen from the moon. He knew what a radio was, and a television, and an airplane, because he had seen them up close, but otherwise his knowledge of contemporary twenty-first century technology was lamentably scant. Another section of the case was full of paper, but to his disgust and disappointment none of it was money. Though colorful, the papers were much too big to be currency; PNG, Aussie, or otherwise. He did not know what they were. Perhaps his roommates Gembogl and Kuikui might know, though they had spent little more time in Mosby than had he.

He was philosophical about his theft. The contents might be worthless, but the case itself was certainly worth something, even with a broken lock. Leaving it under the fragrantly flowering bush, he went once more into the station, this time to beg a length of used twine from his fellow Huli kinsman. With the lock broken, he needed something to secure the case.

When he returned, something inside was beeping persistently.

Slowly and with commendable caution, he opened the case. The noise was coming from one of the small electronic gadgets. Gingerly hefting the rectangular shape, he turned it over in his hands. It was about the size of two packs of cigarettes. On its front were a large number of illuminated buttons above which a small yellow light was blinking. This he eyed in as-

tonishment, wondering how anyone could manufac-
ture so small a bulb.

Could the device hurt him? He knew he should find
a way to stop the beeping, or he might draw unwanted
attention to himself. The Mosby police were not gentle
with thieves, especially those who stole from visiting
Europeans. He had seen how buttons could turn a
radio on and off. Perhaps one of the buttons on the
box could do the same to the insistent beeping sound.

Experimentally, he began pushing them one after
another. Each time he depressed a button, it responded with an electronic chirp, but the continuous
beeping never stopped—until he pushed one of the
buttons near the bottom. Not only did the nerve-
wracking beeping cease, but the yellow light turned
to green.

"Stavros, Stavros . . . *was ist mit ihnen los? Sprechen
sie,* dammit!"

Wahgi almost dropped the device. Then he realized
what it was: some kind of telephone, but unlike any
he had ever seen before. For one thing, it was infi-
nitely smaller than the ones that were fixed in the
public boxes. For another, it was attached to nothing.
From it issued a voice that was as clear as it was
unintelligible.

"Stavros!" The tone was angry and insistent.

Maybe, he thought, there might be a reward for
such a unique and therefore probably expensive telephone. Could he make the irate individual on the
other end understand him?

Leaning toward the device without knowing where
to direct his voice, he said in his best rudimentary
English, "Hello. Good morning. How are you? *Yupela
wantok me?*"

This resulted in a long silence from the tiny telephone, and Wahgi wondered if he had somehow broken it by speaking into it. Then the voice returned,
no longer irate but obviously confused. Confused
and curious.

"*Ya?* Stavros? So you are now speaking English? *Warum*—why?"

Stavros, Wahgi decided, must be the name of one of the four men who he had seen fighting. The owner of the case, or at least its keeper. And like the man on the other end of the line, he had spoken English— as well as other things.

"I no—I am not Stavros," he informed the telephone. "I am Wahgi."

There followed another extended pause that was broken by a stream of furious foreign syllables that the Huli decided he would not have been able to follow even if he had understood the alien tongue. Then another interlude, after which a new voice spoke. It was much more controlled, much calmer than its predecessor, and its English was far better. To Wahgi it sounded like American English, not Aussie or British, but he could not be certain. Sometimes it seemed to him that there were as many varieties of English as there were languages in Papua New Guinea.

"To whom am I speaking, please? You said that your name was Wahgi?"

"Yes." Wahgi was relieved to be talking to someone whom he could understand, and who might be able to understand him in return. But he suspected the person on the other end would have little or no knowledge of pidgin.

"Wahgi," the voice inquired in a sweetly reasonable tone, "where are you?"

"In Mosby—Port Moresby. The capital."

The voice faded, as if its owner was momentarily speaking to someone close to him. In the same room. Perhaps. "At least that fits." Louder, and obviously to Wahgi, it added, "Look at the bottom of the phone you are holding. There should be a word, or words, there. What does it say?"

Wahgi found the single word easily. "I see what you are talking about, but I do not know the word." He added apologetically, "I cannot read."

"How many words? Can you count?"

Of course he could count! Did the other man think he was empty-headed? "Just one."

"How many letters in the word?"

"Six."

A murmur of voices could be heard over the phone. "Good," the other man said. "Now, Wahgi, this is very important. Where did you find this telephone?"

The Huli considered, then decided to plunge ahead. How else was he to find out what the case and phone might be worth, or how big a reward he ought to ask for? "In a small suitcase."

The man's tone changed ever so slightly, but no so slightly that Wahgi failed to pick up on it. "Two men should have been watching this case and its contents. Do you know where they are?"

Wahgi looked up as a pair of fruit bats with four-foot wingspans settled into the tree alongside his resting place. On the busy road, cars and taxis whizzed past without stopping. "Yes. When I left them, they were fighting with two other men. In Boroko." He thought rapidly. "I took the suitcase for safekeeping."

"That was very clever of you, Wahgi. Very clever indeed. And I know that the case—it's called a brief-case, by the way—is safe with you. Now, my friends and I would like to have it back. If you will tell us where you are, we will send other men to take it off your hands."

"It is not heavy," the Huli replied with unconscious irony. "Will I get a reward?"

More muttering on the other end, a few violent words in that strange alien tongue that were overridden by still louder words from the English speaker, and then the voice was back on the line.

"We'll be glad to give you a reward, Wahgi. So long as you return the briefcase in good condition." Anxiety crept unbidden into the man's voice. "It is in good condition, isn't it?"

The Huli decided to be honest. "I broke the lock.

To make certain the contents were okay," he lied easily.

Rather than upset him, this seemed to amuse the other man. "That's all right, Wahgi. The lock is not important. There should be some papers in the brief-case. Papers with colored printing on them and brightly colored borders. Are they still there—in good condition?"

"Oh, yes," Wahgi assured him readily. "They have not been harmed at all."

Softer mutterings from behind the speaker. "That's just fine, Wahgi. Now, what would you like for a reward?"

Large numbers being foreign to traditional Huli culture, Wahgi stalled for time. What was larger than twenty? What was the briefcase, and more importantly, the pretty papers it held, worth to the man on the strange telephone?

"What is your name, and what is the name of your village?" How much should he ask for? He thought tensely. He had heard many numbers on the televisions in the pubs. Which one would be suitable?

For the second time, the other man sounded amused. "My name is Eric Werner von Maltzan, Wahgi, and I am speaking to you from the village of Zurich."

"Zurich. I do not know that village. Is it in Australia?" Australia was the only country Wahgi knew beyond Papua New Guinea.

"A little farther," von Maltzan told him. "About your reward?"

Wahgi had decided. "I want a million kina." "Million" was a term he had heard during sports programs, and it had sounded pretty big to him. Would it be too much? Were the telephone and the papers worth more? Having dealt in pigs, he knew how to bargain. You did not need a big education for that.

His request certainly had an effect on the other man, and those Wahgi believed to be in the room or hut with him. He could hear them arguing in their strange tongues. Crossing his legs under him and watching the flying foxes spit pits from the fruit they were peeling and eating, he waited patiently. With the lateness of the hour, traffic on the nearby main road was becoming infrequent.

Eventually von Maltzan came back on line. "That's about four hundred and fifty thousand American dollars, Wahgi. That's a great deal of money."

Wahgi did not know if it was, but decided to take the other man's word for it. After all, he reasoned, if von Maltzan knew about briefcases and telephones and colored papers, he should know something about money.

"That is the reward I want."

Again von Maltzan could be heard arguing with other men. "All right, Wahgi. You'll get your reward. Now, here's what I want you to do. Go to the airport. Not the public terminal. The private one next to it. In the main building you'll find. . . ."

"No."

The other man hesitated. "What's that?"

"No. I do not know what time it is in Zurich village, but it is very late here, and I am very tired. I am going home, to talk with my friends. Can you call me on this telephone later tonight?"

"Yes, but. . . ."

"Then that is what I want you to do." He started to put the phone back in the briefcase.

Entirely composed up to now, von Maltzan's voice began to crack. "No, Wahgi, *nein!* Don't do that! It's vital that you . . . !"

The Huli was pleased to discover that despite its tiny size, lack of a connecting cord, and strange appearance, the telephone still operated very much like the other telephones he had seen in use around the city. When he found the button that turned it off, he was delighted. The beeping that had so startled him at first and had precipitated the conversation resumed immediately. It continued until Wahgi found another button that turned it off for good. Satisfied, he put the device back in the briefcase and tied it up with the length of twine. Then he resumed his hike back to Koki, dashing across the two lanes of highway.

Gembogl and Kuikui were lying on their torn, bedbug-infested, salvaged mattresses when he arrived. Kuikui lit the single kerosene lantern and put his machete down as soon as he saw who was standing in the doorway.

"Where have you been, Wahgi? We were worried about you."

"Wake Gembogl. I have something show you both."

As the three men sat in a circle on the floor, Wahgi undid the twine and triumphantly showed them the contents of the case. "This is called a 'briefcase,'" he explained with the air of a new schoolteacher.

Not to be outdone, Kuikui added "Brief means 'small' in English."

"That makes sense. And this," he held up the satellite phone, "is a telephone."

A doubtful Gembogl took it and held it closer to the lantern. "It doesn't look like a phone."

"It is. I used it to talk to a man in a village called Zurich. He promised me a reward for finding the briefcase."

That caught his friends' attention. "How big a reward?" Kuikui asked.

"A million kina."

Gembogl burst out laughing. "*Wanem!* A million kina? For a briefcase and a bunch of papers?"

Kuikui was less skeptical. "Wahgi may be telling the truth. You know how peculiar Europeans are about their papers and things. I have seen them in the bank, fussing over them like women over shells."

"A million kina. We could buy car with that." Gembogl sounded wistful.

"Many cars." Kuikui was more economically learned than both of them.

"Then we agree on the amount?" Wahgi's gaze traveled from one man to another. They had shared privation and insults, hunger and spiteful taunts from the more sophisticated townsfolk. Now they would share in his reward.

Gembogl was shaking his head. He was the youngest of the three who had come down from the Highlands to seek work in the city. "I can't believe this. I just can't believe it. It's too good to be true. Of course we agree on the amount," he added as an afterthought.

Kuikui urged his friend. "Call this man back. Tell him we have discussed your proposal and we are all agreed."

"Yes, call him back," Gembogl said excitedly.

"I can't." Wahgi picked up the phone. "I don't know how to use this. But I think he will be calling me." So saying, he pressed the button that had successfully shut off the beeping. It recommenced instantly, as if it had never stopped.

"Now watch." Exaggerating his movements for maximum effect, the Huli pressed the button he had used to activate the device previously.

"This is Eric Werner von Maltzan calling for Wahgi. Eric Werner von Maltzan of Zurich calling for Wahgi of Port Moresby, PNG."

"See?" Proud of his newly acquired technical skill, Wahgi responded. "I am here, *pren* Eric. With two of my friends. How will you get my reward to me?"

"Just leave everything to me, Wahgi. I will take care of. . . ."

"Just a moment." It was Kuikui. He was staring at the open doorway and frowning. "I thought I heard something."

"We should be careful." Gembogl kept his voice down as the older man blew out the lantern. "A million kina is a lot of money."

"Yes. Wait here." Picking up his machete, Kuikui

moved purposefully toward the open doorway. His friends waited in the darkness.

"What is it?" The voice on the phone sounded more anxious than ever. "What's going on?"

"Probably nothing, *pren* Eric." Wahgi spoke in a whisper. "Just some noise outside. My friend Kuikui went to check on. . . ."

The staccato burst of sound splintered in the Huli's eardrums. He had heard that sound before, once during a riot and again during a military parade. It was the sound of a gun going off. An automatic gun that could fire many shots without stopping. Gembogl sprang for his machete while Wahgi grabbed the briefcase and stumbled toward the rear of the shack.

The voice on the phone never stopped talking. "Wahgi! What was that? It sounded like an uzi!"

"We are being shot at!" Clutching the phone in one hand and the briefcase in the other, Wahgi pushed up against the back wall of the shanty. Outside were plank walkways and below, the sewage-saturated part of the harbor that surged back and forth beneath Koki.

"In the briefcase!" the voice on the phone told him. "A plastic egg the size of a man's fist! Put it next to the phone." Fumbling among the devices and papers, Wahgi found the object described and did as he was told. An electronic tone sounded from the phone, in response to which a red light appeared on the side of the container.

"I did what you told me to," he stammered into the phone. "What do I do now?"

"Run, jump, get away, Wahgi—and throw it at the people with the guns!"

"Kuikui, Gembogl, run away!" he shouted. There was no reply as he tossed the container onto the floor and pushed through the flimsy rear wall of the shack. As he did so, three men burst through the doorway. Two were tall and European while the third was Melanesian, but no Highlander. A slim, fine-featured coastal man, Wahgi saw in the glow of the lights they carried, probably from down near Milne Bay.

As he fell toward the outriggers moored below, the sun seemed to come out behind him. It was a sun full of thunder, as the shack, the wooden planks on which it sat, and a portion of the surrounding walkways erupted in a ball of white-hot flame. Screams filled the air as other shanty dwellers explosively roused from their sleep staggered out of their thrown-together homes to gape at the fireball rising in their midst.

Wahgi landed hard in an open outrigger, twisting his ankle and hitting his jaw on the side of the narrow craft. But there was nothing wrong with the rest of him. Carefully placing the briefcase in the bottom of the boat, he untied it and began stroking toward shore, toward Ela Beach. As he paddled, the phone jabbered frantically at him. He ignored it, occasionally looking back over his shoulder. Where the shack had been was a flame-lined hole in the above-water walkway. The supporting stilts had been blown off right down to the water. There was no sign of his temporary home, of the other two men who had lived there, or of the three heavily armed intruders who had burst in on him.

They had not paused to talk or to ask questions, Wahgi reflected. They had simply shot their way in. He was sorry for Gembogl and Kuikui, and angry at what had happened to them, but he now knew one thing for certain: the briefcase and its contents were unquestionably worth a million kina.

Maybe two million, based on what had just happened.

Safely ashore on the narrow city beach, he abandoned the outrigger to the vagaries of the harbor currents. Exhausted and out of breath, his left ankle throbbing, he threw himself down under a coconut palm and opened the briefcase.

". . . are you there, Wahgi! Can you hear . . . ?"

"What happened?" he asked von Maltzan. "What did you do?"

"Those gunmen were after the briefcase," the foreigner explained. He did not need to do that. Of course the gunmen were after the briefcase. Did he still think Wahgi was stupid? "I used the phone to activate the grenade you threw at them. Where are you? Are you all right?"

"Yes, I am all right. But my friends are not."

"I'm sorry. Now will you listen to me and not hang up anymore? If you do, I won't be able to help you."

"Never mind that." Tasting wet saltiness in his mouth, Wahgi felt of his teeth. One was missing, knocked out when he had hit the side of the outrigger, and blood was trickling over his lip and down his chin. To a Huli it was nothing more than an inconvenience. "I want my reward."

"Yes, yes, of course, but. . . ."

"I want it left for me in a paper-wrapped package at the main airport cargo pickup counter, with my name on it. By tomorrow morning."

"It'll be there, Wahgi. No problem. But please, do one thing for me. Leave this phone on in case you run into trouble again. That way I can help you. Keep it close at all times. Other people want what is in the briefcase, and as you have seen this morning. . . ."

"It is night here."

"All right, all right. As you have seen this night, these others are willing to kill to get it."

"I will not turn the phone off again," Wahgi promised.

"Good! Tomorrow morning, at the Jackson's Airport cargo counter. Look for your package."

The voice went away, but the green light remained on. Wahgi surmised that it indicated the line was still open to him if he needed to use it. Looking around, he sought and found a picnic bench across the street from the Ela Beach hotel. In an emergency, he could run in that direction. Port Moresby hotels always had guards on duty around the clock. They would not interfere in a fight to help him, but their presence might well discourage an attacker from using a gun in the presence of armed witnesses.

Stretching out on the warm sand beneath the table, he felt he had done all that he could until morning. Dreaming of a million kina and sorrowing for his dead kinsmen, he fell into a deep and placid sleep.

Parker put the silencer to the side of the sleeping man's head and pulled the trigger once. There was a soft *phut* followed by the sound of bone splintering. Blood spurted briefly, quickly dropped to a trickle. Unscrewing the silencer, he placed it and the gun back in their respective jacket holsters.

"Poor dumb blackfella," he murmured emotionlessly to his companion as the other man picked up the briefcase. "Never had a clue what he was dealing with."

McMurray murmured something into the telephone in the briefcase before turning it off and closing the case. "Probably thought he was safe, he did. Wouldn't have understood if you'd taken the time to try explaining it to him." After a quick look around to ensure that they had not been observed at work they headed for the car parked in the nearby beach lot. "Tracked the phone's location via satellite search from Zurich and its internal GPS pinpointed it for us. There was never any place for the sorry bugger to hide."

"Not as long as he left the phone on sending out its signal." Parker opened the door on the driver's side and slid behind the wheel, nodding at the briefcase as he did so. "The bonds still in there?"

His colleague nodded. "Doesn't look like they've been touched. A hundred and sixty million Swiss francs worth of convertible paper." His eyes gleamed. "It's bloody tempting, you know."

"Now, mate, none o' that." The engine on the rented car coughed to life. "You know they'd send blokes like us after us if we were to try and disappear with that."

"It was just a thought, Eddie."

"Well blow it out your arse. Let's get back to the hotel. First Qantas out of this shithole tomorrow, we're on it."

Gembogl watched the men drive away. When he was sure they had left, he ran to the picnic table. He saw instantly that Wahgi was dead. The car had stopped at the petrol station across the street and he hurried across the road toward it. While one of the men pumped fuel, he slipped inside the station and in a frantic, hushed stream of words began relating what had happened to the silent attendant. The man was a Huli and therefore, however distant, a kinsman.

The knock at the hotel door the following morning prompted McMurray to grab his pistol and station himself flat against the wall to one side of the portal. Nodding to his partner, Parker approached cautiously and without a word put his eye to the peephole set in the door. The tiny fresnel lens showed a small black woman clad entirely in white standing on the other side. She was holding an empty laundry basket.

"What is it?" Making a disgusted face, Parker whispered to his colleague. "It's a maid." Nodding sourly, McMurray put his automatic pistol back in its shoulder holster.

The woman on the other side responded matter-of-factly. "You are checking out this morning, sir. We have a big tour group coming in, and I need to take away your dirty linen."

"But we're not ready to . . . oh, all right!" He unlatched the door. "But be bloody quick about it!" To McMurray he muttered, "We don't need any of the help complaining to management that we're keeping them from their job." Curtly, he pulled the door inward.

The maid entered in. Calling her diminutive would have flattered her. She was maybe four foot six, but perfectly formed. Cradling her basket, she headed toward the beds as Parker closed the door behind her, enjoying the sight of her compact ass twitching from side to side beneath the tight white maid's uniform.

A dozen very short, very muscular men burst through the half-open door like circus midgets shot from a single cannon. They had wild kinky hair that spread out from the sides of their heads, skin dark as bittersweet chocolate, and builds like pocket linebackers. They also wielded knives and machetes like the exploded components of a berserk threshing machine.

Parker was hacked to bits before he could react. McMurray went down with his hand on the stock of his machine pistol, before he could find the trigger. A fire-hardened bamboo arrow caught him in the throat and went completely through his neck. A foot of it emerged from the back. He had time enough to marvel at the incongruity of it. A bloody great arrow! In this day and age!

"Who . . . ?" he gasped before the blood welling up in his throat choked off any further speech.

He did not recognize the young man who came forward to stand over him. It was doubtful he would have made the connection even had he seen his face the night before.

"You killed my friends. Wahgi and Kuikui." He gestured at the watching coterie of small but ferocious men who filled the room. The maid had left to stand watch outside. "This is payback for what you did to them. A friend who worked at the petrol station where you stopped last night after doing your killing owed my village some old payback. We got on his motorbike and followed you here. Madani, who works for the hotel, is Enga, not Huli, so we now owe her tribe big payback. For compensation we will give her village ten pigs for her help this morning in sneaking us into the hotel."

"Ten . . . pigs . . . ?" McMurray choked. He was fast bleeding to death.

He did not get the opportunity to do so. The oldest man in the group; short, white-haired, but straight as an arrow, approached and with a single swing of his bloody machete, cut the European's head half off. He apologized to his companions for not making a better job of it. He was not as strong in the arms as he used to be, he explained.

As they were making preparations to leave, something began beeping within the briefcase. Opening it, Gembogl removed the strange telephone. Remembering how Wahgi had used it, he pushed the appropriate button.

"Parker?" a voice inquired. "You should be leaving with the case in an hour or so. Don't leave any tracks. I know you're not in London or New York, but there's no reason to make things easy for the local police, no matter how primitive they might be, *verstehen?* You never know—one of them might even know how to spell Interpol. I'll be expecting you tomorrow at the airport." The voice paused briefly. "Parker, are you there?"

"It looks valuable." Curious, the wiry elder examined the phone.

"Who said that?" The voice on the other end became alarmed. "Parker, who's in there with you and McMurray?"

"What should we do with it?" Another man was using a bedsheet to wipe blood from his machete.

"It may be valuable, but it killed Wahgi and Kuikui." Raising his arm and ignoring the sudden stream of frantic babble that spouted from the device, Gembogl brought his own blade down sharply. State-of-the-art it might be, but the satellite phone was no match for a honed machete. It splintered into fragments of metal and plastic.

As they were about to leave, Gembogl picked up the briefcase. "And this, what should we do with this? Destroy it also?"

The old man regarded it narrowly. "It killed Wahgi

and Kuikui, too—but you said it was worth a million kina?" The young man nodded. "Then we will keep it, and hide it until we can understand how to make it work for us. Just like we are learning to make other things from the outside world work for us." Turning, he shook his woolly white head as he walked toward the door. "These white people make many magical things work for them, but between you and me, man to man, I will still take a good machete over a device that talks through the air any day."

THE MOJAVE TWO-STEP

by *Norman Partridge*

Norman Partridge was awarded the Bram Stoker
Award for best short story collection for *Mr. Fox
and Other Tales*. Since then he's released two
more collections and three novels, the most recent being *Ten Ounce Siesta*. He also edited *It
Came From the Drive-In*, an anthology that paid
homage to the B movies of the 1950s. He currently lives in California.

THE desert, just past midnight. A lone truck on a
scorched black licorice strip, two men—Anshutes and
Coker—inside.

Outside it's one hundred and twenty-five degrees
under a fat December moon. Frosty weather in the
twilight days of global warming . . . and just in time
for the holiday season.

Sure, driving across the desert was a risk, even in
such balmy weather. Not many people owned cars
anymore, and those who did avoided the wide white
lonesome. Even roadcops were smart enough to leave
the Mojave alone. It was too hot and too empty, and
it could make you as crazy as a scorpion on a sizzling-
hot skillet. If you broke down out here, you ended up

cooked to a beautiful golden brown—just like Tiny Tim's Christmas goose.

But that wasn't going to happen to Coker. He was going to spend New Year's Eve in Las Vegas. The town that Frank and Dean and Sammy had built all those years ago was still the place he wanted to be. Hell on earth outside, air-conditioned splendor within. If you had the long green, Vegas gave you everything a growing boy could desire. A/C to the max, frosty martinis . . . maybe even a woman with blue eyes that sparkled like icebergs.

Let the swells fly into town in air-conditioned jets, Coker figured. He'd take the hard road. The dangerous road. The real gambler's road. He'd ride that scorched highway straight down the thermometer into double digits, and the A/C would frost everything but his dreams. A little business, a couple lucky rolls of the dice, and his life would change for good . . . then *he'd* leave town with a jet of his own. Slice it up like an Eskimo Pie, and that was cool, any way you figured it.

It was all part of the gamble called life. Like always, Lady Luck was rolling the dice. Rattling the bones for Coker and for his partner, too, even though Anshutes would never admit to believing in any airy jazz like that.

Coker believed it. Lady Luck was calling him now. Just up the road in Vegas, she waited for him like a queen. God knew he'd dreamed about her long enough, imagining those iceberg eyes that sparkled like diamonds flashing just for him.

All his life, he'd been waiting for the Lady to give him a sign. Coker knew it was coming soon. Maybe with the next blink of his eyes. Or maybe the one after that.

Yeah. That was the way it was. It had to be.

Really, it was the only explanation.

Check it out. Just two days ago Coker and Anshutes had been on foot. Broiling in Bakersfield with maybe a gallon of water between them, seven bucks, and An-shutes' .357 Magnum . . . which was down to three shells. But with that .357 they'd managed to steal five hundred and seventy-two bucks, a shotgun, and an ice-cream truck tanked with enough juice to get them all the way to Vegas. Plus they still had the Magnum . . . and those three shells.

Now if that wasn't luck, what was?

One-handing the steering wheel, Coker gave the ice cream truck a little juice. Doing seventy on the straightaway, and the electric engine purred quieter than a kitten. The rig wasn't much more than a pick-up with a refrigeration unit mounted on the back, but it did all right. Coker's only complaint was the lack of air-conditioning. Not that many automobiles had A/C anymore . . . these days, the licensing fees for luxuries which negatively impacted the sorry remains of the ozone layer cost more than the cars. But why anyone who could afford the major bucks for a freon-licensed vehicle would forgo the pleasure of A/C, Coker didn't know.

The only guy who had the answer was the owner of the ice cream truck. If he was still alive . . . and Coker kind of doubted that he was. Because Anshutes had excavated the poor bastard's bridgework with the butt of his .357 Magnum, emptied the guy's wallet, and left him tied to a telephone pole on the outskirts of Bakersfield. By now, the ice cream man was either cooked like the ubiquitous Christmas goose or in a hospital somewhere sucking milkshakes through a straw.

Coker's left hand rested on the sideview mirror, de-sert air blasting over his knuckles. Best to forget about the ice cream man. His thoughts returned to the Lady. Like always, those thoughts had a way of sliding over his tongue, no matter how dry it was. Like always, they had a way of parting his chapped lips and finding Anshutes's perennially sunburned ear.

"Know where I'm heading after Vegas?" Coker asked.

"No," Anshutes said. "But I'm sure you're gonna tell me."

Coker smiled. "There's this place called Lake Louise, see? It's up north, in Canada. Fifty years ago it used to be a ski resort. Now the only skiing they do is on the water. They've got palm trees, papayas and mangoes, and girls with skin the color of cocoa butter. Days it's usually about thirty-five Celsius, which is ninety-five degrees American. Some nights it gets as low as sixty."

Anshutes chuckled. "Sounds like you'll have to buy a coat."

"Go ahead and laugh. I'm talking double-digit degrees, partner. Sixty. *Six-oh.* And girls with skin like cocoa butter. If that's not a big slice of paradise, I don't know what is."

"Get real, amigo. A guy with your record isn't exactly a prime candidate for immigration. And our dollar isn't worth shit up north, anyway."

"Drop some luck into that equation."

"Oh, no. Here we go again—"

"Seriously. I can feel it in my bones. Something big is just ahead, waiting for us. I'm gonna take my cut from the ice cream job and hit the tables. I'm not walking away until I have a million bucks in my pocket."

"Even God isn't that lucky." Anshutes snorted. "And luck had nothing to do with this, anyway. Planning did. And hard work. And a little help from a .357 Magnum."

"So what are you gonna do with your money?" Coker asked sarcastically. "Bury it in the ground?"

"Depends on how much we get."

"The way I figure it, we're looking at something large. Forty grand, maybe fifty."

"Well, maybe thirty." Anshutes gnawed on it a minute, doing some quick calculations. "I figure the Push

Ups will go for about fifty a pop. We got five cases of those. The Fudgsicles'll be about sixty-five. Figure seventy-five for the Drumsticks. And the Eskimo Pies—"

"A hundred each, easy," Coker said. "Maybe even a hundred and twenty-five. And don't forget—we've got ten cases."

"You sound pretty sure about the whole thing."

"That's because I believe in luck," Coker said. "Like the song says, she's a lady. And she's smiling on us. Right now. Tonight. And she's gonna keep on smiling for a long, long time."

Coker smiled, too. Screw Anshutes if he wanted to be all sour. "You know what we ought to do?" Coker said. "We ought to pull over and celebrate a little. Have us a couple of Eskimo Pies. Toast Lady Luck, enjoy the moment. Live a little—"

"I've lived a lot," Anshutes said. "And I plan to live a lot longer. I'm not going to play the fool with my money. I'm not going to blow it on some pipe dream. I'm going to play it smart."

"Hey, relax. All I'm saying is—"

"No," Anshutes said, and then he really went verbal. "You've said enough. We're in this to make some real money for a change. And we're not gonna make it by pulling over to the side of the road, and we're not gonna make it by toasting Lady Luck with an Eskimo Pie in the middle of the Mojave Desert, and we're not going to make it by blowing our swag in some casino. . . ."

Anshutes went on like that.

Coker swallowed hard.

He'd had just about enough.

"I'm pulling over," he said. "I'm going to have an Eskimo Pie, and you're goddamn well going to have one with me if you know what's good for you."

"The hell I am!" Ansutes yanked his pistol. "You goddamn fool! You take your foot off the brake right now, or I'll—"

Suddenly, Anshutes' complaints caught in his throat like a chicken bone. Ahead on the road, Coker saw the cause of his partner's distress. Beneath the ripe moon, knee-deep in heat waves that shimmered up from the asphalt, a big man wearing a ten-gallon cowboy hat walked the yellow center line of the highway. He only had one arm, and he was carrying a woman piggyback—her arms wrapped around his neck, her long slim legs scissored around his waist. But the woman wasn't slowing the big guy down. His pace was brisk, and it was one hundred and twenty-five degrees and the rangy bastard didn't even look like he'd broken a sweat—

Coker honked the horn, but the cowboy didn't seem to notice.

"Don't hit him!" Anshutes yelled. "You'll wreck the truck!"

Anshutes closed his eyes as Coker hit the brakes. Tires screamed as the ice cream truck veered right and bounded along the shoulder of the road. Gravel rattled in the wheel wells and slapped against the undercarriage like gunfire, and Coker downshifted from fourth gear to third, from third to second, ice cream visions dancing in his head, visions of Drumsticks and Push Ups bashing around in the refrigeration unit, visions of broken Fudgsicles and mashed Eskimo Pies. . . .

Visions of Lady Luck turning her back. . . .

The electric engine whined as he shifted from second to first and yanked the emergency brake. The truck seized up like a gutshot horse, and the only thing that prevented Coker from doing a header through the windshield was his seat belt.

Coker unbuckled his belt. Anshutes set his pistol on the seat and fumbled with his seat belt. Coker grabbed the .357 and was out of the cab before his partner could complain.

The hot asphalt was like sponge cake beneath Coker's boots as he hurried after the man in the ten-gallon hat. The cowboy didn't turn. Neither did the woman who rode him. In fact, the woman didn't move at all, and as Coker got closer, he noticed a rope around her back. She was tied to the cowboy. Coker figured she was dead.

That was bad news. Two strangers. One alive, one dead. Snake eyes. A jinxed roll if ever he saw one.

Bad enough that the cowboy had nearly killed him. But if he'd put the jinx on Coker's luck—

Coker aimed at the ripe moon and busted a round. "Turn around, cowboy," he yelled. "Unless you want it in the back."

The cowboy turned double-quick, like some marching band marionette. The one-armed man's face was lost under the brim of his ten-gallon hat, but moonlight splashed across his torso and gleamed against his right hand.

Which was wrapped around a pistol.

"Shit!" Coker spit the word fast and fired another shot. The bullet caught the cowboy in the chest, but the big man didn't even stumble. He didn't return fire, either . . . and Coker wasn't going to give him the chance.

Coker fired again, dead center, and this time the bullet made a sound like a marble rattling around in a tin can.

The cowboy's chest lit up. Neon rattlesnakes slithered across it. Golden broncos bucked over his bulging pecs. Glowing Gila monsters hissed and spread their jaws.

Three broncos galloped into place.

The cowboy's chest sprung open like the batwings on an old-fashioned saloon.

Silver dollars rained down on the highway.

And the cowboy kept on coming. Coker couldn't even move now. Couldn't breathe. Oh man, this wasn't a jinx after all. This was the moment he'd been waiting for. This was the omen to end all omens. All of it happening in the blink of an eye.

One more blink, and he'd see things clearly. One more blink and the future would turn up like a Blackjack dealt for high stakes—

But Coker couldn't blink. He couldn't even move—

Anshutes could. He stepped past his partner, scooped up a silver dollar as it rolled along the highway's center line. The cowboy kept on coming, heading for Anshutes now, but Anshutes didn't twitch. He waited until the big man was within spitting distance, and then he slipped the coin between the determined line of the advancing cowboy's lips.

Immediately, the cowboy's gunhand swept in an upward arc.

Then he stopped cold.

Anshutes scooped a handful of silver dollars off the road and tossed them at Coker.

"Guess you've never heard of a one-armed bandit," he said.

Coker's jaw dropped quicker than a bar of soap in a queer bathhouse. Anshutes sighed. Christ, being partnered up with this starry-eyed fool was something else.

"The cowboy here's a robot," Anshutes explained. "Comes from a casino called Johnny Ringo's, named after the gangster who owns the place. Ringo himself came up with the concept for an ambulating slot machine, hired some ex-Disney imagineers to design the things. They walk around his joint twenty-four hours a day. You'd be surprised how many idiots feed dollars into them. I guess they all think they're lucky . . . just like you."

"This thing's a *robot*?" Coker asked.

"That's what I said."

"Why'd it stop moving?"

" 'Cause I fed it a dollar, genius." Anshutes pointed at the machine's lone arm, which was raised in the air. "The Cogwheel Kid here can't do anything until I make my play. I have to pull his arm to set him in motion again. Then those neon wheels will spin, and either he'll cough up some dough or start walking, looking for another mark. Unless, of course, your bullets dug a hole in his motherboard, in which case who knows what the hell he'll do."

Coker blinked several times but said nothing. To Anshutes, he looked like some stupid fish that had just figured out it lived in a tank. Blink-blink-blinking, checking out the big bad pet shop world that lurked beyond the glass.

"It's an omen," Coker said finally. "A sign—"

"Uh-uh, buddy. It's called the Mojave Two-Step."

"The Mojave what?"

"The Mojave Two-Step." Anshutes sighed. "Here's what happened. This little lady crossed Johnny Ringo. Who knows what the hell she did, but it was bad enough that he wanted to kill her good and slow. So he tied her to one of his walking slots, and he pointed the damn thing west and turned it loose. It's happened before. Just a couple months ago, one of these things trudged into Barstow with a dead midget tied to its back. Leastways, folks thought it was a midget. A couple weeks under the Mojave sun is liable to shrink anyone down to size."

"Jesus!" Coker said. "How does Ringo get away with it?"

"He's rich, idiot. And that means you don't mess with him, or anything to do with him, or he'll kill you the same way he killed this girl—"

Right on cue, the girl groaned. Annoyed, Anshutes grabbed her chin and got a look at her. Blue eyes, cold as glaciers. Surprisingly, she wasn't even sunburned.

Anshutes huffed another sigh. There wasn't any mystery to it, really. They weren't that far from Vegas. Twenty, maybe thirty miles. Could be that Ringo had turned the robot loose after dark, that the girl hadn't even been in the sun yet. Of course, if that was the case it would make sense to assume that the robot had followed the highway, taking the most direct route.

Anshutes didn't know what kind of directional devices Ringo had built into his walking slots, but he supposed it was possible. There wasn't anything between Vegas and Barstow. Nobody traveled the desert highway unless they absolutely had to. Even if the robot stuck to the road, it was an odds on cinch that the girl would wind up dead before she encountered another human being.

The girl glanced at Anshutes, and it was like that one glance told her exactly what kind of guy he was. So she turned her gaze on Coker. "Help me," she whispered.

"This is too weird," Coker said. "A woman riding a slot machine . . . a slot machine that paid off on the road to Vegas. It *is* an omen. Or a miracle! Like Lady Luck come to life . . . like Lady Luck *in the flesh—*"

"Like Lady Luck *personified.*" Anshutes dropped a hand on his partner's shoulder. "Now you listen to me, boy—what we've got here is a little Vegas whore riding a walking scrap heap. She doesn't have anything to do with luck, and she isn't our business. *Our* business is over there in that truck. *Our* business is a load of ice cream. *Our* business is getting that ice cream to Vegas before it melts."

Coker's eyes flashed angrily, and Anshutes nearly laughed. Seeing his partner go badass was like watching a goldfish imitate a shark.

"You'd better back down, boy," Anshutes warned.

Coker ignored him. He untied the young woman's wrists and feet. He pulled her off of the Cogwheel Kid's back and cradled her in his arms, and then he started toward the ice cream truck.

Anshutes cleared his throat. "Where do you think you're going?"

"Even if she's not Lady Luck, this lady's hurting," Coker said. "I think she deserves an ice cream. Hell, maybe she deserves two. Maybe I'll let her eat her fill."

Anshutes didn't answer.

Not with words, anyway.

He raised the sawed-off shotgun he'd stolen from the ice cream man, and he cocked both barrels.

Coker said, "You think you're pretty cool, don't you?"

"Cooler than Santa's ass," Anshutes said.

"And you'll shoot me if I give the lady an ice cream?"

"Only way she gets any ice cream is if she pay for it."

Coker turned around. "How about if I pay for it?"

"I don't care who pays. You, the little whore, Lady Luck, or Jesus Christ. As long as I get the money."

"That's fine." Coker smiled. "You'll find your money on the road, asshole."

"What?"

"The jackpot. The money I shot out of the slot machine. It's all yours."

"You're crazy."

"Maybe. But I'm gonna buy me a shitload of ice cream, and this little lady's gonna eat it."

Coker set the girl down at the side of the road, peeling off his shirt and rolling it into a pillow for her head. Then he walked over to the truck and opened the refrigerated compartment.

"No Eskimo Pies," Anshutes said. "Let's get that straight."

"I'm getting what I paid for," Coker said.

Anshutes shook his head. What a moron. Ponying up fistfuls of silver dollars, just so some little Vegas whore could lick a Push Up. If that was the way Coker wanted it, that was fine. In the meantime, Anshutes would make himself some money, and Lady Luck wouldn't have jack to do with it. Hell, for once hard work wouldn't have jack to do with it, either. For once, all Anshutes had to do to make some money was bend over and pick it up.

Silver dollars gleamed in the moonlight. Anshutes put down the shotgun. Not that he was taking any chances—he made sure that the weapon was within reach as he got down to work, filling his pockets with coins.

Behind him, he heard the sound of the refrigerator compartment door slamming closed. Coker. Jesus, what an idiot. Believing that some Vegas slut was Lady Luck. *Personified.*

Anshutes had told the kid a thousand times that luck was an illusion. Now he realized that he could have explained it a million times, and he still wouldn't have made a dent. The kid might as well be deaf. He just wouldn't listen—

Anshutes listened. He heard everything.

The sound of silver dollars jingling in his pocket, like the sound of happiness.

But wait . . . there was another sound, too.

A quiet hum, hardly audible.

The sound of an electric engine accelerating.

Anshutes turned around fast, dropping coins on the roadway. The ice cream truck was coming fast. The shotgun was right there on the double yellow line. He made a grab for it.

Before he touched the gun, the ice cream truck's bumper cracked his skull like a hard-boiled egg.

Kim felt better now.

A couple of Eskimo Pies could do that for a girl.

"Want another?" the guy asked.

"Sure," Kim said. "I could probably eat a whole box."

"I guess it's like they say: a walk in the desert does wonders for the appetite."

The guy smiled and walked over to the ice cream truck. She watched him. He was kind of cute. Not as cute as Johnny Ringo, of course, but Johnny definitely had his downside.

She sat in the dirt and finished her third pie. You had to eat the suckers fast or else they'd melt right in your hand. It was funny—she'd left Vegas worse than flat broke, owing Johnny twenty grand, and now she had three hundred bucks worth of ice cream in her belly. Things were looking up. She kind of felt like a safe deposit box on legs. Kind of a funny feeling. Kind of like she didn't know whether she should laugh or cry.

The guy handed her another Eskimo Pie. "Thanks—" she said, and she said it with a blank that he was sure to fill in.

"Coker," he said. "My first name's Dennis, but I don't like it much."

"It's a nice name," Kim said. Which was a lie, but there was no sense hurting the poor guy's feelings. "Thanks, Dennis."

"My pleasure. You've had a hell of a hard time."

She smiled. Yeah. That was one way of putting it.

"So you're heading for Vegas," she said.

Coker nodded. "Me and my buddy . . . well, we ended up with this truckload of ice cream. We wanted a place where we could sell it without much trouble from the law."

"Vegas is definitely the place."

"You lived there a while?"

She smiled. She guess you could call what she'd done in Vegas living. If you were imaginative enough.

"Kim?" he prodded. "You okay?"

"Yeah," she said. Man, it was tough. She should have been happy . . . because the guy had saved her life. She should have been sad . . . because Johnny Ringo had tried to kill her. But she couldn't seem to hold onto any one emotion.

She had to get a grip.

"You ever been to Vegas?" she asked.

"No," the guy said. "Going there was my partner's idea."

"It's a tough place."

"I don't care how tough it is." He laughed. "As long as it's the kind of place you can sell an ice cream bar for a hundred bucks, I'm there."

She nodded. Ice cream was worth a lot in Vegas.

But other things came pretty cheap.

"It's a rich town," she said, because saying that was really like saying nothing. "It's full of rich men and women. I read somewhere that the entire budget for law enforcement in the United States is about a third of what it costs to power Vegas' air-conditioners for a month."

"Wow. That's amazing."

"Not really. Vegas is a desert. It's an empty place. Everything that's there, someone put it there. Only the rich can afford a place like that. They come and go as they please, jetting in and out in their fancy planes. Everybody else—they're pretty much stuck there. That's what happened to me. I was a dancer. I made pretty good money that way. But every dime I made was already spent on my apartment, or A/C, or water or food. I kept waiting for my lucky break, but it never came. I just couldn't get ahead. Before I knew it, I got behind. And then I got in trouble with my boss—"

"Johnny Ringo?"

"You know about him?"

Coker nodded at the one-armed bandit. "I've heard of the Mojave Two-Step."

Kim swallowed hard. "You never want to dance that one," she said. "I'm here to tell you."

The guy looked down at the road, kind of embarrassed. Like he wanted to know her story, but was too shy to ask for the details.

"Well, maybe your luck's due to change," he said. "It happened to me. Or it's going to happen. It's like I can see it coming."

"Like a dream?"

"Or an omen."

Kim smiled. "I like that word."

"Me too. It's kind of like a dream, only stronger."

"I used to have this dream," Kim said. "When I first came to Vegas. That I was going to hit it big.

That I'd live in a penthouse suite with the A/C set at sixty-eight degrees. That the sun would never touch my skin and I'd be white as a pearl."

The guy didn't say anything. Still shy. Kim had forgotten about that particular emotion. She hadn't run across it much in the last few years. Not with Johnny Ringo, and not with any of his friends. Not even with the two-legged slots that followed her around the casino night after night until she fed them dollars just so they'd leave her alone.

In Vegas, everyone wanted something. At least the walking slots came a lot cheaper than their flesh-and-blood counterparts.

Funny. She didn't feel good about it, but she didn't exactly feel bad, either.

That's just the way it was in Vegas.

It was a rich man's town.

Or a rich woman's.

Kim finished her Eskimo Pie. She liked what the guy (what was his name again?) had said about omens. That they were dreams, only stronger.

She stared at the ice cream truck.

She thought: it's not often you get a second chance.

"You want another?" the guy asked.

She laughed. "Just one more?"

Of course, he thought she was talking about an Eskimo Pie, when that really wasn't what she wanted at all.

He went after the ice cream. She watched him go.

Past the dead guy on the highway.

Past the second chance that lay there on the yellow line.

Kim really didn't have a choice.

She had to pick it up.

She heard the freezer door close. Watched the guy (*Dennis,* that was his name) step from behind the truck.

He was all right about it. He kind of smiled when he saw the shotgun, like he already understood.

"I'm sorry, Dennis," she said. "But dreams die hard. Especially strong ones."

"Yeah," he said. "Yeah."

Coker stood in the middle of the road, eating an Eskimo Pie, listening to "Pop Goes the Weasel."

The ice cream truck was gone from view, but he could still hear its little song. That meant she was up ahead somewhere, playing the tape.

Maybe she was playing it for him. The music drifted through the night like a sweet connection. Coker listened to the song while he finished his Eskimo Pie. Anshutes couldn't stand the music the truck made. He wouldn't let Coker play it at all.

Well, Anshutes didn't have a say in anything anymore. Coker stared at his ex-partner. The big man lay dead on the highway like roadkill of old, his pockets stuffed with silver dollars.

Coker turned them out, filling his own pockets with the coins. Then he walked over to the one-armed bandit.

The Cogwheel Kid was primed for action—Anshutes' coin between his lips, his lone robotic arm held high in the air. Coker pulled the slot machine's arm. Ribbons of neon danced across the one-armed bandit's chest. Bucking broncos, charging buffaloes, jackalopes that laughed in the desert night.

After a while, the neon locked up.

Two tittering jackalopes with a snorting buffalo between them.

Hardly a jackpot.

Coker smiled as the neon flickered out. Losing wasn't a big surprise, really. After all, Lady Luck was gone. She was up ahead, driving an ice cream truck, heading for the land of dreams.

The Cogwheel Kid started walking. He headed east, toward Vegas, looking for another mark.

Coker jumped on the robot's back and held on tight.

He smiled, remembering the look of her frosty blue

eyes. Lady Luck with a shotgun. He should have hated
her. But he was surprised to find that he couldn't do
that.

She was chasing a dream, the same way he was.

He couldn't help hoping she'd catch it.

The same way he hoped he'd catch her.

If he was lucky.

SHAKESPEARE MINUS ONE

by Barbara Paul

Barbara Paul has a Ph.D. in Theater History and Criticism and taught at the University of Pittsburgh until the late '70s when she became a full-time writer. She has written five science-fiction novels and sixteen mysteries, six of which are in the Marian Larch series. Her latest book is *Jack Be Quick and Other Crime Stories*.

"TACKY," Milo said, the expression on his face suggesting someone had just handed him a dead fish. "You're his friend, LaBoz. Can't you tell him how shamelessly exhibitionistic he's being?"

"No one tells Gil anything," LaBoz said mildly.

"That could be his trouble. I really don't want to be here tonight. These little divertissements were intended for one's private amusement. One doesn't invite an *audience*."

LaBoz didn't answer. Milo had a habit of displaying an elegant disdain for the philistine gropings of the not-truly-gifted, but this time LaBoz thought he was right. Gil's inviting an audience to a Minus One was like asking someone over to watch you paste stamps into an album.

But Gil was no glib social mingler, and he'd never

forgiven Milo. Milo had been there the year before when Gil's father drowned; but instead of jumping in the water after him or calling for help, Milo had stood there helplessly flapping his hands as the older man went under. Expecting constructive action from Milo in a time of crisis was perhaps a trifle unrealistic, but Gil had avoided the other man for an entire year. So why tonight's invitation?

They rode the funicular up to the hilltop home that Gil inherited from his father, along with one other passenger, a Eurasian woman older than the two young men. Her name was Shalimar, appropriately exotic, and she lived in the Andaman Islands. She'd never met Gil. "I feel I know him, though," she said amiably. "I was a friend of his father's."

"Ah," said LaBoz, "then you've been here before."

"No, this is my first visit. Gil's father was guest in my house."

"I'm afraid it won't be a scintillating visit," Milo said with a sniff. "Gil has some Minus One play he wants us to look at."

Her eyebrows went up. "I thought it was a Virtual Reality game."

"Good heavens, no!" Milo shuddered theatrically. "It's a Minus One. At least we won't have to harness ourselves into all that cumbersome VR gear. We just have to concentrate on staying awake. Here we are," he said as the funicular door slid open, "and here's our genial host waiting to greet us."

Irony tipping over into sarcasm: Gil looked anything but genial, his face pinched and his eyes hard. He spoke first to the guest he didn't know. "Shalimar— at last. I'm glad you could come."

"It was time we met." She looked closely at his face. "Are you ill?"

"I was, but I'm well now." Gil turned to LaBoz. "Welcome back, old friend. I hope your journey was a pleasant one."

"Very pleasant. But it's good to be home."

Milo stared at LaBoz. "You didn't tell me you'd been away."

"Hello, Milo," Gil said casually. He offered a hand to Shalimar, chatting easily with the woman who had been the last love of his father's life. Gil led them to a reception room where two other guests were waiting.

LaBoz was astonished to see them both. Gil introduced Shalimar first to Phoebe, outspoken and determined Phoebe—to whom Gil had once been married. The other guest was Theodore Kimmel, an older man and business competitor against whom Gil's father had once brought criminal charges of fraud and grand theft. The charges had been dropped: insufficient evidence.

LaBoz went over and exchanged a light kiss with Phoebe. "Surprised to see me here?" she asked with a smile.

He nodded. "I recall a very angry young woman proclaiming she'd never set foot under the same roof as Gil again. Ever."

"I said a lot of things," she answered ruefully. "But Gil can't get to me anymore. He kept saying it was important for me to be here. Do you know what this is all about?"

"I'm as much in the dark as you are."

Across the room, Theodore Kimmel was talking to Gil but staring pointedly at Shalimar. "I've changed my mind. I'll stay."

Gil's mouth twisted wryly. "Whatever it takes."

"Why did you insist I come?"

"I thought it was time we buried the hatchet, Kimmel. Don't you?"

"No, I don't," the older man said bluntly. "I don't trust you, Gil. There's too much of your father in you. He was a hasty man, quick to pass judgment. And I suspect you're just like him."

"But that's what I'm trying to avoid—hasty judgment."

"How? By laying out a little home entertainment for a captive audience?"

"Yes, Gil, do tell us what this is all about," Milo drawled in his most bored tone. "We're all just dying of curiosity."

Gil smiled, his pinched face looking more strained than ever. "Very well. I've asked you all here to help me celebrate the anniversary of a very special day. I want you to cast your minds back exactly one year. Think back to the day that a man who was a strong swimmer somehow managed to fall off a yawl riding at anchor . . . and never rose to the surface."

Today? LaBoz thought in dismay. *This is the day?*

Gil's face looked more strained than ever. "Welcome to my father's deathday party."

The private theater in the hilltop house could accommodate an audience of forty, but tonight thirty-five of the seats would remain empty. Shalimar and Kimmel sat together talking quietly, an island of calm one generation removed from the maneuverings of their intense young host and his contemporaries.

"This is morbid, Gil," Phoebe said. "Unwholesome."

"Hardly that," he answered sharply. "I wish to commemorate my father's passing with a performance of his favorite play. What's morbid about that?" He drew LaBoz aside. "I'll need your help later on. Will you run the stage console for me?"

"Of course. Just tell me when."

"Later. Just sit and watch for now."

LaBoz took a seat in the audience with the others. Gil activated the console. The overhead lights dimmed, and on the stage the setting for the first scene flicked into existence. A hologram projection of a battlement at night, wisps of fog drifting across the stage. Holographic images of actors dressed as old-time soldiers, speaking briefly. Changing of the guard. "For this relief much thanks," one of them said. " 'Tis bitter cold, and I am sick at heart."

The staging was good, and the audience watched attentively as the ghost made its first, mute appearance. LaBoz felt the other actors' fear as tangibly as if he were one of them. More words, a throbbing in the air.

The battlement setting flicked out, and a new scene took its place: a court chamber, with the king and queen and their numerous followers. A brightly lighted, busy scene; LaBoz counted thirty actors on the stage. All holograms—except one: Gil was off to one side, dressed in the black of the mourning prince, his thin face averted from the corrupt celebration of corrupt life going on around him.

LaBoz tensed, wanting Gil to do well even though it was only a private entertainment. And Gil did very well, creating a convincing picture of a royal heir cheated out of his throne, a grieving son still shocked by his mother's hasty remarriage. Gil made only one mistake, inadvertently walking through the hologram of one of the courtiers.

At the end of the scene, Gil paused the projection. "Interesting," Kimmel remarked. "Is it just coincidence that you chose a play about the son of a man who died under questionable circumstances? That son was out for revenge."

Milo said, "Have you cast your guests in the play? Let's see now. Shalimar must be Queen Gertrude, Phoebe is Ophelia—"

Gil laughed. "No, not at all. I thought it might be entertaining if we all took turns playing the lead role. Everybody likes to be the star."

The audience greeted that with three *Oh-no*s and one *Tacky*. "It's a man's role," Phoebe objected.

"Women have played it before," Gil said. "This way you all get to choose the scene you want to play. We can skip the others."

"I have no intention of playing that homicidal maniac," Milo announced indignantly. "He kills *five* people!"

Gil looked amused. "Well, I could dial out Rosencrantz and Guildenstern. You could play both those roles at once." The stooges.

"I'll play," Shalimar said unexpectedly. "Truth is. I've always had a yen to do that advice-to-the-players bit."

"Excellent!" Gil exclaimed. "Step right up. LaBoz, will you run the console now? I want to see this from out front."

Shalimar joined him on the stage, where he fitted the button into her ear that would feed her her lines. Gil handed her a long black cloak to wear over her shimmering green gown and took a seat in the audience.

LaBoz started the scene.

"Speak the speech I pray you as I pronounced it to you," Shalimar declaimed in a strong contralto that was somehow different from her normal speaking voice, "trippingly on the tongue."

The console had a reverse switch, should a player blow his lines and need to start over. LaBoz didn't have to touch it. Shalimar performed with such authority that he guessed she was used to speaking in public. Shalimar moved easily through the scene, not at all self-conscious about being on display. At last LaBoz pressed the HOLD button and joined the applause that greeted the conclusion of the scene.

"Impressive, Shalimar!" Gil's voice soared over the applause. "Quite professional. My father would have enjoyed that—he always did like watching the faces people put on when they appear in public."

She shot him a quick look. "A dubious compliment at best. Leading up to what?"

He spread his hands. "Whatever you will. Name it, it's yours. That's what you're used to, aren't you?" His voice rose. "The rest of you don't know, but we have a VIP in our midst. Shalimar is a member of

the Andamanese Governing Council—a leader, a
politician. A manipulator of lives." Pause. "Ah, Kimmel—your open and honest face tells me you already
knew Shalimar was a national councilwoman. She
told you."

Kimmel mimicked Gil's own hand-spreading gesture.

"This is something new," Phoebe remarked to Gil.
"You used to try to disguise your rudeness." Milo
snickered.

But Gil's attention was back on Shalimar. "Do we
get an encore?"

"I think not." She handed her stage cape to LaBoz
and took her seat.

"How disappointing," Gil mock-groaned. "Remember the man we are honoring. You do remember dear
old dad, don't you? The clown who was willing to
keep your bed warm, for whenever you felt like using
it? Or him."

Oh-ho from Milo.

Gil ignored him. "He turned to you for help, Shalimar. He was at the lowest point of his life and he
went looking for you. Why didn't you help?"

Shalimar took her time answering. "That was between your father and me, Gil. This is no place to—"

"What better? A stage, an audience—"

"Oh, this is *de trop*," Milo moaned. "Honestly, Gil,
there's only so much melodrama one can take in a
single evening! If you're fixated on your father's sex
life, then that's your problem. But for heaven's sake,
leave the rest of us out of it!"

Gil raised an eyebrow and slowly clapped his hands.
"Ver-y good, Milo. Nothing like a little accusatory
Freudianism to discredit me and make yourself look
good. But that's your style, isn't it? Puff yourself up
at the other guy's expense."

Milo stood up. "I want to go home."

"Not yet," Gil said curtly. "Shalimar. When my father returned from the Andamans, he was depressed

to the point of being near-suicidal. He walked around in a trank-haze for three weeks. His judgment was off, his reactions were slow—he should never have taken the yawl out. But he wouldn't have been in a drug stupor if he'd come home in anything like a normal frame of mind. What happened, Shalimar? What did you do to him?"

Milo decided he wanted to hear the answer to that one and sat back down.

Shalimar's eyes were wide. "You're blaming me for your father's death?"

"You contributed. What went wrong? He went to the Andamans with such high hopes."

"High hopes," she repeated. "He came to me hoping for a lifeline. He was already close to a breakdown. Just one business reversal too many. It finally got to him." She slid a quick sideways glance at Kimmel. "He came to the Andamans wanting me to make everything right for him. I couldn't do it. He asked for too much."

"You couldn't?" Gil asked. "Or wouldn't?"

"Probably couldn't," Kimmel interposed. "Your father could be a demanding S.O.B."

Shalimar said, "Gil, I hadn't seen your father for two years. Then he showed up unannounced, expecting me to put my own life on hold to—well, I did what I could, but obviously it wasn't enough. I'm sorry. He and I were close once. But I didn't create your father's problems."

"You merely aggravated them. He came to you looking for relief from pain, and you sent him away with more pain."

Milo abruptly began singing. "Happy deathday to you . . . happy deathday to you. . . ."

"Shut up, Milo," Phoebe snapped. "Gil, stop this. Stop it right now."

Gil blew her a sardonic kiss. "We're just getting started."

Shalimar and Kimmel consulted briefly, stood up. "We're leaving."

"How? No funicular for another hour. And you wouldn't want to miss Milo's sterling performance, would you?"

Milo was back on his feet. "What?"

"Your turn, Milo. Time to put yourself on the line. You can't just lie back and pass judgment all your life, you know."

"Who says I can't? I refuse to take part in this puerile exhibition. The whole thing's absurd."

"Which scene do you prefer?" Gil went on as if the other man hadn't spoken. "Would you like me to choose for you? How about the get-thee-to-a-nunnery scene? You can cavort with Ophelia."

"You might as well do it, Milo," Phoebe said with a sigh. "He's not going to stop this until he's ready."

Milo was pondering. "One scene? And then you'll stop badgering me?"

"One scene," Gil promised.

"In that case, I must have a proper costume. That black thing you wrapped around Shalimar just won't do."

Gil nodded. "There's a costume room backstage. LaBoz?"

"Hurry it up, will you?" Kimmel said in disgust as he and Shalimar sat back down. "Kee-rist."

"He's mad, you know," Milo whispered to LaBoz. "Utterly mad."

LaBoz opened the door to the costume room and watched as Milo selected a broad-brimmed hat with a white plume, hip boots, and a buckle-on sword. "Don't forget a cape," LaBoz said dryly.

"Oh—right." Milo chose a Dracula cape, black velvet with scarlet silk lining.

"Eyepatch?"

Milo considered. "No, I don't want to overdo."

His musketeer appearance brought a burst of laughter from the four in the audience. *"Soft you now—the fair Ophelia!"* Milo bellowed, demanding silence.

The scene had barely gotten underway when it became clear that Gil had pulled a fast one. The holo production he'd chosen presented the nunnery scene as blatant in its sexual teasing. The button in Milo's ear was giving him stage directions as well as lines: *Grasp your codpiece with both hands.* As a result Milo moved through the scene with a perpetually startled look on his face.

His surprise also kept him a consistent few beats behind the set tempo of the scene. Ophelia would react to unsaid lines; then Milo would lunge for her only to find she'd already crossed to the other side of the stage. *Not once* were hero and heroine in sync. By the end of the scene, Milo was so frustrated that he pulled his sword and ran Ophelia through.

With tears in his eyes from laughing, LaBoz almost missed the cut-off at the end of the scene. Milo tore off his costume and stormed back to his seat in the small auditorium.

"For this comic relief, much thanks," Shalimar said, still laughing.

"So glad you were amused," Milo said through clenched teeth.

Gil stood up. "Thank you, Milo. That was exactly the break in tension we needed. And," he faced the others, "I take full credit. I chose the man and the scene. How else could it have worked out? Did you expect him to do it *right?*"

"Oh, Gil," Phoebe said in irritation.

"Milo doesn't do things at all," Gil plowed on. "Milo talks. He talks and talks and talks. But if it's action you want, you'd better look elsewhere. He can't be counted on to act even when he sees a man drowning right before his eyes."

All the color had drained out of Milo's face. "Gil . . . don't. You know I can't swim."

"You could have slipped on a scuba mask and

tied a line around your middle. Hell, you could have yelled for help—you weren't that far from shore. What were you doing on my father's yawl in the first place?"

"Well, I ran into him at the Yacht Club and he invited me aboard—

"You wangled an invitation. My father barely knew you. He was so tranked up he didn't know what he was doing. Was he easy to take advantage of, Milo? And perhaps it was easy to give him a little shove? Over the side of the boat, maybe?"

"Gil!" LaBoz heard the shock in his own voice. He jumped down from the stage. "Do you know what you just said?"

The others were staring. "You're accusing Milo of murder?" Shalimar asked incredulously.

Phoebe was on her feet. "Gil, that's *dumb*. Milo's no killer. Why would he want to kill your father?"

Gil shrugged. "Paid to?"

Everyone started talking at once—everyone except Milo. He sat there pale and shaken, speechless for the first time in his life.

"Look at him, Gil," LaBoz urged. "You've done him a terrible injustice."

Gil stood in front of the stage and spread his arms. "Intermission. Bar's behind the last row." He led the way. The others exchanged a look, shrugged, and followed. All but Milo, who sat slumped in his seat.

"Gil must be losing his mind," Phoebe said to LaBoz, low. "Does he really think his father was murdered?"

LaBoz took a long swallow of his drink. "If he does, this is the first I've heard of it. I can't convince myself he really means it. At least, not the part about Milo."

"I know." Just then, Phoebe saw Gil approaching; without a word she turned her back and walked away.

"Good thing I wasn't hoping for a reconciliation," Gil said wryly. "LaBoz, do you mind being stuck backstage with the console? I do need to watch from out front."

"I don't mind that," LaBoz said, "but I'm not too happy with the direction things are taking."

Phoebe was sitting with Milo, trying to cheer him up. "I hope you're familiar with the laws governing false accusation," Shalimar said to Gil as she drifted back to her seat.

"I didn't accuse," Gil answered her. "I suggested."

A grunt came from the bar, where Kimmel was helping himself. "No, accusation is upfront and straightforward. Innuendo is more your style. Just like your father."

"He accused you," Gil pointed out. "Fraud and grand theft."

"Because he knew I was on the point of bringing charges against him. Anyway, we settled that one out of court."

"Why don't you tell us what was going on?"

Kimmel laughed humorlessly. "Justify myself to you? No, thank you. I see you inherited your father's arrogance along with everything else."

A look of sadness passed over Gil's face. "You really did hate him, didn't you? It wasn't just business—it was personal between you two. Why? I know he wasn't perfect, but he was a good man, Kimmel. You speak of him as if he were a monster. And you must know he was nothing of the kind."

Kimmel studied the face of his old foe's son for a long time. "Some men are one thing at home, another in business. That's the most I can say."

Gil nodded, recognizing the remark as the closest Kimmel could come to conceding the point. "Since you won't enlighten us in one area, how about entertaining us in another? Take the stage. Show us a thing or two."

One corner of Kimmel's mouth turned up. "That's so transparent a ploy that I think I'll let you get away

with it. All right, I'll be your next guinea pig. Do
your damndest."

Gil smiled. "Pick your scene."

The older man thought a minute. "I think it's called
the closet scene. The one where our hero has it out
with his mother."

"How very Oedipal," murmured Milo, beginning
to recover.

LaBoz helped Kimmel into costume. "Why did you
choose that scene?"

The other man grinned. "It was the only one I
could remember."

Oddly, he threw himself into the performance like
an enthusiastic amateur: "Now, Mother, what's the
matter?" The scene was a long one, building in intensity. Kimmel was clearly out of his element, so he took
the pragmatic approach of a man used to problem-
solving as a strategy for living. LaBoz watched fasci-
nated as Kimmel worked at getting the rhythm right,
at pitching his voice to the best level for that size
auditorium. At using his body language to best effect.
The man was teaching himself acting. By scene's end
he was still the amateur—but a less awkward one,
now at least adequate as a performer. When Kimmel
pantomimed dragging Polonius's hologram corpse off
the stage, LaBoz could almost believe it was happening.

The others were equally impressed. "You missed
your calling," Shalimar said dryly. "Or did you?"

Kimmel stood watching Gil, waiting.

"I've just understood something," the younger man
said. "He was afraid of you . . . my father was afraid
of you. If you take that kind of concentration into
everything you do, then he had reason to be. Did you
work that hard at stealing Ferrence from him?"

Ferrence Transportation. A company that operated
short-distance air shuttles between major cities, a
steady but unspectacular earner. "He had the same

chance at a takeover as I did," Kimmel said with a shrug.

"He spent eleven years acquiring Ferrence stock—a little here, a little there. Eleven years, Kimmel. And you came along and stole it right out from under his nose. I don't know how you did it and I don't even care. But, Kimmel, you took something my father wanted *only* because he wanted it."

"Bullshit."

"Is it? You'd never dabbled in transportation before and you haven't expanded since. The one thing that made Ferrence attractive was my father's interest in it. You sent my father into a depression he never recovered from, and you did it out of spite. Just spite. Nothing else."

Kimmel made a sound of exasperation. "Your sainted father played dirty himself often enough." He waved toward the stage. "Where do you think the money for your expensive toys came from? Probably from some company he stole from me."

"So the two of you just kept sticking it to each other."

The other man showed his teeth. "As often and as hard as we could."

Now it was Gil's turn to sound exasperated. "Wouldn't it have solved a helluva lot of problems if you'd just formed a partnership?"

Kimmel threw his head back and laughed in open delight. "My God, I didn't know they still made 'em that naive! Don't you understand, you young idiot? *It was what kept both of us going.*" He snorted. "A partnership!"

Gil reddened. "Then why did you pay Milo to kill him?"

Two feminine voices raised in immediate protest. Milo shouted: "I don't even know this man! I never saw him before tonight!"

Kimmel just raised his arms in a gesture of hopelessness and headed toward the costume room.

LaBoz went down to the edge of the stage and spoke to Gil. "You're going to get yourself sued if you go on saying things like that."

Gil shook his head. "The question had to be asked."

"But why now? Why wait a whole year?"

Gil nodded toward Shalimar. "This is the first time the councilwoman has left the Andamans since he died. And since she's a contributor . . ."

She stared at him. "What a presumptuous puppy you are."

"I wish *I* were in the Andamans," Milo proclaimed in understandable ill temper. "You truly are impossible, Gil. You insist I come here and then you accuse me of murder—I must say that's not my idea of a good time. When's the next funicular due?"

"Relax, Milo. We're almost finished."

Shalimar gestured toward LaBoz. "What about your Horatio? Is he next?"

"LaBoz doesn't perform," Gil said. "He had nothing to do with my father's death."

"And all the rest of us did," Phoebe said neutrally, slowly getting to her feet. "So you saved me until last, Gil. How flattering."

"Have you had time to make your choice?"

"It's obvious, isn't it? The gravedigger scene. The only appropriate conclusion to a deathday party. Besides, that's what this play-acting is all about, isn't it? You're digging someone's grave?"

A silence followed. "When you're ready," Gil finally said.

"No costume," Phoebe announced. "Just the auditory feed." LaBoz fitted the button in her ear, and she took her place center stage. "Start."

A graveyard flicked into view. The gravedigger sang a little song. Phoebe: "Has this fellow no feeling of his business, that 'a sings in grave-making?" Phoebe didn't move at all, ignoring the stage directions murmuring in her ear and speaking all her lines from the spot where she'd positioned herself. The holo figures in the scene moved across her, spoke to an empty place in the stage.

"Alas, poor Daddy! I knew him, Gil," Phoebe was saying. "A fellow of no jest whatsoever."

In the wings, LaBoz felt a chill. Kimmel, now changed back into his own clothes, said, "What's going on?"

"I'm not sure."

Phoebe intoned: "He hath borne grudges a thousand times against me."

"He helped you!" Gil shouted from the audience.

"My gorge rises at it," she said coldly.

LaBoz groped for the volume dial, turned off the sound. Silent images moved back and forth over the stage, Phoebe immobile in their midst.

"He saved the festival for you, Phoebe," Gil said heatedly. "How can you be so thankless?"

It was hard to read Phoebe's expression with the projected images moving over her face. "And do we simply ignore the fact that he was the reason the festival almost closed in the first place?"

"That's not true."

"What festival?" Kimmel asked LaBoz.

"Local music festival. Phoebe was in charge a couple of years ago."

"Gil, it is true," Phoebe was saying. "He knew you and I were on the verge of splitting and he wanted to obligate me to the family, to keep me from embarrassing his little boy. He bought up all our debts and then had his agent call them in. Just so he could step in at the eleventh hour with his big bankroll and play the rescuing hero."

"That's preposterous."

"And it didn't work. I left anyway. That sort of highhanded interference was so typical of your father. And Gil—you were growing more like him every day."

A holographic funeral procession entered in phantom silence from upstage right, then started crossing slowly and majestically to the grave. "For God's sake, somebody turn that thing off!" Milo's voice called out shrilly.

LaBoz took care of it. The graveyard and its spectral figures vanished; a white, harsh light flooded the stage. Kimmel walked out from the wings and faced Gil. "You need to learn how to listen, Gil. You've idealized your father to the point of unrecognizability."

Gil made a dismissive gesture. "You have to paint him a villain to justify your own actions. Phoebe, do you know what he did when I told him you'd gone? He threw up. That's how much he wanted you to stay."

"That was never the question, Gil. Of course he wanted me to stay. A disgruntled ex-spouse is always a vulnerable spot."

"He was so upset he couldn't think straight." Gil spoke slowly and with emphasis. "He couldn't protect himself in the clinches. His defenses were down."

Phoebe eyed him suspiciously. "Now you're saying I am responsible for his death?"

"You are responsible."

"Are you out of your mind? Do you think *I* got Milo to push him overboard?"

"I can't stand it!" Milo roared.

Shalimar stood up. "Gil, you've accused everyone here except LaBoz. Do you have any idea what you're talking about?"

Milo was pounding the back of the seat in front of him. "I—did—not—push him overboard! *I did not push him!*"

Gil looked at him a long moment—and then said: "No, of course you didn't, Milo. I never for one minute thought you did." Five startled faces turned toward him. "Sit down, all of you . . . please. I'll try to explain." He stood with his back to the stage facing them when they were all seated. "LaBoz, I apologize for dragging you through all this. I just needed one friendly face to look at."

LaBoz smiled, nodded.

"As for the rest of you," Gil went on, "I apologize for nothing. I accused each of you in turn because I wanted you to face your own roles in my father's death. Oh, there was no murder in the legal sense—he really did lose his footing and fall overboard, just as the investigators said. He cracked his head on the anchor chain . . . a gruesome way to die. But it wasn't murder. It was an accident."

Phoebe was frowning. "Then why . . . ?"

"Because you four did kill him, you know. At least, the four of you created a set of circumstances that resulted in a man's death. That was not your intention—but you contributed, in various ways and in varying degrees."

Kimmel snorted. "Finger pointing."

"You started it, Kimmel," Gil said. "If it weren't for that stupid, vicious rivalry between the two of you . . . all my life I heard *Gotta get Kimmel.* That was the atmosphere I grew up in." He turned to Phoebe. "It was too rich an atmosphere for my loving wife."

"Too *noxious* an atmosphere," she corrected.

"Tell me something. Did you leave me—or did you leave my father?"

"What difference does it make? You were becoming indistinguishable."

He nodded. "So you walked out just as the Ferrence Transportation deal was coming to a head. You threw him off-balance at a time he needed to be especially sharp. And so he lost out to Kimmel. I don't know why Ferrence was so important to him. But he was crushed at losing it." Gil paused, gathered his thoughts. "Phoebe, you knew how much that deal meant to him. You timed your departure to coincide with the final stages of the negotiations. You chose a moment to leave that would hurt him most."

Phoebe actually smiled. "Tit for tat."

"So one reason my father is dead is that his old enemy defeated him in what was more than just another contest. Another reason is that that defeat was made possible by his own son's wife. Phoebe and Kimmel—you two started him on his downhill slide. The other two of you had a chance to stop that slide—but you didn't."

"He demanded too much," Shalimar said sharply.

"I'm sure he did." Gil answered unhappily. "He expected one hundred percent from everybody. But the fact remains, the third reason my father is dead is that Shalimar did not throw him the lifeline he was looking for. So he came back from the Andamans and doped himself to the gills."

Milo began to squirm.

"Yes, Milo, you're last. I think I know what happened on the yawl. You just froze, didn't you? You saw a man drowning, but you couldn't move—you were paralyzed." Milo was nodding wordlessly. "You didn't mean to let him drown. You just didn't know what to do. The last reason my father is dead is that Milo is the kind of man he is."

There was a long silence. Eventually Kimmel cleared his throat. "You've overlooked the main reason your father is dead. He himself contributed. He let these things defeat him because he was the kind of man *he* was. If we were responsible for his death, so was he."

Gil threw up his hands in frustration. "But his death could have been prevented! If any one of you had acted differently, he'd still be alive. If Kimmel had left Ferrence alone, or Phoebe had waited one more week before leaving . . . if Shalimar had taken a leave of absence from her duties or if Milo had conquered his fear of water . . . if any *one* thing had happened differently—ah, if, if, if! But no, you all did what you did, and my father is dead because of it. Maybe he should have handled his setbacks better—I know he was flawed. He was just a man. But he deserved better from all of you. *He deserved better.*"

No one seemed inclined to argue the point, or to concede it, either. They were all feeling the strain of the past couple of hours; they'd gone as far as they could go. Shalimar stood up, brisk and all business. "When does the next funicular get here?"

LaBoz looked at his wrist. "Ten minutes." Without another word, Shalimar turned and started out.

"Wait—I'm coming, too." Milo hurried after her.

Phoebe got to her feet slowly. "What an incredible evening. All this . . . just to say *Shame on you*? Good-bye. Gil. Let's not meet again."

She was gone.

Gil's pinched face did a poor job of hiding his feelings. LaBoz dropped a friendly hand on his shoulder: *Hang in there.* Gil looked at Kimmel. "I suppose you stayed to tell me what a fool I've been."

"No. I stayed to tell you why your father wanted Ferrence Transportation so badly." The man looked troubled. "He wanted it for you. My spies told me he wanted to make you independent of him, and for his own reasons he'd decided Ferrence was the best way to make it happen. The minute I heard that, I knew I had to get Ferrence away from him." Kimmel rubbed the bridge of his nose. "It never occurred to me he'd go to pieces. It was just another move in the game as far as I was concerned."

Gil was surprised but recovered quickly. "That time it wasn't a game."

"I realize that now. He didn't crack up overnight, not him—it must have been building for a long time. But Ferrence was the trigger." He broke off, thinking. "You want to know something? Nothing has been as much fun since your father died. He was a rotten, underhanded son of a bitch—and I miss him. Maybe I should have left Ferrence alone. You were right about one thing. He deserved better."

Gil swallowed. "Well."

Kimmel made up his mind to something, stood up. "Gil, come see me. We can talk. We'll talk about Ferrence. I could never be partners with your father, but . . . don't get me wrong, I still think my picture of him is more accurate than yours. Yet maybe there's a chance you can still be your own man after all." He paused. "It's time we both laid his ghost to rest. I'm not promising anything, but it won't hurt to talk."

Kimmel nodded to both young men and turned to go. "Come tomorrow," he growled back over his shoulder, and left.

Gil and LaBoz took their drinks out onto the balcony. They leaned against the railing and looked down at the lights on the river that ran past the base of the hill. The funicular had come and gone, carrying the four murderers back to their own lives.

"Kimmel!" Gil said in bemusement. "What an unpredictable man. No wonder my father was afraid of him."

"He's crafty," LaBoz said lazily. "I hope you're taking fifteen lawyers with you tomorrow." LaBoz loved Gil's place; looking down from the hilltop on the world below always made him want to write something.

"Did you notice how they all revealed something essential about themselves when they were acting out their scenes?" Gil asked. "Shalimar's authority and self-possession. Milo's ultimate uselessness. Kimmel's flexibility and his determination. Phoebe's . . . Phoebe's immovableness."

"The play's still the thing," LaBoz murmured. "They say."

"At least I got through to one of them. Not the one I expected, but one anyway."

"Oh? Which one did you think?"

"Phoebe. I thought that now, after he's been dead a year . . . well. There was never any chance of reaching Milo, and Shalimar was an unknown quantity. But Kimmel—I never thought he'd be the one to listen."

Neither of them spoke for a few minutes. Then LaBoz asked, "Is it safe to say *The rest is silence* now?"

Gil smiled. "I think so. Yes, it is."

The funeral was over.

GOOD REPAIR

by Craig Shaw Gardner

Craig Shaw Gardner is the author of more than twenty novels, including the *Ebenezum* trilogy, and his more recent *Dragon Circle* series, which includes the novels *Dragon Sleeping, Dragon Waking,* and *Dragon Burning.* He has also written novelizations of several movies, including *Batman* and *Batman Returns.*

"DONNY? Are you sure you're all right?"

It made him smile. She only called him Donny when she was worried about him.

"Sure, Amy, I'm fine. I finally finished the project, and I think I'm going to enjoy a little down time." That is, he would as soon as he attended to whatever was going wrong in his office. He could hear that annoying error message all over his apartment.

"Well, you're a big boy now." Her image smiled at him as she pulled the long, dark hair out of her face. The crystal display on the portable phone didn't do her justice. "You sure you don't want me to come over?"

He paused before he answered. It was tempting. If he wasn't so tired—

"No, I think I'll just check the Web and get some

sleep. We're still on for the weekend? We'll have plenty of time, then."

Her image winked at him. "We'll always have time."

He always liked it when she said that. They said their good nights. He really shouldn't neglect her like this. If only there wasn't so much to do.

He flipped off the phone and strode back into his office.

"System error," the soothing female voice, not so different from Amy's, really, said over and over again. "System error."

"Yeah, yeah." He looked to the explanation on the wall-sized screen. What the hell? Whatever was wrong with the system, it extended to the screen, which seemed to be printing letters and numbers on top of one another until they were nothing but a white blur.

Well, he had saved all his work before talking to Amy, so no problem there. He hit reset.

He jumped at the scream.

"SUPER STIMS. LIVING LIFE TO THE FULLEST!"

The shout was followed by the blare of Mariachi horns, speedily playing the Super Stims jingle. He took a deep breath, doing his best to still his heart.

The ad-mailers had found some new way around the suppression fields. You always needed another upgrade. All of it was a game in a way, the technology of the ad and anti-ad programs leapfrogging over each other constantly. The ad programs had gotten pretty devious, able to attach themselves to microfiles, viruses, anti-viruses; just about anything. Who knew how this latest one had snaked its way in. He wondered if that alone was enough to screw up the system.

The ad program cut off as abruptly as it had begun. The horns stopped mid-blare. That was odd. Usually it took a quarter of an hour for you to purge the things from your system, by which time the jingle would be permanently embedded in your head.

The view screens had returned to default settings, showing views of the streets immediately around the apartment complex. When he couldn't get out, he liked to scan through the observation cameras; over a dozen different views of the surrounding streets. This late at night, there wasn't much out there; just the occasional vehicle cloaked in a security shield, guaranteed to mask vehicle, occupant, and whatever weapons might have been brought along for Personal Security.

He got his second shock of the night. There was actually somebody out there walking, all alone on the streets at this time of night. Don swore under his breath. The man was dressed all in black. He shuffled down the street, his head down, eyes nearly closed, as if lost in his own private world. This guy was either heavily armed and dangerous, or he was crazy and dangerous.

Whichever it was, Don had the feeling he'd find out soon. Three individuals with shaved heads sauntered down the street only half a block behind the lone man. Rather than hair, the three all sported neon implants, each of the three favoring a different color, yellow, red, and blue. The bright strands on their skulls strobed slowly at first, but faster and faster as they approached the man alone, as if the neon quickened with their adrenaline.

"Hey!" Red Neon called. "We found ourselves a ghost!"

The man alone looked up, pulled from his private thoughts. "What? Leave me alone."

Yellow Neon cackled. "What do you know? A talking ghost!"

"Shame he won't be talking for long," Red Neon added.

The gang thought it was hilarious. Don realized that all three of them were holding knives.

They moved in to have their fun. From the way the blades glowed in the darkness, Don could tell the punks all held Battery Blades, the latest rage in street weapons, designed to both cut and stun. After all, with its high water content, blood was an excellent conductor.

It looked like they were going to kill him. These same cameras fed directly to the building's security system. They'd been at it for a while now. Where were the police?

Knives flashed in the neon glow. The way the three huddled around their fallen victim, Don couldn't see much of anything. But he could certainly hear the screams.

The victim somehow broke free of the others. He slipped once, maybe on his own blood, but kept from falling. He pushed past the punks and lurched straight toward Don's viewpoint. The punks were only a step behind. One raised his knife above his head and plunged it forward, the lighted blade flashing in a downward arc straight into the victim's back.

The camera was covered by spurting blood. As the blood ran down the screen, it formed into red letters against the black background:

"REMEMBER! IF YOU GO OUT BY YOUR-SELF, YOU ONLY HAVE YOURSELF TO BLAME!"

This wasn't even real! It was a goddamned PSA. The ad stims were everywhere. Don jabbed at the reset button.

All his screens went blank. There wasn't even an error message.

This was ridiculous. There were supposed to be safeguards against this kind of system failure. Something, or someone, was messing with him.

A chime sounded. "Don, you have company."

It was the voice of the doorbell. The doorbell? He hardly recognized it. Who besides Amy ever used the doorbell? And after he had entered her handprint ID, even she had bypassed the system.

Don scanned the console on his armrest, pressing the button to show the view outside his apartment.

Somehow, that camera was still working; a view of the hallway outside flashed on his largest screen.

A man in a blue uniform smiled up at the camera. "Service."

"Service?" Don demanded. "Service for what?"

"Basic Systems Error. The whole building's down. I've been monitoring the individual units; that's how I knew you were still up, trying to access your system. Bet you're not having much luck."

"Well," Don answered a bit reluctantly. "Yeah."

"Well, it's a bit of luck for us, actually—the fact you're up this late. If we don't get to each of these units individually, and soon, the whole place could fry."

"I'm sorry, but—"

"We think it's a stealth obsolescence program." The serviceman wasn't going to give Don time to object. "We got news of it this afternoon. We have to purge each subsystem individually. It's a real hands-on experience. If we don't do it now, your whole system might have to be replaced."

Stealth obsolescence? Don had heard of that sort of thing when he'd been out browsing, some of the big conglomerates trying to goose their profits, but he hadn't really paid it any attention. Rumors of that sort were so paranoid, he generally ignored them. Like a lot on the Web, paranoia was a great way to waste your time.

But this was beyond paranoia. This was screwing up his place, messing with his system.

He stared hard at the image of the serviceman. "I assume you have some identification? And a work order?"

The repairman laughed. "What was I thinking about, this time of night, too?" He placed his hand on the apartment palm-reader as he read from his digital clipboard. "Securiteam Member Jason Taylor here to check and clean Unit 21B-Rear, occupant Donald Winslow. Authorization Code B79988—"

The screen went blank. That signal was gone, too.

Don guessed he'd better open the door while he still had electricity. But not before he took some precautions of his own.

He walked quickly into the bedroom and pulled the revolver from the back of his sock drawer. The gun, a Smith and Wesson .38, had been in his family for generations. What had his father always told him? A man had to protect his home.

He tucked the gun into the back of his jeans, and pulled on a loose fitting sweater to hide the bulge. Only when he felt his weapon was secure, and hidden, did he move to the front door.

The identigrid was flashing on the inside of the door. Half the security guard's information had made it here before this system, too, had frozen:

JASON TAYLOR, SECURITEAM AUTHORIZED. PALM PRINT, OK. RETINAL SCAN—the read-out stopped, followed by a whole bunch of garbage.

You had to take some chances in life. Don opened the door.

The repairman smiled at him. He had a very faint scar that ran from his cheekbone down across his chin; the sort of thing low-res cameras didn't pick up. It made him look somewhat more dangerous than his video image.

"All right. I was about to give up on you, Mr. Winslow. Can I call you Don? Everybody calls me Jace." He pushed past Don, into the apartment. "Now we can really get to work."

Don felt like he was already losing control here. "Just what is it exactly that you have to do?"

"I've got to get at the heart of your system. Once I see just what you've got, we can figure out what to do. Where's your primary?"

Don pointed toward his office.

"You're a bachelor, right? Mrs. MacShea, down in 21C-front? She has her primary operating out of her

kitchen. Some women are like that, huh?'' He glanced
back at Don as he reached the office door. "You know
her, right?''

Actually, Don didn't really know any of his neighbors. What with so many people plugged into home
offices, the building's occupants kept wildly different
hours. You certainly didn't talk to anybody out on the
streets these days, and it was impolite to make eye
contact on the elevators. He had seen two or three
middle-aged women in the hallways. He guessed Mrs.
MacShea had to be one of them.

The repairman stepped into Don's office and looked
around. "Pretty up-to-date for this building.'' He
walked over to the main access panel and opened a
pouch at his belt. "Well, Mrs. MacShea—actually, she
asked me to call her Julia—sweet old broad, she could
barely tolerate what we had to do.'' He pulled the
smallest electric screwdriver Don had ever seen from
his pouch and rapidly went about freeing the panel.
"Fooling with her kitchen was like cutting out her
heart, I guess. I had to call in one of the other techs
to take her and sit her in the bedroom until she
calmed down.''

He pulled the panel free and looked inside. "You,
though, a guy living alone like you—I guess you live
alone?'' He glanced back at Don, who didn't give him
an answer one way or the other. This guy was here
to fix a problem, not learn Don's life story.

Jace nodded for him. "Yeah. You go into enough
apartments, after a while you can tell. Well, Don,
being a bachelor, living alone, you're not going to get
emotionally involved in the same way. At least I hope
not. The stealth program gets worse with time. If we
can catch it in the early stages, though . . .'' Jace
shrugged. "Look at it this way. The less time I'm here,
the less problems you're going to have.''

The repairman took a small flashlight from his pack
and shone it into the innards of Don's primary control
panel. He grunted in approval.

"Your system has some built-in safeguards. It'll make my job easier." He pulled out a small set of wire cutters.

What now? Don didn't like this at all. Ever since his system had started shutting down, Don had felt like he was losing control.

"Look," he began. "Why don't you let me handle some of that? I actually know what's inside there pretty well. I personally customized—"

Jace shook the wire cutters at Don. "Don't worry," he chided with that same smile. "I'm not going to mess with anything I can't easily replace."

He flicked the light he had in his left hand on and off and on again, making clicking sounds with his tongue as he examined the computer's innards. "I do like to talk. You wouldn't think so, but it helps me to focus on my work. Say, you wouldn't happen to have something to drink around here, would you? A can of soda or something? This troubleshooting can be thirsty work."

Something to drink? Don supposed that would be polite, but he felt as if he were fixed to the spot. As long as Don stood here and watched the repairman, he was able to maintain some illusion of control. He didn't want to leave Jace alone with the apartment's primary system.

"Ah, hell!" Jace exclaimed as he thrust the wire-cutters into the enclosed darkness. "It's late at night. I've been working for fourteen hours straight. Why don't you make that a beer?"

"A beer?" What was he talking about? How could he drink while he was repairing sensitive electronics? "I'm sorry—"

"Whoops!" Jace called. He shook his head as he looked at Don. "See what you made me do? I meant to get the next one over, but when you distracted me—" He laughed. "We'll just have to fix that." He looked at the wire-cutters still in his hand. "In the wrong hands, this could kill someone."

Now Don was starting to get annoyed. "What do you mean, I distracted you? I'm not the one who barged into someone's home in the middle of the night—"

"Now, now, Don," Jace interrupted. "I'm here to help you. It pays to be nice to me, you know."

Where did this repairman get off? "You're paid to fix the damn thing. Why don't you do that and get out of here!"

Jace sighed. "You're not going to get emotional on me, too? Remember how I told you about Mrs. Mac-Shea? Do you want me to have to call someone to calm you down, too?"

Don stared at the repairman. Could they do something like that? In his own apartment? Don did want to protect his system. He had to calm down. So Jace didn't have very good people skills. Don should be able to put up with his obnoxious behavior for a few more minutes. It was worth it to fix the system, and get the repairman out of here.

Jace pulled out some kind of small gray cube with a digital display. Don figured it had to be some sort of diagnostic device. The repairman put both his hands back in the control box. For a moment, he didn't speak.

"There. I've hooked it back together. You won't even know you had a problem. Fourteen hours on the job, you can get a little shaky." He pulled out the small cube. "What have we got here? Donny boy! You really like those X-rated files, don't you?"

"What?" Don exploded. "What are you—"

"Not that I'm judging you, Don," the repairman continued. "A bachelor's got to have a little fun, right? But maybe we can talk about that some other time. I'm on the clock here, in more ways than one. He reached into his pack again. "Now we'd better do what I came here for."

He pulled a curved, segmented tube that came to a

point at one end. It looked to Don like a wasp cast in metal.

"This baby here will detect any foreign programs or unauthorized codes," Jace said, "and then it will obliterate them." He flicked a small switch on the instrument's side. It made a noise like a dentist's drill.

He plunged it into the open darkness. Another sound came out of the control box, like metal grinding metal.

"Is that thing safe in there?" Don asked.

The repairman winced slightly at the noise, but he kept on smiling. "Oh, it shouldn't damage anything that's supposed to be in here, so long as I'm careful. It will purge anything that's not supposed to be in here, though, software or hardware. So how about that beer?"

This was going too far. First this guy looks at his personal files, then he wants to start drinking.

"Look," Don said firmly, "I never agreed to get you a beer. In fact, I don't think it's a very good—"

"Some of those files, Don," Jace interrupted smoothly, "they have to do with bondage, don't they? Some messy forms of discipline, too. I, of course, only take an academic interest in that sort of thing, but if your mother was to find out . . ."

"My mother?" Don took a step towards the repairman. "I think it's time for you to get out of there."

"Oh, Don. I'll be done in just another minute." The noise from inside the control box changed again, this time to a high whine that made Don's teeth ache. Something popped inside the controls. Sparks shot out past Jace's arms.

The repairman coughed as he waved smoke from his face. "Oops. Another little accident." His brow furrowed as he peered into the darkness. "This one might be a little more serious."

Don took a step forward. "What have you done?"

The repairman froze him with a single glance. "You don't understand, Don. You wanted to stop my work back there. I can't listen to that sort of thing. It makes me nervous." He smiled again. "I make mistakes."

Don really had had enough of this. "You're not going to make any more mistakes here."

Jace shook his head. "Oh, Don, Don. This has to be done now. Do you want me to have to call in the cavalry? I thought you'd be so much more reasonable than Mrs. MacShea. You know women, how they get so emotional."

Don took a deep breath. Maybe punching a repairman wasn't the best course of action. If this was almost over, he could get this character out of his life forever. "How long did you say this was going to take?"

Jace glanced back at the open control grid. "Not long at all. I'd say, Don, that I'm almost done with you." He poked the wasplike instrument back into the hole. For the moment, it hardly made any noise at all.

"Poor Mrs. MacShea," Jace continued as he worked. "She got so very upset. Just because I was a little clumsy with a couple of her family heirlooms. Hey, pottery was meant to be broken, right? She got worse than you, demanding that I leave before I could finish. Well, I had to get her out of the way, didn't I? We actually had to bring in two of my buddies. They took her right out of the kitchen and into her bedroom." He glanced up at Dan and winked. "They were able to keep her occupied until I finished my work."

Don stared at the other man. "Are you threatening me?"

Jace shook his head. "Don, you surprise me. Actually, I was threatening you when I said I'd talk to your mother. She's so frail and sensitive these days, isn't she? It was a shame about the disappearance of your father. Learning about the filth her son's involved in, well, it might just about kill her, wouldn't you say?"

"That's it!" Don shouted. "That's enough! I want you out of here!"

The repairman looked mildly surprised. "No can do, Don. But if you keep interrupting me like this, I may have to call in some of my boys." The smile was back. "They may have to be a little rougher with you than they were with poor Mrs. MacShea."

Don rushed toward him.

"Oh, Don." Jace held the wire-cutters before him. "These cut a lot more than just wires.

Don pulled the gun. "Get out of here!"

"What?" Jace acted like people pulled guns on him every day. "How can I leave before my job is done? That wouldn't be professional at all."

His lack of fear only made Don more angry. "Get out of here, or I'll kill you!"

The repairman shook his head firmly. "I will not leave before I'm done, with you, your system, or your family. You knew that, Donny, from the moment I walked in here."

Don walked forward slowly, the gun aimed between the repairman's eyes. "Move, or I'll kill you."

The smile was gone from Jace's face at last.

"Sir, I have to warn you that shooting repair personnel could void your service contract." He waited a beat before waving the wire-cutters. "Of course, I could always kill you first." He glanced back at the control panel. "And then I'll call up your mother and tell her how you died." He giggled. "Of course, I'll make up the more interesting details."

The repairman thought that was hilarious. He laughed until tears rolled down his cheeks.

"Enough!" Don screamed.

The repairman agreed at last. He jumped up with a yell and lunged for Don.

Don shot him at point blank range. The repairman spasmed, the wire-cutters missing Don's ear by an inch. One bullet in the head, and he was dead.

"Whoo!" Don cheered, throwing the gun down on his chair. What a rush.

The repairman was the first to go, gone from the

floor without even a drop of blood left behind. The
room reestablished itself in under a minute. Besides
the faint smell of burnt cordite, you wouldn't even
know he fired a gun.

Damn, those new holographics were good. The bullet had punched a hole in the console. He supposed
he shouldn't use a real weapon in these things, but,
heck, a gun gave it a real feeling of danger. And the
way he'd juiced up that program, it had almost gotten
away from him. Almost, but not quite. That was the
important thing, to be back in control.

Besides, it didn't look like the bullet had hit anything vital. The new diagnostic repair program should
fix it up in no time. And these repairs would be made
behind the scenes, the way it should be.

Don took a deep breath.

Not a bad night at all; just about the best one he'd
had. He could do it all over again.

The phone rang, right on cue.

"Donny?" Amy asked. "Are you sure you're all
right?"

He held up his end of the conversation, but something didn't feel right. Even though he said the words,
he didn't really feel them. After what had just happened, he needed to challenge himself.

Maybe if he made Amy a blonde.

THE KIDNAPPING OF
RONI TAHR

by Alan Rodgers

Alan Rodgers' short fiction has appeared in such
anthologies as *Miskatonic University, Tales from
the Great Turtle, Masques #3,* and *The Conspiracy Files.* His first published short story, "The
Boy Who Came Back from the Dead" won the
Horror Writers Association's Stoker Award for
Best Novelette. He lives in Hollywood, California.

LONG before the trial, before the spectacle, before
the kidnapping and the apprehension—before all of
that there was a comet in the sky.

Some folks called it the Wise Kings' Star, and said
it was the harbinger of the Second Coming. Other
folks called it the Wishing Star, and said it was the
candle of our dreams.

The scientists were uniformly less romantic.

"It's a menace," they said. "An interplanetary body
in an orbit that will intersect the Earth—catastrophic-
ally."

The reporters who translated that into English said
it meant that we were all about to die.

"This is how the dinosaurs became extinct," Ted
Koppel said on *Nightline.* "A comet—or perhaps it

was a meteor of enormous size—hit ground in Yucatan, remaking our geography, and shattering the world. Weather patterns went into eclipse for centuries and whole ecologies collapsed. Could this be the fate that awaits us in the coming weeks? Will mankind go the way of the Tyrannosaur?"

His guests went on to bolster all of the most frightful speculations.

"We have ten weeks," said Dr. Ken Roman of the Institute for Psychical Research in Tuskegee, Alabama. "The comet's orbit, of course, is relentless; there's no chance that it could turn away. Could we turn it away? All the nuclear force that we possess, concentrated into a solitary Gotterdammerung, might well disperse it—but it might just as well transform the icy menace into a fiery nuclear holocaust, descending on the Earth."

The dirty-looking man beside him—an apocalyptic lyricist who'd written three eerily prophetic numbers released on a grunge rock album the year before—gave a little laugh.

"*'Some say the world will end in fire,'*" he said, quoting Frost. "*'Some say in ice. From what I've tasted of desire, I hold with those who favor fire. But if it had to perish twice, I think I know enough of hate to say that for destruction ice is also great. And would suffice.'*"

Ted gave a little laugh, because Ted Koppel is a literate man who recognized the quote; the other members of the panel looked at the grunge poet as though he'd grown wings and commenced to fly.

"Frost," said the lyricist. "If you don't know him, you should."

At twenty minutes of the hour, newsmen broke into the panel to report the announcement everyone expected: There'd been a big meeting in the secret halls of the United Nations Security Council, and the big powers had agreed to send up all of their thermonuclear munitions under the control of an American shuttle pilot. The technical setup of the mission would take five weeks, at a minimum, but that still left plenty of time on the outside if something went impossibly wrong.

After the news interruption, the panel was a bevy of relief. *Everything's going to be okay,* someone said, *the cavalry's come over the hill.*

And they all believed that for a moment that went on till the camera lights went down.

Believed it through the evening, past dawn into the day.

But at 10:27 AM that next morning, Washington time, one of the astronomers who'd been watching through the night panicked.

And called Reuters.

By noon the hysteria had found us all, consuming us forever.

REUTERS—Astronomers who ask not to be identified report that the Earth-bound comet popularly known as the Wishing Star—one of the largest ice-and-gravel objects ever observed in the solar system—has begun to accelerate out of its orbit.

Astronomers and others were at a loss to explain the acceleration.

"Heavenly bodies don't pick up and soar out of their orbits," the scientist said. "It can't happen. And it doesn't. But we're observing it."

The unnamed scientist refused to speculate on causes. "You want me to talk about woo-woo stuff?" he asked. "I'm not going to do it. Call it a frightening anomaly—because the thing is still moving toward the Earth. Much, much faster, now. It will impact somewhere in the next forty-eight hours if it continues at this rate."

They tried to get a shuttle up in time, but there was none in adequate repair to launch on such short notice—NASA's engineers were still hard at work on the O rings when the Wishing Star sped through the moon's orbital circumference. NORAD did what it could, sending three volleys of ICBMs up through the atmosphere to smash the comet—but the only smashing came when the missiles themselves shattered lifeless and dead against the comet's crystalline façade.

"What happened to the warheads?" Ted asked on *Nightline*. "Those missiles should have blasted bright enough to light the dark side of the moon."

This was the *Nightline* deathwatch show; it started early at 10 PM, Eastern, and was scheduled to run through impact (and the presumed end of the world) at 2:37 AM.

No one had an answer, of course, as to why the NORAD missiles did not detonate. No more than they had a notion why or how a comet could accelerate toward the Earth.

But at seven minutes after one in the morning, the newsmen had more news.

"Ted, we've got a bulletin. It's big."

"Go ahead, Pete, break in. What's up?"

"The comet is decelerating into orbit around the Earth. And the astronomers have gotten a good look at the impact spots where the NORAD missiles died—they say that the comet isn't a comet."

"Isn't a comet?" Ted asked, sounding puzzled and confused. "Well then what the devil is it?"

"They say it looks to be some sort of a spaceship, sheathed in ice."

The engineers in the repair bay managed to solve their O-ring problem somewhere after four o'clock that morning. The lift-prep team went directly into action—fueling, rolling out, and setting up the shuttle. They cut corners that weren't safe to cut, and it's a wonder no one died in the launch that followed. But no one did, and in retrospect the prep crew did the only thing they could, given the emergency; and some folks will try to tell you that they cut their corners prudently at that.

Regardless: At 6:03 AM Eastern the shuttle *Defiance* took off from Canaveral, bound toward the bright new artificial moon that hung above our world.

At 6:32 the *Defiance* eased into an orbit alongside the Wishing Star.

At 6:37 the shuttle crew began trying to hail the crew of the vast icebound spaceship—by radio; with flares. By maneuvering about the alien craft, looking for a portal that might offer entry.

But they found no response.

At length they attempted to breach the alien craft themselves, space-walking about the spaceship's icy surface for hours and hours, looking for some sign of life.

But there was none.

Then they attempted to force an entry, clearing the icy capsule away until they could pry at the hull with their hammers and their bars.

To no avail.

Nothing that the crew of the shuttle *Defiance* attempted to do to the alien vessel had any effect at all—and none of it prompted reaction, either.

In the end, their commanders down in Houston ordered them back home to Edwards Airforce Base.

And then the world began to wait.

It didn't have to wait for long.

Forty-eight hours after the *Defiance* touched down at Edwards, a tiny craft of alien design emerged from an aperture in the great icebound vessel, and slowly slowly slowly it descended.

It didn't bother to slow and burn through orbit; the aliens descended on a plume of force made of fire, dust, and miracles—technologies that no one knew or could imagine let them descend vertically toward Washington.

Washington, D.C.

The unearthly craft descended exactly at the thick of things, toward Pennsylvania Avenue at rush hour,

where a thousand thousand cars and trucks and buses
braced at one another, pushing traffic toward escape
at low velocity.

When the alien shuttle hung a dozen yards above
the ground, it hesitated, as though waiting for the traffic to disperse.

And after a while the traffic *did* disperse.

And the alien module descended to the pavement.

And a portal opened, releasing a ramp.

As Roni Tahr emerged.

That was the first moment that anyone in the
world—anyone on *our* world—caught sight of Roni
Tahr. Till that moment, no human man or woman had
ever seen him or heard tell of him; and while there
are those who claim they always knew he was to walk
among us there isn't any realistic cause to take them
seriously.

The alien shuttle opened, and Roni Tahr emerged;
some people mark that moment as the dawning of
the age.

He didn't look human, Roni Tahr. But he didn't
look so alien then, either.

A child on the sidewalk gasped at the sight of Roni
Tahr. "He's beautiful," the child said. "Is he a person,
Mommy? A people person, like you and me and
Daddy are?"

His mother hesitated, but she knew the answer all
the same.

"Of course he is, Patrick," the mother said. "Never
let yourself think otherwise—a person is a person no
matter who they are."

Roni Tahr heard all of that, and smiled at the
woman. "We come in peace," he said. "We come to
know your world, and cherish it and you."

She was wrong, of course. There were doubters
then, and there are doubters now; even her own son
had doubted till she'd set him straight.

But for all that she was wrong, still she spoke a
fundamental truth: none could see Roni Tahr without

that same stirring of the heart. To see him truly is a spiritual wonder; and while it's true that there are those whose hearts breed hatred deeper than the sea, it's also true that those folks see and love him, too, no matter how they find the rage to loathe him equally or more.

By the time Roni Tahr reached the sidewalk, there were television cameras focused on him, watching; a crowd had already begun to line the streets that led from the landing site on Pennsylvania Avenue to the White House.

Four other aliens—assistants, disciples, or body-guards; no one is certain—four other aliens followed Roni Tahr to the White House from his landing craft. Their names were Ileja, Kure, Orogarn, and Mathos, but little more is known of them.

"They're having a parade, Mommy," the little boy called.

And in a way it was like a parade: the crowd pulled away from the street to line the sidewalk, just as it might line a parade route; despite the hour, traffic cleared from Pennsylvania Avenue in both directions, as far as the eye could see.

Roni Tahr and his four shadowy companions strode easily toward the White House, waving to the onlookers, taking in the welcome and the joy that held the city—

—till they reached the White House gates, and found their way barred by three dozen of the Secret Service.

"I'm sorry, sir," the senior agent said, hat in hand, shamefaced. "We can't allow you to proceed."

Roni Tahr frowned, and nodded sadly. "I understand," he said. "Duty calls us all."

His English was remarkable: utterly unaccented in any way, but colored by a lilt that brought exotic circumstance to mind, a sound that warmed the heart and filled it with all possibility and prospects for the age.

And then the President himself arrived at the gate, followed by his minions.

"Sam," he called, "That isn't necessary, Sam. I'd like to greet these gentlemen myself."

The President smiled the facile homespun and half-sincere smile that was his trademark, and now the Secret Service stood aside.

We know this about the President's meeting with Roni Tahr, because there were witnesses:

We know that the President escorted Roni Tahr and his companions into the White House, and showed him many things: the Oval Office; the famous halls and meeting places. Offices of great officers and small; map rooms, situation rooms.

The president's own quarters, ultimately.

We know that they broke bread together, and went on to share a meal.

We know that their conversation ran long and genial, into the night.

Till finally near midnight the President and Roni Tahr dismissed the aides who'd dined with them, and the President led Roni Tahr into a secure and solitary room, where the two of them spoke privately at length and in substance about the future of the world—and so many things beyond it.

No one knows for certain what was said within those walls, for the room was impossibly secure, and there were no witnesses but the President himself and Roni Tahr.

But there are records from the White House purser that suggest the general form of their discussion: At three o'clock in the morning the President had his valet bring them coffee; at half past four he woke the chef to bring them cognac and fine Dominican cigars.

At five, Roni Tahr rejoined his companions, and the five of them left the White House in a Presidential limousine that took them across the street and through the gathered crowd to the Hotel Washington.

There they took possession of an extensive suite of rooms two floors below the Penthouse, where they rested undisturbed seven hours, seven minutes, and seven seconds.

Undisturbed because a thousand Marines and Secret Service men stood guard in the corridor outside their suite.

When Roni Tahr emerged at last, three Secret Servicemen led him to a room where a dozen junior agents had set up operations to screen their calls.

"You're going to need help, sir," the senior agent said, "to weed through the mass of folks who want to talk to you. Some of them—I think you'll want to talk to some of them. You've come to Earth to meet us, haven't you? There are people here you'll want to see, places that you'll want to go. But you can't deal with all of them yourself—there are just too many folks who want to talk to you."

"There is no need," said Roni Tahr. "We will contact those we must—they have no need to seek us out."

Roni Tahr was as good as his word, of course. When he appeared on the news, he came to us deliberately, in the hour and on the segment of his own choosing; when he spoke to Sam Donaldson on the White House lawn it was at his own instigation—indeed, he took Donaldson and his camera crew entirely off guard, for though they had tried mightily to reach him, their effort had gone unavailing.

When Roni Tahr appeared before the United Nations, that, too, came at his own moment, at his own direction; he came unheralded and unannounced into the Security Council, and regardless of the sentries who sought to bar his way. And then he stood before the captains of the world and spoke peace, without waiting to hear what they might say in turn.

He didn't give them orders, instructions, or directions; he greeted them and offered him his observations of those first days upon our world.

He told them things about our world we always knew but never dared admit to ourselves.

In those first days of the age, Roni Tahr spoke to each of the news organizations, answering their questions, basking in their curiosity. The talk shows all lamented that he would not speak to them, but that hardly gave them pause, in the end—for they were much freer to speak of him when they did not know him than they ever could have been had they interviewed the alien directly.

As on the talk shows and the nets, we all shouted furiously at one another, each of us certain that we and we alone knew the nature of the creature who had come to walk among us.

We each came to our own conclusions, in the end.

And who could say if that was accident or design? No one could—or should.

Cameras followed Roni Tahr and his disciples everywhere; we all watched him hours and hours every day. Telephoto lenses and directional microphones allowed all of us to hang for hours on his every word, live on CSpan 4; no one could ever say we did not know great Roni Tahr before his disappearance.

We saw him spend long hours—whole days at a time—taking in our world, one neighborhood at a time; we all saw him walk the benighted streets of Washington, till the cameramen grew weary and the Secret Service on the street wearied of its charge? Watching people on the streets; gazing up into the shattered windows of the towering apartment-project buildings.

And who ever could forget the sight of Roni Tahr when the child fell from her decrepit bicycle to wound her brow against the pavement? That great slight and powerful alien frame stooping to lift the child in his arms. Whispering sweet comforts to the child as he carried her to her home, up the stairs, through the hall where vermin scattered noisome in their wake; into her apartment where her mother grieved and cried and worried at the wound as she tended to her child.

The cameras caught all of that, and no one who has seen those tapes ever will forget them.

What days those were! All the nation's scandals and disgraces; the turpitudes of nations and the ignominy of regions vast and small; the wars that plagued the world with battle, pestilence, and slaughter—all those things grew small before the eye, and vanished from the mind; in an hour a day, a week those things all vanished from the earth for inattention as surely as they'd vanished from our hearts.

As the world watched Roni Tahr.

Now here at last there *was* Peace in Our Time, because the things that set us against ourselves had made themselves too petty to contemplate. For an hour, a day, a week as we watched Roni Tahr explore our world, the world was as it always should have been.

And then, a week and a day after he'd come to us, the bastards kidnapped Roni Tahr.

And changed the world forever in ways that not even Roni Tahr could ever have foreseen.

No camera saw the kidnappers perform their vile work. No witnesses described them; not one onlooker saw anything untoward. Even to this day the kidnapping of Roni Tahr remains a mystery: how did the xenophobic zealots find their way into the Hotel Washington? How could they begin to make their way into the suites the aliens occupied, past a good thousand Marines and Secret Service men?

And how in all the worlds there ever were or will be did they sneak Roni Tahr and his four companions out of their quarters without attracting the attention of the police, the guards, the soldiers—for God's sake, how could they ever have got past the hundreds of reporters and cameramen who waited inside and outside the hotel?

No one imagines an answer to that question. There are no answers to be had.

But we know this much: we know that the hotel steward entered the alien suite at six forty-five in the morning, Washington time, to set out clean towels, prepare the aliens' breakfast, and generally make ready for the new day.

And what he found inside that suite was chaos of the highest order.

Furniture crushed, broken, scattered hither and yon about the suite; bullet holes and bloodstains in and on the walls; deep stains and singes in the carpet.

And the whole place reeked—not the outré foetor we all recognize from our encounters with the aliens, but something nastier. More feral, and endlessly more primal: the suit stank of burned and rotting human flesh.

Stank powerfully—overwhelmingly, in fact; the odor was so vile and so forceful that from the moment that the steward opened the door to the suite, no one in the hall could mistake it.

Within five minutes the stink had found its way throughout the hotel.

The ransom note demanded seven billion in gold bullion. The sheer size of the demand made many certain that the kidnappers had the help and sanctuary of a hostile power—or perhaps a jealous one?

One paper accused the French. Three others blamed the Chinese.

Some folks knew it had to be the KGB, but the KGB itself found that as amusing as anyone could.

The FBI certainly could have vouched for them. The FBI plunged directly into the investigation, and took assistance everywhere it came to them—and the KGB, uneasy as it was about the kidnapping, offered more assistance than even the historic record would suggest. The American intelligence agencies; the Korean and Japanese services; military and civilian operatives from all around the globe offered what assistance they could render.

In the end, in fact, it was the KGB that led the Americans to the kidnappers' door.

But it took them a long, long time to do it—days and days.

Weeks.

Seventeen days, to be precise.

Seventeen days, ten hours, thirty-nine minutes. And seven seconds.

Roni Tahr himself is the only one of the aliens ever recovered. The others remain missing to this day— their fates and circumstances are mysteries to all of us. Likely, in the end, they'll be enigmas when they write the histories as well.

We have detailed audiovisual records of Roni Tahr's weeks in captivity.

This is an amazing fact. And a painful one: we have a record because one of one of Roni Tahr's warders wore a wire for the KGB.

Wore a datacube recorder, more specifically.

All through Roni Tahr's captivity, he rested in sight of the agents of our authority—and, sadly, beyond our grasp. The KGB mole in the xenophobe cell was a deep, long-term plant; he had damn little desire to blow his cover, even for the sake of Roni Tahr; and in any case had less opportunity than desire.

In a very real sense, the heat surrounding the search for Roni Tahr imprisoned his captors even as they imprisoned him.

"Where am I?" Roni Tahr rasped as he woke. He blinked his unearthly eyes vertically open, shut, open; he swallowed three times, open-mouthed.

"I have your breakfast," his keeper said.

This man's name was Eli, and he spoke English with an accent that suggested the Near East, but could just

as well have marked him as an Eastern European or
a speaker of High German.

"Who are you?" Roni Tahr asked. "What am I
doing here?"

Eli smiled. "I am Eli," he said, proudly. "You are
my guest."

A beat. Another.

"As your guest, then," Roni Tahr responded, "I
would take my leave. Will you bring me to my
companions? My duty calls."

Eli laughed derisively.

"*Sojourner* might be a better word," he said. "You
are not free to leave. It is possible you may never
leave this room." He frowned. "Alive."

Blink. Swallow. Blink.

"I see."

Eli nodded. "I knew you would," he said.

In those first hours the FBI's search was fitful and
uncertain. The monetary demand drew it to question
representatives of hostile foreign powers—for only a
nation state could spend funds into the billions without making its guilt obvious to all and sundry; and
who else had the resources to attempt the impossible?
There were folks who said (quite credibly) that the
aliens themselves had to have had a hand in the disappearance. Terrestrial technologies, after all, don't admit
the disappearance of five persons and an unknown (but
presumably large) number of abductors—not from ul-
trasecure quarters like those on the impregnable Em-
issaries' Quarters of the semi-penultimate floor of the
Hotel Washington.

There simply is no *earthly* way anyone could kidnap
five aliens from those quarters, the argument went,
undetected by the thousands of prying eyes, pacing
sentries, and soldiers standing watch.

But everyone who saw Roni Tahr knew that there
were ways among the stars beyond our ken; unearthly

and extraterrestrial ways that frightful things could happen before the watchful gaze of thousands.

Never mind the details; no one had them. But we all knew, all the same.

Someone's in league with the aliens, the whisper went, *to kidnap Roni Tahr.*

And the answer came: *but Roni Tahr is an alien.*

And the universe is vast enough for menace—and opposition, too.

No one had an answer for that last. It brought the terror to each heart that considered it; it told us everything the feared to know, and assured us of the worst angels of our destiny.

"They're balking at the ransom," Eli said an hour before noon. "If they refuse, alien, you die."

Blink.

"Then I will die," said Roni Tahr.

Eli nodded. "You show a brave face, alien. I admire that in men." Smile. "But you are not a man."

Nod.

"No," said Roni Tahr. "I am not a man. And you are not a Tahr. Is this a concern? We speak; you hear. I understand. Who is a man? What is a Tahr?"

Eli gave a little laugh.

"Yes," he said, pleased. And then he caught himself, for it was him whose body kept the cube. "You are not a man, and you will die."

"Indeed," said Roni Tahr. "Death comes for all of us in time; the ends of all our days are constant as the dictates of the logic of biology."

Eli gave his prisoner a puzzled look. "English," he said. "You're talking nonsense."

Roni Tahr shook his head. "No," he said, "I never would. I meant to tell you only this: everything that God makes will die, returning to the Creator as the breath you draw returns to the sky. Nothing lives immutably forever—because any family that could not change to face the challenges around it would surely die forever."

Eli still didn't follow, but he wearied of the attempt to understand.

"Whatever," he said. "I will now prepare your lunch. Lie there quietly and I will leave you unbound."

"And if I attempt escape?"

Eli laughed.

"There is no escape. You will be civil, or you will not. It does not much concern me."

"I see," said Roni Tahr. And hesitated. "What does concern you, Eli? What brings us to this time, this circumstance? How come you to this place and time?"

Eli smiled.

"I am none of your concern," he said. "Remember that and we will both live longer lives."

The FBI began its search with embassies and safe houses, targeting known hostiles—particularly the ones who were well financed. The Libyans; the Sudanese. Iran. Myanmar, reflexively hostile to the West for decades and now possessed of real wealth from the pillage of its rain forests. Serbia, which found itself awash in Uranium money that year.

It took three and a half days for the FBI to raid and search every known safe house in metropolitan Washington; another two for it to finish all of those in the northeast and upper south.

Searching the embassies was another matter, since embassies are technically the territory of the foreign nation whose envoys they house. On the face of things our government pays great respect to that sovereignty, and expects the same regard in turn—but the Feds have ways to search the embassies, mark my word. They used them that week. They had used them before. And they surely will again.

By noon of the seventh day after the kidnapping of Roni Tahr, the FBI had searched every hostile embassy in Washington, and many of the embassies of friendly powers. Twice agents had been caught in the act—and sent to the FBI for burglary prosecution.

Amazing, that. The FBI can be as slick as its reputation.

But none of those searches, however slick or well conceived they may have been, none of those searches revealed anything of any value, much less a hint as to the whereabouts of Roni Tahr.

The search turned fitful after that. Agents were assigned to investigate the mob, the Cuban—some were even sent to watch madmen like the Unabomber in their prisons.

As the FBI spun its wheels on the eleventh and twelfth days of the search.

Till some genius in accounting had an inspiration at the commissary during lunch.

"You know, Marv," he said to the administrator beside him, "there's only one power in the world with the resources to pull off something like the disappearance of this alien."

"Who's that, Steve?"

"Us."

A laugh.

"You and me? Don't joke. It's serious out there. The aliens in orbit are getting anxious at us."

"No, no—us, the U.S. The Americans. Our country. We could have done that—lots of our government could have done that. So could some of the contractors, big ones like the guys who work for JPL."

"You're out of your mind, Steve," his companion told him.

And that would have been the end of it for days, or weeks, or maybe no one ever would have realized what'd happened to Roni Tahr and his companions.

These men were just accountants, after all. They had no real business with the investigation.

Except for the fact that one of the investigation's lead managers—a hostile and frustrated man named

Johnson Smith—was standing in the commissary line behind the two accountants.

And heard the exchange.

And chewed it for three hours as he reviewed reports of severed leads and pointless burglaries.

Till it came to him that the accountant, Steve Wrightson, had a point.

Someone with serious resources had stolen away with the aliens.

Resources that Johnson Smith didn't know to name, because until that day he'd never had a *need* to know about anything of the sort.

As he picked up his phone.

And dialed one of his associates.

"Roberts," he said. "We need a liaison to the Black Budget people. Can you arrange that for me?"

"Sure," Roberts said. "What're you looking for?"

A sigh.

"Anything. Everything. We need a fishing expedition. Somebody's behind the technology that abducted Tahr—somebody who works for us."

"You're kidding."

"I'm not. You think the Libyans could have done this? Seriously? They couldn't. The Russians? We get better cooperation from them than we get from the CIA. Who else is there—the Chinese? Next year, maybe—ten years from now, maybe. But they honestly don't have the technical capacity right now. I can tell you that for certain."

Eli found Roni Tahr examining the joints in the walls when he returned with their lunch.

"Thought I told you to lie on the bed." he asked. "What exactly do you think you're doing?"

"Exploring my prison."

"Won't do you any good," he said. "Solid concrete. Lined with lead; reinforced with steel. They can't find you in this place."

"I see."

"Heh. I'm sure you do." Eli set the plates on the card table at the center of the room. "Eat up," he said. "Ham sandwiches. You'll like them."

Blink. Swallow. Blink.

"Flesh?"

Eli smiled. "Pig meat. On bread. With mayonnaise."

"Unfortunate."

Eli shrugged. "Eat it or don't. I won't care."

"I will eat."

Eli laughed when he saw Roni Tahr lift the sandwich and begin to pick at it so gingerly; chuckled at the sight of the alien's disgust as he masticated the bread and meat.

"You are *such* a fraud," he said. "Walking around the world like you were the Second Coming. But when you're hungry, you eat, just like anybody else. Even when you're disgusted with yourself."

The alien stopped in mid-chew.

Set his sandwich down. And uttered something in an alien tongue that sounded like a curse. "Who *are* you, Eli?" he asked.

Eli smiled.

"I am your keeper, Roni Tahr. Nothing more; nothing less."

A smile.

"I have never come to you before."

Eli laughed.

"I could have told you that," he said. "It isn't what I meant."

"Say, then."

Another laugh.

"No, there isn't any point. Except that you're still a goddamn fraud."

Blink. Swallow. *Blink.*

It took Johnson Smith most of three days to get the clearances he needed to even start questioning the Black Budget types.

When he finally did get the authorization and the

clearances he needed—directly from eop.gov, because the President was watching the investigation closely—he got damned little in the way of cooperation. Black Budget types have a habit of not answering questions; it makes them hell to deal with when it comes to an investigation.

"I need to know, damn it," Johnson Smith told the nameless major from the Mars project. "The *President* needs to know. Who've you got working on the kind of equipment that could have got the aliens out of that hotel unseen?"

Silence.

"Nobody," the major lied.

More silence.

"We aren't working on anything like that."

Johnson Smith sighed.

"You're lying to me," he said. "What've you got? *Who* have you got?"

"Nothing. I told you that, didn't I?"

It went like that all day, for hours and hours—none of them would answer a straight question, and it didn't do a bit of good to ask the questions at right angles to the point.

At 9 PM, Johnson Smith finally gave up, and resigned himself to heading home to bed.

And then his phone rang.

"Is this line secure?" a scrambled, muffled voice asked.

Johnson Smith hesitated. "Very secure," he said. "Upgrade went in through EOP yesterday."

Pause.

"Good."

Pause.

"What can I do for you?"

"I understand you're looking for the Houdini stuff."

"What?"

"The transport guys. Teleport. Vanishment."

Johnson Smith closed his eyes, trying to imagine. "I don't know what I'm looking for," he said. "I can see what happened. And I've got a hunch what kind of person did it."

"How's that?"

"Crazy xenophobe. Somebody who hates—aliens. Aliens are new, here—I guess I'm looking for a hater."

Silence.

"Yeah, that's him."

"Who?"

Silence.

"Who?"

"I have come to you in peace and with good will," Roni Tahr said. "There is no fraud. I have only come to know and love you."

"Bull spit."

"Bull . . . ?"

"You're lying to me."

Roni Tahr shook his half-inhuman head.

"I do not lie," he said. "I cannot."

"All right, so let's say you aren't lying. Tell me this: What the *hell* are you trying to accomplish, wandering around the world as if you were some kind of a messiah?"

As Roni Tahr finally came upon a word he understood, and his eyes went wide.

"Messiah . . . ?"

"Savior. Augur—prophesier. A holy man, for God's sake—if you were a man instead of an alien."

The alien closed his eyes. Shook his head. Moaned.

"Oh, no," he said. "That is not what I meant." Opened his eyes, and looked away. "That is not it. At all."

They found the xenophobe sleeper in his office, in the Pentagon; they raided his home at the same hour, and found more than enough evidence to convict him.

Souvenirs. From Orogarn and Kure.

Bits of anatomy—things they couldn't live without.

Couldn't? Who could say? They were aliens, and their nature was more uncertain than the wind.

They took the sleeper—whose name was Ron Thomason, and who had been a ranking civilian on a DIA project that's still subject to serious classification—they took the sleeper to a small, dark room in the basement of a safe house in Langley.

And they asked him many, many things.

Asked hard, and long, using every technique they could legally apply.

And quite a few that might've got the questioners prosecuted.

If they'd left their marks behind. If anyone could have proven anything at all.

But all the same, in the end they could only go so far: there was no way any man in our government's employ could bring himself to commit the kind of torment that will always bring an answer from a man.

"Maybe we ought to loan him to our new friends in the KGB," somebody joked. "God, remember what they did in Lebanon?"

And everyone in the room laughed a long rude laugh, except for Ron Thomason, who lay strapped to the padded examination table in the center of the room, turgic and unmoving, staring at the ceiling.

And that was an odd coincidence. Because at that moment word came down from the secure line in the house above that there was a call for Johnson Smith.

And when he answered it, he found himself speaking to the third-ranking director of the KGB.

"Johnson Smith," he said. "We have a locus for you."

"If you aren't here to act out the Second Coming," asked Eli, "what the devil do you think you *are* trying to accomplish?"

"We only wish to know you," Roni Tahr responded. "To know you and to love you."

Eli sneered.

"And doesn't it occur to you that your presence just might have an effect of its own?"

"We come in peace," said Roni Tahr. "We mean no harm."

"You're turning us into a world of mind-numbed idiots!"

Blink. *Swallow.* Blink.

"I never could," said Roni Tahr. "I never would."

"What do you think it does to people, having you show up here, acting like an angel? You think they can make their own decisions in any sensible way with some half-divine watching over their shoulders? Protecting them from harm?"

Pause.

"You are mad, Eli. No evil comes of kindness."

"I'm not," Eli said. "I've seen them. They're already losing all their passion for the world, their will to thrive. They need a challenge, alien. And the fact that you are here to comfort them removes it."

"Show me," the alien insisted. "How could that ever be?"

"Damn you," Eli said. "I will!"

And Eli grabbed the alien by the wrist, and dragged him to the kitchen.

Stepped onto the ladder at the far corner of the kitchen—and started to climb.

At the top of the ladder there was a portal secured by a wheel-lock—the sort of lock they use on battleships, and tanks.

The kind of lock they use in the construction of bomb shelters.

For they were in a bomb shelter—a deep shelter designed to withstand the force of many megatons of thermonuclear force; a place intended to take a direct hit on Washington—

As Eli opened the hatch, to lead Roni Tahr out into the world and show him the ennui of the earth—

—he opened the hatch into the face of six FBI SWAT agents.

And another dozen from the KGB.

Nobody's sure who started shooting first. Was it Igor, who'd spent six years in Lebanon during the civil war? Was it Leroy Watkins, who'd stood inches from the hatch as it opened into his face?

Some people say that it was Johnson Smith, who'd got in so far over his head that he was high-strung and overwrought, beyond the exercise of his best judgment.

Others still clam that it was Eli himself, surprised and caught off guard, who started shooting first. The EMTs who dragged Eli and Roni Tahr from the tunnel found a pistol in his hand—but there's no record of that pistol in the datacube, and the general wisdom is that it was a drop gun, the sort of unmarked and untraceable weapon law enforcement personnel carry to cover themselves for occasions just like these.

Whoever started the shooting, the outcome was straightforward: a dozen and a half FBI and KGB agents dressed in SWAT armor fired down into that shelter.

And in a matter of some moments both Eli and Roni Tahr lay on the floor in seeping bloody heaps of flesh.

And how the world grieved and mourned that hour! As the EMTs descended into the miles-deep tunnels, and came out in a concrete courtyard just off the Washington Mall, bearing stretchers soaked with blood and unearthly ichor, and the children in the crowd wailed, and a woman screamed in despair for she knew that she could not go on.

"Roni Tahr," she shouted, "Roni Tahr awake, awake. The world is lost without you!"

And then the strangest thing began to happen.

As the woman forced her shrieking screaming hysterical way through the soldiers and the guards and the FBI types pressed around the corpse; as she cast herself upon the shattered alien corpse—

As she embraced Roni Tahr and screamed that all

life on earth was lost without him, the alien began to stir.

And Roni Tahr woke to see the broken woman mourn him.

And he said, "No, no, no, this is not what I meant, this is not what I meant."

And he tore away the straps that had fasted his seemingly lifeless form to that stretcher.

And stood.

And lifted the woman roughly by the arms, and shouted to her.

"You could never be more wrong," he said. "I am not here to save you. I never could! I could destroy you without intending, don't you see?"

And the woman wept, and she kissed his blood-stained cheek.

"No, Roni Tahr," she said. "We *believe* in you."

As Roni Tahr screamed and shoved her from him, roughly.

"You must not!" he shouted. "You *may* not!"

The woman, shaken but none the worse for wear, shook her head.

"We always will," she said.

"Then I will stop you," said the alien.

As he seized the M16 from the arms of the Marine beside him.

And fired and fired and fired into the crowd, until the entire Mall ran red with blood.

IN MEMORIAM

by Mike Stotter

Having written five pulp western fiction novels
and two children's historical nonfiction novels,
Mike Stotter has now turned his hand to the
crime and thriller genre. Having written for *Mystery Scene* and *The Mystery Review* he now also
edits *Shots*—a British magazine for crime and
mystery. What spare time he has is spent writing
western and mystery short stories. He lives in
Essex and is married with three sons eating him
out of house and home.

DOWN here he was a ghost.

Among the flickering computer screens and background hiss, the soft tap-tap of keypads and the crackling static of loudspeakers Jerry Lane was no one. Just
one more number in the army of workers.

Yet another fruitless day stuck in the bowels of hell
and nothing to show for it was coming to an end.
Lately he'd been growing resentful of his recent promotion to the Biometrics Information Corporation,
considering it a bad move. He'd taken umbrage at his
wife's interference in obtaining the move. A move he
didn't want in the first place. His career in the Criminal Intelligence Section had been an enjoyable time.

The B.I. section was for dead-headed, keyboard-tapping drongos.

He looked up at the clock—another five minutes and he could log off and get home. He began closing down his workstation, feeling his muscles at the back of his neck tense as they always did when finishing for the day. The act of turning off the monitor was like the final turn of the screw before all the tension could disperse.

He had actually made it into his jacket when the monitor screen sprang to life.

"Card gone active. Card gone active," the speaker boomed.

"Ah, shit!"

Lane threw off his jacket and went back to his workstation. "Details," he ordered.

The screen flashed up a large-scale quadrant map where a tiny red speck oscillated in its center. "Mile End Gate, Citizen 246317216 using smartcard at credit facility." The computer announced.

Smartcard? The citizen was well behind the times. Lane ordered an enhancement of the street plan. The computer showed him the junction of Mile End Road and Burdett Road. It was just on the limits of the Outer City; any further and Lane would need to call for armed backup. But this was one he could handle himself. This particular citizen had slipped out of his grasp on two previous occasions. Lane had programmed the computer to download a tracking device into the smartcard the next time it was used, so maybe he could get lucky this time. Happy to be actually doing something, he ordered up a patrol car as he strapped on his webbing belt.

So what if I get caught?

All he could think of was getting something extra to eat and drink; getting back to the safety and comfort of his hideout and shutting out the rest of the world. He knew that he shouldn't have used his card, but there was no other way, no other legal way, of getting those extra rations. The center had provided his one meal for the day, but his stomach growled in protest. Now he wished he hadn't left home. A stupid row with his parents and now look at him.

No home, no parents, no comforts, no love.

What they fought about was long forgotten, only the fact remained that they didn't want him back and had even relocated. For the last eight months he had had to fend for himself.

The sky darkened dramatically, and a few spots of rain splattered down on to his unprotected head. A jagged fork of lightning lit up the street for a split-second. He began to count: one, two, three, four, five . . . the crash of thunder rolled and echoed against the buildings. Ian Palmer wondered who taught him to do that—to count the seconds between the thunder and lightning to guess the distance of the storm.

He hunched his shoulders against the sudden tropical downpour and protected his food against his body. The rain fell harder, driving people off the street to scuttle for shelter. With no protection, Ian was soaked through within minutes. The rain plastered his hair against his head, ran down his collar, and seeped through his cheap footwear. He turned down a side alley away from the cars and people, finding himself a little bit of protection within a shop doorway.

A car stopped at the mouth of the alley. It was too narrow for it to get down, so it pulled up a couple of yards farther on, and stood idling for a minute before shutting down. But Ian was too busy to notice; he had popped the can and was drinking the water like he'd spent a week in a desert.

"ID card."

The voice came out of nowhere.

Ian almost dropped the can, but instincts got the better of him. His other reaction was slow.

"ID card," the voice repeated.

Playing for time, the youngster fumbled in his

pocket then tried a sudden break, but the man was ready for him. With his arms trapped against his body, he was shoved back hard against the door.

"One more stupid move like that . . ."

Defeated, Ian brought out his ID card and held it for inspection.

"You think I'm going to do all this standing out in the rain and getting pissed on?" Jerry Lane took Ian by the arm and frog-marched him over to his patrol car and threw him in the back. The locks went on automatically.

From the driver's seat Lane turned around and demanded Ian's smartcard. The boy handed it over. It was fed into the computer console and both waited for the results to come spilling out.

As they were waiting Lane said, "A few questions for you, citizen."

"Depends on what questions."

The answer came with an attitude. It never ceased to amaze Lane that his job could arouse so much animosity.

Lane said, "I'm with Biometrics, not the law."

"Same difference."

"Believe what you want." He leaned over the console, checking out the name. "Citizen Palmer. I'm not going to go into the whys and whatfors for you."

"Cops, Biometrics Cops, what's the difference?"

Lane held his breath for a beat, then said, "You've not been at the facility for five months—why?"

Palmer shrugged.

"You know we'd come out and get you. What's the problem?"

Again the shrug.

"Aw, cut the crappy tough guy image, son. You aren't old enough to shave yet, so let's have some answers."

Ian made eye contact with Lane for the first time. What he saw was a pale-faced older man, who was probably around his father's age, with hard gray eyes that seemed to bore into his very soul. His hair was regulation length, and his mouth had a down turn which made him look sour.

Ian quietly said, "I didn't feel so good when I come out of there last time."

Lane was suddenly struck with Ian's childlike quality. The simplicity of truth.

"You go there, get your vitamin shots, a medical, you're fed, and then you're freed. That's it."

The console beeped. Lane tore off the strip of print-out and read it.

"Hmm."

"What's 'hmm'?"

"I've got to take you in. Smartcards are no longer valid. You need to go through a biometrics reprogram."

Ian sank back in the seat.

"Hey, don't get all worked up. It's not as bad as you think."

"Have you had it done?"

" 'Course," he said easily. In explanation he added, "You don't get to be my age without having entered the program."

He stood by the large picture window and looked out over the cityscape. Night was taking over the city, and the lights from the tower blocks started to blink on. Every now and then he would catch a brief glimpse of firelight out beyond the city walls. Then the white beam of light from the watchtowers would blind him for a second before passing on.

"What's the matter with you tonight, Jer?"

His wife always called him Jer. She was the only one he allowed to do that.

"Nothing."

"Jer, I know there's something wrong. Whenever you got something on your mind, you stare out of the window. Like you're the guardian of the city."

Dani Lane moved up behind him and draped her

arms around his neck; her fingers followed a lazy circle over his chest.

"Not really," he insisted.

"Is it something at work?"

Lane knew she wouldn't give up, so he turned around to face her. He slipped his arms around her waist and drew her closer into him saying, "Okay, okay. There was this citizen pickup a couple of days back. We talked on the way into the facility."

Dani smiled. "And?"

"He was frightened to go back into the program."

"So what? I bet there are citizens out there in the same situation. What makes him any different?"

"He couldn't remember his date of birth."

She shrugged. "So?"

"Well, it's not the type of thing you forget, is it?"

"Suppose not." She kissed him on the mouth and broke free of his embrace. She moved across to a small table and helped herself to a cup of tea. It smelled of lemon.

Lane followed her and retrieved his drink. "Or about the Year of the Storm. The year that changed all our lives when solar storms shut down all the computers. It knocked the Millennium bug into a cocked-hat."

Dani lifted the cup to her lips, eyeing him above the rim. She knew all this and didn't need a lecture. "You're going somewhere with this?"

Now it was his turn to smile. "And he knew nothing about the City."

"What about it?"

"Why the walls went back up after hundreds of years." Lane crossed to an easy chair and lowered himself into it. "In fact, he was quite ignorant about a lot of things that you and I take for granted."

"Why has this affected you? What's so special about the boy?"

Lane said, "He's perhaps the fifth or sixth citizen

I've picked up in the last eight weeks who seems to have trouble with his memory."

"A coincidence?" Dani suggested.

Lane shook his head.

"Then what?"

"I don't know," he replied honestly. "It might be something, or it might be nothing."

"That's the old policeman in you coming out, Jer," she said softly. "You're not in that line of work anymore. You're with BIC, remember?"

"Yeah, no need to remind me."

"You're still not bitter that I got Dad to get you out of that dead-end job, are you?"

Ah, not the same old argument, he thought. She always threw that up into his face at every opportunity. It was Burke Foster, his father-in-law, who had been instrumental in getting him out of the police force and landing him the job at BIC.

"No," he said. "Perhaps curiosity gets the better of me sometimes."

"You know what curiosity did, don't you?"

"Yeah, but I've got a feeling in my bones about this." He crossed over to the window again but leaned against the glass, his back to the City. "What if someone, somewhere, is monkeying around with us?"

"In what way?" Dani sat upright, paying attention.

"Say that they could adjust people's memories. Like they can do with our own biometrics."

She blinked and looked at him. "That's a touch melodramatic, isn't it?"

"Is it? Just think about it for a minute. If we can put our own DNA, eye-dentification, fingerprints, geometry, and whatever else into a computer system, what's stopping the computer putting something into our biological system?"

She said, "So that they can control our thoughts, you reckon?"

"No, not control—more like deselect them."

"Okay, but what does whoever get out of this?"

Lane shrugged. "I don't know. Don't know even if I'm right."

Dani slowly shook her head. "Jer, you're reading too much into this."

About five minutes later Lane said, "Have you thought any more about having another child?"

His change of tack threw her. She stumbled for words.

"I still think it's too soon."

He shook his head. "What has it been—nine months?"

She nodded.

"Then it's time to move on. To try again."

She refused to look at him.

He said, "Dani, are you listening to me? What's the problem of trying for another child?"

"I . . . I can't."

"How long are you going to keep this up? You aren't the only one who's hurting."

"Later, Jer. Later," she said through her tears.

He knelt down in front of her and took her face in both hands, lifting it up. He looked into her eyes. He could see the hurt, the anxiety and the fear of a second and final failure in them. Even being the daughter of one of the top directors of BIC didn't allow her the privilege of trying for a third child. The rule was set in concrete. Two children per couple in any partnership. Having lost their first child during pregnancy, he knew Dani's fear of another miscarriage, thus ending her chance of having children.

He said, "Don't leave it too late."

And wiped away the tears with his fingertips.

In the basement office Lane threw his jacket over the back of his chair. He looked at the monitor for messages, then asked Rosi, the shift leader, if there'd been any calls.

"Quiet as the old proverbial," came the reply.

Lane thanked him and dropped into his chair. He

had had a troubled night's sleep in which his dreams were haunted by images of zombielike citizens wandering aimlessly in the streets; of babies lying in the gutter, their mouths opened in silent screams; and always at the periphery of the dream, a figure dressed in long robes, his face hidden by a hooded cowl, shouting words that were snatched away by the wind, never reaching the citizens below.

The dream's images stayed with him into the waking hours. They haunted him over breakfast, which he couldn't finish, and during the drive into work.

Lane said to Rosi, "That's good—I've got a batch of inputting to finish, then a couple of follow-up interviews, so don't be surprised if I'm not around this afternoon."

"No worries," Rosi replied, then switched his attention back to the monitor screens.

For the next three hours Lane set about feeding data into his PC; cross-referencing his information into the mainframe computer, then waiting for the results. Lane had the data downloaded to his recorder, removed the mini-disk, and slipped it into his pocket. What started out as a half-baked idea at the back of his mind had now turned into a substantiated reason to carry out an investigation. At the same time, he didn't want to explain his actions to his supervisor before he could corroborate his evidence.

Lane followed the same routine over four days, and on the fifth considered he had gathered enough of the information he needed. He told Rosi that he was going out on the streets to carry out his investigation and received a barely audible answer. Lane smiled; that was the beauty of working with Rosi. The man had his mind on other things, so he could get away with whatever he wanted to do. He took his patrol car and headed out of the city.

He went back to Mile End Gate and cruised around for a while. The image of Ian Palmer's face was imprinted on his mind's eye. Lane slowed down when-

ever he saw a teenager, but after an hour he had found
no sign of him. It was almost midday, the office hadn't
been in touch with him, and he was hungry. Lane
pulled into a supermarket car park that was virtually
empty, maybe ten cars, and sat there for a moment
getting his thoughts together.

Then he saw Ian Palmer exiting the store with a
gang of other boys. Obviously, he was just one of the
gang; the leader walked in front, his exaggerated swag-
gering walk and animated expression marked him out.
Palmer walked alongside a pasty-faced youth some six
inches taller. Lane stayed behind the wheel, his hands
gripping it so tight his knuckles showed white. When
the group were a few yards off, Lane got out of the
car.

The gang came toward him. The leader noticed
Lane leaning casually against the patrol car, arms
folded across his chest, his eyes staring intently at
Palmer. He stopped a yard or so away. The others
bundled to a halt behind him.

Lane said, "I want to speak to Citizen Palmer."

The leader gave a lopsided grin. "Palmer?"

Lane jabbed a finger at Ian.

Palmer said to the leader, "Malc?"

"He don't have anything to do with you, cop," said
the leader.

"In the car, Palmer."

The boy made no move. Lane remained against the
car, his muscles coiled tight as springs, and repeated
his order.

"What d'you want?" Palmer asked.

"Some questions and forms that the center forgot
to get done," Lane lied.

As Palmer moved to comply Malc put out an arm
to bar his way.

Lane moved in quickly. He grabbed Malc's wrist
and jerked it violently away, spinning the youth
around. An ankle sweep had him face down on the
ground in seconds.

"Into the car, Palmer," he said over his shoulder.

Malc was sweating. Lane felt like kicking him in the ribs but didn't. He waited until Palmer was in the passenger seat before taking his foot off the leader's back.

"Okay, Malc," he said, "you showed you're the boss but to the wrong person. You remember my face. Go on take a good look. The next time we meet I may not be so nice. You may not get to keep your kneecaps."

Lane released his wristlock and walked around to the driver's side. By the time he got into the car, he found himself shaking. Sweat leaked from every pore. He sped away from the parking area.

Lane parked up outside a derelict building that fifty years ago had been a famous department store. Now the windows were gone, and the building had been taken over by an army of citizens without their own assigned residences. There was nothing but blackened stumps where an avenue of trees once gave the street a countrified feeling. Litter blew across the surface, stirred by a hot wind blowing in from the south. The air grew heavy, and both passengers silently thanked the car's air-conditioning.

"I want to tell you something, Ian." Lane began. "Well, quite a lot of things really." He'd already explained that he had lied to him earlier, that what he wanted was to talk to him.

Ian was unsure. "What things?"

By the time Lane had finished talking, it was late in the afternoon. His voice was dry and hoarse, his hunger forgotten. He couldn't be sure how much Ian had taken in, but the youngster had sat and listened to everything Lane had said. At the end of it Lane put in the mini-disk into the on-board computer and pressed the play button.

Ian watched the screen and learned much more in fifteen minutes than in the whole of his lifetime. Lane watched him. The teenager's face seemed to have added lines that hadn't been present moments before.

Lane thought he might have pushed him just that bit too far, but Ian's eyes were bright and alert.

The disk finished and Lane switched on the car's communication. Listened for a minute: calls about track-downs, ID abuse at a supermarket, a computer blackout, and more of the usual calls. He switched it off.

They sat there, listening to the car's air-conditioner humming in the background, both silent and lost deep in their own thoughts.

Finally Ian said, "Why?"

"Because I thought you had a right to know."

There was a long pause.

"What do you want me to do with all this?"

Lane shrugged. "Tell others, tell Malc—let them know what happened, what's happening."

"And what about you?"

Lane looked away and said a moment later, "Don't have to worry about me, I'll be okay."

"I got to think about this. It's all . . . well, just too much to take in."

"It's a beginning."

They were waiting for him when he got back home.

Dani was standing by the window; Burke Foster was leaning up against the breakfast bar, and the two security men stood close to him.

Dani turned around as the door opened.

Lane stepped into the room and felt a sudden sinking sensation in his stomach.

"You didn't think you'd get away with it, did you?" said Foster.

Lane walked into the room, ignoring the question, and headed over to his wife.

"You okay?" he asked.

She nodded her head but couldn't force herself to look at him.

"You should be worried about yourself," said Foster.

"Not really."

"Don't be so arrogant!"

"Don't preach to me about arrogance!"

The security guards made to move in, but Foster waved them off. He signaled to one to leave the room. To Lane he said, "How you could compromise my daughter?"

"She had nothing to do with it."

"You put her at risk."

Lane admitted to himself that obviously there had been risks but felt that he was in a position not to exactly stop what was going on but to minimize what he considered the misuse of biometric technology.

He said to Foster, "The risks were mine alone. No one, no government or power has the right to do what you and your biometrics henchmen have been doing."

"That's such a narrow-minded view, Jerry."

"At least I can use my mind. What about all those people you've robbed of their past—their heritage?"

Foster rubbed a hand over his face. "What gives you the right to decide to play God? Everything we've done has been for a reason—a very good reason."

Lane certainly knew some of the things the Biometrics Information Corporation had been doing. That over the last three years they had been systematically erasing the memories of those living in the outer city. The computer and electrical collapse brought about by the solar flares at the beginning of the century had given BIC the opportunity to bring about a massive change in society. Those not selected to be involved in the rebirth had been ostracized outside the city walls and gradually had been brought to the centers to be given vaccines. The Corporation had defiled their minds. Another freedom stripped from the less fortunate. And in the meantime those living within London's city walls benefited from BICs technological advances. He had proof in the data stored in the mini-disk.

The security guard came back into the room carrying the mini-disk that Lane thought he had hidden. He waved it in the air, silently goading Lane, before handing it over to Foster.

Lane's shoulders slumped in resignation as though the discovery of the disk had drained him of the fight.

Foster turned the disk over and over in his hands. "What you have here is far more dangerous than anything we have done. The whole infrastructure of our society could have been undermined and set us back a hundred years or more. I'm only too glad that Dani had the sense to contact me." He saw the couple exchange looks. "That's right Lane, she told me of her fears; Rosi did, too, and this disk confirms everything."

Lane said, "You'll do whatever you'll need to do."

Foster moved away from the breakfast bar saying, "There's no way we can overlook this. You realize that, don't you?"

Lane wasn't in a position to make ultimatums. He had ruined himself for a worthwhile cause but still had some dignity left. "You'll leave Dani out of this. She wasn't involved. I'm the one who's to be punished, not her," he demanded.

Foster silently nodded his consent. If Lane had him labeled as a plutocrat, then at least he could be magnanimous to his own flesh and blood.

Lane walked over to Dani and put a hand on her shoulder. She flinched away from him. Untouched by Dani's rejection, Lane looked out over the landscape and inside his heart was reassured that whatever Foster had in store for him, Ian Palmer was out there. Everything wasn't lost.

SLEEP THAT BURNS

by Jerry Sykes

Jerry Sykes's short stories have appeared in a number of magazines and anthologies including *Cemetery Dance, Ellery Queen's Mystery Magazine* and *The Year's 25 Finest Crime and Mystery Stories*. He is the editor of *Mean Time,* a collection of crime stories set around the end of the millennium. In 1998 he was awarded the Crime Writers' Association Gold Dagger for Short Story of the Year.

MY first assignment as a cop had been to herd rubberneckers away from the broken suicides that lay at the foot of the Millennium Ferris Wheel. Twenty years on and I was still herding people away, only this time the wheel was on its side and the people were the vagrants who made their home in the giant rusted cage that was all that was left of the wheel.

It was a hot evening, and the sun burned a moving red spectrum on the glass towers of the City making it look like they were on fire. I drove slowly along the embankment to Millennium Park, windows open, the acrid smell of the Thames in my nostrils, and looked out over the river. It was low tide, and I could see beachcombers down by the water. On either side of the river, barely a hundred feet wide at this time of year, people moved in slow motion, eyes scanning the baked mud, twists of wood, and metal breaking the surface like the bones of a desiccated corpse. Many of the searchers carried Hessian sacks on their shoulders, others huddled their findings to their chests, distrustful of their neighbors.

I backed the shuttle up to the gate and killed the engine.

The Ferris Wheel, with a span of over five hundred feet, had once been the centerpiece of the Millennium Festival, visible from Blackheath to Primrose Hill, when the night sky would be filled with the cries of the innocent rolling through scrolled neon and into new worlds limited only by their imaginations. The structure had long since been formally abandoned, and lowered on to its side to prevent further suicides, and was now a makeshift shelter to the constant flow of vagrants that ghosted through London. The top and sides of the wheel were covered with an urgent tapestry of plastic sheets, blankets, and tarpaulins; inside, the wheel was divided into separate dwellings by more tarpaulins and blankets.

My remit as a shuttle operator was to move these vagrants out to holding camps until they could be allocated government support through the Realignment Bill. Twice a week I would come down to the park and herd fifty of them into the shuttle and ship them out. It was a never-ending cycle, not least because the process of realignment took so long, many people would often drift away from the camps and make their own way back to where they had come from before they could be processed.

Across the street a group of vagrants climbed over the embankment wall; they had the staccato movements and the jaundiced look of donors.

I turned to Denny. "Anyone for the slab?"

He looked at me with flat eyes. "Man, I need a hit tonight or that last interest hike's gonna blow me outta the water. I'm gonna end up out here with these fuckin' meltdowns." He jerked his thumb out of the window.

Denny was a freelance agent for the NHS and it was his job to find people willing to part with one of their kidneys—for a price, the right price. More than fifty percent of the people in this country between the ages of forty and fifty suffer from kidney damage, a direct legacy of the drug culture at the close of the millennium; more than fifty percent of the people in this country between the ages of forty and fifty can afford to buy a new kidney.

A seller's market.

But such was the lack of post-op care afforded donors, many didn't live long enough to enjoy their windfall and soon ended up in the morgue on the slab.

"Let's see what we can do," I said.

We climbed out of the shuttle.

Around the edge of the wheel each dwelling had its own entrance; the dwellings on the inside were reached by a communal entrance in front. Denny headed for the main entrance; I turned to go clockwise around the wheel.

I walked slowly, pulling aside makeshift curtains to get a look at the occupants, barking commands for people to get on the shuttle, trying to keep the mix right; I didn't want a load of juiceheads and runners.

Every now and then I could hear Denny shouting at someone, and the occasional thump of metal on flesh from within the wheel. Denny was the kind of guy who liked to throw his weight around. He was a qualified paramedic, but he chose to ride shotgun with me because he got to beat up on people.

A third of the way around the wheel I came across an old guy I had seen many times before.

"Hey, Wally, how you doin'?" I squatted down beside the small fire. He was cooking some eggs on the lid of an old paint tin.

He looked up at me, eyes swimming with a milky

discoloration. His face bore the lines of someone who had learned to live with pain at an early age.

"You gonna come for the ride?" I said. Wally had been a regular passenger on the shuttle for a long time, but for a variety of reasons he had never been processed, the latest being that he was just too fuckin' old. But sometimes he liked to tag along and make out like old times.

He poked at the eggs with a long handled fork. "Where you headed?"

"Does it matter?" I said.

He snorted, and his head wobbled around on his shoulders.

My legs were cramping, and I stood up. I took a pack of cigarettes out of my jacket and tossed one on the ground next to Wally. He picked it up and lit it from the coals of the fire.

"Maybe I'll give it a miss this time, huh?" Feathers of smoke drifted from his mouth as he spoke.

"One of these days I'm gonna come at you wi' this," I said, slapping the gun on my hip. "Then maybe you ain't got no choice." I smiled at him.

I moved on, walking between broken belongings that lay scattered on the parched grass. It took me twenty minutes to walk around the wheel and when I returned to the shuttle it was already full. Denny was twisted 'round in his seat, shouting at someone in back.

"—and for the last time, no fuckin' jugs of booze in the Medibag, okay?"

I climbed into the driver's seat. "What's goin' on?" I said, looking in the rearview mirror.

"These fuckin' guys are fiends, man. They wanna use my Medibag to cool their juice. You believe that?" He sighed and shook his head.

I stifled a laugh. On the last trip out, someone had used Denny's Medibag, the icebox he used for transporting kidneys, to keep their jug of beer cold. The next kidney to occupy the bag had become contaminated and worthless. It had cost Denny his month's rent; he relied on those little extras to meet his bills.

"Any troublemakers?" I asked. Normally, when confronted with Denny, people will just get on the shuttle as if under hypnosis, rarely is there any trouble. But occasionally he will find some reason for stomping some poor guy's head.

"Just go," he said, his eyes beaming straight ahead.

I hit the ignition and we moved slowly out of the park. A light rain had begun to fall, and the vagrants moving through the mist looked like after-images of the people they had once been. Clouds of smoke curling out of slits in the tarpaulins glowed blue in the twilight.

We drove upriver and crossed the Thames at Westminster Bridge.

It was now four years since my son had been killed.

Eleven months into his National Service, Cal was pulling down extra hours to try and wind up early so he could get back to college with a running start on his final year. The extra workload was no hardship; for the whole of his time he had been stationed at a center for people with Alzheimer's and he had gotten to know a lot of the patients as friends, often staying late and trying to follow the scant logic of their conversations. But the extra hours meant late nights, and late nights meant running risks out on the street.

He was killed by a single bullet from the gun of a juicehead out on his stag night.

Once Virtual Reality had faded into the mainstream and become just another tired thread in the cultural fabric of the world, for a few dark souls a new frontier in entertainment was needed. And this time, the kill had to be for real. Guys like Billy Hendry were quick to fill the gap in the market; his White Hunter had been one of the first organized trips into the cold heart of the professional killer. For a price, you could take your pick of game: Cal—young, white, male—cheap at ten thousand.

The shooter had been easy to track down; a security camera by the ATM that Cal had been using at the time of his death had caught the murder on videotape: the jeep pulling up to the curb, the pistol appearing through the open window, the face twisted in cruel intensity as it drew a bead on the back of Cal's head. . . .

Together with a patrol cop I pulled the juicehead from his bed and executed him in his own back yard. In the morning, the cop had called the church and canceled the wedding.

After six months the official investigation was wound up. Our life savings and the services of a bounty hunter fueled our hopes and frustration and anger for another two months, but the bounty hunter could only come up with one sure thing: Billy Hendry had disappeared.

Soon after, Jolie walked out on me. She said that in shadow my profile was the same as that of Cal, and as her world was now full of shadows . . .

Last I heard she was running computer security for a telecommunications group up near Liverpool.

Some nights I watch the video from the security camera until I drift into a troubled sleep that burns images from the tape deep into my mind, so that every action, every thought, every memory is controlled by them.

The following morning I wake to static filling the screen and white noise filling my ears.

At nine I pulled into a service station to refuel and grab a bite to eat. Denny was asleep and I had to dig him in the ribs. "You comin' in?" I asked him.

"I better get these fuckers sorted first," he said, nodding to the rear of the shuttle. He rubbed at his face with the palms of his hands.

"I'll get you some coffee."

The restaurant was quiet, the only other customer a young kid in dark green overalls up at the counter. His eyes were molded to the rear end of the waitress, sharply defined by her tight uniform. I walked to the rear and took a booth against the window. I held my hand up to the glass and saw Denny leading a group from the shuttle toward the back of the restaurant where the kitchen staff would hand out G-rations. He had his hand on the butt of his gun and his eyes flitted anxiously over the group.

I ordered coffee for two and lamb chops and reflected on Denny's suitability for the job. Realistically, the post was little more than that of driver's gopher, but with his medical credentials and his bloodlust he had turned the shuttle into a carrier for his freelance kidney trading. Not that it bothered me; he always gave me a slice of his fee, and I enjoyed having to put my foot down when the temperature alarm on his Medibag showed red.

After a few minutes Denny came in through the back and slid into the booth opposite me. A crooked grin hung on his face like a broken mask.

"You okay?" I said.

"Those dogs out back?" He looked toward the back door, as if expecting the dogs to walk in at any moment. "Those dogs—they were eating some guy's head this morning. You believe that?"

"Eating someone's head?" I said, raising my eyebrows.

"The guy out back, the chef, guy out having a smoke?"

"The dogs were eating the chef's head?"

"Hey, you wanna hear this, slap the wise guy, okay?"

"Okay, go on." I forked some lamb chop into my mouth.

Denny shuffled in his seat, looked over at the back door once more. "You know the estate out back of here? Quarter mile or so?" I nodded. "Well, the other

day they found this old guy out there that'd been dead
for seventeen months. *Seventeen months.* You believe
that? Imagine, so little presence, so little life . . ." He
held his thumb and forefinger together and tapped out
the words slowly in the air. ". . . no one cares, no one
knows, no one gives a *fuck* when you're dead." His
eyes drifted into the distance for a moment before
snapping back. "Anyway, right after they found him,
they threw out all this shitty old furniture, hundred
years old, most of it. Stuck it in the garbage room.
And it drives the dogs fuckin' wild. They're jumpin'
around, going crazy, trying to get in the garbage, kicking up a tornado. Somehow they eventually get in and
they're going mad chewing on the mattress, ripping it
apart. No one knows what the fuck's happening,
what's sending all these mutts crazy. There a sudden
doggy craze in duck feathers or what?" He picked
up his coffee and took a sip. "Anyhow, the caretaker
eventually manages to chase the hounds away. Shoots
in the air or somethin', I don't know. And he's curious, you know, he wants to know what's happening,
what turned the dogs on like that. So he takes what's
left of the mattress for a DNA scan." Denny leaned
over the table conspiratorially. "Now get this." His
eyes flicked momentarily to the back door again.
"Turns out when they took the guy's body outta there,
or what was left of it, part of his head got left behind
on the mattress." He jabbed his finger on the table.
"*That's* what the dogs were going wild over. Flesh,
human flesh. Fuckin' wild about it." He leaned back
on the seat, a big grin slapped across his face.

"You ready to order now?" I asked him.

It was another two hours before we hit the holding camp.
The camps were originally built as low-cost housing
projects for the dispossessed in the '80s and '90s, but
the standards were such that within ten years they
began to fall apart. Coupled with the general migra-

tion of businesses and family homes to the new green areas, the projects were eventually abandoned and now served solely as holding camps.

At the entrance to the camp was a low red-brick building with a flat roof, the control center. I left Denny to unload the shuttle while I let myself into the center and logged in the vagrants.

Denny was leaning against the wall waiting for me when I stepped back outside. A plastic cigarette poked out from between his lips. I nodded to the pad of donor release forms stuffed in his pocket.

"You got someone lined up?" I said.

"Some old guy. Lives over by the school." The cigarette bobbed in his mouth.

"Old guy?" I said. The kidneys of most people over fifty were usually shot to fuck by years of additives and expellants; even on the black market they were difficult to shift.

He took the cigarette out of his mouth. "There's some desperate people out there."

I raised my eyebrows. "You're tellin' me."

I looked at my watch: almost eleven.

"It's getting late," I said. "Where do we find this guy?"

Denny gestured for me to follow him, and we went into the camp.

We walked across a gravel car park painted silver by a hawk moon, our footsteps counterpoint to the random noises of the camp at night. The car park led to a sheltered walkway with doors hidden in darkness on our right. Shadows moved across the edge of my vision, and occasionally I would catch a glimpse of a face, a slice of skin pale in the moonlight.

I followed Denny along the walkway until we came to a dark green door; a pale light shone through the peephole. Denny took out his notebook and checked the number. "This is the place," he said. He rapped his knuckles on the door. A cool breeze blew along the walkway and I could smell burned food and urine.

I turned away to avoid the smell, and that's when I saw him.

A group of men had emerged from a stairwell at the end of the walkway, no more than fifty feet away. They threaded themselves between abandoned cars and headed for the opposite corner of the square. They shuffled over the gravel car park, their footsteps a continuous growling noise. As they passed beneath a streetlamp, each face was washed in pale orange, and there he was. There was no mistaking the twist of the nose or the eyes that burned with the fear of a trapped animal.

Billy Hendry, the man who had arranged the killing of my son.

I stepped off the walkway and headed toward the group. At first no one seemed to notice me, but then I made the mistake of calling out, "Hey! Wait!," and my voice was like a gunshot in the still air. The group fragmented and ran in all directions.

Hendry cut loose for the stairwell he had appeared from. I knew that just beyond was an old strip mall and a group of tenement blocks that was like a three-dimensional maze. If he reached that, I would lose him for certain.

I took off after him.

As I ran, the only sounds I could hear were the rasping of my breath and the violent crunch of my boots on the gravel. I reached the entrance to the mall with Hendry still in my sights, fifty feet ahead.

And then he fell; in the darkness he tripped and went flying, stretching out his hand to break his fall and skidding across the tarmac. I heard him cry out in pain.

And then I made a mistake.

I slowed to watch him, thinking he was trapped. I slowed to a jog—and then he was up and running again, limping slightly but having lost none of his pace. Seconds later the ringing sounds of his footsteps disappeared into the maze and into the night air.

I had lost him.

I bent over, my hands on my knees, and breathed deeply. The air seemed to burn in my chest; perspiration ran into my eyes. I stood up and looked around, walked toward the mall. The beating of my heart echoed from the buildings around me.

I came to the point where he had fallen and lowered myself to one knee and peered at the ground. I could just make out . . . what? I took out my penline torch and shone it over the ground. Drops of blood appeared like rubies in the dust.

I stood and looked around again. I thought about going into the maze, but the chances of finding Hendry—if it was Hendry, I had only glimpsed the man briefly; the speed with which he had taken off suggested he was guilty of *something,* but was it Hendry?

I looked at the ground in front of me, drawing circles with the torch beam around the drops of blood.

I took a handkerchief from my jacket and placed it carefully over the blood; tiny red flowers bloomed in the cotton. I then took a plastic evidence bag from my jacket and dropped the handkerchief into the bag. I put the bag in my pocket and headed back to the camp.

Denny was sitting in the cab of the shuttle when I reached the car park. A solitary lamp burned above the control center, and all I could see were his hands flipping the top of the Zippo. I knocked on the glass. He lowered the window and peered down at me, his face deep in shadow.

"What the fuck happened to you?" snapped Denny.

"I saw—"

"I lost him. That old guy, remember? He was watching us from upstairs. I heard him rattling the window when you scooted. He musta thought we were the goon squad or somethin', scared the shit outta him—"

"Denny—"

"—the fuck's goin' on?" He leaned out of the window and glared down at me. The ridge of muscle along his jawline pulsed violently.

I took a deep breath. "I saw him. Hendry—"

"You saw Hendry? Why— Why didn't you say? I coulda—"

"I'm tellin' you now," I said, keeping my voice level. "Okay?"

Denny withdrew into the cab. I heard a rustling sound, and then his Zippo flared, splashing his face with white light. He lit a cigarette and smoke drifted from his nostrils.

"Hendry. He was in that bunch of vagrants across the way. When we were waiting for the old guy?" I pointed vaguely in the direction of the stairwell.

"Scaring the shit outta him," muttered Denny, still rankling from my knocking him back.

"Hey, lose the fuckin' attitude, okay? I'm talkin' 'bout the guy that whacked my son, not some fuckin' meltdown that pissed in your pocket."

"Hey, I didn't mean—"

I pushed his objection aside. "I chased him into the maze, but . . ." Thoughts ran away from me. "Anyway, look." I took the bag containing the handkerchief out of my pocket.

Denny looked at the bag and then up at me. "What? You get a nosebleed or somethin'?"

"It's Hendry's. The blood. I was chasing him and he tripped over a curb or something." I suddenly felt uncomfortable and lifted the bag for a closer look as if I might be able to recognize the blood. "I'm not sure it was him, though."

"Hey, he ran. Sounds guilty to me," Denny reasoned.

"So would a whole pile of other people." I put the bag back in my pocket. "I'm gonna run a DNA scan on it, anyway."

Denny climbed out of the cab, and we walked over to the control center. I swiped my ID card and pushed through the wooden door into the lobby. A heavyset man in a gray uniform with a dark complexion was sitting behind the console reading a paperback. Reflections from the monitors before him danced across his glasses, as if he were playing scenes from the book on them. He looked up as we approached.

"Still here? Thought you'd be long gone by now." He delivered the words one at a time; it was a wonder anyone ever let him finish what he was saying.

"We ran into a bit of trouble. We need to head on up to the Datacenter, check something out. Okay if we go on through?"

The guard's eyes flicked to a monitor, back again. "Sure," he said, and rolled his huge shoulders.

He buzzed us through the main door. It opened onto a short corridor with two further doors on either side. A large metal door stood at the far end. As we walked through the corridor, the sign on the door gradually came into focus: TRANSIT LABORATORY—AUTHORIZED PERSONNEL ONLY.

We reached the door, and I gave it a gentle push with the palm of my hand. It was locked. I knew the guard was watching us on a monitor, so I turned to the camera above the door and gave him the finger. I heard a soft click, and when I pushed the door again, it was open.

Another corridor stretched before us. I walked on, looking at the sign on each door. I could hear Denny breathing heavily behind me and his footsteps clipping the tile floor.

We came to a door marked DNA SCANNER and stopped. I squeezed the plastic bag containing the handkerchief in my pocket and then knocked. After a few moments there was the sound of soft footsteps behind the door and then it was slowly opened. A man about my height, six two, with thinning red hair stood there, white lab coat wrapped around his shoulders. He looked us up and down through half-moon glasses on the end of his nose. I felt my DNA twitch.

"Yes?" He kept one hand on the doorknob and the other on the frame, blocking our entrance.

"Blon." I held up my ID card. "Detective Blon. We've come to run a scan on some blood?"

"I know who you are." His voice sounded weary.

Denny looked at me, at the technician, shrugged. "So now we all know each other, what are we waiting for?"

The technician looked at his watch.

"Hey, don't you worry 'bout the time. We got all night," said Denny and gently but forcefully pushed the door open.

The technician sighed and stepped back. He seemed to deflate as if his skeleton had crumbled, leaving only tired flesh.

I followed Denny into the lab.

It was a small room, ten by ten, with computer hardware floor to ceiling on three walls; on the fourth wall a solitary window overlooked the camp. In the glass I could see my reflection: a face drawn by shadows, pale and cold. One eye seemed to be twitching, but I could feel no movement in my face.

The technician pulled himself up to his full height. "Detective Blon, this is not a private lab, and we are not here to service your private actions. You are in breach of everything you have ever learned in the force and you know it." He held my stare.

A minute passed, our eyes locked. I felt every muscle in my body tense.

Eventually his eyes flicked away. "You think you got him this time?" he said. There was genuine concern in his voice.

I shrugged and handed him the evidence bag. He disappeared through a door next to a large glass case. Inside the case were rows of bottles of blood in deepening shades of red.

"You better hope this is the real thing," said Denny, "or you're gonna get yourself a reputation." He pulled himself up on to a desk and leaned back with his head under the extractor fan and the cool pulse of the air. "You gotta take this guy out. And soon. You understand?"

I knew what he meant. This was not the first time I had been to the lab with a blood sample. But I had to be sure I had the right man. That way it wouldn't matter when I killed him, shot him in the back. That was something Victims' Rights allowed me to do, administer my own punishment. Damn, it even *encouraged* me to do it, go right out and shoot the guy in the back of the head and not feel like a coward.

It took the technician ninety minutes to run the scan. I was watching shadows shifting around in the camp when he came back into the room. Denny still had his head under the extractor fan.

The technician was trying to hide a smile and not having much success.

"We got him?" I said. My heart thumped deep in my chest.

"Ninety-eight percent match. I ran it twice, just to be sure. I didn't wanna fuck up and have you coming back here in a couple of weeks with another dirty handkerchief."

The camp covered two square miles and held an average of twenty-six-hundred vagrants at any one time. Finding Hendry was not going to be easy, and there was always the possibility he had already left the camp. It was not a prison, people were free to move on as they pleased.

With only the two of us, there was no point in being too systematic about the search. We took off in opposite directions.

Cold blue moonlight threw the camp into dark relief as I made my way to the first tenement. In my right hand I carried my pistol, in my left a heavy duty torch. The building seemed to shift in the darkness as I approached, and the splintered glass of the broken windows looked like burned-out stars captured in wooden frames. Occasionally I heard signs of life: a barking cough, the death rattle of the bronchitic; feral screams dragged from the deepest of sleeps; angry calls to silence. I hoped that somewhere among the grumbling mess of people was Hendry.

Denny had still been pissed off with me for losing him the kidney, and I had had to agree to rush him a couple of thousand for helping me out, more if we caught the guy. But he was under threat of death himself not to shoot him. That was my gig.

The stairwell smelled of stale alcohol and decaying flesh, and I was reminded of the dogs behind the diner on the freeway. I hurried up the stairs.

At the top of the building were two doors, with tribal markings slashed across them in red and green. The one on my right was open. I lifted my gun and followed the torch beam into the room.

The concrete floor was covered with the tools of the dead and the defeated: cigarette butts, broken vials, cracked needles. The bundle of rags against the far wall were probably vagrants. I crossed the room and kicked the first one on the foot; gently, I didn't want to break it off.

A hand appeared from beneath the rags and dragged them to one side. I shone the torch into a face that twisted to look up at me, blinked in the strange light. The eyes were sunk deep into the skull and the mouth hung loose, saliva spooling from the corner.

I moved the beam off the face. "Go back to sleep," I said.

I lifted the blankets from the other two mounds in the room and saw identical faces, a single mask that took on the contours rent by the latest hurt.

I walked back down the stairs with heavy steps.

I searched on through the night, tired, pointing my torch into faces until ghosts swam before my eyes and I could no longer trust what I was seeing. Occasionally I caught glimpses of running shadows in the distance and at first I thought they were cops, but my mind was so tired and twisted they could just as well have been the shadows of clouds scooting across the moon.

I was heading back to the main block, ready to call it a night, when my radio squawked into life. "Denny, you still around? I thought you'd—"

"Get your fuckin' ass down to the Clark block," Denny snapped. "Now!"

"Wha— What's happening?" My mind wheeled.

"I've got the fucker."

A cold wave passed through me. "Hendry? You found him—?"

"Just get the fuck over here fast, or you ain't gonna get the pleasure of the pop."

My legs were already rolling. "You shot him?" Anger welled in me. "Denny—"

"Relax. I just—I just settled him down a little, that's all. I ain't gonna deprive you."

I clipped the radio back on my belt and started running toward the Clark block.

Denny was standing in the open doorway. A bare lightbulb burned directly above him, turning his hair into a halo. His hands hung loose at his sides, thick veins cording his forearms. I was panting by the time I reached him and took a moment to calm my breathing.

I nodded at Denny.

He pointed into the building. "Through that door, second on the right."

I followed his directions. My legs felt weak, and my face was glazed with sweat. The floor was swimming with urine and I reached my arms out to the walls to steady myself and felt something sticky. I looked up. Angry fingerpaintings in blood covered the wall on my right. I followed the trail, ending in the room where Denny had directed me.

The pale early morning sun burned through the grime on the windows and picked out a hunched figure against the far wall. He was sitting with his knees drawn up, his head resting on his knees. A trail of blood led from the door. The man's clothes were ragged and dirty; the soles of his shoes flapped loose like grotesque tongues. The small of feces assaulted my nostrils and I found myself gagging. I crossed to open the window. It was rusted shut, so I popped it with the butt of my gun. Shards of glass rattled on the floor at my feet.

The man stirred and raised his head, and I saw the full extent of Denny's handiwork; a quick death would be a relief to this man. A deep cut ran from above the left eye down to the jawline; it had sliced through a nerve and the upper lid twitched as if shot through with electricity. Beads of blood as dark as leeches clung to the cut. The eyes were as dead as glass marbles. His jaw was broken, the right side of his mouth hanging loose.

The man's head fell back on to his arms.

I flashed on video images from deep memory.

I moved closer, careful not to slip in the blood. I knelt in front of the man and put my gun against his forehead and pushed his head back, cracking it against the wall.

The face of a stranger leaped out at me, and my senses froze, unable to deal with the information. A stranger. A complete stranger. All I could think of was why had Denny led me to a stranger? For a brief moment I had been blinded by the mask of injuries, but the more I looked at the man before me, the more I couldn't understand what Denny had done.

But in the end it didn't matter; all that mattered was that Hendry was still out there.

I pulled my radio from my belt and called for a paramedic.

The freeway was quiet heading south, and I was able to run on cruise control. It had turned eight, the sun was burning a track in the sky, and the tarmac shimmered before my eyes. Denny was asleep in the

back, and I could hear him snoring gently. The fact
that he had almost just beaten a man to death didn't
seem to have jagged his rhythm.

We must have been an hour out of the camp when
I noticed the red light on Denny's Medibag. I remembered Denny telling the juiceheads to leave the bag
alone and I could only assume that despite his warning
one of them had managed to hide their juice in the
bag on the trip out and had left it switched on.

I shouted at Denny to take a look, but he just rolled
over in his sleep, dreams of torture playing across
his eyelids.

The light was still on, and Denny was still asleep
twenty minutes later when I pulled into the service
station. I drove over to the far side of the car park
and stopped next to a green Bullet van.

I climbed down from my seat and opened the rear
door. I pulled myself into the back and walked over
to the Medibag. Normally, Denny keeps it locked, but
when I flipped the lid it opened. A cold mist crept
over the edges and began to spread across the floor
of the shuttle. I waved it away with my hand and knelt
down to take a better look. There was something in
there. It looked like a sheet of paper all crumpled up.
I reached in to lift the paper out, and there it was.

A human heart.

Deep blue and covered with a fur of frost but still
a human heart.

I fell forward on to my knees, a burning pulse beating in my head. I could do nothing but stare into the
box, at the cold air swirling around the heart, as if
pumped by the organ itself.

I still had the sheet of paper in my hand. I lifted it
and read. It was a printout from a DNA scan, the
information identical to the one the technician had
shown me back at the Datacenter, identifying the
blood as belonging to Hendry.

I didn't understand. Was the heart Hendry's? It
didn't make sense. How . . . ?

I looked at the sheet of paper again for some sign; spidery handwriting near the bottom; blood was smeared across most of it but I could make out the tail end: ". . . now that his heart is still, we may be at rest." It was signed Jolie.

Jolie.

She must have hacked into the DNA database and put a trip on it so that when anyone accessed the records of Hendry, she would know immediately. I flashed on running shadows—telecommunications security turned bounty hunters? And Jolie—had she cut out the heart of the man who had killed her son? I screwed my eyes tight, but images of Jolie scooping a knife in a man's chest still burned on my retina.

I stared at the heart for a long time, the distant rhythmic sounds of traffic on the freeway calming me.

The whole mad spiral of events that had led to my being here, from the shooting of Cal to the bloody heart in my hands, played out in a continuous violent loop in my head, over and over. . . .

Eventually I picked up the heart and wrapped it in the sheet of paper. I jumped down from the shuttle and walked across to the far side of the car park where a chainlink fence separated me from the yard. I listened carefully but for a long time I could only hear the sound of my own breathing.

When I heard the sound of the dogs fighting over scraps behind the building I drew back my arm and threw the heart as hard as I could toward the noise.

The frozen heart shattered on hitting the ground, splinters of viscera already melting on the hot tarmac.

THE DEATH OF WINSTON FOSTER

by R. Davis

R. Davis currently resides in Green Bay, Wisconsin, with his very patient wife Monica and his beautiful daughter Morgan Storm. He holds a BA in English from the University of Wisconsin, and writes both fiction and poetry. His current projects include a book-length manuscript of poems entitled *In the Absence of Language* and several novel projects that may never see the light of day.

> "*. . . so if you've found yourself dreaming of killing your abusive husband, take it as a sign that a significant part of you has already done the deed. It is unfortunate that the dream itself is not nearly as gratifying or effective as actually doing him in . . .*"
> —Maxwell Centouro, 2075 AD

THERE are good days and bad days when you make your living as a police detective. Most of them, including this one, were bad. I made an effort to think about the good days as I steered my air car to the home of a recently—very recently—widowed lady by the name of Francis Foster. She knew I was coming, and from the tone of her voice when I'd called, she had already heard the news. Her husband was dead.

I'd spent the first part of my morning at the scene of the accident, which didn't get my day off to a flying start. Her husband, Winston Foster, had been killed on his way to the office by a hypertrain traveling at 380 miles per hour. When it hit Foster's car, it had spread his body like raspberry jam down the tracks and into the ditch. He'd been initially identified by a fingerprint scan from his left hand, which was attached to his left arm, which wasn't attached to anything at all. The arm had been found among the weeds in the ditch by a rookie cop who'd promptly thrown up at the sight.

The problem, and the reason I was involved at all, was that there are numerous safety systems built into a car to prevent just such an occurrence. I had been assigned the rather grim task of breaking the news to Mrs. Foster, as well as investigating what—if any— reasons might exist for the accident. All in all, it was building up to be a banner bad day.

I arrived at her home, parked the air car on the pad, and walked to her door. The house was beautiful. Maroon colored plasi-bricks lined the walkways and flawless ivy crawled up the chimney. I palmed the touch pad next to the door. A feminine-computer voice said, "Identify please."

Yep, I thought, *definitely wealthy to afford this kind of security system.* "Bridges, Jacob R.," I said. "Detective 1st class, Omaha Police Department."

The pleasant, if slightly metallic, voice responded, "Please wait."

I stood there for a moment while the computer ran a check against my hand print and did a voice analysis. Finally, "Identity confirmed. Please stand by."

"Please come in, detective," Mrs. Foster said over the security speaker. Her voice automatically triggered the door locks.

I stepped through the doorway, and heard her say,

"Come to the dining room please. Straight down the hallway on your right."

I followed her directions to the dining room and saw her standing, dry-eyed, next to the mahogany dining table. We stood there looking at each other, and I could see that she'd been crying earlier even if she wasn't now. She had a look of concentration in her large brown eyes as she absently fingered an overripe plum from the fruit basket on the table. A slight smile lingered around the corners of her mouth. I could tell she was assessing me, and I was suddenly reminded of a wild animal testing the air for signs of danger.

"Mrs. Foster, I'm Detective Bridges, Omaha P.D.," I said, extending my hand.

"Yes, I know," she said. "The security system said so, and I recognize your voice from your call earlier, of course."

"I see," I said. "Mrs. Foster, I'm sorry to have to tell you this, but—"

She held up a hand. "I know. Winston died in a hypertrain accident at approximately 8:13 this morning." Her voice seemed rote, as though she were hypnotized or in a trance.

I nodded, having expected this. Still, I was curious. "How did you find out?" I asked.

"Oh, there's no mystery there, detective. I know because I killed him."

I stood there, my jaw hanging somewhere between my belt and my knees. "I beg your pardon?" I asked.

"I said I killed him," she repeated, sounding vaguely annoyed.

Trying to catch up, and assuming that this was her grief talking, I said, "How did you do that, Mrs. Foster?"

She waved her hands at me in exasperation. "Listen, detective. Why don't we get down to brass tacks? This isn't me feeling guilty or upset that he's dead. I don't. In fact, I'm relieved.

"The simple fact is that I killed him. Unfortunately,

my confession is null and void because I could be grief-stricken right now. I don't have my attorney present. I couldn't possibly know what I'm saying. All of which leads me to ask you something. Do you want to hear the story, or just take me downtown and have me released within the day?"

A lot of detective work depends on instinct and intuition. Trusting your gut feelings. At that moment, my gut had a sinking feeling in it that made me want to sit down and put my head between my knees. I took a deep breath and made an effort to control myself. I could tell she was serious, but I could also tell she was scared. I shook my head in bewilderment. *How in the world,* I thought, *do you kill someone with a hypertrain? She must be delusional.* "Okay, Mrs. Foster, why don't you tell me the whole story?" I asked.

"I'm a Ms. now," she said. "You may, if you choose, call me Fran."

"All right, Fran. I'll listen to what you have to say," I said.

"One condition," she said. "After you've heard my story, you'll have to decide whether or not you want to arrest me. That means I want as fair a hearing from you as possible—meaning no interruptions, no questions, and," she pointed at me and tugged her earlobe, "no recordings. I know that police have a recording chip built in. If you understand what you hear, you file a report that clears me. If you don't, I'll come with you and confess for real."

She was one gutsy lady, I had to give her that. And I was intrigued. I'd only heard of one other case of a car hitting a hypertrain, and that was because the driver had smashed into it on purpose. Normally, the automatic braking system would stop the vehicle before it even tapped the blocking bar to the tracks. *If she really had killed him, how had she done it? Still, I couldn't promise the moon.*

"Just a second, Fran. I'll agree to everything you said, but I can't promise not to arrest you. I'm a cop, not a judge, remember? But I'll listen to your story, and we'll go from there. And I have a condition, too," I added.

She looked at me suspiciously, and I realized that Frannie Foster knew all the rules of the game. She knew I had to file a report on what I'd learned. She also knew that sometimes, given a good enough reason, a cop would lie.

"What's that?" she asked.

I smiled at her. "Call me Jacob," I said. I thought a soft touch interview would draw her out. If I scared her, she'd probably just freeze on me, and then I'd be stuck.

She nodded. "I'll get us some coffee," she said, and turned away, heading for the kitchen area. "I gave the servant the day off."

I took the opportunity to really assess her. The vision chip I use told me she was 5.531 feet tall and weighed 110.223 pounds in her current clothing. She was small, almost tiny compared to me. She carried herself in a defensive manner, as though at any moment she expected to be tackled. She was also, I thought, quite pretty. I really couldn't picture her plotting murder. But it's always the ones you least suspect.

As she reentered the room, backing through the swinging partition between the kitchen and the dining room and holding a tray with two coffee cups on it, I attempted to ask a question. Pulling out my palm-top, I said, "Fran, could I ask about Mr.—"

She turned so quickly that she nearly spilled the coffee. "I said 'no questions,' and I meant it," she snapped.

"Whoa, hold on a minute!" I said. "You're going to have to give me a break here. First, I'm a cop, and that's part of my job. If I'm going to understand everything, I need some background."

Her shoulders sagged a little. "You're right, of course," she said. "I'm sorry, Jacob. It's just, well, I need to do this in my own way." She smiled ruefully and shrugged. "Ask your questions, then, but please be brief. I don't really know if I have the strength to tell this twice."

"No problem. I just wanted to clarify the events of this morning. Sort of set the end in sight, so I can see where we're going."

She shrugged again, and said, "Okay."

"Why don't you start by telling me a little about your husband? What was he like?" I asked.

She didn't say anything for nearly a full minute, but I waited. I didn't want to set her off again. I wanted her story, but I wanted it coherent. Her eyes were cast down and to the left, body language that told me she was remembering something.

Softly, so soft that her voice had changed almost entirely, she said, "Big."

"I beg your pardon?" I asked.

"He was big. A big man, very strong. Very smart. He was an investment banker."

I knew all that, of course, from the crime scene and arm scan this morning as well as the preliminary computer report I'd run on Mr. Foster. Still, it was a start.

"Did he say anything to you this morning before he left? Something to make you angry?"

"No," she giggled a little under her breath. "He told me to take out the garbage." She was still remembering, not looking at me directly. "I guess I did," she said.

Wanting to catch her in this reflective mood, I quietly asked, "Did you really kill your husband, Fran?"

"Oh, yes, Detective Jacob Bridges. I killed him in self-defense."

For the second time that morning, I sat there dumbfounded. *Self-defense? How the hell do you kill someone in self-defense with a hypertrain?* She laughed again, lightly, and waited for my reply. Finally, I said, "Self-defense, huh? I guess you'll have to explain that one to me."

"I know," she said. "And that's the story I'm going to tell you. The story you need to hear."

"Well, then, I guess I'm done asking questions. At least for now."

"Very well," she said, "then I can begin."

Her eyes went down-left again, and we both ignored the coffee. Her soft melodic voice was the only sound in the room. She said, "It all goes back to an anonymous e-mail I received last summer. It said that the person knew I was an abused wife, and if I wanted to get out of the situation, I should come to a secure virtual chat to hear this man speak.

"Winston would've killed me if he'd known. But I went anyway. By then, I was so desperate for a way out that I would've done anything at all. The one time I went to the police, he beat the hell out of me. Of course, he knew a judge, so the matter just 'disappeared' from the official records." She laughed bitterly. "Still, I thought maybe this chat was my last hope. So I went."

I nodded, and said, "I understand what you must've been feeling. My sister was abused. It only ended when my father died. What happened at the chat?" I asked.

"My whole life changed," she said.

"I sat in the fourteenth row of the dark auditorium and wondered what I was doing. I stopped there by accident really, or maybe it was curiosity. Hope was not something I was feeling. Mostly, I was afraid that my husband would come home while I was online and plug in to see what I was doing.

"The speaker was a blond man, in his early thirties. He was dressed in a cream-colored sweater and blue jeans. I remember because he seemed so confident and relaxed. His voice wasn't deep, but he spoke well. I thought he sounded like a minister.

" *'Ladies,'* he said, *"my name is Maxwell Centouro. I am here to help you, and if you listen to me, your*

*troubles—at least those with your husbands—will soon
be over.*

" 'My father was an alcoholic and an abuser. On the
last night of his wretched life, he beat my mother for the
very last time. Because he killed her. And I killed him.

" 'What I didn't know at the time was this: I should
have done it in such a way as to leave no doubt that
it was an accident. But I didn't. Instead, I got sent to
prison for seven long years. But while I was there, I
made one vow to myself. When I got out, I would teach
others—women like yourselves, whose husbands hurt
them—how to escape the situation.' "

"I remember thinking at the time that it was like a
dream. Winston would never allow me to escape.
Never allow me to leave him. Still, I listened. It
seemed I had no choice."

" 'You can't rely on the law, ladies. My mother tried
that. And he won't get better if you just do the right
thing. All he will do is get worse and worse. Because
he likes hurting you. And I'm here today to teach you
how to stop him.' "

"I remember how silent it was in that room. All
around me the women were completely quiet, though
a few of them cried softly to themselves as Maxwell
talked. They sounded like wounded animals. I probably would have left then, but I was already hooked. I
felt hope again.

"Winston hit me all the time, and every time it got
worse. I would've left but for one thing. Something so
small that Winston had already forgotten it, I'm sure.
Two weeks before I came to this lecture, Winston had
beat me with a belt in this very room. Not far from
where you're sitting, Jacob.

"And as I lay on the floor, crying and begging for
him to stop, he stood over me with that damn belt in
his hand and he smiled. He was enjoying my misery.
I realized then that I'd do anything to be free of that
smile for the rest of my life.

"I learned a lot that day. I learned that it must

appear to be an accident, and just in case, to document
the abuse. I also learned four techniques that Maxwell
said would 'take care of your husband permanently.'
The best one for me, or rather for Winston, was number three. Maxwell called it: *For the man who has a
daily pattern.* It was perfect.

"You see, Jacob, Winston had a pattern. Was a man
in love with patterns. If I let him fall behind schedule
for any reason, his wrath was terrifying. So I planned
a way to use it against him.

"It took me six months to figure it out. To find the
'hole' in his pattern where an accident could happen.
It took me another three months of online study to
figure out how to make the accident happen. During
this time, I documented as much as I could about what
Winston was doing to me. I took pictures and wrote
everything down. My biggest fear was that he would
find them."

I finally interrupted. "Hold on a minute. Do you
still have those pictures and stuff?"

"Yes," she said. "I do. Maxwell taught us very well.
But I thought we'd agreed on no more questions?"

"You're right," I said. "Sorry, go ahead." I noticed
when she spoke her voice automatically lowered in
tone. Another body language sign of submission.

She continued, "Of course, he beat me during those
months. But in some ways it was worth it. For the
first time in nine long years I had a secret. Something
Winston didn't know. I think, maybe, that a mad little
part of me was in love with the very idea of secrecy.
Of having something to myself. I hid the pictures and
letters under the grill vent of the refrigerator. And I
watched Winston.

"Each day, I learned more about his schedule. Finally, I spotted the hole. He insisted on driving to
work. In that ridiculous 'classic' car of his, rather than
take an air car or use the city train. Every morning at
8:04 sharp, Winston left for work. Not at 8:05, and not
at 8:03. As I said, he was really stuck on his schedule.

"The hypertrain crosses the tracks at 8:13. I know because I timed it every damn day for a month. I told Winston I wanted to lose some weight, so I left the house right at 8:00 to bicycle down there and check the time. It was hell, Jacob, to get on the bike and pedal like crazy in order to get there and be away before Winston drove by.

"Always, the train got there at 8:13. So, just like Winston, the hypertrains ran on time. I just needed to get him there at the right time. And he needed to be distracted, just enough to take his mind off the train and his car. It wasn't that difficult really. Once I figured it out, I was surprised that I hadn't thought of it sooner." Her voice trailed off, and she looked at me. "Jacob, do you ever feel that way?" she asked.

"Yeah, Fran, sometimes I do. Like now, except I don't have all the answers yet. How did you do it?"

"I set his watch back. His big, fancy watch that could tell him right down to the second what time it was."

I knew the watch, having seen it that morning. "Okay, but what made him crash?"

"Simple. Last night, while he slept, I went out to the garage to accomplish two things that I learned. You see, what I studied online during those months was mechanics. 'Classic Vehicle Maintenance 101' was the actual course title," she said.

I looked at her with some admiration. "You shorted the automatic braking system, didn't you?" I asked.

She smiled proudly for a moment, and nodded. "Yes I did. It was really easy. All the older cars had the system wired in as an after-market product. It wasn't something that the manufacturers put in back then."

"What was the second thing?" I asked. "You said 'two things'."

"Oh, yes. The distraction. His 'classic' car is—was—air-cooled. I sprayed mace into the vents on the front of his windshield, and on his hood. When it pulls air in from the outside, I guessed that it would pull the spray in, too."

"But how could you know he would turn on the air inside the car?" I objected.

"I couldn't. I took a gamble that it would be another hot day, and it paid off. I estimated that as soon as he was out of the driveway, he would turn on the air. It takes about seven minutes to cycle the air system into full operation. I guessed that the spray would hit him about sixty seconds before he crossed the tracks. I assume it did."

I sat there for a few minutes, saying nothing. It was stunning how she'd worked it out. Essentially, she'd made his eyes water just seconds before he would cross the tracks. The tracks were at the bottom of a steep hill and surrounded by a ditch on either side. Even if the spray hadn't worked, he probably would have crashed with no brakes at that speed. Had he left at his normal time, the train would have been there and gone before him. I had to admire it.

I looked at her, and could see the desperate hope on her face. "Can I see those pictures, please?" I asked.

"Sure," she said, and rose to go get them. When she returned, she tossed me a large envelope. Inside were pictures of her bruised body. In one photo, I could see welt marks on her ribs from a strap or a belt of some kind. In another, there were cigar shaped burns on the inside of her thighs. I shuddered. It was enough.

Smiling at her, I said, "Sorry about your husband, Fran."

"Yes," she said, "thank you." This time her smile was real. "It's a shame he had to go that way, but at least he felt no pain."

"You're a generous woman, Fran. He deserved far worse than what he got."

"I know," she said, "but accidents happen."

I left the home of Francis Foster, and got back in my air car. As the autodrive engaged, I reported in to the station that I was headed home for lunch, and that I would report in later. I listened to her story on my ear chip as the traffic flew by.

The air car landed on the roof pad of the apartment building where I lived. Walking down the steps, I erased the recording I'd made of Fran's story. I believed her, Foster was an abuser of the highest order, and I'd promised her no recordings. I entered my apartment and tossed my coat on the kitchen table.

I ordered up a sandwich and a beer from the auto-chef. While it was synthesizing my lunch, I turned on my computer system. Grabbing my meal, I sat down at my console and plugged myself in through the neural jack on the back of my skull. Entering virtual reality has always been a pleasant escape for me.

Soaring over numerous sites, I activated my security program, and located the chat "room" where I spent most of my spare time. I chose my persona, this time a distinguished-looking gentleman with gray hair at his temples, dressed in an immaculate three-piece suit. I stepped in, and looked out into the room. It was, in actuality, an auditorium. Filled with women.

There are good days and bad days when you make your living as a police detective. Today had turned out pretty well.

I stepped out onto the auditorium stage, and said, "Ladies, my name is Maxwell Centouro. I am here to help you, and if you listen to me, your troubles—at least those with your husbands—will soon be over. . . ."

GLORY HAND IN THE
SOFT CITY

by Jay Bonansinga

Jay Bonansinga is the author of the novels *The
Black Mariah*, *Sick*, *The Killer's Game*, *Head
Case*, and *Bloodhound*. His short fiction and arti-
cles have appeared in *Grue*, *Filmfax*, *Cemetery
Dance*, and *It Came From the Drive-In*. He lives
in Evanston, Illinois, with his wife and son.

I woke up in the middle of the night thinking I still
had my right hand.

It threw me for a moment.

I lay there in a cold sweat, my heart thumping. I
brought my stump up in front of my face, waving invisible fingers back and forth. I could feel the twinges of
phantom pain, the sharp aching in the knuckles that
weren't there anymore, and the hot, itchy sensations
like sunburn tingling in the heart of my nonexistent
palm.

"What's'matter, Glory?" The hooker lying next to
me was stirring awake, gazing up at me through heavy-
lidded eyes. She called herself Porsche, and her hair
had that bizarre coppery color of laboratory-grown
follicles. Earlier in the evening we had humped for
twenty minutes, until I had climaxed my routine one-
and-a-half fluid ounces of sterile semen and Porsche

146

had fallen fast asleep. I hadn't had the heart to boot her out.

Now I was telling her I was fine.

"You're sweating," she insisted, sitting up, reaching for her box of synth-cigs.

"Nightmares."

"You're shitting me. You're still sleeping natural?" Porsche lit a syn-stick, sucking a mouthful of pale blue smoke. "I sleep like a baby since I got the alpha implant put in. Word to the wise, Robert: Get an alpha implant."

"Already tried it—didn't work," I said, flexing my nonfingers, concentrating on the ghostly feelings. The heat, the tingling: They were my first true neural sensations since I had lost the hand in a nasty kendo-fight with a couple of transgenic Sikhs in a juice den last month. I was on a missing person case that had gotten me mixed up with the Indo-Burmese Chimera Triad, and I was trying to fight my way out. It took a pair of emergency techs working nonstop just to save my hand's nerve network and get the thing frozen before the cells shut down. They told me they could probably save the hand and restore the nerves, but I was devastated. My pipeline to true bio-touch had been inexorably threatened.

That's when I started thinking about checking out of the private investigation game.

"When do you get *that* back?" The prostitute nodded toward my stump, toward the cap of surgical mesh and the network of medical tattoos drawn around my wrist for calibration during the reattachment.

I told her next Thursday, and then I glanced across the shadows of my measly little studio flat. The cracked plastic calendar was hanging by the autoclave, the digital face reading Friday, March 7, 2053, and I realized I had only six days left until my biological hand was done. And then I realized my right hand was all I had left in the world. The rest of my body had been grafted and treated so many times, there wasn't much left with a decent nerve ending. Like most of the regular army, I had lost ninety percent of the skin on my arms and legs during the war in Pakistan. All those new viruses mingling, nasty hybrids surfacing everywhere. Of course, the plague years got the rest of me. My left hand, much of my torso, and a good portion of my left shoulder had atrophied during the Hanta plague in '24; and most of it had to be reseeded with test tube tissue. Even my ass had ninety percent lab-flesh on it.

But nobody was smart enough to see the shutdown coming.

They called it Miller's Syndrome: the gradual atrophy of the nerve endings due to some faulty connection between laboratory grown skin and the natural subcutaneous fascia. In English: The world went numb. Four out of five survivors of the new plagues experienced the deadening effects within a year of being treated. I got it myself. After my discharge, I started going numb. And even throughout my years as a beat cop, I felt the nerve endings closing down.

Of course, I was lucky. I had fared a lot better than most of the poor schmucks creeping around the HardCity nowadays. Most folks born after the turn of the twenty-first had a hundred percent reworked tissue, and the closest thing to a real neural sensation for them was jacking into a nerve-net box and letting some virtual Hindu mama jerk them off. I, on the other hand, possessed . . . well . . . *the other hand.* I was one of the small percentage of old timers who still owned a biological hand. A stretch of skin with its original nerve bundle intact.

And right now I wanted it back.

"Ouch!" I jerked back against the fibersteel headboard with a start. My unseen fingers were shrieking. The invisible heat was erupting.

"What is it, honey?" Porsche had managed to slip out of bed and climb into her sari. Now she was standing a few feet away, nervously puffing her cig.

"I dunno—I can—I can feel—*OUCH!*" I convulsed against the wall.

My phantom hand was going up in flames.

"Should I buzz somebody?" Porsche was gawking at me, chewing her lip.

"No—I'm just—I can feel the—" I climbed out of bed and turned on the halogens. With my numb left hand I managed to pull on my leather pants and guide my feet into my boots. The heat was like a cymbal crashing in my brain. I took a few deep breaths, then walked over to the window.

I looked out through the gray ozone filter.

My invisible hand throbbed.

The HardCity was shimmering in the toxic darkness, the sodium-bright residential blocks glowing sickly silver. At this hour the streets were still humming, the threads of directional lasers still stitching through the haze, looking like cat's cradles. Off in the distance, I could see the blue flames on the horizon, the Microsoft farms growing bio-circuits twenty-four hours a day. They owned everything. Even me: my skin, my organs. Either Microsoft or Dupont. They owned the patents on everything.

I started to say, "I think it's just a twitch or something—"

Then it hit me.

The phantom pain could be a signal from some remote transmission. A warning. Something happening to my physical hand. *My own flesh and blood.*

A distress call.

"I gotta go check on something," I muttered, heading for the closet.

"At this hour?" Porsche looked like an apparition, standing there in her coppery hair and re-gen silk.

"Help yourself to some coffee, whatever you want," I said, pulling on my ozone jacket, shades, and gloves. There was an advisory tonight, and I didn't want to jeopardize my preoperative site.

I walked over to the door, paused and added, "Make yourself at home, Porsche, I'll be back in a flash."

"But what about—?"

I had already shut the door in her face and was halfway to the elevator.

The handi-cab skimmed along the slotted macadam of the HardCity, the sound of air circulators rattling in unison with the aging motor. I was sitting in back, my ghost-hand screaming at me, the pain constant now. I could barely see through the safe-shades tonight. There were several atmospheric advisories on the RT, and the air outside the shields was the color of pewter. Every few moments the belly of the cab would thump over another magnetic terminal, clocking the distance to the Brooksfield industrial park.

A moment later I saw the flames.

A quarter mile away, the salmon-colored smoke rose in a dense curtain above the smooth gray walls of the Re-Gen Center. Panic squeezed my heart. Tendrils of lights were cutting through the haze, reflecting off mirrored windows all around me, the whine of sirens seeping through the cab's welded joints. I blinked the sting from my eyes, then I rubbed the cab's grimy side-shield as the maelstrom loomed ahead of me.

I recognized one of the squad cars pulling up behind a fire wagon.

"Program stop! Right here!" I ordered the cab over to the side-track.

The cab rattled to a halt, and I snicked open the door with my money-chit.

"Jesus Criminy, Glory—whaddya doing here?" The voice bellowed behind me as I climbed out of the handi-cab. I whirled around and saw the behemoth coming at me. A pituitary case named Zander, he was an old watch commander from my former precinct. He was built like a freight barge, with half a dozen chins and beady little eyes set deep in his fleshy face like two little raisins. He wore a safe suit under his flak vest. "How'd you know about this so fast?"

"What happened, Zanny?" I couldn't take my eyes off the burning building.

"How'd you know about this?"

"What happened here?"

"Answer my question, Glory."

I told him it was hard to explain . . . but I felt it. I felt the fire.

"You what?" The fat man was staring at me now, his eyes contracting into tiny black diamonds.

I looked at him. "My hand's in there, Zanny, I gotta go make sure it's okay."

I started walking toward the fire scene, toward the giant burning monolith. The building was as wide as a city block, as high as the clouds, with thirty-inch-thick walls carved out of super-slate and artificial mortar. Another wholly owned subsidiary of Microsoft, the Re-Gen Center was a place where amputated limbs and cancerous organs could be given another chance, cleansed through hyper-radiation, reconstructed through genetic engineering. My hand was in there somewhere, in its final stages of regeneration, and now the top floors were blazing bright liquid silver. Goddamn idiots had too many alkaline metals stored in the vaults again. These magnesium fires could burn through Fort Knox. I could feel the dry heat on my face as I approached, my phantom hand tingling.

Then a steel-vice grip was on my shoulder, yanking me backward.

"Easy does it, sweetheart," Zander growled at me, spinning me around. And there might have been a scintilla of sympathy in his tiny cinder eyes, I'm not sure. Two other plainclothes cops were approaching us, the pink glow refracting off their mirrored shades.

"Lemme go, Zanny!"

"You don't get it—"

"Let go!"

I tried to wriggle free, but his grip was like a channel lock on my neck, so I just gave him a sharp nudge to the rib cage, trying to shove him off me, but it must have triggered his goons because they were on me in a blink, driving rock-hard fists into my kidney, then a few knuckle-balls to my gut, their genetically-enhanced hands like sledgehammers. They snapped my feet out from under me, and I just folded up like a paper doll, the ground coming up and smacking me in the side of my face.

Zander leaned down close enough for me to smell the beans on his breath. "Bad news, Glory," he was saying. "The fire's a diversionary thing."

"—what?—"

"Whole thing's a boost job." His big meaty face was glowing magenta-pink, melting before my eyes.

I managed to utter, "What are you telling me?"

"I'm telling you the place was knocked over. Scumbags pinched a buncha organs, extremities, and what-not."

Everything was going dark, and I got one last question out: "My hand—?"

Zander sighed. "Sorry, sweetheart . . . they got it. They got your paw."

I shivered suddenly, adrenaline coursing through me. I tried to stand up, tried to yell, tried to grab for Zander's sidearm. I didn't even notice the other cop coming toward me. His fist came out of nowhere.

Tagged me square across the bridge of my nose.

It was like a switch being turned off.

I woke up in a holding cell. They brought me some food, and I got my bearings. And then I started pacing, and I must have paced the length of that cell for hours, thinking.

I just couldn't figure out why some second-story man would risk life and limb to get himself a natural hand? Sure, there was a healthy black market for natural organs, but nowadays test-tube extremities were being farmed everywhere, and they worked a lot better than the originals. All you needed was a plastic scaffold that mimicked the shape of a hand—and a few cells to "seed" it with—and pretty soon the cells assembled, and the plastic degraded, and voila! You got a brand new hand, stronger and more dexterous than the original. It just didn't make any kind of sense that a local cat would try to boost one.

Funny thing was, I had no idea how close I was to the answer.

Around five o'clock that night, Zander showed up and sprang me.

"Dicks ain't exactly supposed to brief 'civvies' on law enforcement matters," Zander grumbled as he led me through a narrow corridor toward the processing bay. He was chewing a stinky cheroot, and the brown smoke swirled around his huge head as he walked. The "civvies" reference was definitely a dig. Cops hated ex-cops. But for some reason—be it pity, amusement, or what-have-you—Zander had a soft spot for yours truly. "I'll tell ya this much," he went on. "We've already recovered ninety-five percent of the organs."

"Ninety-five percent?" I gave him a sidelong glance as we strode through pools of halogen.

"That's what I said, Glory."

I tried to control my emotions. "My hand's been recovered?"

"No, sir, I didn't say that."

"My hand's in the five percent?"

"Yessir, unfortunately, yes."

"Where's my hand?"

"Go home, Glory," he said, pausing by the gigantic exit door, punching out a code on the keyboard.

I stood there, gaping at him. "Do they know who cribbed it?"

"I said go home."

"Has it been fenced yet?"

The door hissed open. Zander turned to me and grasped a handful of my collar and very softly, very patiently, asked me to vacate the premises.

I knew it was the last time his request would be soft or patient.

I waited two days.

Pacing the length of my place, zoned out on restrex, flexing fingers which were once attached but were now noisy ghosts, sputtering, tingling, sparking, I could feel my sanity—what was left of it—denaturing into something primal. Something black and poisonous. I've been known to have a temper—I won't lie—but now a new kind of rage was coursing through me with each twinge of phantom pain.

I had to do something.

On the second evening, I jacked into the net, trying to scare up some of my own leads. I threw out some cockamaimie call for bone marrow cells as bait, and started sorting through all the fences working angles on hot tissue. Process of elimination got it down to a single shitbird.

Georgie Quine was a small-time scrounger. Specialized in hot molecules copped from indie labs, research schools, and the like. He lived under a co-op down near the hover station; I decided to take a chance and pay him a visit.

By the time I got down there, the night air had turned gelid, the city a rancid melange like too many perfume counters clashing. The clouds were faded black muslin, cracked and veined with yellow age and pollution.

"Who dat?" The blurred image of Georgie Quine was flickering on the rez-box moments after I pushed the toggle.

"It's Glory," I told him.

"Glory?" the pallid face on the screen crackled at me. "What's the panic?"

"Got questions need answers."

"No can do, Brother. Sick as a dog."

I told him he'd better get well quick or I'd make him terminally ill.

A minute later the door seal hissed, and the little stick figure poked his wan face out the crack. "I got the blue lung, Glory," he wheezed. "Chrissake, I can't hardly take in a breath."

"All I want to know is who stuck the Re-Gen Center, and don't give me any noise about you not knowing anything."

The junkie sucked his sallow cheek for a moment. Dressed in gray leather and a moleskin mask, he was a couple of years away from the incinerator, his skinny body riddled with genetic dissonance. He had one good laboratory eye left, which flashed and sputtered like a dying lightbulb as he replied. "You didn't hear this from me, okay? All right?"

I grabbed him with my jacked-up lab-hand and slammed him hard against the jamb, hard enough to rattle his brain. Made his eye flash *tilt*. My phantom hand was cold now and twinging with filaments of pain, and I was losing control. "I'm on a goddamn schedule!" I barked at him. "Tell me who did the goddamn job and you can keep your teeth in your skull!"

"Stains, Stains did the job, Stains did it, Rupert Stains, that's the guy."

I blinked, incredulous. Rupert Stains was a major player in the biotech arena, a genetic designer with more awards than the head of Rotary. Rupert Stains was also a boy-wonder who had made designer-in-residence at Big Softie before his thirtieth birthday.

Word was, Stains had started to decline in recent years, contracting an especially virulent form of Miller's syndrome. But who the hell needs natural tissue when you're rich, right? Word was, Stains had replaced every major organ and every square centimeter of his flesh with the finest tissue money could buy. His delicate little physique was trimmer than ever, his handsome mug more handsome than his press pictures. But rumors were also rampant that Stains had gone completely bug-fuck loony. Maybe it was the loss of all that feeling, or maybe it was just the natural course of a genius intellect. Regardless, it made no kind of sense that a guy like Stains would do a B&E job on a re-gen lab. He had a family, according to news reports, and was not the type of guy to get caught with his pants down.

"Stains was behind the job?" I finally managed to ask, clutching at Quine's throat.

"No, no, amigo, no—Stains *did* the thing. Along with Hawkhurst and Black Jimmy."

"You're telling me Stains did this thing *himself* with a couple of second-floor men?"

Quine's eye pulsed. "My hand to the almighty." He glanced at my stump. "No offense intended."

"They still in the HardCity?"

Quine swallowed dryly. "Cops already got two of 'em, Glory, I swear to you, they're coming down hard on everybody. Nobody's moving a thing—"

"Who's left?" I tightened my grip. It looked as though Quine's eyeball was about to pop out.

"Stains—Stains is still running—somewhere north of Blackchappel—"

I started slamming the back of his head against the jamb, a thin membrane of scarlet drawing down over my vision. "They took one of the naturals! A hand! A right hand! Where the fuck is it?!"

The words wheezed out of Quine's turkey neck: "—Stains has it—"

I hurled the little hoodlum to the floor of the foyer,

cracking his skull against the wall. His eyeball flickered and strobed.

I turned and started toward the north, the vapor
lights going red and hazey.

I barely heard Quine's slurred speech behind me, a
sickly bird singing one last tune.

"Better hurry, Glory . . . Stains has already been to
the transplant team. . . ."

The words were barely audible as I began to run.

Blackchappel was a vast graveyard of decaying, oxi-
dized quonset huts buried in hardpack like fossilized
dinosaurs, their metal spines gleaming in the sodium
wash. The air was hotter around here. Toxic. Veined
with static electricity. Handi-cabs wouldn't run this far,
and the cops rarely bothered patrolling the place. But
as I approached the east bridge on foot, breathing
mask-filtered air, lenses down, heart hammering, I saw
the commotion a hundred yards away, out by the ancient switchyard.

Zander and his posse—three squad cruisers in all—
inching along the edge of the tracks.

My invisible fingers were fuses now, lit and crackling
hotly, the pain making me crazy, and I started trotting
along the shadowy footpath, staying low, moving
toward the switchyard, toward those slow-moving
cruisers. I was all jigged up on hate and adrenalin,
and I was clenching my phantom hand, tasting hot
magnesium on my tongue.

Ahead of me, the cruisers jerked to a halt, one by
one, their doors springing open, the shadowy figures of
Zander and his men piling out, guns raised, infrareds
snapped on, search-strobes sweeping the cobalt haze
in front of them. And my heart was jittering wildly in
my chest as I realized, all at once, just exactly what
was going on.

One of the quonset huts a quarter kilometer away
was lit up inside.

An underground clinic.

Rupert Stains was in there—I was sure of it now—my missing hand growing on his arm.

The revelation coursed through me like nitro, all the tiles in the puzzle-box clicking in place in my brain: the son of a bitch in that silver warehouse, richer than God, taking the last vestige of sensation from me, taking my hand, my touch, taking it from me and assimilating it like a worm growing segments. And now the rage was erupting in me, all the pain, all the longing, longing to feel something, longing to touch, and before I knew what was happening, I was running full bore toward that goddamned quonset hut with my gun drawn.

Two hundred meters ahead of me the doors to the quonset burst open.

I fumbled the safety off, and I ran as fast as my lab-legs would carry me.

Zander and his men were already fanning out when they saw me approaching. Zander did a sort of comical double-take, his infrareds whirling toward me, a glint of sodium light catching his eyepiece and blossoming. Almost fell on his big fat ass. "Glory!" His rasp filtered through the pox mask. "What the fuck—?"

He couldn't finish his thought because things were happening very quickly now.

A hundred meters ahead of me, the shadows were disgorging three figures, and I sprinted toward them, ignoring the cops off to my right, ignoring the pain in my chest, ignoring Zanny's warning calls, ignoring everything but the three men fleeing the hot house, and I fixed my iris on the smallest of the three. The little one was dressed in leathers, jackboots, and old flying ace goggles. He had broken off from the group and was hightailing it toward the East Sprawl Bridge.

Stains.

I fixed my sights on the bridge and made a beeline, the first tracer shots popping behind me, Zander's plasma-pellets buzzing over my head, buzzing white-hot, making the darkness flicker and crackle. I stayed

low, my gun raised, aimed straight ahead at the little
millionaire racing across the bridge fifty meters away.

Stains was heading toward the far gates, toward the
luminous threads of blue laser-light demarcating the
outskirts, and as he approached the end of the line,
he swam through a pool of chrome-yellow arc light,
and I got a momentary glimpse of his right arm . . .
and the pale, pink fingers clutching the tiny vintage
Walther PPK handgun.

My right hand.

I was about to shriek at the top of my lungs when
I saw him skid to a halt, then spin around with the
Walther raised, then the four silver florettes sparking
from the barrel. I dove to the ground just as the dumb
bells sizzled above my left shoulder, striking the bridge
behind me, chewing through the ancient teflon span.

Behind me, pandemonium erupted, the sounds of
angry cop voices, and more sirens coming from the
distance, and Zander's men firing off high-V slugs, and
I managed to rise to a crouch in a hail of gunfire and
squeeze off half a dozen smart-slugs with my stupid
left hand. The heat seekers arced out into the darkness
and pinwheeled every which way, but it was too late:
Stains had crossed over into the SoftCity—a vast re-
stricted area where superbacteria had broken down
the cells in the concrete, metal, and glass, and now
everything was literally soft and waxy—and nobody, I
mean *nobody,* was reckless enough to chase him into
that quagmire.

Except me.

I crossed the far threshold and plunged into the
indigo fog, the blue terminal lasers vibrating all
around me, and I descended a steep slope of ashes
into the wasteland, my boots sinking ankle deep into
the detritus, and I kept the gun raised in case Stains
was waiting to ambush me, but I knew I was doomed.
My right hand—its natural nerves intact—was far too
fast. My right hand was a killer. I could never outshoot
my own right hand.

The only thing I had going for me was the searing rage pumping through my veins.

A building rose out of the mist—some sort of gothic ruin from some twentieth-century train station—and I caught a fleeting glimpse of the millionaire ducking behind a rotting rampart twenty meters away, and I started firing wildly, sapphire flames barking out of my gun, and the smart-bullets curled around the side of the building, puffing through steel girders: needles through pudding.

And then my gun was empty, and I started toward the building, awkwardly reloading a magazine with my left hand and right stump, my brain fizzing, overloading, a cognitive tape-loop parroting: Why? Why would this son of a bitch with more money than God risk everything for a little taste of the natural touch, a little bit of feeling?

Why?

I was approaching the building when the adjacent wall erupted in my face.

The little rich man was bursting through the softened mortar like a toy through a vacu-form.

Gunfire exploded all around me as I dove for cover behind a fossilized train engine, and I felt the heat on the top of my skull as the fireworks display swirled over my head, piercing the softened iron of the Sky-Chief, and I opened my mouth and wailed through my mask, my voice drowned in a hurricane of fire, and I finally managed to look up. Stains was running away across an old decaying trestle.

Then I saw the world go haywire.

It happened so quickly I barely had time to focus, my eyes flash-blind and blurry, and I blinked and blinked because I couldn't believe what I was seeing: The ancient iron of the trestle turning all rubbery under Stains like a Salvador Dali nightmare.

Then the walkway dipped and flexed and stretched down into the darkness of the gorge like taffy, and Stains went with it, screaming all the way, his voice drowned by the sound of a gargantuan metal spring uncoiling.

The bridge finally snapped, and Stains landed hard on a slag heap.

I made my way over to the edge of the gorge and looked down. I could see Stains lying semiconscious down there, half buried in the metal mush, and I saw something else that pressed down on my heart, made my blood vibrate in my veins, and made my phantom fingers tingle, and even as the sounds of Zander and his men were approaching behind me on the poison winds, I kept staring at that horrible still-life down in the rotting shadows.

My right hand was down there, all pale and pink, still attached to Stains' arm, still gripping the Walther PPK.

It took three days for the boys and girls in the fifth precinct to sort out the whole mess. I was on Zander's shit-list for meddling; but considering my personal interests, I don't think he really blamed me.

At the end of the week, they moved Stains to the federal clinic in Eastminster for the transplant.

I showed up early on Friday morning for the big show, and they ran me through the pre-op procedures. They prepped my stump, got me dressed in surgical robes, started drips, and made me wait forever in a sterile green-tiled room in the bowels of the building. It was well into the afternoon when I finally buzzed for the nurse. Her face flickered across the screen above me, and I told her I was tired of waiting and I wanted to know just where the hell they were keeping my hand.

She told me the other patient was still with the clinic psychologist, and there would be a slight delay.

"What delay?" I asked.

"I'm not sure, sir. Would you like me to call the psychologist?"

"What the hell's going on?" I felt a strange twinge, something feathery on my phantom fingers.

"Sir, it'll just be a few more minutes—"

"This guy's a goddamn thief, he stole my hand, and you've got him seeing a shrink?"

"Sir, if you'd just—"

"I want to know what the hell's going on!"

She sighed, her image flickering for a moment, and then she said, "Look, I'm not supposed to do this, but I think under the circumstances . . ."

She reached down and flipped a switch, and the picture on the screen changed.

The new image was of another room, a stark little lounge in another wing of the building. A table in the center, a couple of chairs, the venetian blinds drawn. Stains was sitting at the table, dressed in hospital robes. Standing behind him were the shrink and a couple of armed guards.

Across the table sat a little girl in a cotton jumper and pigtails. She was Stains' little girl; I had seen pictures of her on the Web-news. She couldn't have been more than six years old, and she was clutching a little stuffed turtle with one hand, holding her daddy's hand with the other.

Her daddy's hot hand.

My hand.

I gazed at the screen, my throat drying up, filling with sawdust, my eyes welling, elephants standing on my chest. It was as though I was a ghost caught in some other dimension watching my shadow-self, and I felt the moist warmth of the child's touch on my phantom fingers, and I watched the screen, transfixed, as the millionaire held his daughter's delicate little hand one last time.

And then it occurred to me: *This* was why Stains had gone to all the trouble.

To hold his little girl's hand just once.

To feel her touch.

I stared at the screen for as long as I could tolerate

the intimacy, memorizing every movement, every gesture, every quiet exchange between the child and the man, and I realized it was my hand that was doing the holding, *my* hand, God help me, it was my own flesh and blood in there. When I finally looked away, I was fighting the tears. "Nurse!" My voice was like metal tearing apart. "Nurse! Nurse!"

The screen flickered, and the nurse's placid face came back on. "What is it?"

"Changed my mind."

"Pardon me?"

"The operation," I said. "I changed my mind, I don't want to go through with it."

There was a beat of silence. "You what?"

"I said I don't want to do the transplant anymore. Is that all right with you?"

There was more silence, and then the nurse finally shook her head. "I'll get Doctor Burgess on the line. He'll want to know about this right away."

The screen went black.

And I turned away and let the tears come.

Lately the nights seem to have grown more silent in my little cubicle. The ticking of the air filters above me, the distant muffled drone of the city outside my windows, and the slow, steady pulse of my own heart are the only sounds. I prefer it this way. I haven't seen Porsche for weeks. Haven't been in the mood for that noise for a while now. Got too much thinking to do. I read a lot. Started a diary last week, but I forget to write in it sometimes. Mostly I just lie on my contour couch and stare at the hepa filters embedded in the ceiling, clocking endlessly in the darkness, silent sentinels tirelessly guarding against some lethal strain of mush floating into my space.

Funny thing is, I've never been this happy, going through the motions each day, playing detective, then coming home each night, alone.

So much quiet time.

I can feel her touch every few days. It's fading now, but it's still there. It'll always be there. That warm, moist, powdery touch against my ghost-fingers. The sweet, delicate hand of a little girl nestled in my own phantom palm. She'll always be there.

Always.

THE CRIME OF TRANSFIGURATION

by Will Murray

Will Murray is a professional psychic and the author of nearly fifty pseudonymous novels in the long-running *Destroyer, Doc Savage,* and *Executioner* series. Other short fiction by him is found in *Miskatonic University, The UFO Files,* and *100 Wicked Little Witch Stories.*

THE Chairwoman of the Virtual WorldBank vanished on 6/6/66, at 6:66 PM Uniform Global Time, from her 66th floor office at 666 6th Avenue in New NYC. It was the exact minute she wiped her desk system clean, eradicating all ID and healthcare files, V-money accounts—insuring that, from an economic and political sense, she no longer existed—or could exist—in Beta society.

An FBI team was on site by 11:45 UGT the next morning, vacuuming up latent prints and executing a full systems sift.

"Wiped clean," the technician pronounced gloomily.

FBI Special Agent in Charge Gill Murrillo turned to the fingerprint expert. "Now give me the *bad* news."

The print-tech finished scanning the office windows

and hit the Sort Function key. "Processing," the FID chirped.

"Latents match prints found at the prior crime scenes," he chanted. "Readout: Unknown Alpha Person."

Murrillo lifted his voice. "Okay. Wrap it up, everybody. I'm calling in a Divination Team."

The D-Team were air-dropped onto the roof so their distinctive sky-blue jumpsuits and yin-yang shoulder patches wouldn't create a public relations problem with the more militant super-Betas. It was led by a Native American who identified herself in a honeyed contralto voice: "Dawn/Fawn O'Leary."

That made her an Alpha-Beta. Murrillo eyed her holotag ID and asked, "Which one am I talking to?"

"Dawn is my Beta name; in Alpha, I'm Fawn. I'm presently in an Alpha state, so I would appreciate it if you would still your mind until we've completed our Alpha sweep to avoid sensory leakage."

Murrillo watched as the team went to work. One took a turn around the room absorbed in what looked like a FIDbox, except the readout cycled through the major and minor arcana of a digital tarot deck. Another dropped into a Theta trance and began describing what she saw in her mind's eye while another D-teamer drew the described face on a tablet with an old-fashioned greasepencil. Fawn O'Leary psychometrized the desktop system, caressing it like an ethereal harpist.

After twenty minutes, the D-team conferred briefly.

"She's not dead," Fawn reported. "Nor kidnapped. We feel she left of her own free will."

Murrillo nodded. "That fits the pattern to date."

"She's still on our side of the Rockies, but I sense her ultimate destination is Alphaside."

Murrillo grabbed his handphone. "I'll inform the Director."

"There's more. She underwent a sudden spiritual emergency." Her voice darkened. "It was *induced.*"

Murrillo disconnected. "What do you mean— induced?"

"The person with whom she was meeting induced a spontaneous spiritual crisis. This was not a conversion, chakra blow-open, or a typical psychic breakthrough. Her temporal lobes were artificially overstimulated. I would classify it as a high-level transfiguration of some hitherto-undocumented type."

"Don't tell me she's not reclaimable. . . ."

"If you capture her, you will find her Beta brain functions have been nuked. She won't be able to balance a checkbook or drive a lightcar. She will be in a permanent state of bliss, and exhibit other outward signs of Williams Syndrome. And she will be operationally psychic. You might as well let her go Alphaside; she's no longer of any use to Beta society."

"And she's too psychic to be easily caught . . ." Murrillo growled. "Who the hell could have done this?"

Fawn presented the tablet to Murrillo. It showed a rather goatish-looking bearded male face. "Look familiar?"

"Except for the thick eyebrows, that's the face the other teams conjured up."

"I'd appreciate a more respectful choice of words."

"Sorry. Anything else?"

"I picked up a name clairaudiently. Mel Drum."

"That helps. Nobody got a name before."

"I read him as an unlicensed psychic. He also has an agenda."

"Go ahead."

"He's trying to crash the economy."

"If this keeps up, he'll succeed," Murrillo growled. "Okay. Stand by with your team. I gotta get instructions."

FBI Director Silverglate took the news in silence.

"We have to find this Alpha terrorist, Mr. Director. We have a face, a name, and a pattern. And we know he's targeting high-level banking officials. But we don't know why."

"With undergrounded Alphas, there is no why," the Director snapped. "Maybe he takes 'Money is the Root of All Evil' literally. Maybe he has a stash of old currency and thinks if V-money is discredited, he can cash in at pre-Schism rates. Motives don't matter. We have to find this individual. Squirt your data to Central Processing."

"Done, sir. They show no such person. He's an Alpha illegal—virtually untraceable."

The Director cleared his throat.

"If you can't find the perpetrator, then it is your job to identify his next victim. Can you work with the D-Team onsite?"

"If I have to. . . ."

"That's a politically correct answer. This won't appear on your permanent record, if that's your wish."

"It is," Murrillo admitted.

"Go to it. Just don't lose another one."

"Yes, sir." Murrillo snapped off. He found Fawn.

"Fawn—"

"I'm Dawn now." Her voice had a professional edge to it.

"I need you in Alpha. You are now under my operational direction. We've been tasked to identify the next victim."

"Easier assigned than carried out."

The D-Team took two hours. Murrillo didn't watch this time. It always gave him a weird feeling to watch Alpha-state people at work. Like a vague memory was stirring, haunting, half-remembered. He had taken St. John's Wort at Harvard—a lot of people were doing SJW at the close of the Second Millennium—and had experienced lucid dreaming. That was as far as his flirtation with Alpha had gone, but the memories lingered.

When Agent O'Leary found him drinking coffee-flavored herbal tea in the hardbeam-secured corridor, she had that mellow lift to her voice that told him she was back in Alpha.

"Our man is blocking us. He's got his walls up and my belief is that he's not consciously preselected his next victim precisely to thwart us."

"That means he knows FBI has off-the-books divination teams."

Fawn shrugged. "It's an open secret."

"Who works precognitively on your team?"

"I do. But you know how it goes. Given ninety percent psychic reliability factors drop to twenty or thirty when you go precog. Time is not recognizable in Alpha, so I might pick up on victim five or six, instead of four. Assuming I catch the correct timeline."

"Okay, okay. Spare me the quantum quasi-physics lesson. If we're blocked, we're blocked. We're just going to have to go public."

Fawn lifted a quelling hand. "There *is* another way."

"Name it."

"There's a man who used to do this kind of work. A legend."

"A super-psychic?"

"He *is* psychic, but that's not his forte. He used to work with the police, but after the Schism, he went underground. Not wanting to give up his Beta life, he didn't care to go full Alpha. So he dropped out of sight." Her dark brows knit together. "Funny, he should pop into my head. I haven't thought of him in years."

Murrillo raised an impatient eyebrow. "So?"

"He's an astrologer. One of the best."

"Astrology is not a sanctioned procedure. You know that."

"You know as well as I do it's a valid operational system."

"I don't want to hear this, O'Leary," Murrillo growled.

"Then I must prepare myself." She turned to go.

*   *   *

Former Virtual WorldBank President Loris Rainer turned up in Day-OH. No one could figure out how she got so far so fast without ID cards or personal transportation. She was found wandering the campus of the University of Dayton by campus security police, and placed under protective custody for being an unregistered Alpha Person.

SAC Murrillo made the jump to Day-OH in twenty minutes flat.

"Has she talked?" he asked the special agent in charge.

"Actually, she's singing."

If it was singing, it was aphonetic. Loris was emitting a high, keening sound that made Murrillo's feet lift off the floor as if walking over vibrating glass. The cell doors split open. He stepped in—quickly retreating with his hands pressuring his ears.

He returned to the cell wearing a white-noise headset. Loris Rainer sang on without acknowledging his presence. This was not the same woman whose face Gil had seen at televised news conferences. Her coiled black hair hung in wispy ringlets, lips a shocking natural pink. But her eyes sparkled. Gone was that Beta steel that could wither investment bankers with a glance.

There was something wrong. Her left temple was . . .

"Christ," Murrillo muttered. He reached out to touch her left temple. Quieting, Loris brushed back the loose tendrils for him.

The area over her ear was a long bulging ridge. Murrillo shifted her chin to expose the opposite temple. It, too, looked as if her brain had swelled to force the bony skull outward in two matched ridges that precisely corresponded to the psychically-sensitive temporal lobes of the brain. A vein pulsed visibly.

"What happened to you, Ms. Rainer?"

Her smile was radiant. "Something wonderful."

"Who did you meet last night in your office?"

"God."

"Was it an illegal confidential consultant? What was his name? What did he do to you?"

She raised a hand and Gil withdrew from the powerful energy field. "Don't you know that you are part of something greater? We all are. . . ."

There was no getting through to her. A neurobiologist examined her with a portaPETscanner and reported: "Both lobes look like they've doubled in size. But they're undamaged."

"She's operating?"

"She lives in Alpha now. And that singing? It's not her. It's coming through her from the Other Side."

"What is it?"

"Angels. Demons pretending to be angels. No way to know. I don't like to think about the Other Side. I'm a lapsed Catholic. It never made sense to me when they called it the Afterlife, and it makes even less sense now that we've established contact."

Murrillo looked at Loris Rainer and shook his brushcut head. "Why people with everything going for them dabble in this stuff never fails to baffle me."

Director Silverglate listened to Murrillo's report and hesitated only a moment.

"I'm declaring a Blue Moon Situational Condition," he said. "That means anything goes."

Murrillo swallowed. "Anything?"

"Just don't put it in your report."

Dawn O'Leary had some good news when Gil paged her.

"I have the name of the probable next victim. I couldn't get it in Alpha, so I dropped into a Theta trance and threw my consciousness forward to—"

"Just give me the name, O'Leary."

"Carla Braun. Another banking official. I picked up a sunburst pattern around her. That's the corporate logo of—"

"—Astoria BanCorp," Murrillo finished. "And you

picked up the previous victim. Been missing since the middle of August.''

"Oh."

"This is why I hate Alpha . . ."

"I was in Theta, sir."

"For your information, O'Leary, Braun was the second of what are now three violently spiritually transfigured victims."

"Should I be privy to that information?"

"No choice now. I've been sanctioned to resort to any means necessary to find this perpetrator. What was that astrologer's name?"

"He's known as Smith."

"Can you find him for me?"

"He's a Capricorn Sun by reputation. That means he's always at work. Since we know exactly what his work is, it's just a matter of—"

"Just do it."

It looked like any number of licensed sex parlors catering to the clients with a more Kundalini bent than normally found in the Chelsea District of lower Manhattan. The building was a nine-story brick tomb. The original bricks had long since been remineralized to prevent crumbling; otherwise it was strictly Second Millennium.

The window holo sign said *Tantric Sex* in lavender script.

"You sure about this?" Murrillo asked Dawn O'Leary as they paused outside the entrance.

"It's a known front for confidential consulting."

Gil spat. "Call it what it is: damned fortune telling."

Dawn indicated a red-lit hematite statue in a window. A nude woman had an equally-nude bearded man in a painful hammerlock.

"That's Shirley MacLaine getting the best of the Amazing Randi," she said dryly.

Murrillo pushed his way in, ignoring the Entry Scanner and the hostess, and announced: "FBI. This establishment is hereby federalized under Section Four of the Spiritual Privacy Act of 2012."

Several holo-clad females scampered for the back rooms as a matronly woman with aluminized hair emerged from behind a beaded curtain and threw out her ample chest.

"Not again! Why don't you people just put us on retainer?"

Murrillo swallowed his surprise. "If you cooperate, we won't interfere with business. I'm looking for a rogue astrologer named Smith."

The woman called over her shoulder. "Smitty! It's for you!"

Smith looked like a typical pre-Schism holdover— droopy mustache, gold pirate earring, and a bluish M tattooed on the back of one hairy hand. A stale contraband Lucky Strike hung off his lower lip. Eyeing Murrillo, Smith asked, "Leo Sun?"

Gil flinched at the direct hit. "Ever see this man?"

Smith took the greasepencil suspect drawing. "No, but I guarantee you he's an eighth house person. Heavy-duty Scorpio influences. Death is written all over his face."

"All we have to go on is the name Mel or Melvin Drum. Help us find him and you won't be charged with Contributing to the Undermining of Free Will, and other violations of the Spiritual Privacy Act."

"Deal. But I gotta have something in return." He smiled broadly. "Pizza. A real one. Red onions and red peppers."

When the pizza was laid out before him, Smith sprinkled it liberally with a white crystalline substance from a pocket tube.

Murrillo paled. "Is that . . . *salt?*"

"My blood pressure medicine," Smith explained, lifting a wedge to his mouth.

Dawn stepped in. "There have been three victims, all high-level banking executives, and all spiritually transfigured against their will in an identical manner."

Smith snapped impatient fingers. "Dates. I need birthdates."

Three butts cooled in an ashtray after Smith finished running charts on a pocket system. He consulted a battered blue book entitled, *Ephemeris of the Years 2000–3000.*

"The next one will disappear in two weeks," he announced.

"How do you know that?" Murrillo demanded.

"He's doing this on the full and new moons. It's a pattern. The next victim goes on the next new moon. That means you have a clock running and a head's up on when the alarm will ring."

"We'd prefer to find the perpetrator before then."

"Good luck," Smitty said dryly, reaching for the last cold slice of heavily-salted pizza.

"Don't you ever think about your HDL count?" Dawn wondered.

"Cholesterol," said Smitty, "is voodoo." He continued. "All three victims had chart warning indicators for massive psychic breakthroughs—Scorpio moons, Pluto going over the ascendant, a heavily aspected Uranus. They were super-Alphas just waiting to happen. Especially under the present Neptune transit. If it wasn't this Mel Drum, it would have been something else. He's just shooting fish in a barrel."

"Karmic bullshit," snapped Gil.

"Welcome to the harsh world of natal astrology, where your life has been charted *for* you," Smith said archly. "Based on his facial features, I want to say your perp is a Capricorn."

"You can tell that by his face?" Dawn asked.

Smith grinned mischievously. "Takes one to know one. Note the coarse hair and heavy brows. But these cold cobra eyes mark a Scorpio moon, ascendant and probably a flock of other Scorpionic planets. Scorps merge with their environment like chameleons. He'll be as tough to find as a rainbow during a lunar eclipse.

Makes me thank my lucky stars my moon's in Virgo. It's a very sane moon."

Gil interrupted, "Can you or can't you ID the next victim?"

Smith frowned darkly. "My money's on Richard Castle. He's got an afflicted Neptune, not to mention a clusterfuck of planets—that's a stellium to you civilians—in his twelfth house, the house of secrets. Pluto's dead on his natal moon, so however it happens, he's looking to get hammered by the next new full one. Sit on him, and see."

"I get Friday Farrell as next," Dawn said. Gil looked at her. "It just came to me," she explained.

Smith said, "She's the Taurus? You can sit on her, too, but you'll be wasting your time. Taurus is about as psychic as a brick." He clapped the *Ephemeris* shut.

"That's it?" Gil asked.

Smith's voice turned brittle. "I just saved you a barrel of work, and all it cost you was a pizza. You can leave my *tip* with the hostess."

"Tell me, how is it you never went over the Rockies, Smith?"

Smith's mustache frowned. "Three reasons: Alpha doesn't believe in pizza, nicotine, or time. I live on pizza and cigarettes, and astrology is all about timing."

Gil frowned. "We'll be in touch."

"Not if I see you coming." Smith's smoky laugh followed them out of the building.

Roberta Chung took no chances. Not in business, not in love. She booked a room whenever the call of Kundalini stirred her hormones. She had been only four when America split into two polar opposites— the materialistic Beta and the spiritual Alphas—and although the Schism was largely nonviolent, America discovered Alpha and Beta could not coexist unless everyone was psychic, or no one was. Beta was where money could be made, so she left Los-CAL at 22, not abandoning Alpha-state pleasures, merely compartmentalizing them. Thus, the hotel room in New-NJ, and the anonymous call to a Tantric Sex Practitioner.

He came wearing apricot and smelling of apricots. She wore a holo-veil to ensure confidentiality. They assumed facing lotus positions on the floormat, and began rubbing scented pheromones on each other's pliant skin in preparation for a luxurious six hours of transcendent sexual bliss.

Fifty minutes but only seven orgasms in, she felt the Kundalini energy building at the base of her spine and stopped breathing to heighten the effect. Her nameless lover produced from nowhere a silver something resembling an old-fashioned laser pointer and touched the lambent blue end to her left temple . . . and the Universe cracked open in a dazzling bloom of transcendent light.

The light was alive, it was love, it was everything. And nothing else mattered. Not love, not sex. Not even money.

Dawn O'Leary took the call at her office monitor.

"Murrillo here." His voice was raw. "We just lost Chung to a Kundalini breakthrough. She's under police guard, wearing only her birthday suit and a spuckled smile."

"Impossible. I foresaw Friday—"

"And that twice-damned Smith promised us Richard Castle."

"I don't understand. Smith is the best astrologer this side of—"

"Screw the moon, stars, and planets. We're down to a small handful of candidate victims. Continue monitoring them. It's a matter of a month or so before we catch this madman in the act."

"Or we lose our top bankers. Global markets have been off seventeen percent on rumors. We can't keep the lid on this much longer."

"Stay mindlinked with Friday Farrell until further notice," snapped Murrillo.

"I'd like to check back with Smith."

"Do it on your own time. I don't trust that nicotine-sucking stargazer." The monitor screen imploded into a gray void.

Dawn settled back into her chair, popped 0.3 milligrams of prescription-strength St. John's Wort and slipped into an Alpha trance.

Punching up a mandela screen-saver, she focused on it. The lines blurred, and she fell into its field. She was Fawn now.

As Fawn, she cast her mind back to the interview with Smith. His tattoo surfaced on the placid pond of her still mind. She had noted it only in passing. A feminine M. A first name? An old girlfriend's initial? Concentrating, she brought the exact contours to mind. An M with an extra loop. It resembled the glyph for Virgo—no, for Scorpio. They were similar, she recalled. Fawn clearly visualized a tail instead of a closed loop. Odd. Why would a Capricorn have the glyph of Scorpio tattooed to his hand?

Fawn popped out of Alpha. She punched up a number.

"Tantric Sex," a thin voice said.

"Is Smith available?"

"Out today. Would you like an appointment?"

"No. I would like his address."

"We do not provide personal information."

"This is an FBI request."

"Sorry."

"Give me his first name, then."

"As far as we know, Smith *is* his first name."

Fawn changed tactics. "Would you know his sign?"

"We do not give out *confidential* information, either," the woman said frostily.

Frowning, Fawn disconnected. Touching her throat-mike, she said: "Birth Records check."

The system beeped. "Name?"

"Smith. First Name Unknown. Global." Then she settled back in her chair as every living Smith born in

Beta territory was sorted and displayed in long, te-
dious chains of text. It was going to be a long day . . .

Gil Murrillo was making explanations to the Director of the FBI. The Director was having none of it.

"No more astrological hunches. Is that understood?"

"Yes, sir."

"And have that Smith picked up. Nobody makes
the Bureau look spuckle-faced. Clear?"

"Clear." Murrillo disconnected. The handset chirped
instantly. "Murrillo."

"Dawn here. I have something. Remember the
name I received clairaudiently—Mel Drum?"

"Yeah."

"Global search turns up a Meldrum Smith, born
October 27, 2011 at 7:48 UGT, Bo-MA."

"So?"

"A man born at that time would be a Scorpio Sun,
with his moon, ascendant, Mercury, and Venus all in
Scorpio. In short, a super-Scorpio. Those conjunctions
are very rare."

"Forget it. The Director has instructed me to aban-
don all astrological investigations."

"Listen! The astrological profile Smith described fits
this Meldrum Smith. He could be our spiritual
terrorist."

"Is he locatable?"

"Yes and no. Gil, I think our Smith is Meldrum
Smith."

"That's crazy, Dawn! He's a damn Alpha holdover,
clinging to the last century like a kid with his blankie.
And didn't Smith claim he was Capricorn with a
Virgo moon?"

"We have only his word on that. Just hear me out.
He could have lied about his chart. A lot of astrolo-
gers guard their planetary picture jealously. But Smith
volunteered the information. I think he's a quadruple
Scorpio passing as a Capricorn. This side of the Rock-

ies, who would know differently? And his demeanor is extremely Scorpionic."

"What about the suspect sketch your people came up with?"

"They're never perfect. You know that. And Smith's mustache might be the remnants of a shaven beard. Think about it. We know our terrorist doesn't preselect his victims in order to foil precog scans. When we consulted Smith, we fell into his hands. He pointed us where he didn't want us looking. It's classic misdirection."

"Too much of a coincidence," Murrillo snapped. "We just *happened* to consult the one Betaside guy who's our man?"

"Maybe it wasn't a coincidence," Dawn said levelly. "I thought it was odd his name just popped into my head when this all started. Maybe it didn't. Maybe Smith planted the thought in my mind. It's a given our man is monitoring all operations against him. If he intuited the existence of FBI D-teams, he'd know it was only a matter of time before we found him, one way or another. So he drew *us* to *him.*"

"I don't buy it." The harshness left Murrillo's voice. "But the Director wants Smith picked up for practicing an illegal system of divination, and being a smug jerk. I'll let you audit the interrogation, okay?"

Dawn's voice climbed to a shrill note. "Gil. Don't treat this as a routine pickup. I have a strong feeling about—"

The sudden catch in Dawn's voice was like a sob. When it came back, her voice was hushed and thick with fear.

"Gil! I think I'm being remotely viewed. I sense a presence. It's . . . why am I smelling apricots?"

"Apricots! The odor of apricots was all over Roberta Chung."

"Gil! Gil!" The line went dead.

*   *   *

An FBI lightcar whisked Gil Murrillo to Dawn/ Fawn O'Leary's co-opt overlooking HudsonRiver. His override card defeated all building security lockouts until O'Leary's door fell open before him.

Polypistol in hand, he eased his way in. "Fawn? Dawn? Either of you here?" Silence came back. He inched forward, every sense keyed up.

FBI SAC Gil Murrillo found Dawn/Fawn O'Leary seated at her desk system. Her head came up at his approach. She smiled gloriously—a radiant, beatific smile. Her entire being seemed to glow, as if her auric field were becoming palpable.

"Hello. . . ." Her voice was dreamy.

"Agent O'Leary, what happened to you? Talk to me, Dawn."

"I'm Fawn. I'm Fawn forever. . . ."

"Was it Smith? Tell me. Who did this to you?"

Her hands came up, open, inviting, almost eager.

Carefully holstering his polypistol, Murrillo approached. Her hands took his. They were strangely cool to the touch, her obsidian eyes luminous. "Just talk to me, Fawn," he coaxed.

Gil Murrillo never had a solid hunch or psychic flash in his entire life. But in the moment Fawn's hands clutched his in a grip that was warm and loving, yet as unshakable as steel, a strange fluttering touched his left temporal lobe—and his gut grew cold with fear.

"Nothing will hurt you again," Fawn promised. "Ever."

The hand wielding the stainless steel beampointer was hairy and masculine. Murrillo caught a momentary glimpse of a faded bluish tattoo. A letter M— but with an extra fillip. A loop that stuck out like a barbed tail.

Perhaps it was an old subconscious memory. Maybe it was a true psychic insight. But in that flash of knowing Gil Murrillo understood with perfect knowledge that he was looking at a dual symbol: The ancient glyph of Scorpio—which also stood for a man's name: Meldrum.

A familiar husky male voice said, "Astrology is timing. It's all timing."

A coolness touched Gil's temple and a cold blue light flashed. It pierced his skull, illuminated his brain, interpenetrating his soul. In the next exquisite moment he saw a greater, whiter light. Even though he had never seen it before, Gil recognized the light.

It was God, the Universe, everything. His ego, his mind, his individuality melted into a warm oneness that was utter bliss.

Gil Murrillo was one with God, and God was pure, perfect Alpha.

PIA AND THE KING OF SIAM

by Janet Berliner

In her twenty-five years as a writer, editor, and publishing consultant, Janet Berliner has worked with such authors as Peter S. Beagle, David Copperfield, Michael Crichton, and Joyce Carol Oates. Among her most recent books are the anthology *David Copperfield's Beyond Imagination,* which she created and edited, and *Children of the Dusk,* the final book of *The Madagascar Manifesto,* a three-book series coauthored with George Guthridge. Currently Janet divides her time between Las Vegas, where she lives and works, and Grenada, West Indies, where her heart is.

IN order to more completely answer the dichotomy of her present and her future, Pia took a trip into her past. Borrowing from Peter, promising herself that she would repay Paul later, she ordered the archival tape of her grandmother's memories.

When the tape arrived, she delighted her understudy by taking two days of her allotted personal time off from the Company's musical production of *Hamlet.* Headset in place, she entered her grandmother's archival experience and toured her life, her world, her stomping grounds, starting in East Berlin, as it was called then, in the early sixties.

She was eight years old, standing with her bicycle at the Brandenburger Turm. This was her weekly pilgrimage to the Wall which rose menacingly between her and her best friend, Daniel, who had escaped the East the year before. "Danny," she called out. "Are you there?" His voice rose thinly into the crisp autumn day. "I'm here, Rachel. I'll come and see you next week. We have a pass to come through." "Mutti says bring coffee," she called out. "Next week, then."

She wheeled the bike down the boulevard, away from the monument, playing their game, hers and Danny's. Looking for litter was a foolish game at best, and one they could never win, but they'd always played it anyway. Sometimes they found a small branch that had detached itself from one of the linden trees that lined the boulevard; the occasional stray leaf. That was it. Nothing else ever disturbed the street's antisepsis. Not even one small piece of debris. . . .

Briefly, Pia removed the headphones. She had expected to feel discomfort in the mind of someone she'd never known, in a time and country she'd seen only in old movies. Instead, she felt more comfortable than she did in her own skin. It was a puzzlement, she thought, quoting the King of Siam. Her mother and grandmother had parted ways long before she was born. Her mother fitted perfectly into the late nineties. Judgmentalism was the order of the day, a perfect environment for her. But not for Pia, who had never quite managed to fit the mold, and apparently not for her grandmother.

She replaced the headset and fast-forwarded it.

She was nineteen, sitting in a theater, watching her friend Tanya play Anna in The King and I. *"I want to play Anna, too, one day," she told the Herr Direktor*

*of Tanya's Company later, when her friend introduced
her to him. "You're not the type," he said. "You will
be Nellie Forbush in* South Pacific, *perhaps, but not
Anna. Never Anna." She buried the dream deep down
in her soul. Every once in a while she disinterred it and
looked at it, letting it grow, deciding that she not only
wanted to play Anna, she wanted to do so in the grand
ballroom of the Schloss Charlottenburg, the castle
across the street from the Reichstag. The fact that the
castle was in West Berlin only added to the grandiose
quality of her fantasy. No one she knew had ever
danced in the West, let alone at the Schloss. She'd only
heard about the castle and the ballroom from people
who'd seen it in the days when the old people were
given passes once a year to cross the border.*

Pia was enchanted. She, too, adored Anna and
wanted to play her; she, too, had been told that Nellie
Forbush was more her style. Returning to the tape,
she experienced her grandmother's escape to West
Berlin. She saw the luxury and the decadence and
smelled the dog droppings in the less-than-pristine
streets. Then, frightened, she heard the announcement
that the Wall had tumbled. "They" had taken over
the West and it was now without light and heat. The
shops on the Kurfurstendam stood empty and the streets
were clean.

Then the parties began, the farewell bashes for the
forty-somethings, the ones who were being sent
away. Somewhere.

Pia removed the headset and took something to
help her sleep. She awoke in the middle of the night
and returned to her grandmother's life. She escaped
with her from Berlin, arrived with her in New York,
journeyed with her to San Francisco and a new life,
in the Haight. The going-away parties hadn't yet
started in America. The streets were filled with musi-
cians and clowns and mimes, people openly smoked
all manner of things, including cigarettes, and every-

one talked of flower children and behaved like it was
still the Age of Aquarius. She experienced her grandmother's joyous reunion with her friend Tanya, a
grown woman now and performing in *Jesus Christ,
Superstar.* Pia had never seen the show before, though
she'd heard of it in the coffee shops, before the Juicers
took over. Heard that it was banned at the turn of
the century, when she was just a little girl and the
Clinton fiasco allowed the Moral Majority to take hold
of the country.

Pia loved the show. She loved her grandmother for
their shared passions for old musicals and old movies.
Were her grandmother alive, she'd have embraced her
and taken care of her, the way they used to take care
of elderly people in the olden days.

Discarding the headset, she was beset by a deep
sense of longing. There had to be something out there
for her, something better than what she had now. This
thing she had—this excuse for a life—was hardly
worth clinging to.

Throwing on a coat to shield herself from San Francisco's wind, Pia headed for Sacramento. She notified
the courts that she would be there first thing in the
morning, spent the evening walking around the ruins
of the old city, and was at the courthouse when it
opened. At nine o'clock sharp, she was called before
the judge.

Leaning against his desk to steady herself, she took
the document that had been prepared for her and
began to read.

"Just sign on the bottom line." The judge's voice
was rasping, metallic, his eyes expressionless.

"That's it?" she said.

"What did you expect? A song and dance routine?
You know the regulations."

Yes, she knew the regulations, Pia thought. Ending
her marriage was simply a matter of sending in an
application and coming here to take care of the me-

chanics. She wanted the divorce, but there was something obscene about the lack of intricacy. Ten years with one person deserved more than that. Even Max, with his impassioned highs and suicidal lows, deserved more than that.

"On the bottom line," the judge repeated. He held out a pen. "Your full name."

If you only had a heart, Tin Woodsman, you'd understand, Pia thought. But she wasn't Dorothy, and Sacramento circa 2031 was hardly Oz.

Pushing back the strand of hair that had loosened itself from her neat chignon, she took the pen and signed her name. Olympia Hoffman. Carefully. As if neatness counted. Feeling nothing. A mandatory year of lectures, counseling, red tape, before they'd granted a marriage license. Now this inglorious sixty-second procedure. It was like instant surgery—tidy and efficient while it was happening, to fool you into forgetting that the pain would come later, during recovery.

"Next."

Pia moved out of the way. She knew she should leave; she was providing no function being there. But she stood and watched the next person in line, a man with the trim body and controlled movements of an athlete. She timed him through the process. Thirty seconds for the judge to check the list on the monitor to his right; a fifteen-second paper-shuffling pause; another fifteen seconds and it was over.

"Next."

"And to whom do you belong?" The athlete, smiling, had stopped at her side.

Pia glanced at the judge. He was staring right at her. "To Them," she said, wondering as she gave the requisite answer why she didn't feel uncomfortable under his scrutiny. It was like that with all of Their messengers. They were enforcers, yet they carried with them a sense of familiarity that made their actions palatable.

"Next."

She was leaving the building now, moving across the square and heading toward the bus station. The athlete was still with her, making an effort to tone down his long stride to match her slower pace.

"Name's Jim," he said. "You headed to San Francisco?" he asked.

She didn't answer. Jim, John, Joe, she thought. Who cares?

"Me, too. I mean, I also live in San Francisco," he said. Taking her silence for assent, he helped her board the bus. "Isn't it wonderful how They make everything simple for us?"

"Yes. They're wonderful," Pia said. Out of earshot of the judge, she felt relatively safe in allowing a touch of sarcasm to filter into her words. They. The rule-makers, she thought. Hidden away, attending to the greater design of the world and insisting that she and everyone else fit into Their pattern.

"Let's celebrate when we get back," the athlete said.

Pia shook her head. He looked puzzled. Hurt. As if his daily ration of protein had been arbitrarily denied him. They trained his body but not his instincts, Pia thought. A modicum of sensitivity would have told him she was in no mood for what he had in mind.

"You're not supposed to be alone this afternoon or tonight. You know the rules."

"I won't be alone," Pia said, wishing he would scout the bus for another candidate.

He had taken the seat next to hers. Now he removed his hand from her arm where it had rested possessively. "We have the rest of the day off," he said, making one last-ditch attempt to change her mind.

"Sorry."

"Too bad. You have a good body. Another time, huh?"

"Yes. Another time."

Pia was consciously sidestepping the rules again. By

Their lights, she was committing a crime and could be punished—whatever *that* meant. It was all very well for Them to sit around like fat cats, doing what They wanted and issuing directives to everyone else, she thought. Handing out lollipops for obedience to Their rules without ever defining the punishments for what They defined as crimes. By her lights, this directive was pure insanity. The idea of forcing herself to spend her few hours before Liz's going-away-party with this stranger was intolerable. Nor was she lying, when she said she wouldn't be alone, at least not entirely. Rick was waiting for her at home. She'd be spending the time in Paris and in his café in Casablanca. Thinking about him made her heart beat faster. For a few sweet hours she would be Ilsa.

Apparently accepting defeat, the athlete mumbled and took a seat next to a more likely candidate. Pia watched him go, in some small way envious of his easy acceptance of the system, he and the others who felt at home with Their mandates. Then she thought about the sweet hours of solitude she had just bought herself and smiled. Her defiances were small ones, to be sure, but they pleased her. She thought briefly about not showing up at the party. That would be a larger defiance, and one that might provide her with a great deal of satisfaction, if she got away with it. If not, the worst that could happen was . . . what? She had never been caught, so she didn't know the answer.

The idea of staying at home alone all evening was almost sensually tempting, but Pia dismissed it. If she was going to try it, she would have to choose another night, another party. Tonight she would surely be missed; she was the entertainment. At least, she thought, she was dancing *Coppelia.* Though she preferred musical comedies, she had an affinity for De-libes' music and Offenbach's doll. Besides, she wanted to see Liz, to wish her . . . what?

Deliberately, Pia ceased to think about the party. She left the bus a few stops early, resisted the temptation to see if Jim was watching her through the bus window or, worse yet, had followed her out of the bus. She had the creepy feeling that he was trailing her as she walked the rest of the way to her apartment, but she did not look back.

Nearing the building, Pia gave thanks to Max for having agreed to move out until she could find somewhere else to live, and to Them for lifting the ban on an increasing number of musical comedies. She adored *Swan Lake,* of course, and *Giselle* and *Coppelia,* but she'd been passionately in love with musical comedy ever since she'd seen her first one. She let herself into her apartment. In one fluid movement, she kicked the door shut behind her, pushed the button to start the video cassette, and removed her coat. As she settled into her favorite chair, she remembered the way her husband—ex-husband—complained about its being out of sync with the decor of the room. She still didn't know whether it had become her favorite before or after his comment, she thought.

Deliberately emptying her mind of everything except what was happening on the screen in front of her, she commanded Rick to divert her. Within seconds, she was captivated by a world that never failed her. Paddle fans. Rick's café. North African intrigue. That was her reality. Not performing *Coppelia* or living with Max Hoffman . . .

A blinking light on Pia's wall demanded her attention. She ignored it as long as she could before picking up the telephone.

"Olympia?" her sister asked. "You sound so far away."

"Only mentally. I was watching—"

"Don't tell me. Let me guess. *The King and I* or *Casablanca,* which is it? Don't you ever get tired of that stuff? I mean, it's all right in its place, but you take it too seriously. I think that's why you couldn't make it with a real man like Hoff. Sometimes I think

you just married him because you wanted your last
name to be Hoffman."

There was no need to say anything, Pia thought.
Nothing short of a firing squad could stop Mira once
she started on her favorite topic, and the truth was
that one of the reasons she had married Hoff was
because she wanted to be Olympia Hoffman.

"I remember those nightmares you were having
when you met Hoff," Mira went on. "You began to
believe that Dr. Coppelius was going to come for you
so that he could chop you into little pieces. . . ."

Pia stopped listening to her sister. She didn't want
to think about the dreams ever again, and especially
not tonight when she was dancing Coppelia at Liz's
farewell party. It had all begun after she'd danced the
role at several parties in a row, night after night the
same dream. Dr. Coppelius searching for her. Wanting
to destroy her so that he could shape another, more
obedient, doll. And then she'd met Max Hoffman. She
hadn't even liked him very much but she'd kept thinking about Offenbach's Hoffmann and wondering what
might have happened to Coppelia if he'd succeeded
in spiriting her away. Dr. Coppelius might never have
found her. . . .

"Pia? Are you listening to me?"

She tuned back in. "I'm listening, Mira."

"If you're having those dreams again, I'll come
over. You're not supposed to be alone today anyway."

"I'm not alone." Pia said nothing about the dreams.
They had never really stopped, but it didn't seem to
matter anymore. They were as much a part of her life
as getting up in the morning.

"You mean you have someone with you?" Mira's
relief was apparent. Her voice rose several decibels.
"I'm so glad. I won't disturb you. . . ."

The telephone light went out, and Pia smiled. Mira
would be happy for a while, believing her sister was
following orders. It made her so uncomfortable to

think that she was related to someone who habitually questioned Their wisdom.

Changing her position slightly, Pia returned to the world she preferred. Eventually she would have to think about Their reality but not now. Not while she had an hour of solitude left.

The figure in the trenchcoat became a dot on the rain-soaked Casablanca runway and Pia started to cry. For a while, she let her tears flow freely. Then, wondering how she'd have made it through the years without Bogart's help, she replaced her worn *Casablanca* cassette in her collection and took out *The King and I*. The catharsis was over, and she needed Anna.

Fingering the cassette lovingly, Pia thought about what it must have been like to play Anna at that premiere performance sixty years ago. She balanced the cassette on high. Delicately. Like a glass of champagne. Taking the hem of her skirt in her other hand, she waltzed around her small living room until, out of breath, she fell abruptly back onto the sofa. Dammit, she thought. If she could afford a holograph machine, she'd know what it felt like to be a woman like Anna. Proud. Magnificently proud. Unafraid even of the King of Siam.

If she couldn't have a holograph machine, Pia told herself, the least she could do was to keep expanding her collection. The party tonight was her one shot at acquiring a complete Valentino collection. Liz would have no need of antiquated musicals where she was going, or of anything else for that matter. Besides, it would be her last chance to see her mentor before she was taken away.

Poor Liz, Pia thought. So what if she was turning sixty tonight. She was healthy and happy and deserved to stay. At forty, Pia still had twenty years to think about where it was They took you. To a better world, They said.

Pia remained unconvinced. As far as she was concerned, Liz would cease to exist. Like all of the others They had sent away since the new system began. Her parents; her friends' parents; her neighbors. She had tried to believe there was a place where they gathered, that if she only knew where to go, she could see them all again. Alive. Smiling. For a while, she'd even agreed with Mira that they'd undergone some magical process and were living forever like the heroes and heroines in her cassette world.

Her sister had kept right on believing, but for Pia the delusion had been short-lived. If she could only see one of Them, one of the lawmakers, she thought, she'd learn the truth about the old people—and about so many other things. Truth was something you could read in people's eyes, like fear and love. If Their way was the only one that precluded chaos, why wouldn't They show themselves? How could she trust edicts from rulers who told her they were the creators and orderers of her universe, yet refused to walk at her side? She couldn't. Nor could she believe in Their messengers—those strangers who blindly enforced Their rules and carried that aura of familiarity that comforted her into doing Their bidding.

Reluctantly, Pia packed her costume and dressed for the party. She chose her clothes carefully and made herself up with great attention to detail, hoping that seeing the finished product would lighten her mood. It did, but only temporarily. Once she was at the party, her depression returned. It was triggered by the sure knowledge that she was going to lose out on the Valentino collection. At least three other people in the room wanted those cassettes, and they were all better qualified than she. The first two requirements were no problem: she was there, and she wanted it. Coveted it. Probably more than the others did. Her problem lay in the third regulation; her acceptance level of Them and Their system. It was down again. Way down. She had measured it on Liz's machine.

"Are you all right?" Liz asked. She put her arms around Pia and hugged her.

"I'll be okay," Pia said, wondering at the lack of fear in her friend's eyes. "You're the one. . . ."

"They're going to love me there," Liz said. "Look at me, Pia. I've lost thirty pounds." She executed a graceful pirouette, her face as expectant as Coppelia come to life in the toy shop and her body as fragile again as the young woman who'd first taught Pia the role.

That was when two strangers appeared. As they moved closer to her, she saw that one of them was Jim. That Jim. The one in the courthouse, on the bus, and probably on the street dogging her trail. He looked different, better, in his formal evening attire. If he recognized her, he did not show it. She watched him move easily toward Liz and turned her attention to the other stranger, who was passing among the guests like a dancer floating lightly across thin ice. Spallanzini come to claim his creation, Pia thought, not realizing until the tall, slender figure came closer that it was a woman. She wore a black jumpsuit, and her dark hair was drawn tightly into a dancer's bun. Her face was pale, translucent, as if her skin had never touched the sun.

Because the light was dim, it took Pia a while to realize that the woman's careful progress was inspired by the enormous crystal bowl of cut fruit that she was carrying, balancing its fragility as if she held a slice of a rainbow.

Drawn to her, Pia took a step toward the stranger. Before she had time to say anything, the woman placed her gift on a table and turned around to face Pia. "And to whom do you belong?" she said, using the standard greeting.

Pia began the required response but stopped. Saying "To Them" had always been as natural as breathing. Now the words stuck in her throat.

"What's your name?" the woman continued as if

the traditional exchange had been completed. She looked fragile up close, like a piece of Dresden china.

Pia looked across the room at Liz, glowing with her regained delicacy of motion.

"Your name?" the woman asked again.

Suddenly she knew who the woman was. Why she was there. With the knowledge came an urgent need to do something, anything, that was an act of defiance against Them. "Would you believe me if I told you my name was Liz?" Pia said.

"You're too young to be Liz."

"Have you come to take her away? Are you one of Them?"

"I'm a messenger."

"Is she going to die?"

The woman's expression didn't change. "There's no need to be afraid for her," she said. "As long as she obeys the rules—"

"All of her needs will be satisfied," Pia said, finishing the litany. The words fit comfortably. "Satisfy *my* needs. Take *me*. Look at her. Her spirit is young. Mine's not."

"I can't take you."

"Why not? Did anyone instruct you not to take me? You could come back later for Liz."

The woman put her arm around Pia's shoulder. She smelled of lavender and lemons. "Do you really want to go?"

"I don't want to stay. I want to go where there's noise and laughter and tumult," Pia said. It was something she had once said to her mother, so many years ago that she had thought the memory erased. Her mother had responded with a rare moment of gentleness by telling her a story, one she had recognized as fact, though it was presented as fiction. It wasn't the story itself that had stayed with her; it was the setting. She had often wondered since if such places really existed, somewhere out there beyond the boundaries that she was forbidden to cross.

"I want to go to a casino," Pia said now. She rolled the words around on her tongue, as if she were savoring a taste so subtle that the flavor would escape her the moment she swallowed.

The woman nodded. She looked almost as if she'd been expecting the request.

"Is there still such a place?" Pia asked.

Again the woman nodded.

"Are you telling me it's possible for me to go there?"

"It can be arranged, in special cases."

"Special? In what way?"

The woman didn't answer.

"How long would I be allowed to stay?" Pia went on.

"You'd be given money. When that runs out—"

"Will They come for me then, to punish me?"

"A messenger will come for you."

"To take me to Them?"

Releasing Pia's shoulders, the woman reached out and stroked her cheek. "Patience, child," she said, as if she were promising Pia that she would be grown up soon enough and then she'd know everything.

"Who are you?"

The woman smiled and took Pia's hand. "I am whoever you want me to be," she said. "Come. It's time to leave."

She led Pia through the guests. They moved aside without question, thinking only that Pia was leaving to warm up for her performance. Liz disengaged herself from Jim and waved, blowing a kiss instead of her usual "See you later" farewell, and Pia waved back, wondering if her mentor would wait all night for a messenger who had already come and gone.

Noise and laughter and tumult, Pia thought, looking around the casino. It was hard to remember that there had ever been anything else in her life; no one talked about Them here, or about obedience and order. She had a clear picture of following the woman through Liz's front door, and then a series of fuzzy ones: crossing the California border into Nevada; barreling along the E.T. Highway toward Area 51; a sign that read, *You are entering Last Chance, Nevada*; a sense that she was playing a role in a tape soon to be archived.

She had no idea how long she'd been here, but nothing seemed as real to her as this place of no clocks and noise and laughter and tumult. They'd lied to her, to everyone. There *was* a world of lights and warmth, a world where everyone was her family.

Even the security man bending over her now was her friend.

He was undoubtedly the ugliest man she'd ever seen, but the sight of him had amused her when she'd arrived. She'd watched him storming the aisles between machines, masquerading as authority in his white linen suit and dark sunglasses. Whispering "Play it, Sam" to her trim image in the mirror behind the roulette wheel, she'd imagined Sydney Greenstreet somewhere close by, in a smoke-filled room, sweating beneath a huge wooden fan.

"No bare feet in here," the security man said now, his practiced voice soft and low.

Pia watched the traces of a smile hover around the corners of the man's mouth as he lowered his skinhead toward her, his breath making contact with the ash piled around her cigarette butts. As he bent over her, his body declared her in violation of his domain because her purse was empty.

How long has it been, Pia wondered, pushing her toes back into their leather shackles and pulling her shoulders closer to her knees to protect the pile of useless Keno tickets she had gathered on her skirt; how many hours, days, weeks of too many cigarettes and no sleep. She sank deeper into the red vinyl chair, though she knew her body would adhere her thighs to the plastic surface.

The man straightened up. His mouth was moving,

but Pia couldn't hear what he was saying above the clatter of coins and the shouts of gamblers. Mesmerized, she watched his manicured index finger reprimanding her; the nail's quick was a half-moon in a sky of mirrors and imitation gaslight stars.

Forcing her eyes away, Pia concentrated on the numbers lighting up the Keno board. They danced into view to the music of coins forced between metal lips by little old ladies drunk with the joy of stuffing the slots of their one-armed lovers. Crap shooters screamed their delight as a red-headed roller won them yet another pile of chips. Pia had won with her earlier, laughed with her as she punctuated each new roll with a toss of her head, kissing the dice that had been warmed at her breast.

In the Keno lounge, the numbers kept coming. Pia watched the little white balls being blown out of their container and into two long arms that held the winners. Ten balls on each side. Twenty numbers, and only one of them hers. Crumpling her useless Keno ticket in her sweating fist, she cursed whoever had installed the equipment and the Chinese for being the first to play games with numbers. She swore at the digits themselves, and more than anything she cursed the lifeless balls as they lay silent in their silver cage.

How long, Pia thought again. How long had she been winning a little, losing more? She ripped her thighs off the vinyl seat and walked toward the Keno counter.

"Same card?" the Keno marker asked. Pia nodded and pushed the crumpled paper at the girl. She couldn't change her numbers now. Not when she had only one coin left. If her old numbers came up, she'd never forgive herself, she thought, forgetting that if she didn't win now, she wouldn't have a chance at regret. She'd be broke and facing the next bend in the road she'd chosen without any concept of its destination. The flash of the electronic camera recorded the empty Keno board. "Number twenty-three," the Keno girl called out in a board voice. It was one of Pia's numbers.

"I go off duty in half an hour," the security man whispered, leaning over her again.

Pia nodded mechanically as she checked her card against the numbers on the lit board. One more and she'd get her money back. She'd be able to play again.

"Last number—fifty-eight."

"No. It can't be the last number," Pia said, without realizing that she was shouting.

The whirling stopped. "I have three out of eight. I should get something for that," Pia said to the white balls that lay lifeless once more in their metal prison.

"Same card?"

Pia fumbled in her pockets, hoping for a forgotten coin. Her fingers came up empty. She shook her head and turned away, feeling her body in revolt against its broken regimen.

Seeking the order and quiet she'd abandoned, Pia made for the ladies' room. There she inspected herself in the mirror for the first time since she'd entered the casino. To her amazement, she looked no different. Behind her, she could see a middle-aged matron sleeping in a pink-and-white chair that faced discreetly away from the toilets, and overhead she could see the speaker that was piping in "As Time Goes By" from the bar.

The ladies' room door opened. Like the voice of an old lover, the casino called out to her. If you had just one coin, you could try one more spin of the wheel, one last roll of the dice, another Keno ticket.

Leaning over the sink to splash her face with cold water, Pia caught sight of an ashtray overflowing with coins. It lay on the stained counter, beckoning to her. Dreamily, she put out her hand and caressed the money with her fingertips, the way she had done to her cassette collection on Liz's birthday.

"Can I help you?"

Pia pulled her hand away and smiled, hoping the

attendant would think she'd been making a contribution. The woman came closer. There was something
familiar about her—a scent of lavender and lemons.

Pia fled into the casino. They couldn't send for her.
Not yet. She wasn't ready. Opening her bag, she tore
at its lining. One more coin, she begged; one spin of
the wheel.

She found nothing.

At the roulette table next to her, the croupier's eyes
promised her a winner. He poised his fingers above
the wheel, and she dropped to her knees to search the
coarse weave of the carpet under his table for the
careless droppings of a winner.

"Sixty," the croupier announced.

He was teasing her, she thought. Amusing himself
while he waited. He had to be—there were only thirty-
six numbers on the wheel.

The whirr of the wheel began again.

"Sixty." She heard the click of his Lucite marker.

She sat perfectly still and waited, knowing she had
run out of time. Then soft pink fingers lifted her up
the length of an immaculate white linen suit, and the
security man crooked his arm.

"And to whom do you belong?" he asked, removing
his dark glasses.

Desperately afraid, hoping to save herself, Pia
began the required response. It was no use. She had
come too far to retract now.

"To myself," she said quietly, with as much dignity
as she could muster.

To her amazement, the man bowed his head
slightly, as if acknowledging that she had said the right
thing. She watched the gaslights reflect off his bald
head.

"Who are you?" she said, when he stood erect once
more. "Are you one of Their messengers? One of
Them?"

He smiled and she noticed the fine wrinkles around
his eyes. He's not ugly after all, she thought. The

woman's words came back to her: *"I am whoever you want me to be."* He's the King of Siam, she decided, waiting for the messenger to answer.

"I'm a dreamer like you," he said.

"Aren't you a messenger?"

"Yes. We're all dreamers. Rebels."

Slowly, Pia was beginning to understand. "How old are you?" she asked.

"Sixty-five. I have ten more years of apprenticeship to serve."

"Before you become one of Them?" The man nodded. Pia looked back at the casino; it was the antithesis of everything she had left behind, yet it was neither better nor worse.

"What happens to me now?" she asked.

"If you wish, you may become one of us."

"One of Them, or a messenger? An enforcer of the rules I've always detested?"

He looked amused at her anger. "Most people prefer narrow boundaries. Strict rules," he said. "It makes life easier for them."

She started to protest. *"Isn't it wonderful how They make everything simple for us,"* the athlete's voice echoed back at her.

"What about those of us who'd prefer the challenge of a less simple life? What about those of us who'd rather control our own destinies?"

He gestured at the casino but said nothing, as if the answer to Pia's question only counted if she found it for herself.

"Is that why They let me come here?" she asked. "To show me that making choices results in chaos? I don't believe it. There has to be something in between."

"I'm giving you a choice now," the man said. "You can go back to California and conform. You can stay here and try to make it as one of the have-nots, or you can come with me."

"And do what?"

"Try to make as many people as possible happy while you help us search for the road in between."

He crooked his arm and waited. Once again, he was bowing slightly, waiting for her decision.

It was there again, Pia thought, that comfortable sense of familiarity that she had always felt around the messengers and enforcers. That was when, suddenly, she knew. The man read her face and smiled as she slid her arm through the triangle of his elbow. She should have known when he'd said he was a rebel and a dreamer. They were the ones like her, the ones who survived despite the rules and the rule-makers, or perhaps even because of the restrictions.

"Would there be any need for rebels and dreamers if things were perfect?" Pia asked as, together, she and the King of Siam moved toward the door marked EXIT. If she was right, she thought, she'd at least be trying to find a middle path between rigidity and decadence, a moderate road that allowed room for both leaders and followers. And if she was wrong . . .

She looked up at the tall man at her side. Even if she was wrong, she thought, she was leaving with the King of Siam. If nothing else, she was playing Anna at last.

THE SERPENT WAS MORE SUBTLE

by Tom Piccirilli

Tom Piccirilli is the author of *Dark Father,
Hexes, Shards,* and *The Dead Past.* He is the
assistant editor of *Pirate Writings* magazine and
reviews books for *Mystery Scene* and *Mystery
News.* His short fiction has sold to *Hot Blood 6*
and *7, 100 Wicked Little Witch, 365 Scary Stories,
Deathrealm, Hardboiled, Terminal Fright,* and
others. A collection of five intertwined stories
entitled *Pentacle* was recently published by Pirate Writings Press. All of the stories therein
have made the Honorable Mention list of Dat-
low and Windling's *Year's Best Fantasy and
Horror.*

A furious, burning wind tearing east off the desert
sand-blasted the windows as the hydrocephalic kid,
heaving his immense head forward out of the foam-
lined cranial clamps, pressed his cracked lips to the
glass and whimpered, "From the Well."

Schaffer's team had done a good job remaking Jeffy
Grant's bedroom and bringing it up to hospital specs—
blindingly white, sterile, and packed with whining
equipment that looked impressive and didn't do anything at all. Even in the strictly regulated antiseptic

environment, the new chief deprogrammer and his medical assistants stank of nervous sweat, bile, and single malt scotch. I didn't much blame them.

Sandra Grant quieted her son and resettled him into the angled platform that served as his bed. He couldn't lie flat or the shunts wouldn't drain properly; if he tried to turn over, the shards of his damaged skull would stab inward and kill him. She smoothed his cherubic cheek and stared down for another minute before letting Schaffer's team return to study their patient and pretend they were deeply involved with curing him.

She dipped her face into her hands, and I spotted the barely noticeable surgical scars on the back of her neck, like faint love scratches made in the early morning. She appeared to be only in her mid-fifties, but ductile derma-polymers hadn't even been used in the last twenty years. She must've been among one of the first trial groups to undergo the expensive, painful process before the new transplantation techniques were developed to rebuke infirmity and old age. I could tell the most recent procedures had fixed up a couple of earlier botched facial alterations.

She had to be at least ninety now, and I admired the will it would've taken her to suffer a synthetic uterus implant so she could bear more children at that stage of her life. Being married to a millionaire husband had its advantages, even if Fredrik Grant proved to be stupid enough to hire an idiot like Schaffer.

Her hair, once blonde like the few remaining wisps hanging above her son's ears, had converted to a tangy saffron. Her eyes were brown and angry and fertile, but they'd probably been replaced at least twice by now. A crucifix dangled around her throat, shedding a reflected drop of light against the ceiling, but I could see by the ingrained grime that she'd just started wearing it again. She'd put it on out of a willfulness to hold tightly to something—even a lost God—from an age before the coming of the Tenfew, Children of the Well.

Jeffy clapped and giggled, pointing. "Mom, from the Few, from the Well."

Sandra Grant turned to me, her face so filled with the conflicts of the earth that I saw somebody else there for a second, familiar to me. "That's all he says. Maybe it's all any of them can say, dancing and splashing, trying to drown themselves or whatever it is they think they're doing." She smiled at him as he watched the dust swirling and pecking at the glass. "But at least he still calls me Mom. I suppose that means he recognizes me, somewhere, and wants to share what he's found." Mahogany eyes she hadn't been born with narrowed and hardened. "Cultist maniacs. They did this to my child. They're doing this to everyone's children. They destroyed my son."

Technically, they hadn't, so far as the boy's current state went. Schaffer had introduced the streamlined viral infection when they'd retrieved Jeffy from the Tenfew. It had been meant to recomprise his personality, memory, and everything else that makes up a normal fourteen-year-old kid. Instead the modified virus had shattered his central nervous system and gutted his mind. A flawed, self-perpetuating neural-nanotech interface had blitzkrieged through the tender convoluted matter of his brain and continued to breed, swelling first the cerebrum, destroying the thalamus, the temporal lobe, followed closely by the cerebellum, causing massive organic damage. His head was now four times larger than normal, full of microscopic machinery and viruses, with shunts in front, back, and along the sides to drain off fluid and nanotech waste. It didn't help.

He sat up gaping in the direction of the Citadel, still smiling with only about a tenth of his intellect left. That remaining portion couldn't recall his name or how to tie his shoes or what it meant to be depressed for being a hydrocephalic incapable of lying flat on his back without killing himself. He did remember the Tenfew, though, and the power of water and rebirth; nothing they did could challenge or change that, and so nothing they did could ever make him anything less than happy.

Schaffer, the former chief deprogrammer who'd led the assault on the Citadel and created the deprogramming bug, a man known to botch jobs but who had a genius for shifting blame, was no longer a member of his own team. I suspected he was also no longer among the living.

"What's your name?" Sandra Grant asked.

I started to answer but stopped short, almost gurgling. "Will. . . ."

My tongue felt too sleek in my mouth, and freezing sweat erupted and rolled on my upper lip and crawled over my chest. It was just as terrifying to remember your own name as it was to forget it. My forehead heated with the molten millennia, and I drove the heel of my hand against my brow, digging.

I knew myself.

I cleared my throat and tried once more, but couldn't get my tongue around the taste of sweetness. It had been so long since I'd spoken my real name that it took a while to find it, but then I remembered who I was, and what I had done, and had to do again.

I whispered, "Seth."

She didn't hear me. "Is something the matter?"

The acknowledgment of my true nature staggered me, and I reached out to keep from stumbling. Wind bucked madly outside and the oak rafters moaned. The surge of myself made me powerful for an instant, and then intensely sad and lonely. The time had come again.

"My name is Will Gardner."

"You seemed . . . distracted . . . or. . . ."

"Not at all."

She led me into the study where her husband Fredrik Grant sat sipping wine and grimacing through the windows at the Citadel glowing in the distance. The room, like the man himself and the ten thousand desert acres he owned, seemed to breathe the very law of survival. Dry and primitive, with an air of savagery tempered by objective. Dozens of rifles with convertible magna-fire, mini-frag launchers, and laser rangefinder/digital compass assembly stock lined the walls, old-style and new collapsibles, set beside medals representing successful wars fought around the globe.

After leaving the military, he'd formed his own private regiment of nearly two hundred men, remnants of armies, mercenaries, and death squads from several nations. Scattered over his land were towers and tunnels and units latched deep into cliff dwellings. He patrolled the school system and sent his men out as far as Durango and Picotown, waiting for the Tenfew to preach their message in university dormitories, airports, funeral homes. Black vans and buses rolled out among the cities and returned to the complex, one after the other, depositing new believers in the Tenfew Citadel. Dozens of them daily, perhaps more. They'd go on to become priests, acolytes, nuns, the dancers in their veils and robes, and those who lived continuously in grotesque fountains and pools—brothers and sisters of the well.

An ex-Marine Colonel with a cracked Militia father, Grant had learned early to dig in deep and gather as many guns to him as he could. But it hadn't helped him save his children, and the realization had broken him as surely as if he'd stepped on a Bouncing Betty or butterfly fragmentation mine. He was old but still had strength, and although they'd never get rid of all the scar tissue, if he kept taking care of himself, he could add another two or three decades to his already aching hundred years. He'd had skeletal transplants to stave off the osteoporosis.

"Hello, Will," he said.

"Hello, Fred."

There were a number of framed photos of Jeffy piled

on his desk, facing outward, as if Grant meant to use them to lure me into his vengeance against the Children of the Well. Alongside were pictures of his daughter, Elaine. Both teenagers were blond and blue-eyed, smiling with only a hint of the world's ancient concerns in their faces, so young that I could feel the ashes stirring thickly in my veins.

He said, "You were right when you warned me off Schaffer. The ineffectual cretin ruined the entire assault and failed to get Elaine out. You've already seen what his unrealistic promises did to Jeffy."

"I'm sorry."

"The government doesn't realize what maniacs these Tenfew cultists are. I don't give a damn if they are a recognized religion sanctioned by the world order." He leaned back, as if to drawn me in further toward him, so that the photographs of his children would be inches from my nose. The padded flesh around his eyes fell in on itself. "I've watched them grow these last fifty years. Runaways, the hungry, the damned, they snatch whoever they can and absorb the numbers. I remember when the Tenfew were just a small gathering in a hut, digging a well where there was no water."

"But there was."

"Yes," he admitted, "and now there's a honeycomb city of one hundred thousand nestled between those cliffs. I need you to prepare and lead the next mission." He continued on for a while, but I could no longer quite connect myself to the man I had been five minutes ago. In the much larger truth, that small segment had already drifted into the overwhelming ocean of my name and duty.

"I lost six men bringing Jeffy out. Schaffer planned it too damn poorly."

"You were foolish to go in with force."

"They had my children," he groaned, his rage so much a part of him that it barely slipped into his voice. He talked about love and murder and failed pre-dawn raids. At one point I cackled, because I like to laugh, and he reared away, startled and fuming for a moment, before telling me more. "Omega and Beta squads each had transmission, but not all the cameras worked."

"Show me the film."

He keyed the pad at his desk and the 3-D Silicon graphics ONYX workstation came alive, giving a fairly accurate modeling and simulation of what had occurred that night Schaffer had attacked the Few.

That scene filled the room until we were inside it, and we sat watching them come down in front of us through the cliffs, gazing over the compound, four of them stupid enough to break radio silence and whisper in awe at the Citadel. Grant growled and looked like he wanted to stand up and kick Schaffer in the face. Beta squad made a couple of crude comments on the beautiful fountain dancers, translucent girls who lay naked rolling in the pools washing their pigment off, splashing and arching their backs in joy for the Well, giggling, some making love. Omega team mimicked the chants and songs they heard. Somewhere inside myself the assassin I'd been grew disgusted with their performance.

Soon Schaffer clambered into the complex, cut the throats of two unarmed, smiling acolytes, and used the weapon subsystem M78 close-combat optic to sight the next objective. We could see the wavering shades of green come through on the thermal scope as he crawled and propped the rifle in the dirt, utilizing infrared pointer/illuminators to weed out the chest cavities of two Tenfew priests wandering past lost deep in prayer. The squads ran rampant through the waterfall dormitories until they hauled the nonresisting Jeffy Grant out of the geyser where he hummed to himself, and dragged him from the foaming room. Omega team led, carrying the boy, while Beta squad followed and set off a few poorly-placed and improperly timed charges.

Six cameras went dead at that moment, and Schaffer

and the other five men dragged Jeffy from the Children of the Well, never turning back to check on what had happened to the others.

The scene ended and we sat in silence, sipping wine. The ethereal glow of the Citadel slid into the room, igniting the darkness with a haze.

"I'll get you the best, not mercenary filth like these," Grant said. "How many men will you need?"

"None."

"What?"

"I'm going alone."

"It's impossible. You'll never get Elaine out by yourself. There're too many of them, and they toil on that abomination of a temple day and night. You'll need point men, a backup team. . . ." He drifted off, unable to finish, realizing he sounded as inane as any other frightened old man. I got a vague and distanced sense of heartache. Wearily, he asked, "Can you do it before the month is out?"

"I'll leave within the hour."

He shook his head and threw his glass at the wall, and fell back in his chair without a word, hardly breathing. Sandra Grant appeared in the doorway and he told her, "Show, Mr. Gardner out."

His hands were soft and weak and trembling, like those of a keeper of sheep. I knew he hadn't been the one who ordered Schaffer's death. Mrs. Grant led me down the hall and past Jeffy's room, the machines louder than before because the staff had turned up the volume to make up for the fact they couldn't do anything for him. When I shook hands with her, I recognized her angry clench, full of conflict and resolution, thick with the world and full of responsibility and choices, and realized that she would have the strength to murder her son.

"Thank you, Seth," she said.

Four paths ran into the city of the Tenfew, like four rivers churning among the cliffs, choked with pilgrims

seeking salvation and sanctuary. The black vans and
buses eased forward, lined up by the dozen while a
sea of people roamed in the dust. Others drove up in
overheated cars packed and strapped with goods,
ready to turn over all their possessions to the Well. I
walked among them, filing past the aides and acolytes,
the bleached-bone pale nuns who carried huge earthen
jugs of water, letting the thirsty drink and washing the
faces and backs of the severely sunburned.

Organization meant nothing, though symbolism still
did. Carved into the cliffs for all to see were the gods
of the Tenfew, Children of the Well.

Every deity of the pantheon appeared happy and
weak. Ten beings who ruled the earth and sky and
moon, most of them slack-jawed, hollow-eyed, so hor-
ribly thin and bent they looked as though any child
of the Crusades could beat them to death. Only the
first two and the last mattered, the rest were aspects
and scarecrows: man with his unbearably stony
glare, and woman stooped as if listening to whispers.
And at the end, the other man, trailing out of step
behind the rest, jigging a mischievous jig and seeming much weaker than any of them despite his being
the evil one.

The temple stood thirty stories, and they worked on
it the way the Jews had slaved in Egypt, except they
did it smiling. I couldn't tell what it represented, if
anything. Somebody had become much more aes-
thetic, or simply gone insane across the years. Unlike
the building of the pyramids or Stonehenge or the
heads of Easter Island, this had nothing to do with
the calendar or position of the stars, not even with
ego. Maybe we were all losing our touch.

It didn't take long to find the blood on the stones
and steel, where mishaps had occurred and kids had
been crushed. It didn't slow the fervor of the devoted.
Like all temples, this one was alive, and its hunger
continued to grow.

I had power but didn't know what it might be—perhaps only memory, perhaps chance.

I looked for guards, weapons, sentries, automated or human, and saw nothing. Maybe Schaffer's men had simply blown themselves up with one of their last charges. The pale, wet priests wore sopping robes and vestments, and ushered the pilgrims into the fountains where they bathed in the cooling shadows of the towers and obelisks of the Citadel. Nuns danced in the water among corpses of the drowned that tumbled and heaved in the pools. Maybe they'd finally found the means of building a religion capable of crossing the horrifying barrier between life and death—or maybe they'd simply forgotten just who was still alive and who was already dead.

The hymns grew deafening along with the gut-shot wailing of the wind. I felt comfortable in the sun, listening to their familiar rhetoric, appeals, and litanies. They sang and prayed to the Well, danced and preached and pontificated to the Well, called up and called down and called over the Well, but after three hours of searching the insane city I still couldn't find the damn thing.

Eventually a girl who could have been Elaine Grant, if it mattered anymore, with a beatific smile so wide and empty it had almost worn out at the edges of her mouth, approached and brought me a jug. "Drink from the Well."

"Elaine Grant?"

She nodded happily. "Drink." She kept nodding at nothing and the sway of her soaked hair as she brushed it behind her ears reminded me of her brother. "It is from the Well."

"Where are the labs?"

"Labs?" Her mouth couldn't completely close, her sublime grin holding it open like that of a fish. "Drink from the Well."

"Where is the Well?"

"Drink."

"Is there a Well?"

"Drink."

"Where do you draw your water?"

"From the Well."

"Elaine, most other gods allow for light conversation. Consider that point."

I grabbed the jug, took a sip, and could taste the high nutrient content and sweet recombinant DNA agents immediately trying to change my genomes at the first base pair. I chuckled and shook my head—they were going all out this time, no fooling around.

All eighty thousand genes abruptly started shifting sequences in the three billion chemical base pairs that make up human genome DNA, altering the long protein strands from the beginning to end. The Children of the Well weren't waiting tens of thousands of years the way they had changed humanity before with the introduction of each new faith. Asians, the Middle Eastern faiths, Mayans, Africans, Native Americans, Egyptians, even the lost Anasazi and Incas and Roanoke Settlement—with each new belief came a little more dabbling into genetics, and a slightly altered new human race.

I allowed the virus to run its course and could feel the changes the Tenfew were attempting to effect: an enlarging of the thalamus in the diencephalon, which would function as a tighter link between the psyche and the soma-body. Greater conduction of neural axon impulses: the water had to be nutrient-heavy because these people wouldn't care much for eating. A modification from twelve pairs of nerves on the undersurface of the brain to fifteen. Less muscle tone in specific areas of the body, especially the face. It was difficult to frown or look pensive. Tear ducts shrank— less crying, less ability to show fear or sadness. I'd been wrong: Schaffer's nanotech virus hadn't destroyed Jeffy Grant's intelligence. The Children of the Well had already stolen most of it.

"Nice touch," I whispered, and the assassin's hands snapped shut and shattered the jug. What bitter tricks.

"Is there a garden?" I asked her.

She wanted to look angry about the broken jug but couldn't pull it off with the weakened muscles of her blissful visage, so she pointed to the east and strode off. It was just as well she never saw home again; her mother would be doomed to another killing. I walked east through the complex, finally catching the scent of fruit among the dust, and followed until I found the garden.

Twined with Creosote Bush and Desert Willows, draped with limbs of Joshua and Smoke Trees and Screwbean Mesquite, they'd refashioned Eden. Colors exploded from every direction with blooms of Freesia and Belladonna, the Mariposa Lilies and brilliant Ghost Flowers. Clusters of fine, tiny, barbed spines hid among the ropes and tendrils of plants, sap drooling across branches. Numerous erect stems with bright, red-to-orange blossoms and white leaves flowed into the brush and trees. I slipped between the bushes, careful of the Saguaro Cacti and Crucifixion Thorns, and heard laughter.

At last, the Well. Dozens of people gathered in a much larger pool, the young and ancient and the naked dead stewed together in the frothing mix. They swam and drowned and made love in the water, one huge clot of roiling bodies. I pressed my way among the throng, plunged in, and could feel the cold currents sweeping up from the depths. Vibrations of machinery thrummed in my ears and on the edge of memory. The Tenfew's filtration system and reticulation pipes had to be perfect in order to clean out the corpses. The man I'd been had a background in underwater demolitions and enjoyed the feel of slicing through the water. It took two minutes to fully oxygenate my lungs, and then I dove and kicked for the bottom.

At least one of the entry ports would backflush as

part of the filtration system. The drowned were
dragged down in a long train, the subtle undertow
drawing them as they spun and waved and shimmied
into the darkness. I followed the dead, as I usually
did, and descended to about a hundred feet, the effec-
tive three atmospheres starting to drive into my skull,
my chest burning, and allowed the distillation to draw
me into the pipe. If I could hold out another ninety
seconds, I'd be at the heart of the labs, where the
Tenfew would still be experimenting with humanity
and god after all these millennia. If I couldn't hold
out, I'd have to start all over again inside another
man. The thought didn't please me or the assassin
I'd been.

Carcasses tightened around me as the piping grew
smaller, and my breath bubbled between my lips in
agony. Death and life grew even more into one as
mouths brushed my own for a moment, and were
tugged away.

With an enormous roar and splashing purge, I came
free into a much wider funnel and came up for breath
inside a large tank where the debris was divided into
separate streams that whirled along. Bodies wove past
me like fish trapped in towing nets of a trawler.

I flopped out of the filtration tanks and fell on my
face sucking sterile air. This was the distillation center
of a much cleaner religion. The labs would be directly
next door, as they had been since the crypts of Egypt
when they'd studied and catalogued brains before em-
balming and mummifying the dead.

I struggled to the door and found it locked with a
simple keypad numerical combination. They could
never remember if the 666 was the number of the
savior or the serpent, or if there was any difference.
There wasn't. I slid into the lab and found their computers and machines whirring and droning as loudly
and emptily as those machines in Jeffy Grant's
bedroom.

Schematics, readouts, and charts on the social, genealogical, ethnic, and theological evolution of the world filled the screens. I called up diagrams and scales on the growth of the Tenfew, their architectural plans, new government order, history, the eager spread of the racial virus, the presumed rise of beautiful island cities. They still had no reason for the temple, they just liked it. In a caustic glowing red one computer spat all Epidemiological records for food, air, and water-borne and sexually-transmitted diseases: cholera, meningitis, hemorrhagic fever, AIDS, influenza, transmissible spongiform encephalopathy, yellow fever, and Western Equine Encephalitis. They'd found a cure to all major diseases and most of the smaller ones as well, but would have to allow the vaccinations out step by step over the next century. In creating the vaccines, they'd also stumbled onto and mutated other infections, including the bubonic and pneumonic forms of our old friend *Yersinia pestis,* the Black Plague.

All samples were kept in the black box room, a separate hyper-insulated lab used for storing hot zone samples. Using the automatoid robotic arms and skeletal plasti-steel claws, I enabled the controls, cracked open the protective seals in the chamber, and stared through the window at the now lethal air in the black box the same way Jeffy Grant had stared at the dust. I brought my lips to the glass, for the hell of it.

She entered.

Her hair was wet, as it had been on that first day of the world. She turned and peered at me, and I watched as our entire history welled in her eyes. It staggered her as it had done me, and she reached for my hand as she always did. I took her in my arms and felt the blood tide beneath her flesh, and knew my wife.

For a moment I had no idea what to call her. She hadn't gone by her name since her sheepherding son had been murdered by his brother. The queen of these new gods was known as Katha, I recalled, or maybe it was Hatha or Latha, and I didn't find them to be

any worse than Hera or Freya or Isis, but none quite
as lovely as Sequana or Ninmah.

"Hello," I said.

"Oh. Hello, Seth."

She would hope to kill me now, as I pressed my
cheek to nuzzle her neck—she usually made a half-
hearted attempt before sobbing beneath the abject
weight of the sorrow that had befallen us. I waited,
but she merely held me as we slowly swayed together.

"So, what do you think?" she asked.

"Pretty hokey. The Tenfew? Children of the Well?
About the worst you've come up with yet. You don't
even have a holy book this time."

"It gets more difficult."

"Yes, I know."

We looked to the lab door because this was his cue,
and always had been.

He entered with a young man following at his side,
an adolescent who didn't smile insanely and whose
hair was dry. His son, no doubt, or perhaps mine. The
Fruiteater had difficulty in ever forgoing the past or
learning from it. He still looked the way he had when
I'd first met him, just as all his sons had looked
through the ages. I, too, always looked like Seth, and
the sons of Seth, and the sons of Adam, and we were
all exactly the same.

Even his rage had worn as thin as a leaf, and when
he grimaced at me it seemed more like a child trying
to hold in a laugh. "You're a liar," he said. "An assassin, a deceiver." The puerile words came to him by
rote, without meaning or intent or fear of what was
going to happen next. "You've always been a be-
guiler."

We'd said these sentences many times in many
ways, but at least I hadn't tired of them yet. "I simply
offered you a choice. You took it. You made it."

He held a collapsible rifle with magna-fire that he'd
taken off of one of the lost team members, the laser
rangefinder aimed at my heart. I took a step toward

him, and he spoke with such a monotone that it sounded like the voice of emptiness itself. "Stop, no closer."

"Stop? You actually said that to me?" For a man with the knowledge of all humanity under his tongue, who'd been able to build empires and cure murder and find water where there was none, he wasn't very bright anymore.

"Don't take another step."

"You get more foolish every time I see you."

I've rarely pulled the trick on him, but it had to be done again. I moved in fast and low, and he pulled the trigger and shot the assassin Will Gardner and blew out the entire chest cavity. I sighed inside his son and reached out and disarmed him and threw the rifle across the room. He had a puzzled expression on his face like he was having a difficult time remembering the last time this scene unfolded in this fashion. He'd grown so forgetful.

"Don't you understand? This is complete bliss," he argued, because like all men and gods he was doomed by his own conceit. "They do have a choice, they've always had a choice, and they choose to be at peace with us. They are my children."

"They're mine as well, and most of them don't even make love anymore. Soon none of them will. You've doomed them to stagnation. You've damned them with harmony and serenity."

"You don't have the right."

"Yes, I do. I'm the only one who does."

I had been the serpent, Loki, Coyote, that same genetic component embedded in all men and mischief-makers who stepped out of line and lived by their own set of values, leaving a barren, blank-faced world behind, teaching them how to dance, to fight, to cause trouble and garner their own will. "I opened their eyes. I opened your eyes."

"You tricked my wife."

"She's my wife, too, and I saved her."

What he lacked in verve he made up for in patience. He'd become as drowned by his antiquity as any of the corpses that had bobbed beside me in the pipe. "Have the offspring of Seth done so much better with the world? They've brought it to the edge of ruin."

"I know, they botched it, too, but at least they came by their triumphs honestly. They may have made the wrong choices, but at least they were genuine."

"Genuine? Using organ donors to prolong their lives and viral nano-infections that can alter their personal traits? Men who cut throats in the darkness?"

I thought about it. In the early days, in the garden, back when First Man and Monster Slayer strode the earth before the face of the Great Spirit, and Adam slumbered naked without knowing he was naked, things had been much simpler. He refused to remember that we existed in all men, and always would. I'd forever rise against him with whispers to his wife, my wife, because that was our fate, and the fate of the world.

"Don't you understand yet?" I said. "You always *invite* me in."

I reached for the door of the black box hot zone. It lacked the subtlety I'd been known for, but I didn't have much choice.

"Oh, God, what are you doing?" he said. He still called on God, even now as the purveyor of new races and deities, and I didn't know what to make of that. "No. No, you're insane."

"Maybe."

"You'll destroy the world."

"Not all of it. Anybody who struggles hard enough to survive will live. They'll have the choice to fight or to die. That's what I'm supposed to do."

I gave him credit because he lunged for me then and tightened his hands around my throat. I respected him more in that moment than ever before in our endless lives. His hands were my hands, and it was like staring into my own furious eyes as we wrestled and spun across the floor in the cool room where the earth might be saved or doomed.

I called to her. "Open it."

"No!" he shrieked, just as he had after they'd tasted the fruit.

She moved forward shakily, always so beautiful and unsure, but listening to me because she listened to her heart. She unlocked the door to the black box, and gripped the handle.

I gasped, "You know that it's the right choice to make."

"No, I'm not sure I do know that, Seth. I'm not certain of anything anymore."

"Don't!" he screamed at her, as he forever would though she never listened. He chewed his lips until they bled. "I'll still be here," he hissed at me as we pressed nose to nose. "Even if only a handful of people survive in a world of murdered children, I'll be inside one of them."

"So will I."

Her knuckles turned white, then blue, as she clutched the handle of the hot box. In the warm glow of the past and the burning, needy fate of the future that would befall us again, groping for what lay ahead and hoping it would be like that day in the garden before the Lord God tempted me too boldly, when I dripped the venom of love upon my wife, we could feel earth and heaven about to tilt in a new direction. He tightened his hold on my throat, on his own throat. Our lives and souls set in our duty, I wondered which of us would crawl on our bellies in the dust next time, and which would stand and whisper warm words of temptation to our beautiful love, and taste the sweetness of her sugar-smeared lips in the next unbearable Eden.

TINKER'S LAST CASE

by Ron Goulart

The work of Ron Goulart has its roots in many
genres. His science fiction has elements of mystery, his mysteries have elements of fantasy, and
almost everything is infused with wit. Under numerous pseudonyms he has written dozens of
novels, short stories, novelizations, and comic
strips, including recent nonfiction in *The Big
Book of Noir*.

THE dog started complaining even before he was
completely unpacked. "Quit goosing me with that
crowbar," he requested in his piping voice as he spit
out twists of plaz excelsior.

"You might as well stay in the crate, Tinker," suggested Jack Bowers, setting the crowbar down on his
lucite desk next to the packing container. "You're obviously far from repaired."

"And you, Jack, are still a dimbulb," said Tinker/
236–HMX, poking his chrome-plated nose over the
edge of the partially opened neowood crate. "My quick
wits and gift for sparkling repartee are innate qualities of
this particular model of Forensic Computerbot/Compact
Policehound Format."

"Sparkling repartee is one thing, Tinker, and wise-ass insults are something else again."

"Suppose we get down to business," suggested the robot dog. "I was languishing in the Stemwinder Electronics International Repair Shop in the benighted Pasadena Sector of Greater Los Angeles for nigh on to a full frapping week. If I know you, the detective agency is on the brink of being in the toilet by now."

"Actually, Jack Bowers, Hollywood Detectives, Inc. has been thriving while you were getting overhauled."

"Hooey," said Tinker. "If you go more than another couple of days without me on the staff, you'll have to sign up for the SoCal Dole." Giving an impatient snarl, the chrome-plated little bot lifted his silvery right forepaw.

A thin beam of purplish light emanated from the paw. When it touched the neowood slats, they swiftly disintegrated into sooty powder.

"I told them to deactivate that disintegrator of yours."

Tinker hopped free of the confines of the packing crate, booted it with a glittering hind foot, and sent it sliding free off the desktop and onto the paisley thermocarpet, along with Jack's electropen and three faxmemos. "Sounder minds prevailed."

"When I pay $7,400 for a complete tune-up and overhaul, I expect those halfwits at SEI to follow the instructions that—"

"Being a shade wiser than you, kiddo, they had the good sense to consult me before performing any sacrilegious acts upon my person." The dog hopped off the desk and landed in Jack's chair. "What sort of caseload has been piling up in my absence?"

Jack eyed his forensic bot. "Did they at least repair your built-in cameras?"

"Sure, all fixed and shipshape. You got a surveillance job for me, boss?" The metallic hound curled up into a comfortable sprawl on the private investigator's cushion.

"Yeah, a couple of adultery cases," Jack told him. "Plus a possible industrial spying thing. I've been handling that and Reisberson's working on one of the fooling around cases, but—"

"Reisberson?" Tinker produced a derisive noise. "It's a real pity they can't send humans to repair shops. There's a lad who is in serious need of an overhaul."

Resting his backside against the desk edge, Jack said, "Apparently they didn't adjust your snide gear either."

"Truth is never snide," Tinker pointed out. "Okay, here's how we . . . Oops! What time is it anyway?" He held his left forepaw up to his ear, consulting his voxwatch. "Holy shit, three minutes after eleven AM. All your distractions nearly made me miss my favorite vidwall show."

"Nope, no, not at all. You aren't going to watch that henceforward," he informed the dog. "Those halfwits at the repair shop were also supposed to curb your admiration for her broadcasts."

"They did, sure, but it wasn't tough modifying their adjustments." Rising up on the chair on his hind legs, Tinker pointed his right forepaw at the wall opposite.

The vast vidwall screen came to life.

A thickset man in his fifties, clad in a pale yellow bizsuit was smiling behind a large rubberoid desk. ". . . though I control Stemwinder Electronics International, the Waterworks Potable Water Company, Latin American Sweatshops, Inc., Total Multimedia, and other monopolies and trusts too numerous to list, I am still humble and awed in the presence of certain exceptional talents," he was saying. "That's right, folks, Erle Trafalgar is a simple fan like you when it comes to the lady I'm about to introduce. Here she is, Polly Bowers, Hollywood Detective."

The plump tycoon vanished. Now on the immense screen appeared a sunlit bedroom. There was a large, unmade floating oval bed in the shades-of-blue room's exact center. From an arched doorway a very pretty naked red-haired young woman came hurrying in.

"Jesus," observed Jack, "it gets worse and worse."

"Hey, Polly's got an impressive figure. She may as well display it." Tinker rested his metal chin on the desk top, let his plaz tongue loll.

"Not to 3,500,000 viewers."

"3,700,000, according to *E-Variety.*"

Polly halted beside the bed, catching her breath. "I stayed in the darn sonic shower too long," she apologized. "I got to woolgathering, you know, and . . ." She shrugged her bare shoulders. "That's why I'm late."

Smiling, she located a pair of all-season sinsilk panties among the tangle of bedding and started slipping them on. "Oh, and don't let me forget to make the required dippy disclaimer." She undulated as the underwear reached her hips. "I'm compelled to inform you that I'm Polly Bowers, Hollywood Detective, and that I have absolutely no connection with Jack Bowers, Hollywood Detective." She gave an exasperated shake of her head as she plucked a one-size-fits-all bra off the bed. "As if anybody would confuse my top-of-the-line detective agency with that rundown pesthole operated, barely, by that doddering old coot to whom I . . ." Frowning, bra only partially in place, she glanced off camera. "Huh? What?"

Polly shrugged and put on the bra. "Yeah, okay," she said resignedly. "My darn producer reminds me that, even though I'm speaking God's truth, I'm to refrain, for legal reasons, from mentioning that my erstwhile husband is an inept private eye or a superannuated old fogy."

Jack said, "Being forty-two doesn't put me in the old fogy category."

"You're forty-six, chief," reminded the robot dog.

"That still isn't old."

"Polly's twenty-eight, so to a kid like that, you seem—"

"She's thirty-one."

"You've never been able to prove that."

Polly had pulled on a pair of skinfit crimson slax and was wandering around her bedroom in search of a suitable singlet. "Lots of you have called in asking about the next issue of *Polly Bowers' Mystery Magazine*," she was saying. "Well, I'm happy to announce that the latest multimedia edition will be out next week, coming to you from dear Erle Trafalgar's Stranglehold House division. And, yep, for the thousands of you who've been demanding it, there will be another installment of my ongoing memoir, *I Married A Nitwit But Had The Good Sense Not To Renew Our 3-Year Marriage Contract And Instead Founded My Own Detective Agency And Am A Huge Success Today And Happy As A Clam To Boot.* You'll also find fiction, puzzles, recipes and . . . Hold it, folks." She frowned off camera. "Huh? What?"

"She's not supposed to call me a nitwit," said Jack.

Polly said, "My producer reminds me that I was conned into agreeing not to call Jack Bowers a nitwit on my show anymore. So what's left? Can I call him a dumbbell, a schmuck, a moron, a buffoon, jerk?" Eyes narrowing slightly, she glanced again toward the unseen producer. "Goof? That's it? That's all I'm allowed to use? Goof? Well, okay. I can use nitwit in my magazine but not on the air. But a nitwit by any other name . . ." Bending from the waist, she picked up a candy-striped singlet from the floor.

"You'd better," Jack told the robot dog, "get in touch with my attorneys."

"Already did. They say you can't afford any more lawsuits. We still owe them for the last one."

"Shit," observed the private eye.

On the wall his former wife was pulling on the singlet over her head. "Before I show you the interview I did with the GLA DA," she said, "I want to make an important announcement."

"She'd better not call me anything else." Jack left the desk and eased closer to the vidwall.

"Every one of you out there in Greater Los Angeles has been living in abject fear over the past two weeks," Polly said, sitting on the edge of her floating bed and crossing her long legs. "I'm referring, of course, to the latest serial killer to emerge in our area. The one the media's dubbed The Malibu Slicer. You've no way of knowing if this maniac, who strikes at random, will come stalking you next. Will you be found sliced neatly into three portions with a lazrod?" She uncrossed her legs and stood. "I'm concerned for you and for every citizen of Greater LA. So, without in any way implying any criticism of the wonderful SoCal State Police or the GLA Homicide Squad, I am volunteering to go to work on the case." Smiling, Polly spread her hands wide. "I'll be doing this as a community service, not charging anyone my usual impressive fee. From the moment I go off the air this morning, I'll be putting the entire resources of Polly Bowers, Hollywood Detective, to work on cracking this case. And I'll bet you that you won't see a certain senile private op daring to make a similar offer on . . . Huh? What?"

Jack turned off the wall. "That's sufficient Polly for one day, Tinker."

The dog hopped up atop the desk. "Suppose," he suggested, "we take up the challenge?"

"What challenge?" He moved over to one of the tinted viewindows of his tower office.

"How many challenges have come your way today so far?" inquired the dog. "I mean the gauntlet that your ex-wife just tossed in your puss. What say *we* go after the Malibu Slicer?"

Jack stood watching the hazy morning outside, the towers and the flickering skycars going by. "I'd enjoy beating Polly in a contest," he said after a moment. "But can I do it?"

Tinker chuckled. "With me back on the job, boss," he assured him, "it'll be a cinch."

Tinker, after scanning the menuscreen on his side of the small, round restaurant table, said, "The cloned-veal on sawdust-rye sounds tasty. I think I'll try that and a side order of—"

"You can't eat," reminded Jack from his side of the table. "You're a robot."

"I can simulate eating, however, chief." He nodded up at the hovering android waitress. "The cloned-veal san, hon, and the mouse-gene-lettuce tossed salad and a mug of simulated café blanco."

"What kind of sugasub?" inquired the pretty blonde mechanism. "Suga . . . suga . . . sub . . . up . . . bup . . . wang!"

The robot dog, who was sitting in an adjustable hichair, reached out his left forepaw and slipped it inside the andy's sinsilk blouse. "Voxbox on the fritz, sweetheart," he told her. "Fix it in a jiffy. *Voila.*"

"Oh, thanks," she said, smiling. "That feels lots better."

"You can extract your paw now," suggested the detective.

"If I hadn't been sidetracked into the gumshoe trade," observed Tinker as he withdrew his silvery forepaw, "I would've made a great healer. Got the touch."

The healed android waitress asked Jack, "And what'll you have, sir?"

"What's the catch of the day?"

"Cloned-abalone, sir, with synthetic polenta on the side."

"Fine." He made a go-away-now gesture.

The dog watched her walk away from their table on the second level of Natural Nat's in the New Westwood Sector of GLA. "Her backside needs realigning," he said. "How did your morning's interviews go, boss?"

"Where'd you acquire the ability to repair androids?"

"Little knack I taught myself," answered Tinker. "It may come in handy when I go into business on my own, sahib."

"How're you planning to do that? I own you."

"Just kidding." The robot dog made a tinny chuckling noise. "While you were out pumping informants and stool pigeons, I hooked myself up with the SoCal State Police main computer and read everything they have on the Malibu Slicer."

"I assume you did that discreetly. The state cops don't take kindly to—"

"Do you honestly believe that any dimwit cop is going to tumble to the deft intrusion maneuvers that I practice?"

"Okay, spare me the sales pitch. What'd you find out?"

"Want me to print out my concise, pithy, and informative summation of all I've learned about the case to date?" Tinker touched a slot on his chrome-plated side.

"Verbally for now." Jack glanced around the restaurant. As yet there were no patrons at the tables nearest to them. "And in a low, confidential tone of voice, huh?"

Tinker produced a raspberry sound with his plaz tongue. "As you know, the killer was dubbed the Malibu Slicer because the first two victims resided in that tacky paradise. The next chopped-up victim, however, lived in the Old Westwood Sector, and the one after that was based in the Pasadena Sector. So far, there doesn't seem to be a discernable geographic pattern to the slayings. The information the SoCal cops have made public contains a minimum of bullshit," reported the dog. "I haven't uncovered any indication that they know a hell of a lot more than they're telling the media."

Jack leaned forward, resting his elbows on the table

top. "Okay, they can't link the locations—how about the victims?"

Tinker hesitated. "They can't, no."

Jack leaned farther forward. "But you can?"

"I'm still working on it," Tinker answered finally.

"That's interesting," said the private investigator. "One of my informants this morning hinted that the whole serial killer idea is a diversion."

Tinker nodded his silvery head. "Been done before," he agreed. "Kill a bunch of people, make it look like the handiwork of a certifiable loon. And out of all the victims, there're maybe only one or two you really wanted knocked off."

"That's what I'm thinking about. Have you dug up anything that—"

"I'm still burrowing, boss."

Jack leaned back. "Maybe you shouldn't have sent out that press release this morning," he told the dog. "That's going to irritate both the law *and* Polly."

"We're doing this for publicity," reminded Tinker. "The first step in going after publicity is to alert the populace as to what you're up to. If that annoys anybody, well, tough taffy." When he shrugged his shoulders, they made a faint ratcheting sound.

"But annoying Polly might—"

"What an interesting coincidence." The dog cocked his head to the left.

Polly Bowers, fully dressed in an orange sinsilk lunchsuit, was striding across the see-through floor toward them. Clutched in her tanned right hand was a single sheet of buff-colored recycle paper. "Listen, you . . ." She halted beside the table, taking a deep breath. "I'm trying to remember what I can call you in public without having those doddering shysters who represent you sue my ass."

"Goof," supplied Tinker. "That's allowed, as are sap and moron."

"Listen, you goof," said Jack's former spouse, "what's the big idea of challenging me?" She slapped the sheet of paper down on the table over his menuscreen.

It was a small newspaper titled *The Nitwit News.*

He asked, "What the hell is this?"

"My computer prints this out for me every morning, sap," explained Polly, angry. "It sums up what you've been up to during the previous twenty-four hours. Usually it's a dinky little thing and one can stuff all the news about a nonentity like you . . ." She paused, glanced at Tinker. "Am I allowed nonentity?"

"Perfectly acceptable," replied the dog.

"You can stuff all the news about a nonentity like you in a gnat's butt. But today, no, today you hand out your insipid press release and have the temerity to—"

"Actually, Polly, it was Tinker who—"

"Typical, passing the buck yet again," she accused. "The point is that only someone suffering from severe delusions would dare pit his dinky little pathetic detective agency against mine and claim he's going to beat me to the solution of the Slicer case. I've already got it nearly solved now."

"So don't worry, then, Polly."

"It exasperates me when a pitiful shamus like you sticks his snoot in my business," continued his onetime wife. "Just make sure, Jack, that you don't get underfoot and screw up my investigation."

"We are no longer wed," he reminded her. "As I understand SoCal law, Polly, I am therefore no longer obliged to listen to your hectoring and fishwifery. Begone, shoo."

She snatched up the copy of *The Nitwit News.* "You better move fast on this, moron," she told him. "Because I'm within a day of clearing the whole mess up." She turned on her heel and went walking away.

"Say what you will about her," commented Tinker, "*her* rear end is still in great shape."

*   *   *

The voxbox in the rattling elevator wheezed when it announced, "Lower Depths, last stop, coming up."

Through the dirt-blurred plaz walls of the descending car, Jack could see the shadowy streets of the Ground Level Sector of Greater Los Angeles. The neometal pillars that held up the pedramps were scrawled with curses and protests; scraps and tatters were abundant on the rutted pavements. Near the gutted remains of an overturned landcar two wild mutt dogs were having a snarling fight over what looked to be somebody's arm.

The cage came to a thumping, thunking landing. "You sure you want to get out here, pal?" inquired the dangling voxbox. "I can run you back up to Level Ten."

"That's okay." He absently patted the stungun in his shoulder holster. "This is a business call."

"I'd hate to be in your business," wheezed the elevator as the door shimmied open.

"You ought to do something about that wheeze." He stepped out into the hot, gray afternoon.

"No kidding? Hell, I've been on the repair waiting list for nearly five months."

Easing around a sprawled cyborg whose left foot was missing, Jack started for his destination.

On the next corner three skinny teens were, roughly, dismantling a Salvation Army robot. It kept saying, in a squeaky voice, "Bless you, my children. Bless you, my children."

The skinniest of the youths, wearing a ragged overall suit, eyed Jack. "We're collecting for charity, asshole. Let's have a contribution."

"What a shame. I left my Banx card at the office." The detective yanked out his stungun, set it on the lowest setting with a nudge of his thumb and shot the thin young man.

"Son of a bitch," remarked one of his companions.

The stungunned youth lost the use of his legs and fell down. "Hey, that's no fair," he muttered as his head bonked against the broad metal chest of the fallen SA bot.

"If there's no objection, I'll continue on my way."

"You've crippled Oskar for life," accused the lean youth in the sequinned overcoat.

"Nope, only for an hour." Keeping his stungun in the open, the detective moved along.

TeaHouse 23 was in middle of the next block, scrunched between a defunct ponic farmers market and a MedCal Free Crematorium.

"Out of the way." A battered landhearse was pulled up to the curb and two black-enameled robots were worrying a body out of the rear of the vehicle.

Jack stepped aside, waiting until they'd carried the gaunt dead woman inside the cremation facility.

One of her shoes fell off as they were hauling her. A neoleather pump, it bounced on the paving.

After it fell into the gutter, Jack approached the door of TeaHouse 23.

The metallic door inquired, "Yeah?"

"I have an appointment with Willis."

"You're alluding to Mr. Marryat?"

"That Willis, yeah."

"Hold it, while we confirm."

Roughly a minute later the door jerked open inward.

There were ten small square tables in the little tea-room. All were occupied, and at six of those customers were having their fortunes told by a variety of mystics and seers.

Walking through the room, Jack pushed through a curtained doorway.

"You must really be up the creek, Jack." A lean, bearded man was sitting in a plaz armchair near the far wall.

"I need some psi help on a case, Willis," he admitted, sitting in a rubberoid rocker.

On the wall behind the bearded man were mounted

six small monitor screens. Without looking back at them, Marryat said, "Screen five."

A very fuzzy image formed on that screen.

"What is it, Willis?"

"What the hell does it look like?"

Narrowing his eyes, Jack leaned forward. "Give me a hint."

"Sweet Christ, it's a projection from my brain."

"I know that, what I'm trying to convey is that it's too blurry for me to—"

Marryat frowned, turning to get a look at the screen. "That is a lousy picture, isn't it? Must be the spell of sinusitis I've been suffering through is futzing up my—"

"You could simply tell me what it was supposed to be."

"That's never as impressive, though."

"Even so."

Marryat sighed, facing Jack again. "A corpse sliced in three."

Jack studied the image. "Now that you tell me, yeah, I can sort of make that out."

The screen went blank. "The picture was to point out that I've already sensed what case you're worried about."

"It's been on all the Newz vidwall broadcasts today. You don't have to be psychic to—"

"You're on to something," cut in Marryat. "You want to see if I can confirm your suspicions by extra-sensory means."

Jack nodded. "I've got Tinker working on this with me, handling the tech stuff," he told the psychic. "What I'm starting to suspect is . . . what's the matter?"

Marryat was pressing his hands to his stomach, bent far forward. "Something," he murmured.

"What?"

The bearded man shook his head. "Lost it."

After a moment Jack said, "The cops seem to think

that the Malibu Slicer is just one more goofy pattern killer. I've got a hunch, based on what's coming in from various informants, that this whole chain of killings has a definite rational purpose."

Marryat leaned back, closed his eyes.

"What I believe," continued Jack, "is that somebody wants to kill one or maybe two people and that they invented a serial murderer to cover the—"

"Back off." The psychic sat up straight, eyes opening.

"That's a warning?"

Marryat said, "I'm not getting anything clear, Jack. But I keep seeing the door of your office."

"And?"

"There's a funeral wreath hanging on it."

"C'mon, nobody uses funeral wreaths anymore. That's an archaic—"

"It's a symbol."

"Does that mean my hunch is right?"

"That would be how I . . ." Marryat suddenly doubled up again. "Don't do that, Jack. No, don't."

"Do what?" He popped free of his chair, put a hand on the psychic's narrow shoulder.

Breathing shallowly through his open mouth, Marryat said, "It wouldn't be a good idea. You're in enough danger already."

"Exactly which idea are you talking about?"

"I'm getting the strong impression that you've been thinking about attempting a copycat killing of your own," said Marryat slowly. "The Malibu Slicer would be blamed and you'd be rid of a serious rival."

Frowning, Jack shook his head. "Nope, I'd never do anything like that," he assured the psychic. "Kill Polly and rig it to look like the Slicer did it because she was getting too close to solving the case." He sat again in the rocker. "Although it's an intriguing idea, isn't it?"

* * *

The rain had begun at dusk. By eight it was falling heavily all across Greater Los Angeles.

As he guided his skycar toward the Sherman Oaks Sector, Jack, alone, replayed the voxmail message that had been waiting for him when he'd returned to his underground beach condo a half hour ago.

"I want to call a temporary truce," Polly's voice had proposed. "I've dug up something strange that concerns both of us. Might be a good idea if we worked on this Slicer business together. Come over to my place as soon as you can."

The message had been logged in at 6:39 PM. When he'd tried to pixphone his one-time wife, a phonebot had told him there was a temporary lapse in service.

Dropping down through the rainy night, Jack said to himself, "She must've come up with something exceedingly strange to prompt her to suggest a collaboration."

The skycar set down on the landing lot behind Polly's cottage. Lights were showing at most of the windows but, for some reason all the simulated shrubbery that surrounded the neowood house was snapping off and on.

Jack sprinted through the hard-falling rain to the front door.

The door was open about three inches.

Frowning, he called out, "Polly? It's me."

Nothing from inside.

He eased out his stungun, shoved the door fully open with his knee and then, after a ten second wait, dived across the threshold.

"Jesus," he said, lowering the gun and hugging himself. He had to fight to start breathing again, fight to keep from being sick.

Polly's remains, in three sections, were scattered over the living room's floor.

"Pretty gruesome, huh?"

He pivoted to his right, gun swinging up again. "I thought you were stowed at the office. Reisberson was supposed to check you into the equipment locker when you got back from—"

"Boss, please, use the old coco." Tinker was sitting in a highback black armchair. "In a battle of wits, would you actually put your money on yours truly or on a pea-brain like Reisberson?"

Jack tried not to look at what was left of his ex-wife. He started shivering, his head was filling with zigzags of pain. "How the hell did you get here?" he asked the robot dog. "Did you get a look at the Slicer or see—"

"Sit down, boss."

Jack, very unsteady, attempted to walk further into the room and reach the chair that Tinker had nodded at. His legs weren't working very well anymore. "Shit," he said, slowly trudging along the edge of the carpeting, working his way toward the plaz chair.

"Don't step in the blood," cautioned the dog.

"Listen, you tinplated little putz, Polly and I didn't exactly like one another, but you can't—"

"Didn't like her?" Tinker chuckled. "It went way beyond that, boss. I mean, doing this to her indicates a deep-rooted hatred and—"

Jack stopped beside the chair, stared across at the robot. "What the hell are you talking about?"

"Sit down, will you?" recommended the dog. "I'll explain the setup."

Jack remained standing. "Who really killed her?"

The dog said, "You need some back story first."

"Skip that, just—"

"First off, I'm resigning," Tinker informed him. "Not that it'll matter to you, but—"

"You can't resign. I own you. You're nothing more than a gifted appliance, Tinker."

"Once perhaps, but I've been improving myself," he told the detective. "Did a good job, too. Well, for example, just look at how I solved the Malibu Slicer case."

"Solved it? Then who killed Polly?"

"You did. Aren't you paying attention?"

Jack sat, eyeing the silvery robot animal. "You're suggesting that I'm going to be framed for this?"

"For all the murders actually," amplified Tinker. "Trafalgar and I decided somebody had to take the fall, play the patsy, and so forth. You're perfect for the frame. Erle suggested we play it the other way, make it look like Polly did you in and then made a voxmail confession." He shook his glittering metallic head. "Naw, I told the tycoon. Jack fits better. He's a washed-up private eye, got a violent temper, hates and envies his successful former mate. And just today he got into a near brawl with her at Natural Nat's restaurant."

"How does Erle Trafalgar fit into this mess?"

"He's behind the Malibu Slicer killings, dimbulb," said Tinker. "Geeze, I figured that out even before I met you for lunch, boss. The cops were too dumb to spot this, but I figured out that two of the victims, in different and not obvious ways, stood in the way of a new takeover Trafalgar's planning. So he cooked up this Slicer business and—"

"You dropped in on him and told him what you knew," said Jake. "Rather than telling me or the police."

"Bingo," said Tinker. "You couldn't pay me anything, neither could the cops. With the money I'm getting from Erle, I'll be setting up my own detective agency in Greater LA. Tinker & Associates. This is my last case as a stooge. From now on I'm the boss and not a flunky."

"But you're not supposed to have any ambitions like that. You're a robot, and they—"

"You really don't attend to me," said the dog. "I've been telling you that I'm not your ordinary dogbot anymore."

Jack still kept himself from looking at what was left of his former wife. "What's to stop Trafalgar from arranging an accident for you?"

"He would've tried that had I not informed the gink that there are several copies of the dossier I whipped up about his activities in the case," explained the robot dog. "So cleverly hidden electronically that he and all his goons'll never find them. But if I don't perform certain tasks each and every day, those several copies will find their way to the minions of the law."

Jack started to stand up. "You killed Polly, didn't you?"

"Wasn't that difficult," said Tinker. "And the method that Trafalgar and his toadies worked out for the other killings is a cinch to imitate. Cops, trust me, won't be able to tell the difference."

Jack lunged for the dog. "You're not going to—"

"Sit." A thin beam of yellowish light shot out of Tinker's right eye. It hit him in the left knee.

He cried out in pain, tottered back, sat.

"Lowest setting," explained the dog. "You can still talk, but you can't walk at all."

"How are you going to convince the police that I—"

"Oh, you're going to be long gone when they get here, a suicide," Tinker said. "What's going to clinch it, in addition to the clues I'll plant is the voxmail confession you're going to send to the SoCal State Police right before you do away with yourself."

"You're not going to be able to force me to make a confession, Tinker," Jack assured the robot dog. "And there goes your halfwit plan."

Tinker sighed. "It looks like you're going to keep underestimating me right up to the bitter end," he said in a flawless imitation of Jack's voice.

ALL THE UNLIVED MOMENTS

by Gary A. Braunbeck

Gary A. Braunbeck writes poetically dark suspense and horror fiction, rich in detail and scope. Recent stories have appeared in *Robert Bloch's Psychos, Once Upon a Crime,* and *The Conspiracy Files.* His occasional foray into the mystery genre is no less accomplished, having appeared in anthologies such as *Danger in D.C.* and *Cat Crimes Takes a Vacation.* His recent short story collection, *Things Left Behind,* received excellent critical notice. He lives in Columbus, Ohio.

"Secret of my universe: imagining God without
human immortality."
—Camus, *Notebook IV,* January 1942–
September 1945

I found the guy outside one of the downtown VR cult temples just like the thin-voiced tipster said I would. He was around thirty-two, thirty-three years old, dressed in clothes at least two sizes too small for the cold December dusk. There were blisters on his forehead, face, and neck. One look in his eyes told me that his mind—or what might be left of it—was still lost somewhere in cyberspace, floating without direction down corridors formed wherever electricity runs with intelligence; billowing, coursing, glittering, humming, a Borgesian library filled with volumes he'd never understand, lost in a 3D city; intimate, immense, firm, liquid, recognizable and unrecognizable at once. The Twenty-First Century Schizoid Man, in the flesh.

I gently placed one of my hands on his shoulder. My other hand firmly clasped the butt of my tranquilizer pistol, just in case.

"You okay?"

He turned slowly toward me, his eyes glassy, uncomprehending. "Who're you, mister?"

"A friend. I'm here to help you."

"D–d–did . . . did he ever find that girl?"

"Who?"

"John Wayne?"

He seemed so much like a child, lost, lonely, frightened. A lot of VR cultists end up like this. Sometimes I wondered if the mass-suicides of religious cults in the past were really such a tragedy, after all. At least then the cultists—sad, odd, damaged people who turned to manufactured religions and plasticine gods— were released, were freed forever from the Machiavellian will- and mind-benders who turned them into semi-ignorant, unquestioning, shuffling zomboids. Worse, though, were the families who hired me and my partner to get their kids back and deprogram them. They always thought that familial love and compassion would break through the brainwashing—and don't try to PC my ass, because brainwashing is the only thing to call it—but then they find out all too soon that you don't need surgical equipment to perform some lobotomies. Seven times out of ten the kids wound up in private institutions; at least one of the other three are dumped at state-run facilities where they're snowed on lithium for six months, spoon-fed first-year graduate school psychobabble, then put out on the streets to join the other modern ghosts, adorned in rags, living in shadows, extending their hands for some change if you can spare it, and wondering in some part of their mind why the god they had worshiped from the altar of their computer monitor has abandoned them.

"That's my car over there. C'mon, I'll take you someplace safe and warm. You can eat."

". . . 'kay . . ." His voice and gestures seemed even more childlike as he started toward my hover-car. "How . . . how come your car don't got no wheels?" He seemed genuinely mystified, as if he'd never seen a hover-car before. We were nineteen years into the twenty-first century and hover-cars had been in use for the last five. Okay, so they weren't exactly commonplace yet, but there were more than enough in the air at any given time that, unless you'd been on Mars since 2014, you'd have seen at least a couple.

"It flies."

His eyes grew wide, awed. *"Really?"*

I smiled at him. "Sure thing. Why don't you get in . . . uh . . . what's your name? Mine's Carl."

"Mine's Jimmy Waggoner."

"Get in, Jimmy Waggoner."

He did. I locked his door from outside (the passenger-side door cannot be opened from within), then took my place behind the controls, and soon we were airborne, gliding smoothly and quickly over the cityscape.

Jimmy looked out the window and down on the world he was no longer a part of. "This is *soooooooooo* neat!"

"Glad you like it."

"Uh-huh, I really do. This is the best birthday present I ever got, *ever!*"

"It your birthday today, Jimmy? December eighteenth?"

"Uh-huh. Mommy says I was her 'Christmas Baby.' She let me watch *The Searchers* on tape and then she gave me some pizza money."

Something cold and ugly crept up my back. "How, uh . . . how old are you today, Jimmy?"

"I'm seven," he said proudly, pointing to his chest. Then he saw his hand—

—the thick hair on his arms—

—felt the beard on his face—

—and before I could I activate the autopilot and stop him from doing so, he grabbed the rearview mirror and turned it toward himself, getting a good look at his face.

"That ain't me!" he cried, his voice breaking. *"Where'd I go, mister? Where'd I go?"*

I had to sedate him a few seconds later. If I hadn't, we would have crashed.

Jimmy was one strong child.

I put the hover-car down in a clearing right smack in the middle of a patch of woodland that surrounds three quarters of our safe-house. A long time ago Parsons and I agreed that the more remote our workplace, the better. This area was nearly impossible to get to by standard automobile, and if anyone ever did manage to get this far, there was only one road leading to the house. Even without the hidden security cameras that lined the final stretch of that road, we'd see them coming from three miles away.

I radioed in for a medical team to bring a stretcher. Parsons got on the horn and asked me if I'd managed to get any information from the kid—and *kid* is how I thought of Jimmy, his age be damned.

"Just enough to give me the creeps," I replied.

Jimmy was still out of it from the tranquilizer shot I'd given him earlier, and as I stared at his peaceful, sleeping form, I figured it was probably for the best.

I didn't know which VR cult this kid had belonged to—there were dozens that had temples in this part of the country—but what I did know was that none of them were in the habit of simply dumping their converts in the street and then calling the likes of us to come and clean up the mess.

The VR cult phenomenon didn't really get going until 2003, though it had its genesis back in the mid-1990s. Back in the '90s, personal VR equipment was bulky, clumsy to use, and expensive—forget that virtual reality itself on the net was more of a curiosity than anything else, and most of the VR worlds were fairly crude by today's standards. Then there were the computers and servers themselves; the '90s saw the beginnings of the ISDN proliferation, the introduction of NFSnet—God bless fiber-optic cable—but even those couldn't manage a transfer rate faster than 2Gb/sec. Then, around 2002, slowly but surely, the faceless Powers-That-Be began giving people a taste of the Next Big Thing, and like lemmings to the sea they lined up.

Now—Christ, *now* you were in the dark ages if your system functioned under 1000 MIPS and transferred less than four million polygons/sec. The power required for color- and illumination-rendered, real-time, user-controlled animation of (and interaction with) complex, evolving, three-dimensional scenes and beings was widely available. The VR equipment needed to function in these worlds was streamlined into little more than a pair of thin black gloves, a lightweight pair of headphones, and some slightly oversized black glasses with a small pair of sensory clips; one for your nose (to evoke smell) and one that you tucked into the corner of your mouth (to evoke taste). In a world overrun with people, where personal space was moving its way up the endangered species list, VR worlds and servers offered people the chance to "get away from it all" without leaving the confines of their computer terminal.

Problem was, when you give an apple-pie American something with endless possibilities, they find a quick way to either pervert or trivialize it. It wasn't long before "cyber-diets" were all the rage—Lose Weight

Fast! Slim Down for Summer! Log in, and we'll give your senses the *illusion* of being fed. 3D interactive kiddie porn. Sites where you could virtually torture your enemies.

Oh, yeah—and the gods of cyberspace. Any nutcase with a religious manifesto could buy space and set up a virtual temple to beckon worshipers. Create-A-Deity, online twenty-four hours a day for your salvation, can I get a witness. Some of the bigger ersatz-religions—Mansonism, Gargoylists, Apostles of the Central Motion, Vonnegutionism (my personal favorite, they used a cat's cradle as their symbol), the Resurrected Peoples' Temple, and the Church of the One-Hundred-and-Eightieth Second—were granted licenses to set up their own servers—and because of that, Parsons and me would always have jobs. There would always be lost souls like Jimmy. First get them hooked on the net, alienate them from the world they know, then draw them into your virtual fold, blur the lines between the person they are on the net and the person they are off the net until you trap them forever in the spaceless space between, imprison them in the *consensual loci.*

I was snapped from my reverie by the medical team, who gently loaded Jimmy onto the stretcher and into the ambulance. I signaled them I would walk to the house.

I had a feeling that walk was going to be the last quiet time I'd have for a while.

Jimmy was still asleep in the recovery area when Parsons met me outside the computer room.

"You say he thinks he's seven?"

"Yes. You should have seen him flip out when he finally got a look at himself."

"Did he give you any indication what cult he belonged to?"

"None."

"So where does that leave us?"

"We know his name. Let's run it through and see if any bells go off."

"You just love talking in tough-guy clichés, don't you?"

I grinned. "Watched too many Clint Eastwood movies when I was a kid."

Parsons laughed. "You were never a kid."

"I feel so good about myself now."

I liked Parsons a lot. A former VR cult member himself, there was no scam, no form of reasoning so out there, no logic so convoluted, that he couldn't work his way through it to awaken what lay at a subject's core. In the six years we'd been working together, I'd only seen him lose two subjects—one to suicide after her family took her away too soon, the other to law school.

Parsons hates that joke, too.

One of our latest residents, Cindy (she wouldn't yet tell us her last name, even though we already knew what it was), age seventeen, approached Parsons and asked him about Jimmy.

"I saw them bring him in downstairs," she said.

Parsons put a reassuring hand on her arm. "You don't need to worry about him, Cindy; Jimmy'll be fine."

"You don't know him, do you?" I asked.

"I don't think—I mean, I don't know. Something about him seems familiar, I guess." She thought about it for a second, then shrugged and said, "I guess not. Sorry."

Parsons looked at his watch. "Shouldn't you be helping with dinner preparation in the kitchen?"

"Omigosh, I forgot all about it." She hurried away toward the elevator.

I stared after her. "She seems a lot friendlier than she did last week."

"I know," whispered Parsons. "Amazing how fast she's progressed, don't you think?"

We looked at each other.

"Think she'll try it tonight?" I asked.

"Not tonight, but definitely before Christmas."

"I'll double outside security."

"You do that."

Escape attempts are commonplace here during the first three weeks; week one, they fight us tooth-and-nail because they see us as the evil ones who took them away from salvation and home; week two, they loosen up a bit, then decide to play along, hoping to give us a false sense of accomplishment; week three, they try to run for it. Cindy was a Third Weeker. Time to try.

We parted after that, Parsons going off to a scheduled session with some twelve-year-old from Indiana we snatched from the Resurrected Peoples' Temple. I went into the computer room to run down Jimmy's name.

One of the things I've learned over the years is that you must take nothing for granted when tracking down a subject's past. Not that we have to do it all that often; usually the family provides us with more than enough information to go on. There have been, however, a handful of burn-out cases that have simply stumbled into our hands. These always take extra effort, but I rarely mind.

At least with Jimmy Waggoner I had a name—and a possible temple affiliation.

Cindy of the No-Last-Name-Given had been snatched from the Church of the One-Hundred-and-Eightieth Second, who believed that they and they alone postponed the end of the world because they and they alone owned the last three minutes of existence. Their literature even claimed that these last three minutes were a physical object, one that their Most Holy Timekeeper, Brother Tick-Tock (I'm not kidding) kept safely hidden away, watched over by the One and True God of All Moments, Lord Relativity.

I doubted that Cindy actually knew Jimmy, but at

this stage anything was worth a shot. I fed all the information into the system, sat back, and waited.

It took about thirty minutes. I'd guessed about Jimmy having come from the tri-state area; most VR cults are localized religions and recruit their members close to home as a rule.

I'd almost nodded off when the computer cleared its throat (a .wav file I installed as a signal) and the words MATCH FOUND appeared on the screen. I rubbed my eyes and pressed the mouse button—

—and there it was.

All the information on Jimmy Waggoner that there was to be found.

Only thing was, it came from the last place I'd expected.

The Center for Missing and Exploited Children.

Parsons looked up at me from behind his desk. "Don't bother to knock."

I shoved the printouts in his face. "James Edgar Waggoner, born December 19, 1986. Disappeared on his birthday, 1993, on his way to a pizza parlor half a block from his home. It's all there, his kindergarten and first grade report cards, school pictures, health records, dental charts, all of it."

Parsons scanned the printouts, all the time shaking his head. "Dear God in Heaven."

"Do you have the medical report yet?"

"Um . . . yeah, yes . . . it's right here." He handed it to me but I didn't take it.

"Why don't you just give me the *Readers' Digest* version?" I said.

He put down the printouts and rubbed his eyes. "Those marks on his face and neck? There were identical marks on his chest, forearms, and thighs."

"Burns?"

"No. Medical adhesive irritation."

"In English."

"That guy's been hooked up to both an EKG and

EEG for a very long time. Plus, there was an unusually high trace of muscle relaxants in his system."

"*Muscle* relaxants?"

"That, and about a half-dozen different types of hypno-therapeutic medications."

We stared at each other.

"Any traces of hallucinogenic?"

"Good old-fashioned Lucy-in-the-Sky-with-Diamonds."

I felt my gut go numb. "So whoever took him has . . . has—"

"—has kept him more or less snowed out of his skull for a good while, especially the last year or so," said Parsons. "Tests indicate definite brain damage, but we're not yet sure of the extent."

". . . Jesus . . ."

"I'll second that. You got an address on his family?"

I nodded my head. "The father died a couple of years ago. Coronary. His mother still lives in town at the same house."

"You suppose she stayed there because she believed he'd come back some day?"

"Seeing as how it was the father who petitioned for the declaration of death, my guess is probably."

"Need anything to take with you?"

"A photograph of the way he looks now."

"I'll take it myself."

I stood staring out at I-don't-know-what.

"You okay, Carl?"

"Twenty-six years," I whispered. "What the hell were they doing with him for twenty-six years?"

"I've got a better question."

"What's that?"

"One minute the kid's seven years old and off to buy a birthday-in-December slice of pizza, the next—*wham!*—he finds himself in a thirty-three-year-old body and doesn't know how he got there. How do you explain to someone that they've been robbed of over one-third of their life and will never get that time back?"

Joyce Waggoner was fifty-seven but looked seventy. Still, she carried herself with the kind of hard-won dignity which, with the passage of time and accumulation of burdens, becomes a sad sort of grace.

Her reaction to the news that her son was still alive was curiously subdued. I supposed (and rightly so, as it turned out), that she'd been scammed countless times over the years by dozens of so-called "cult busters" who, for a nominal fee, promise quick results. I assured her that I was not after any money, and even went so far as to give her the name and number of our contact on the police force. She told me to wait while she made the call, but then she did the damnedest thing—she stopped on her way to the phone, looked at me, smiled, and asked if I'd like some fresh coffee. "It's really no trouble," she said in a voice as thin as tissue paper. "I usually have myself some coffee about this time of day."

"That would be very kind of you," I replied, suddenly feeling like a welcomed guest.

She first made the coffee, then called Sherwood, our police contact, who assured her that Parsons and I were on the level and could be trusted.

"May I see that photograph again?" she asked when she came in with the coffee. I handed it to her and spent several moments adding cream and sugar to my cup while she examined the picture Parsons had taken not two hours ago.

"I guess it could be him," she whispered, then looked up at me. "I'm sorry if I don't seem overjoyed at your news, but I've been duped by a lot of people over the years who claim to've had news of Jimmy's whereabouts."

"I understand."

She looked up at the mantel. There were only three framed photographs there: one showed Jimmy as a newborn, still swaddled in his hospital blanket; the next, in the center, was a picture of herself with her late husband that had apparently been taken shortly before his death; and the last, at the far end of the mantel, was of Jimmy, taken on his fifth birthday. I raged at the emptiness up there, for all the photographs that should have been present but hadn't been and now never would be—Jimmy graduating from grade school, his high school senior picture, college graduation, all the moments in between, silly moments with Mom and Dad, maybe a picture of himself with his prom date, both of them looking embarrassed as Mom stood in tears while Dad recorded the Historic Moment on film . . . all the empty spaces where precious memories should have been, filled only with a thin layer of dust and a heavy one of regret. Even with the smell of air-freshener and what I suspected was freshly-shampooed carpeting in the air, there was a smell underneath everything that had to be grief. It had been clogging my nostrils since I'd come into the house.

"He was watching *The Searchers,*" she said. "You know, that John Wayne movie?"

"Yes, I've seen it many times."

"It was his father's favorite movie, you know. Anyway, he was watching it while I was making some last-minute arrangements for his surprise party later that afternoon and . . . you have to understand, Jimmy was always the sort of child who *liked* being kept in suspense. I guess that way he always had something to look forward to. So, about two-thirds of the way through the movie—and boy, was he immersed in the story—he had to use the bathroom, so he put the tape on "pause" and did his business, and about the time he was coming out of the bathroom his father was coming in the back door with Jimmy's birthday present—his own VCR. Well, I didn't want Jimmy to see it, so I gave him a couple of dollars and told him to walk up to Louie's Pizza and get himself a couple of slices. Louie's—it's been gone for a lot of years now—it was right at the end of our block, so Jimmy didn't have to cross the street or anything like that, and he *loved* Louie's pizza. So he said, 'Okay. I'll have it when I watch the rest of the movie,' and he took off. That's . . . that's the last we ever saw of him.''

"Mrs. Waggoner, I have to ask this question: in the weeks, days, or hours before Jimmy disappeared, do you remember seeing any—"

"Yes."

The immediacy of her answer surprised me.

She saw my surprise and laughed. "I didn't mean to stun you, but the police and FBI must have asked me that about a thousand times. Yes, there was a man I saw walking through the neighborhood that I didn't recognize and, yes, Jimmy once told me about this man trying to talk to him."

"Did you contact the police?"

"You bet your ass we did. My husband had several friends on the force, and for several weeks afterward I noticed more frequent patrols through our area. After Jimmy was taken, my husband started buying all sorts of guns, most of them from his friends on the force—old pieces of evidence, no serial numbers, like that. At one point, he had two guns in every room in our house. After he died, I got rid of most of them."

"How much time elapsed between Jimmy telling you about this man and his disappearing?"

"About five months."

"Did this man say anything to Jimmy that might—"

"I'm way ahead of you." She reached into the breast pocket of her blouse and removed a small, age-browned business card. "He gave this to Jimmy."

She handed me the card. It was a sketch of a man meant to resemble Jesus, his face turned heavenward, his arms parted wide, a clock in the center of his chest.

The time on the clock was three minutes until twelve.

The logo for the Church of the One-Hundred-and-Eightieth Second.

She stared at me. "You recognize it, don't you?"

"Yes." And I did something then that I'd never done before.

I told her everything.

This is not SOP with me, understand. Usually Parsons and I try to feed the information to the families in bits and pieces so as to make the sordid whole a bit easier to swallow, but this woman, this good, graceful, lonely woman had moved something in me, and I felt she deserved nothing more than the whole truth.

She listened stone-faced, the only sign of her grief and rage the way her folded hands balled slowly into white-knuckled fists.

I finished telling her everything, then poured myself some more coffee while the news set in. I still couldn't get that underneath-things-smell out of my nose.

"The police checked it out, that card, but that church, they denied that any of their 'apostles' had given it to Jimmy. I guess they've got thousands of those cards floating all around; anyone can get their hands on them."

"Can I keep this?" I asked.

"Don't see why not." She stared off in the distance for a minute, then shook herself from her reverie, looked at me, and smiled. She looked like someone had stuck a gun in her back and told her to act natural.

"I still have that damn VCR we got for him," she said. Her voice was so tight I thought the words might shatter like glass before they exited her throat. "Still wrapped up in birthday paper. They don't even make the damn things anymore. Still got that tape of *The Searchers,* too."

I reached over and took hold of one of her hands. It was like gripping a piece of granite. "At least that'll give him something to look forward to."

She nodded, and for the first time I saw the tears forming in her eyes.

"I don't so much mind what they robbed me of," she said. "Seeing him grow up, mature, riding a bike for the first time . . . I don't mind that so much. But *for him* . . . I very much mind what those fuckers robbed him of. Childhood ends all too soon anyway, but to be . . . to be *stripped* of it like that, to have it expunged, to never, ever experience it . . . that's worse than simply robbing a boy of his childhood. It's a hideous form of rape in a way, isn't it?"

"We'll get them for this, Mrs. Waggoner. I swear it."

She wiped her eyes, looked at me, and tried to smile. "I don't doubt it for a minute."

I readied myself to leave and take her back to the safe-house. To my surprise, she didn't want to come along.

"I, uh . . . I don't exactly look my best right now," she said. "I want to clean up a bit, put on a good dress, you know."

"Of course. I'll have someone come for you later this afternoon."

"Around five would be wonderful." She took my hand and kissed me once on the cheek. "Thank you, Carl. I don't know what kind of a life my son and I will have from here on, but at least we'll have one. Together."

I smiled at her as best I could and nodded, then quickly trotted out to the hover-car and took off.

I didn't want her to see how badly I was shaking.

Something had clicked into place while she was speaking to me.

And when she'd craned to kiss my cheek, that underneath-things-smell was on her.

And I recognized it for what it was.

And the implications scared the hell out of me.

"Detective Sherwood."

"Ian, it's me."

"Carl. How goes the spirit-saving business?"

Usually I'd have had a snappy reply, but not today. Sherwood sensed something in my silence and asked: "Okay, you're in no mood for jokes. How serious is it?"

"It may just be my imagination running wild with me—"

"You don't *have* an imagination, pal."

"Everyone's complimenting me today, first Parsons, now you. I feel giddy."

"*There* you are."

"Look, Ian, this might be damned serious. I need you to get your hands on some phone records for me, can you do that?"

"I'll need a couple of good reasons."

I listed three.

Now it was Sherwood's turn to be silent.

"Still there, Ian?"

"Uh . . . yeah, yes, I'm just . . . wow."

"Like I said, it might just be my imagination, but if it isn't—"

"—if it isn't, a lot of people are going to be in deep sewage."

"I figured."

"How far back do you want me to check?"

"Start with a week ago, going through today."

"I'll dispatch some plainclothes in an unmarked car to keep an eye on the place."

"Tell them not to apprehend, just follow."

"So now you're my boss?"

"Please, Ian? This one feels bad."

He sighed in resignation. "That last name was W-A-G-G-O-N-E-R?"

"Must've been your junior-high spelling bee champ."

"National finalist."

"You're kidding?"

"I'm kidding . . . but then *I'm* the one with the sense of humor."

"I gotta get new friends."

"No one but us'd have you. Call me back in an hour and I'll let you know."

"Cindy?"

She looked up from the dishes, surprised to see me. "Yes?"

"I want you to tell me about the place where Brother Tick-Tock takes all new apostles."

She stared. "That's private. Sacred."

I came toward her. There must have been something in my eyes, because she turned slightly pale and backed up a few paces.

"You listen to me, Cindy. That boy who came in here today, Jimmy, you *know* him, don't you?"

"I don't know, like I said."

I had her backed to the wall. "Tell me about Lord Relativity, then."

This caught her off-guard, but at the same time seemed to perk her up a bit. "He is the One and True God of All Moments, available to His followers on-line at all times."

"And what does He say to His followers?"

"Nothing. We simply log on and become One with His Presence."

"You . . . you *feel* him, then?"

"Yes, his thoughts and the beating of his heart. Lord Relativity was inspired by Jesus. It was in His Seventh Year that he became aware of His greatness, and in His thirty-third year, he falls into the ashes of cyberspace and emerges reborn."

"Reborn. At age seven?"

"Yes. Praise His name and the realization of the New World He promises all."

I grabbed her by the shoulders. "Where does Brother Tick-Tock initiate the new apostles, Cindy?"

"That's a secret, I told you."

"Then try this: Unless you tell me where this sacred

place is, I think someone is going to try and kill
Brother Tick-Tock before the day is over."

"No! Without Brother Tick-Tock to guide us, to
interpret what Lord Relativity thinks in His Cyber
Palace, we will be lost and—"

I slapped her. I couldn't help it.

I didn't know how much time might be left.

"Dammit, girl, tell me!"

"CARL!"

I turned to see Parsons standing in the kitchen doorway. He looked livid. "How dare you strike her like
that!"

"I don't have time for your subtleties, my friend.
Have you talked with Jimmy yet?"

"A little."

"There's a huge hole in his memory, right?"

"Yes."

"One that you're going to have to use hypnosis to
fill in?"

"Probably."

"Let me save you a little guesswork. You've got the
latest incarnation of Lord Relativity up there."

Cindy gasped.

Parsons tilted his head, looking confused. "How do you
know—what do you mean the *latest* incarnation of—"

"Get on the horn and see if any seven-year-old boys
have disappeared in the last three days, then call Detective Sherwood and tell him to get a squad over to
the address Cindy is about to tell us." I glared at
her. "Well?"

"How can that man be Lord Relativity. He exists
only in cyberspace, where all intellect and electricity
meet to form a new consciousness and—"

I drew back to slap her again.

"Because Brother Tick-Tock and the elders of the
church have been kidnapping little boys, drugging
them, then hooking them up to medical equipment
which is tied into the church's mainframe server so

that followers like you can get online and commune with Lord Relativity. I have no idea how many times they might have done it, or how often your precious lord rises like a phoenix from the ashes of cyberspace, but I *do know* that Brother Tick-Tock may be dead soon, and if you don't tell me where the sacred initiation site is, it'll be your fault."

Parsons must have heard it in my voice, because he did not contradict what I said. We try never to use threats with people here, but if what I suspected was true, there was no time.

"Are you telling me the truth?" whispered Cindy, looking so scared and broken I almost took her in my arms.

"Yes, Cindy, I am."

She gave me the address.

On my way to the address Cindy had given, I put the hover-car on autopilot while I tidied myself up and removed the detective's shield and ID from the glove compartment—a gift from Sherwood at the police department. Sometimes I had to impersonate a detective in order to gain access to certain people. Thus far I'd never been called on it, and Sherwood had always promised to take care of any problems that might arise should I get busted.

I hoped he was a man of his word.

My phone beeped, and, the car still on auto, I answered.

It was Sherwood.

"You nailed it, my friend," he said. "One call to the church, two from. All within the last twenty hours."

"Your plainclothes boys there?"

"They are, but I don't think anyone's there."

"I'm listening."

"Right after you left, she called the local precinct and was connected to the Records Division."

"Unlisted phone numbers, legal name changes, private addresses, and the like?"

"Two cigars for you."

"Parsons called you, right?"

"I've got two cars on the way, and as soon as I hang up, I'm on the way my own self."

"Good-bye, then."

I broke the connection and landed right in front of the upscale condo and went inside to find the security guard unconscious at his desk.

Not bothering to remove my gloves, I checked the computer for Roger Buchanan's (a.k.a. Brother Tick-Tock's) apartment number, then grabbed the first elevator.

The ride to the twentieth-floor penthouse seemed to take forever.

When the door opened, I came out with my gun drawn. Across from me stood the door to Brother Tick-Tock's personal initiation space where, I suspected, he'd seduced both boys and girls into the fold.

The door was open.

I nudged it farther with my foot, then slipped in, my gun in front of me.

There was no sound.

I went from room to room, until at last I came to a large set of oak doors that had to lead into an office.

I opened them slowly and quietly.

Brother Tick-Tock sat in a plush chair behind his desk, a small splotch of blood staining the center of his shirt.

I could still smell the shot in the air.

Not unlike the dying aroma of gunpowder that I'd sniffed in Joyce Waggoner's sad and hollow home.

I walked over, very slowly, to the person sitting in the chair on the other side of the desk.

Joyce Waggoner was still holding the gun, an automatic with silencer attachment.

There was no doubt in my mind that it was one of the untraceable weapons her husband had bought.

It took a moment for her to register my presence,

and when she did, she simply shrugged and smiled. "He didn't deserve to live, not after all he's done."

I stepped behind the desk and felt for a pulse.

Brother Tick-Tock was still very much alive.

I came back around and took the automatic from her hands. "You called in the tip, didn't you?"

"Yes." She lifted up her open handbag. It was stuffed to bursting with platinum credit chips. The smallest one I saw was a thousand.

"Jimmy got away from them somehow," she said. "I was so stunned to see him, to know that he was alive, that I just . . . I just held him a lot last night. Made cocoa. But then I got mad. I called the church and told them that I knew they'd taken my son from me and I was going to make them pay. They called me back, Brother Tick-Tock himself here. I hung up on him and he called right back. He offered . . . he offered me a lot of money to keep quiet. I don't have a lot of money to live on anymore, you see, and Jimmy, well, he's going to require a lot of care and . . . and . . ."

"So you said yes to a deal?"

"Yes. But then it occurred to me that they might try to . . . to take Jimmy back when they came with the money."

"So you took him to the VR temple downtown and called us to come get him?"

"I wanted him to be safe, somewhere they wouldn't dare try getting to him."

"How many men from the church showed up at your house with the money?"

"Only two. One of them slapped me, threatened to hurt me if I didn't tell them where Jimmy was."

"So you killed them both? Shot them?"

"How did you know?"

"I caught a whiff of gunpowder on you when you kissed me good-bye."

"I thought you seemed awfully sharp."

"Where are the bodies?"

"In the cellar. I have no idea how I'm going to get rid of them . . . of course, I guess that's all moot now anyway, isn't it?"

Brother Tick-Tock moaned but did not regain full consciousness.

Then I heard another sound.

A whimper; very small, very thin.

Behind a door to the left of the desk.

Not taking my eyes off Mrs. Waggoner, I backed toward the door and kicked it open with my foot.

On a bed not four feet away lay a small boy, dressed in winter clothes, who was tied to the bedposts and all-too-obviously drugged.

I looked at the child.

Then Mrs. Waggoner.

Then Brother Tick-Tock.

And I thought then of Jimmy, of the childhood he'd been robbed of, of the dust on Mrs. Waggoner's mantel, of the hysteria that the parents of this new boy must be feeling, and a last thought, unbidden, came to me: How many times had Brother Tick-Tock done this? How many seven-year-old boys had he kidnapped, drugged, then hooked up to the church's computer so the followers could log on to see the Reborn Lord Relativity?

In this age gods, like their followers, can be easily manufactured.

I stepped into the room and saw all of the children's toys that littered the floor—balls to bounce, fire trucks, tiny robots, puzzles; a kiddie's paradise.

Then I saw the bank of monitors from the corner of my eye.

I turned to face them.

There were eighteen in all, most of them showing very small rooms with very small occupants on medium-sized beds.

None of the children were alone.

I will not describe the depravities these children

were being subjected to by their roommates. I had to turn away for a moment before I threw up.

I saw a second door, set between two bookcases on the far side of the room. I walked very slowly over to the door and pushed it open. A winding stone staircase led downward.

On autopilot myself, I picked up one of the small bouncing balls, a blue one, and tossed it down the stairs.

I turned back toward the monitors and stared at the one in the center.

It showed a stone archway where a stone staircase ended.

I waited, forgetting to breathe.

A few seconds later, the blue ball bounced from the stairs onto the monitor screen.

I stared again at the empty, glassy eyes of the children on the other monitors, wondering if they knew their degradations were being recorded.

I had been wrong about what was really going on.

In my worst moments, I'd never imagined that I'd ever encountered anything as unspeakable as this.

I knelt down for a moment and pulled open a set of drawers under the monitors.

Hundreds upon hundreds of digital video disks were stored there, identified only by labels such as: LARRY, age 6, blonde; Little Boy Blue; Jessica, age 4, brunette; Little Miss Muffet.

So all of this, all of it—the church, the temple, the cyber-crusades of Lord Relativity and Brother Tick-Tock—all it was an elaborate front for a child pornography ring.

Then I noticed a label on one of the disks: ONE USE ONLY; red and noisy.

There were at least twenty more with the same label.

ONE USE ONLY: New cyber-speak for snuff movie.

All of this flashed through my mind in a second, and, knowing that Sherwood and his men would be here any minute, I made a decision that I knew would change the man I was for the rest of my life.

I came back into the office. "Mrs. Waggoner? You with me?"

"Of course."

"Don't ask questions, just listen and answer 'yes' or 'no,' all right?"

"Yes."

"Do you have a heart condition of any sort?"

She looked at me, puzzled. "No . . . ?"

"Do you have any sort of condition that might endanger your life should you suffer a form of body trauma?"

"No."

I exhaled, nodded my head, made sure my gloves were still firmly covering my hands, then took her gun from her hands and shot her in the shoulder.

She fell off the chair with a shriek.

I stood over her. "Listen to me, Joyce, listen very carefully. You came here to confront Buchanan about what he had done. You were out of your head with anger—that's why you knocked out the security guard downstairs. You came up here and the two of you argued."

I picked up her handbag and slammed it against the side of Brother Tick-Tock's head. "He came at you and you hit him in the head with your purse." I jumped back over to her and punched her in the nose. "He hit you in the face and you went down right where you are—don't move. Still with me?"

". . . yes . . ." she said through a haze of pain.

"Good." I went behind the desk and began opening the drawers, hoping to find a concealed weapon of some sort. I did, second drawer on the left, in a metal box that was unlocked. I removed the pistol and shoved it through my belt under my coat, then pressed Joyce's gun into Tick-Tock's hand. "He went for his gun and shot you in the shoulder." I hauled Tick-Tock's limp form from his chair, Joyce's gun still in his hand, and threw him on the floor beside her. "He came around after you went down and you kicked him in the balls."

I kicked Tick-Tock in the balls.

"He went down, and the two of you struggled with the gun." I placed her hands on the pistol as well. "You shot him twice, once in the chest, and then—" I put the gun up to Tick-Tock's face and pulled the trigger. Blood spattered Joyce's face and clothes and my gloves. I dropped their hands and the gun, then quickly removed my gloves and shoved them in my pockets. "You killed him in self-defense, Joyce. I came in here just in time to see the end of it, understand?"

". . . yes . . ."

"Can you remember all that?"

"Yes." She was recovering from the pain somewhat. This was one tough lady.

"I'll get rid of the bodies in your cellar later, don't worry about that. I hate to admit it, but I've got friends who have experience in that area." I scooped up her purse and removed all the credit chips, shoving them into my pockets. There was still enough junk inside—medicine bottles, makeup, checkbook, etcetera—to give it some good weight. "You're going to keep this money, Joyce, because you'll need it."

I heard the elevator bell.

She looked up at me, then at Brother Tick-Tock's body. "Why did you do this?"

"Because you're right, he didn't deserve to live . . . and every little boy deserves to see whether or not John Wayne rescues Natalie Wood."

She smiled at me, and as Sherwood and his men came running from the elevator, I went into the small room to untie the little boy whose childhood would not be stolen from him for the sake of false gods and their followers.

I held the child in my arms, and in the darkness I

wept, thinking, *I can feel you breathe like the ocean, your life burning bright, all the unlived moments before you; may that fire be your friend and the sea rock you gently.*

I don't do as much fieldwork these days; that I leave to Sherwood, who retired from the force a few years ago and came to work with us. Mostly I trace cyber-trails, gather info, make calls. Every once in a while I'll go on an assignment with Sherwood, but my conscience always manages to get in the way.

When at last it all becomes personal, you're no good in the field.

And I am a murderer whose greatest guilt is that he feels no remorse for his crime.

Jimmy and his mother are doing fine. I stop by their home frequently, and I'm glad to report it's a happy home.

Happy enough.

Joyce now has the mantel filled with photos of her and Jimmy. It looks like a family has lived their whole life there.

Jimmy loves his VCR. We have now watched *The Searchers* twenty-six times. He never gets tired of it.

Come to think of it, neither do I.

Amen to that, pilgrim.

THE WHITE CITY

by *Alan Brennert*

Alan Brennert is a Nebula award-winning author who has also worked in the television and film industries. He was a contributing writer and producer of the *The New Twilight Zone* television series. His work has also appeared in *The Magazine of Fantasy & Science Fiction* and other magazines. He lives in California.

I'VE never seen his face; his real face. Sometimes he wears one of those malleable FunFlesh masks, the kind kids wear on Halloween, its features molded into the likenesses of people I recognize vaguely if at all: Jeffrey Dahmer, John Wayne Gacy, Albert Fish. So long ago, such distant infamy. Sometimes he wears white robes and a squared-off hood, a ghostly evocation of someone he calls "Zodiac"—like all his heroes, a psychopath dead two centuries or more—and when I look through the ragged eyeholes of the hood, I see clear, blue, intelligent eyes; eyes that even seem for a moment warm, and friendly. And that's when I'm most afraid. That I'll never leave this place alive.

Today my captor is a dapper man in what looks like a nineteenth-century business suit—dark wool pants, vest, jacket, a derby hat atop a mustached face, a black

doctor's bag swinging from one hand. He stands in
the open doorway of my brightly-lit cell; smiles at me,
as I lie immobile on my cot.

"*Good* morning." Cheerful. Hail-fellow-well-met, I
think they used to call it. "Sleep well?"

Sleep? I sleep only when I can no longer stay
awake, when my exhaustion is greater than the tor-
ments of my body. Sometimes only a few minutes;
sometimes close to an hour; rarely longer, before the
pain wakes me again. But sleep *well?* I offer up an
obscenity to him, and he laughs what anyone else
might take for a good-natured laugh.

"Can't say I blame you, old man," he says, approaching. Even if the mag straps binding me here
were to suddenly fail, I doubt I'd have the strength to
attack him; he's seen to that. Above me the ceiling is
a jigsaw of video images barely three molecules thick,
dozens of angles and amplifications, all of the same
depressing subject: my own wasting, emaciated body.
Here a view of my swollen, nearly useless feet; there
a shot of sunken cheeks and shadowed eyes. How long
have I been here, like this? Four weeks? Five? There's
no telling. No windows, no sunlight, no way to mea-
sure the passage of days except in escalating degrees
of pain.

He is at my side now; he smells like apples, isn't
that strange? Above us I can see the crown of his hat
reflected in one of the video fragments. "Breakfast?"

He opens his little black bag, takes out a syringe,
presses it against my arm; with a hiss a nutrient solution penetrates my skin, finds its way into my blood-
stream. Electrolytes, amino acids, saline . . . just
enough to keep me alive and conscious, in delicate
equilibrium between life and death. . . .

Another smile. "Do you know who I am today?"

I don't know. I don't care. I close my eyes as he
tells me about somebody named H. H. Holmes, a
nineteenth-century physician whose Victorian home in
Chicago was a house of horrors—many of his victims

were lodgers in Holmes' mansion, dying in sealed rooms pumped full of poison gas, bodies dumped like so much laundry down long metal chutes and laid open like crayfish on dissecting slabs in the basement.

"Many of them were tourists," he says, reaching again into his medical bag. "This was 1893; Chicago was hosting the World Columbian Exposition—what was once known as a 'World's Fair.' Interesting to think of these hapless travelers as they rode the world's first Ferris Wheel, or watched a demonstration of Electricity, or marveled at the sparkling collection of buildings known as the 'White City'—marveling at the future! And when they return to their rented rooms, why, the future is waiting for them there, too, though not one that the Utopian architects of the Fair could possibly have anticipated. . . ."

He changes the fluid in his syringe with a casual dexterity that makes me wonder if he, like Holmes, is a doctor. Another jolt of injection; this time it is almost certainly not nutrients but the opposite, genetically engineered organisms designed to slowly eat away at specifically targeted organs—pancreas, liver, spleen. Or nannites that even now cluster inside the veins of my heart, deconstructing them slowly, stripping away cell by cell the inner layer, the connective tissue, the smooth muscle . . . even as other nannites work to keep my mind clear and unclouded, alert and aware of all that's happening to me. He explained as much to me early on, a bright darkness in his eyes as he detailed the microscopic tortures he's devised.

The cloud of pain which envelops me seems suddenly to grow sharper; stronger. As much as I don't want to, I cry out. My captor smiles an anaconda smile; starts to turn away.

"Kill me," I say, and he stops, looks back, eyes wide and innocent.

"But I have," he says, laughing, and then he's gone.

As the door slides shut, the mag straps automatically let go, and I'm free to move about the cell—to use the toilet, to pace the length of my ten by twenty foot cage. My feet are so swollen now that it's all I can manage to stagger to the bare commode squatting obscenely in the middle of the cell. Once, early on, I tried to outwit him—sleeping on the floor, hoping to evade the electromagnetic field which paralyzes most of my motor functions as I lay on the cot—only to discover that the field worked equally well no matter where I came to rest in this torture cell.

I sit on the toilet, voiding myself, knowing he is watching, knowing he derives pleasure from my humiliation and loss of privacy. Above me the video fragments mirror my movements—a tremor in my leg; the small movement of my rib cage as I take shallow breaths—recording them for my persecutor's future enjoyment. And I think of this record outliving me, the last mark I will leave on this world . . . and I start to cry. Tears of grief, and shame, and helpless anger. He enjoys this, too, I know . . . but I just can't stop myself.

I was a teacher. History; junior college. I think now that's why he chose me—someone who had at least a nodding acquaintance with the past, someone who could appreciate what was happening to him. Perhaps he was one of my old students, though he denies this. I was chosen, he claims, entirely at random—"within certain logistical parameters," including location, access, predictability of daily movements.

It was that predictability which no doubt made me such an appealing target. Spring Quarter, April: Nine o'clock to ten-thirty, Delacroix Hall, first floor, Nineteenth-Century European History; ten-thirty, up to the second floor, Interactive Study Group until noon, then lunch, either in the commissary or a restaurant somewhere on State Street; one o'clock, Gower Hall, Twentieth-Century American History until two-thirty, followed by Twenty-first Century until four, back to Delacroix for another Interactive Study Group until five, and then home.

I never saw his face then, either. I was on one of the quiet, shaded paths between Delacroix and Gower after my four o'clock study group when I felt the press of a blunt object in the small of my back, followed by a tingling sensation, followed by—oblivion. A neural suppressor, I imagine, shutting down the higher brain functions while handing over most motor control to him. If anyone saw us leave campus, all they would have glimpsed was the two of us walking together toward the parking structure—his arm, perhaps, draped across my shoulders in what appeared to be good fellowship but was in fact gentle guidance of my usurped body. And when I regained consciousness. . . .

I was here. In this windowless box, soundproofed, white walls neither cold nor warm to the touch, hidden nanovids refracting and reflecting my image above me. Am I above ground? Below? I'd guess below, a converted cellar perhaps, but I have no way of knowing for sure. In the middle of a city—like Dr. Holmes' murder castle—or in some rural corner far from urban sprawl? I have no idea.

I yelled for help. I yelled to be set free. I yelled until I was hoarse, until my hands were bloodied from pounding away at the steel door . . . and as I sank onto the cot, rubbing my bruised and battered hands, experiencing the first taste of pain in my captivity . . . the door slid open. I jumped to my feet, managing no more than two steps before the mag kicked in and I fell back onto the cot, helpless.

Then my captor appeared, towering above me . . . his Zodiac hood forbidding, frightening. The only parts of me I could move, obviously by his design, were my eyes and my mouth.

"Who are you? Why are you *doing* this?"

He squatted down beside me, his voice muffled by the fabric of the hood. "You're the history teacher," he said. "What comes to mind?"

"Please . . . I have a family—"

"Parents, brother, no wife, no children. Does the name Edward Gein mean anything to you? Kenneth Bianchi, Cleo Green, Heinrich Pommerencke?"

"No. I don't—"

"Albert DeSalvo? Fritz Haarmann? Coral Watts?"

"Who the hell *are* you, why am I—"

"You may not know the names, but perhaps you'll recognize the handiwork." Above us the video fragments shattered and reformed into a horrifying collage of death, torture, mutilation. Men, women, children, the sovereignty of their bodies violated by monsters the likes of which I could barely comprehend; though the implications for me were becoming clear.

"No," I said, my voice hoarse, "Jesus, you can't be— I mean, things like this don't *happen* anymore—"

"How do you know they don't?"

"Look," fighting to stay calm, to be rational, "it's not the twentieth century, for God's sake, you can't get *away* with this—"

I thought I saw a smile in those clear blue eyes. "Murder is not extinct in your White City."

At the time I had no inkling of what he meant by that. "No, of course not, but—the last *serial* murderer in the U.S. was, what, fifty *years* ago—?"

"Forty-three," he corrected me. "Theodore McCoy, killed and mutilated three women in Seattle, Washington; Tacoma; San Francisco." Voice calm, collected, as though he were a student in my classroom, pleased to offer up an answer to a question from his professor. Before I could point out the obvious, he beat me to it: "By examining the bodies of the three women— the pattern of mutilation, means of death, probable instruments—and comparing it to neural signatures of other known serial killers, FBI and local authorities were able to construct a neural profile of the killer. Signature tracking of the area yielded three close matches, one of whom turned out to be McCoy."

Maybe he wanted me to talk him out of it; maybe

I was supposed to play the role of teacher, or conscience. "Yes. Right," I said. "And that was before genescan. Today you can't even dispose of a single body without being found out, much less commit multiple murders without being—"

I felt a jolt in my arm. He had pulled a syringe from his robes and injected me with what turned out to be the first of his tiny agents. He stood.

His eyes seemed to smile again. "We'll see," he said, turning away, the door sliding open, and once again I was alone. Even as the mag straps let go, I felt a sharp stab in my chest. I cried out—my pain, soon to become my only companion in this cell, mirrored above me. And so it began.

It will end soon. I know that for certain. The small intruders in my system are thriving, multiplying, feasting on blood and bone; my body feels less and less my own, more and more merely a landscape on which the designs of others are forcibly writ. Soon this fragile biosphere will burst, the last battlements of flesh will be overwhelmed, and I will die.

I look back on my forty-odd years of life, and I try to visualize every woman I ever made love to. Julia, Colleen, Laurie, Mikaela. I try to block out the pain and conjure again the feel of their lips, the brush of their skin against mine. Chandra, Brianne, Mei . . . I could have married Mei, why didn't I? Could have had a son, a daughter, something that would have outlived me; I might not even *be* here if I had, my life not so proscribed and easily usurped, or at the least I'd be here thinking of someone I love, knowing I had lived a genuine *life* and not . . . whatever it is I have lived. Oh, God . . . Mei. Tears well in my eyes, I repeat her name over and over, wishing my words back in time, and for a moment I seem to be there, some quiet night at home with her, whispering to my younger self: *Marry her, you idiot! For God's sake ask her, ask her now!* But the young me doesn't hear or if he does doesn't believe, I lose sight of him amid the wrong turns and blind alleys of his future, my past . . . and I find myself once again here, alone, with tears in my eyes and a lover's name dying on my breath.

The door opens. To my surprise the mag straps do not activate, but I'm too weak even to sit up; it's all I can do just to turn my head and look up at my captor as he enters. His mask today is a clown's face, garish crescents of red and white around nose, mouth, cheeks. I've seen this one before. The leering face of some long-dead psychotic who killed by night, and made balloon animals for ailing children by day. What the hell did he call himself? "Pogo"?

For the first time, he sits down on the cot beside me. I wish desperately that I had the strength to reach up, to claw at him, wrestle him to the ground . . . but my body fails me, as he knew it would. He takes a small notebook from a pocket . . . places it beside me.

I look at it, then at him. "What?" An effort to force out even one word.

He produces a pen from another pocket; folds it into one of my hands. "In case there's anything you want to say. To . . . whomever." I must look incredulous, because he laughs and says, "I'm serious. There's nothing you can tell them that can hurt me, after all; you have no idea where you are, you've never seen my face. I have nothing to lose. Go on." He pushes the notebook closer to me, then stands up. Smiles impishly. "Have I ever lied to you?"

In moments he's left again. It takes an enormous effort just to roll over on my side; I reach for the notebook, open it. Blank pages stare out at me, beckoning with the promise of a last good-bye, apology, declaration of love—anything I wish, to whomever I wish.

Mei? Long married, mother of three . . . and not in a million years will I give this madman her name and address (assuming he doesn't already have them).

Who, then? I think of my father, my mother, regretting the years of unease and distance between us. My captor already knows their names, where they live . . . but the thought of giving him an excuse to contact them is too horrifying, I can't risk it.

And besides: I know why he's offered me this. Not for me, but for him: a grisly souvenir, a *memento mori*—a reminder of my own impending death, written in my own hand. His leering interest in whatever I might say rendering it unclean; worthless. I hurl the notebook away from me; it just barely makes it halfway across the room, where it falls open, its empty pages reflected in the video fragments above. Something satisfying about this: pages and screens staring blankly at one another, offering nothing for voyeuristic eyes.

As if in response to my action, something wet and cold seems to break loose inside me, and I scream as I realize that it is my life itself which has finally ruptured—whatever years I had left to me stolen by this ridiculous anachronism, this monster out of time.

"Bastard!" Where do I get the strength to shout, the breath to curse him? *"Bastard!"* The video images seem to recede from me, as I at long last make my escape from this place. "I'm your last victim!" I cry out, even as the walls of the cell seem to bend and constrict into a tube, a dark tunnel with no beginning and no end. He's succeeded in killing me, but I can take bleak comfort in knowing he won't kill another; that in this White City he reviles, *no one* can kill repeatedly and remain at large—and that someday death will come for him as it now comes for me. But oh, how beautiful it is! A light sings at the farthest end of the tunnel, a light I seem to ride like a wave; I am no longer flesh, nothing so perishable, I am photons riding a solar wind, riding *backward* into the blinding warmth of the sun, its bright beckoning disk growing larger with each thousandth of a second. . . .

Until . . . I suddenly begin to slow. The sun becomes

less perceptibly bigger; a hundredth of a second more, and it ceases to grow larger at all. I've . . . stopped.

The sun now starts to move away from me, or me from it, the solar wind reversing direction; I find myself hurled away from its warmth and light and, voiceless, I try to scream in protest, begging to go back, to go—home? I drop below *c* and feel myself growing heavier, photons reverting to gross flesh, thought changing to voice, *Take me back, take me back,* as the walls of the tunnel close in around me, and the sun, long set, gives me over to the night.

The light returns slowly. Not as bright as before— but just as warm, and just as welcome. My eyes open, but I have to shield them against the glare. I'm staring into . . . the sky?

And then I notice . . . the pain. Or rather, the lack of it. Impossible as it seems, nothing *hurts* inside; and I know, as only someone who has experienced it can know, that nothing *is* inside . . . that I am alone in my own body once again.

I sit up; look around me. Trees, grass, a ribbon of concrete threading through shady arbors. My briefcase lies on the ground not three feet away, ungraded term papers scattered around it. With a start I realize where I am.

On campus. That building over there—my God, it's Gower Hall! I jump to my feet, my heart pounding. Jesus—can it *be?* Am I really here? I roll back the sleeves of my jacket; my shirt. My skin is unbroken, unscarred. I take a deep breath of air and hold it. My lungs are strong; my heart races. My God, I am— I'm *alive.*

I break into laughter—relieved, delighted laughter. Was the nightmare only that—a dream, a delusion? It seemed so real—so hideously, perversely real. But clearly it wasn't. I think suddenly of Mei, of my parents, of all the paths I am free to take again, the blind alleys I newly dedicate myself to avoid. Another chance: I have another chance!

I pick up my briefcase, shuffle the fallen papers back into it, snap it closed. I fairly well jaunt along the path; I feel like breaking into dance, or song. As a compromise I start humming, which turns again into laughter. A short distance from Gower Hall I pause at an automated kiosk offering free copies of the college paper. I press the screen, opting for hard copy rather than audio or electronic. A copy slides out, and I eagerly scan the masthead, looking for the date—April 2nd, wasn't it?—that will serve as the final confirmation that my nightmare was just that.

The date on the paper . . . is May 14th.

My heart skips a beat. I drop the paper to the ground.

I feel the press of a blunt object in the small of my back.

The scream dies in my throat as my body seizes up and I find myself quickly paralyzed. This time, however, he doesn't shut down all of my higher brain functions. Trapped inside a body which no longer responds to my wishes, I can see him out of the corner of my eye as he steps up beside me—feel him as he drapes a friendly arm across my shoulders.

"Good *morning*." His eyes are bright, warm, and friendly. "Feeling better?" Better. Yes. Amazing what nannites can do, isn't it? Heal as well as hurt. Reclaim that which seemed . . . forever lost. . . .

My legs begin to move of their own accord. I can't stop them. Can't do anything.

I was right, and I was wrong. Wrong in thinking that he'll be caught; that his pattern of murder—the bodies and depredations and choice of victims—creating a profile that will eventually, inevitably, lead the authorities to him. That won't happen. He's found a way around it, a way to kill and kill and never, ever get caught, never betray himself.

I'm your last victim, I told him. That much was right. Last . . . and only. Now and forever.

I try to scream, but, in a touch of characteristic irony, he's rewired my neurals so that any expression of fear or panic turns into a smile, or a laugh.

"Yes," he says, smiling, patting me on the back, "good to see you, too." He ushers me into the parking structure. I laugh again. And again. And again. My laughter fills the parking garage, and my companion, ever amiable, laughs with me.

SETTING FREE THE DAUGHTERS OF EARTH

by Peter Crowther

Peter Crowther is the editor or coeditor of nine anthologies and the coauthor (with James Lovegrove) of the novel *Escardy Gap.* Since the early 1990s, he has sold some seventy short stories and poems to a wide variety of magazines and chapbooks on both sides of the Atlantic. He has also recently added two chapbooks, *Forest Plains* and *Fugue on a G-String,* to his credits. His review columns and critical essays on the fields of fantasy, horror, and science fiction appear regularly in *Interzone* and the *Hellnotes* internet magazine. He was appointed to the Board of Trustees of the Horror Writers' Association. He lives in Harrogate, England, with his wife and two sons.

"Oaths are but words, and words but wind."
—Samuel Butler

THE addict hunkered down beneath the bridge, leaned into the support, and blew warm air into his cupped hands. His breath came out like steam, pooled around his hands, and then drifted slowly up against the blackened stonework of the bridge, weaving its way through the filigreed metalwork of the railings to mingle with the exhaust fumes of the occasional overhead traffic.

Somewhere off in the distance, beyond the towering Residential Blocks that littered the Edge, sirens sounded—maybe a traffic accident, another Midtown thruway littered with fallen debris. The addict knew it had to be Midtown because the Prowlcars didn't come out here often—hadn't come out here regularly for a long time, long before the addict had become hooked.

He looked over his shoulder, surveying the litter-strewn dry canal bottom whose bank he now crouched upon, and stared out into the night, watching the pirouetting light beams scratch the sky around the Business Blocks, where the surrounding blackness was already lightened by the glow of life, a glow that never went out. Not like the old days, the days he had heard folks talk about around the occasional fires here on the Edge, days when work stopped on an evening, slowed down on a weekend, that mythical pause in commercial motion when all but the most essential services ceased for a day.

Sunday, it had been called.

The seventh day. A day of rest.

But Sunday had long gone.

Now time was marked strictly by the Julian calendar, a five-digit identification that did not recognize individual days or their characteristics.

His mother, before she died, had told him all about Sunday, and about the other days, information passed down to her by *her* mother who had had it passed down to her by *her* mother!

About how his mother's great-grandfather, in that long-ago mythical time before the addict was born, would go out for A Drink on Friday, the sixth day, with his friends.

And about how, on a Thursday—which had been the day before Friday—the two of them, his mother's great-grandparents, would sometimes go out to see a

moving picture show . . . in the days before TAP came
in. And about how some folks had gone to Church
on Sunday.

That was long gone, too.

And she had told him about how the different
months used to have different characteristics.

Months? he had asked.

His mother had smiled and ruffled his hair. Months
had been groups of four weeks, sometimes four and
a half, which occurred at different times of the year.
The seasons, his mother had called them, speaking
their names reverently . . . though she had never
known them herself.

The addict could remember their names—summer,
winter, autumn, spring—but not their order. It didn't
matter.

The seasons, his mother had explained, had been
differentiated by the weather. Sometimes it was hot.
Sometimes it was cold. And sometimes it was getting
close to being one or the other, but not quite there yet.

One season, his mother had been told, the sun
shone and people got out of doors, walking around or
lying on the grass, drinking in the sunshine, feeling it
recharge their bodies.

Then, in another season, folks started to wrap up
more, had started to wear more clothes, and the trees
had started losing their leaves.

And still another one, the one after that one, snow
would fall out of the sky. Snow . . . even the word
had a magical resonance to it. In reality it was rain,
frozen into tiny white cereal flakes of coldness, that
fluttered down and lay on the ground, blown by the
wind into banks and drifts of white against buildings
and fences. The addict did not know snow. But he
hoped that, one day, he would see it . . . watch it
falling from the sky.

And then, last of all, she had told him about how,
after all the coldness and the snow, the temperature

would ease off and plants would start to sprout new shoots, the trees would grow new leaves, and people would rummage through closets and wardrobes and old chests in the hallway, sifting through piles of clothing until they found the light stuff, the stuff with hardly any sleeves or hardly any pants legs . . . getting ready for the heat.

But that had gone, too. All gone.

Everything was gone.

The snow, the wind, the heat.

No days. No seasons. No weather. No beliefs.

People worked. And people TAPped.

And that was it.

For those who did not work, those lost souls who had drifted out into the dead areas of the Edge, on the periphery of the dome-covered Cities that now covered the inhospitable world, a brief nomadic existence was on offer . . . brief because they invariably drifted out of the domes, pulled by the lure of the open land glimpsed through the murky Plexiglas. Then there was only lingering death. But there was a sense of the way things used to be . . . if you were interested and if you could be bothered to look for it.

On this night, as it was with every night, the addict looked.

Still crouched down, the addict carefully stepped out from beneath the bridge and breathed in, fighting off the urge to cough.

Once free of the overhang, he looked up and saw a skybus negotiating the tight corner of Vicar Lane and The Headrow, a handful of empty emotionless faces staring out of the fluorescent-lit interior and down into the gloom of the streets and the darkened buildings. The bus stopped against a loading platform and a stooped figure carefully stepped down. The addict imagined he could hear the sibilant rush of the pneumatic doors—*ssssshhhh!*—opening and closing, and then the bus moved off into the stream of inter-

mittent traffic, steam jets pumping from its rear and
its underside.

The stooped figure watched the bus for a minute
and then turned away, lugging what looked like two
huge mallbags, limping onto the railed walkway that
traversed the residential block.

The addict watched the figure go and then allowed
his eyes to drift down the building, floor by floor, until
he was staring straight at a man sitting on the stone
armguard of the bridge. The addict was about to duck
out of sight, but it was clear that the man was not
interested in him. The man wasn't interested in anything at all, save the current running from the box in
his lap—the addict assumed that was where the box
was although he couldn't actually see it—and up the
wires to the terminal bolts grafted into his temples.

The man was a TAPper or a Frankie, oblivious of
everyone and everything while his bolts were being
fed, thrusting whatever particular images and sensations made up his own particular pleasure.

A cab passed overhead, its underside light sweeping
the bridge and then the ground before returning to
the bridge and fixing momentarily on the man. An
airhorn sounded—*horrrk!*—as the cab wheeled left
and passed over the addict, moving toward the dense
forest of residential blocks closer to the dome edge.

The addict turned to watch it go, watched its tail
lights blinking, and, just for a second, before the cab
turned again to move along Boar Lane, he saw the
distant reflection of its headlights in the Plexiglas between two blocks on the corner of Boar Lane and
Commercial Street. Then the glass was dull again, unseen, just a wall of darkness at the end of Commercial Street.

He looked back at the bridge and saw the man
shaking, watched him near the end of his hit. The man
would be in heaven for a few hours now, swirling
down the blissful aftermath of the hit until reality

crowded in again and he would have to seek out another supply.

The addict shrugged his coat up on his shoulders and scrambled up the side of the embankment onto the walkway. Everyone had his or her way of dealing with life in the domes, particularly those who lived on the Edge . . . his or her way of escaping the way things really were.

But some methods of cerebral escape were considered to be even more heinous than the artificial stimuli that could be scored for a few credits from any street corner or in the shadowed recesses of the second-cellar bars in Downtown. Of these—of all the recreational drugs openly tolerated (and even encouraged) by an increasingly dependent society—one and only one was completely forbidden. And this was the substance favored by the addict.

The penalty for being caught with his particular tipple was termination.

No questions, no excuses, no trial. Just lights out, and good-bye.

He shrugged his shoulders and stared along the walkway.

The sound of the city was stronger up here, so strong that the addict could barely hear the man on the bridge coming to the end of his hit. But he could still hear it just a little, and he hurried his step to get out of range.

The air smelled of smoke, cold, and fuel.

The puddles on the walkway and the rain-slicked ledges of the buildings were all rainbow-hued, the constant drizzle of fuel particles having eaten into the surface to come out with the water and swirl in eddies of various shapes and colors. The addict looked up into the darkness. He couldn't see the dome's ceiling, let alone the sky beyond, but he could feel the gentle drizzle from the sprinkler system, drifting down over the town.

Now and again, when the system broke down, the

authorities would send rainships circling the building tops. He had seen one once, coming down onto the dock at the filling station across town, its bulbous tanks gleaming in the fluorescent lights, its contents spread across the streets.

With crops grown outside the dome in separate covered areas and all water for domestic use fed into the city, rain was something the population didn't actually need any longer. The official line was that the daily spraying was a token gesture to simpler times: the consensus, however, was that the nightly downpours were used to quell disenchantment and insurrection.

Sometimes, when he was feeling particularly low and particularly bold, the addict thought about leaving the city.

Sometimes, at night, lying in his cot, wrapped up in his coats, he dreamed of the deadly open spaces beyond the Plexiglas.

He dreamed of dusty roads winding between grassy hills, and of clouds silently drifting across an endless blue sky.

He dreamed of wooden shacks and picket-fenced garden areas, of clear lakes and a vast ocean lapping a sandy shoreline. He even dreamed of gleaming, brightly-colored automobiles humming along rolling highways, attached to the roads themselves instead of flying around the building-sides, and he dreamed of panting trains hammering along a ribbon of track that snaked between frozen-rain-topped mountains . . . and grass . . . and forests.

He dreamed these dreams because of his addiction. And his addiction was a direct result of those dreams.

A voice spoke from the darkness.

The addict stopped and squinted into the gloom beneath the canopy of a block entrance, his hands out of his pockets and ready for confrontation.

"I said, you *need* anything?" the voice said, the words accompanied by a thick waft of smoke pouring out into the street.

"Uh-uh," the addict lied. He did not want to detail his problem without first seeing the identity of the person asking the question. There were too many dummy-dealers out in the darkened streets, Prowlers looking to pull you in for few hours . . . to spend some time in the Prowlhouses. In there, amidst the old tried and tested methods of persuasion, the Prowlers could find out all they wanted to know.

A man stepped out of the entrance, the darkness peeling away from him like a cellophane covering. The man took a deep draw on his pipette and, throwing his head back, blew out more smoke, making a circle of his mouth at the end to cause smoke rings, which shimmered and then dissipated.

"What you need?" the man asked.

The addict took a step back. "I said I don't need anything."

The man nodded. He removed the pipette from his mouth, wound it up until the bowl was fixed into the center and then placed a shiny clip around the stem. He dropped the apparatus into an already bulging pocket in his ankle-length coat and said, "Everybody need *some*thing."

"Not me."

The man nodded but carried on. "You want uppers or downers? You want head games?"

He leaned forward, and the addict shuffled back some more.

"I not hurt you," the man said, "just looking see you been fitted . . . see if you a TAPper."

The addict subconsciously lifted a hand to the skin of his left temple and then dropped the arm to his side. "Well, I haven't," he said. "There's no such thing as Total Audience Participation. It's a con."

The man nodded, not wanting to get into a conversation. Maybe not even knowing what this guy was talking about. "Just looking, too, see you Prowler," he added, although he had clearly decided that such was not the case.

The addict raised his arms in supplication. "Do I look like a Prowler?" he asked.

The man considered this and then said, "*Every*body look like Prowler."

The addict relaxed. "Well, I'm not," he said.

"I can see." The man leant back against the wall. "So, maybe you need smoke, little weed maybe."

"No," said the addict.

"Glue capsules? DNA droppers, wood-burners, sharkfins?"

"Never use 'em," said the addict.

"How's 'bout some dreamboats—got new supply in this week, help you sleep for month, sleep so long you wake up starving. Got some LDs, too—keep you going for 'nother month, never need to sleep, laugh all time."

"Don't need to go Long Distance," the addict said. "And I get all the sleep I need. Every night. Like a baby."

The man gave out a raucous laugh. "Ain't nobody sleep like baby, man," he said.

"Well, I do."

"Okay," the man said with a carefree shrug. "You don't need nothing, I might 'swell go."

"Wait." The addict looked back along the path. A limo-car was passing overhead, a couple of levels up, its headlight beams splaying the embankment where he had just been. The TAPper from the bridge had gone. Maybe he had fallen or even jumped, his head filled with ejaculation thoughts, his mind convinced that he would survive the drop . . . or maybe hoping that he wouldn't.

"Hey, listen," the man was saying, "I got places—"

"Okay," the addict said. "Show me."

"Show you? Show you *what?*"

He shrugged. "Everything. I want to see it all."

Now it was the man's turn to be suspicious. "You *sure* you not Prowler?" He drew the word out, emphasizing the two syllables, "prow" and "lurrr."

The addict shook his head and stepped closer to the man. He could smell the man's dirt now, could smell his sweat and the smoke on his clothes, the piss stains on his plastic coverall pants, the oil and grime in his matted hair . . . which the addict now saw was gathered into two small pigtails resting on the upturned collar of his coat, each one tethered with a tiny length of tubing. He had stepped so close that he was touching the man, could feel the man's body up against his own, could feel the man's hand trapped against his own stomach.

"I just want to be sure before I make a decision."

"Yeah?"

The addict nodded. "Call it window-shopping. I don't know what I want until I see it." He looked into the man's face, stared into the hooded squinting eyes. "You can understand that," he said.

The man waited for a few seconds, watching the addict, and then straightened up. He lifted his right arm, pulling it up between them, and showed a long bladed stiletto tube-knife, a capsule already loaded into the see-through trigger guard. He smiled and flipped the safety. A sheath unfurled along the blade and the guard slid into the handle. The addict's eyes were wide open.

"Had be sure," the man said. "You coming on strong."

The addict nodded and gave a shrug, watching the man drop the tube-knife into his coat pocket, heard it clunk against the pipette.

"Okay," the man said, unfastening the toggle-catches down the front of his coat, "take look." He pulled the two flaps open. "Take *good* look."

Somewhere behind him in the night, the addict heard air horns. They sounded like he imagined humpbacked whales might sound, or dolphins, swimming lazily beneath a dark sky, not fully knowing where they were going or even where they had been . . . only that they *were*.

It was a sound of exhilaration and of simply being.

But it was also something else. It was a fanfare for
the contents of the man's coast, each item held into
place against the lining by carefully sewn straps and
inlaid pockets. It was true, the addict thought, his eyes
jumping from one attachment to the next. You really
could get anything here, here in this shadowed entrance to a seedy residential block, with the rain falling
in a thin spray. He allowed his eyes to wander, drinking in the sights inside the man's coat in the passing
overhead glare of a limocab.

There were gaudily-colored packets, shining phials
and glow-in-the-dark tubes, and alongside them,
against the man's right armpit—the smell!—were electrical bolt-leads with cushioned clamps; and long,
winding pipettes and smoking bulbs; long-nosed syrin-
ges and dum-dum needle-heads; speed-dipped nipple-
pins, testosterone pustules, and a whole array of penile
and labia adornments and sex embellishments.

Against the other armpit were sublimated chest-
pads, toe-capsules for a guaranteed slow climb, and
heavy-duty army surplus amphetamine suppositories
for the instant peak.

Down around the man's upper thighs an array of
bottles hung suspended from his plastic coveralls by
the slimmest of threads, their contents like the sweets
of old, varying colors and shapes and sizes . . . SUN-
SHINE YELLOWS, one label proclaimed; MEADOW
GREENS boasted another; BLUE DOWNS said a third, all
in the same shaky writing.

Some were cylindrical capsules, mostly for anal or
vaginal insertion, and of the oral varieties some were
flat and circular while others were square or cuboid
to delay movement into the stomach.

A sewer-cover rattled over to the right of them and
steam bellowed from the depths beneath. At the same
time, a distant siren wailed and someone howled to
the night, the aggression of the single drawn-out cry

quickly dissipating into a deep-throated sob of anguish. The cry was abruptly cut off.

"You see something?" the man asked.

The addict turned back from looking along the deserted walkway and shook his head. "Just a little jumpy," he said.

The man shook his head in exasperation. "No, I mean you *see* something?" He let go of one side of his opened coat and pointed to the rows of bottles and packets and artificial stimulants. "You see something *here!*"

"No," the addict said sadly. "You have nothing I need."

The man grunted and fastened his coat. "What you need, then? I get it for you. What you need?"

The addict stared at the shadowed outline of the man's head, wondering if it were safe to tell him. He looked back along the walkway, saw a news broadcast and share information feeding its was silently around one of the Residential Blocks, and breathed in deeply. Looking back, he said, "Pages."

The man took a step back against the doorway.

"You said," the addict reminded the man. "You said you could get me what I needed. Well, I need pages."

The man moved quickly out of the doorway and stood in front of the addict on the walkway, his face now exposed to the dim light, his eyes wide open. "You mad," the man said. "No pages." He waved his hands to underline the statement. "No pages," he said again, to underline the underline.

"You said." The addict reached into his back pocket with one hand and pulled out a thick wad of credit notes. With the other, he reached down between his legs, flipped open the Velcro prosthetic flap on his left upper thigh and produced an old Prowler gun, its greased-up snub-nose coated in talcum powder.

The man raised his hands. *"Prowler!"* he whispered.

"No, I'm not a Prowler," the addict said.

The man pointed. "Prowler *gun.*"

"Yes, it is a Prowler *gun,* but I'm not a *Prowler.*" He waved the credits, wafting them in front of the man's face. "I will pay you," he said, spreading the words out so that the man would be able to understand.

"Pages bad."

"Yes, pages are dangerous," the addict agreed. "If you get *caught.* We will not get caught." He pushed the wad of notes back into his coat pocket and pulled out three forties. He reached out and stuffed these inside the lapel of the man's coat. Then he slipped the gun into his other pocket, raised both hands to show that they were completely empty. "I pay you well."

The man was clearly considering his chances . . . wondering whether to break for it, to run a zigzag path along the walkway, risking being shot in the back for—how much? he pulled the notes from his lapel and looked . . . 120 credits—when maybe he could get more. Maybe much more.

"You come," he said at last, pocketing the credits as he turned and started to walk.

The addict followed.

In all his days and nights of wandering the City, the addict had never been this way. It was as though the way was a special secret way, one which could only be traversed at a certain time on a certain day.

There was a strange sentience to the darkened walkways, and the pair moved carefully and slowly, feeling the dank silent doorways and the hooded windows sightlessly following their passage. The addict listened for signs of movement amidst the shadows but heard only the sound of his feet and those of his guide, occasionally echoing on girders, and occasionally thudding on stone flagging or rotting boardwalks.

The man led the addict into parts of Downtown that he had not realized existed, and it was not until they had been walking for several minutes that the addict noticed that the sounds of the city had disappeared.

He halted for a moment, and the man in front stopped also, turning to look at him through the gloom. "Okay?" he whispered.

"Listen," said the addict.

The man cocked his head to one side and then to the other. "Don't hear nothing," he said.

"That's right," said the addict. "No sounds."

"Good," came the response.

"No," the addict said. "There are no sounds of *any*thing."

The man appeared to consider this. "Good," he said again and, turning sharply, he resumed the trek.

Along they went, then down twisting narrow steps that led to a thin walkway along a culvert, its sides curving steeply to meet below a silent stretch of still water.

They walked along the side, trailing their left hands across the wall as they passed, leaning slightly to avoid the feeling of falling . . . or of wanting to jump. Beneath a curved stone bridge, they came to more steps, this time going up. The man ran up the steps two at a time, his coat-tails wafting behind him, and the addict followed, pleased to be leaving the culvert behind.

At the top of the steps they turned sharp right along a narrow street between what appeared to be warehouses. The road here was cobbled and uneven, its surface shiny with water and slick with something else. Now there was a smell.

The addict breathed in deeply.

The scent of decay and oldness was at once repellent and attractive. He thought it might be like the smell of the sea.

At the end of the street they turned left, the man glancing over his shoulder to make sure the addict was still there. The addict suspected that the man could not care less either way, and, as they continued, he half-expected the man to make a break for it. He wondered what he would do if that happened. He had absolutely no idea where they were.

A little way along another street, that sloped gently downhill, the man stopped and moved to the side where he stopped and pressed his back against the wall.

"Are we there yet?" the addict asked, pausing for breath.

"Where?" the man asked.

The addict shrugged. "Wherever it is that we're going."

The man did not respond. Instead, he backed along the wall until he reached a section of boarding. He backed onto the boarding and began to tap with his knuckles, beating out a discordant rhythm that seemed to go on and on. After a few seconds, the addict thought that the man was simply playing for time . . . that the rapping was a nervous tic . . . but then he stopped.

The addict sensed that they were now waiting for something.

He listened.

Then, there it was . . . a distant and faint rapping, a faraway syncopated melody of hand on wood. It came from behind the boarding.

The man rapped again. And waited.

A sudden litany of noise sounded, and stopped.

The man stepped aside and waved for the addict to join him against the wall. As he stepped forward, the addict heard a faint scratching rasp, metal on metal, from behind the door. He leaned back against the wall and waited, hardly daring to breathe.

At the far end of the alley a figure appeared, seeming to step straight out of the wall itself. Without moving his back from the wall, the addict craned forward to see if he could discern some kind of door but the wall seemed to go on right to the end of the street.

The figure jogged noiselessly across the street, where it disappeared momentarily, folding itself into the shadows. Then it reemerged and jogged to the end of the street, its bulbous head darting first one way and then the other, checking the street that crossed the end of the alley for any signs of movement. The figure came back and stood for a few seconds looking down at the addict and the dealer. Then, with a short wave of an arm, it backed up into the shadows.

"Is he waving at us?" the addict whispered.

The dealer shook his head and pointed down the alley, away from the waving figure.

The addict looked around and saw a second figure, its head as huge and unwieldy as the first, stepping back into the shadows. The wave had clearly been some kind of signal, perhaps confirming that the streets were clear of Prowlers, and the addict waited quietly for further developments. He did not have long to wait.

The rasping noise came again, louder this time as though whoever or whatever was making it no longer felt such a need for stealth. The noise grew louder still until it stopped with a dull thud. Then came a metallic jingle and the sound of keys being inserted and turned to give a solid thunk.

The dealer stepped away from the wall and held out his hand to the addict. "Credits," he said. "Give to me."

Momentarily wrong-footed by the sudden use of the preposition, the addict pulled out his wad of notes without thinking and peeled off five.

The dealer took them, gave them a quick flick and shook his head. "More."

"How much more?" the addict asked. "I haven't even seen anything yet."

The wood paneled boarding began to rise.

"Many pages in there," the dealer hissed, nodding to the rising boarding. "Give ten like others."

"Which others? You brought other people here?"

"No," the dealer snapped. "Like other *notes*." He patted his coat pocket.

"Forties!" The addict made a quick mental calculation. "That's more than five hundred credits," he said.

The other man thrust the notes he already had into his pocket and then jabbed his empty hand out again. "Yeah, right. Give."

The addict counted off the forties and placed them in the dealer's hand. The man thrust his payment into his coat pocket and ran off down the street, his steps echoing through the gloom.

Turning around, the addict watched as the boarding reached the top of the surrounding brick and stonework and stopped. The addict frowned. There had only been a wall behind the boarding. He was about to turn and shout to one of the shadowy figures at either end of the street when the wall shimmered and another figure stepped through it and out onto the pavement.

Before he stepped out of the shadows, the addict transferred the old Prowler gun from his pocket to the prosthetic flap on his upper thigh.

The new figure wore plastic coveralls and a large bulbous helmet. Holding the gun steady, its muzzle pointing straight at him, the figure lifted its free arm and flicked a button on the helmet. Amidst a blur of crackling static, a deep male voice said, "Who was he?"

"Who?"

"Your friend. The guy ran off?"

The addict shrugged. "Dealer. He brought me here. I asked him."

"Why'd you do that?"

"I wanted something he didn't have."

"What was that?"

"Pages," the addict said. "I need some pages."

"You carrying?"

The addict shook his head.

"Lemme check."

The addict lifted his hands and fell forward against the wall while the man frisked him.

"Okay," the man said. He turned slightly and looked up the street. "Hill . . . see anything? That other guy gone?" he said. The addict looked up at the figure at the top end of the street and saw it walking down towards them. Clearly, they were communicating by some sort of shortwave system.

The figure with the weapon turned to the other end of the street. The deep voice said, "How 'bout you Brooks? Things look okay?"

The addict turned and saw the third figure walking toward them from the lower end. It waved an arm.

"Seems you okay," the deep voice said.

The addict nodded, fighting back his excitement. "I am. I just need some pages."

The man hefted the weapon onto his shoulder and said, "Okay. Walk through the wall." He raised an arm and pointed. "Merry . . . switch it on. Our guest is coming through."

The addict stepped up to the wall, hesitated and then stepped forward. There was a brief blurring and the addict was inside . . .

. . . in another world.

He looked ahead and he looked upward.

He looked to the left and he looked to the right.

He even looked down.

And he breathed in the smell.

Around him and above him and below him were metal gantries, walkways similar to the one on which he now stood, stretching forward and crisscrossing each other, layer upon layer, tier upon tier, with each one traversed by silent people, men and women, each dressed in a similar garb of green and white, sweater and pants. To either side of them, be they up or down or to left or right, set back behind protective rails, were huge piles of paper sheets, littered with colored marking cards jutting out sometimes at angles and sometimes straight ahead or at 90 degrees to one side. Each pile was held in place by what appeared to be plastic sidings, their sides a graffiti mosaic of scribbled

writing and accompanying numbers, the numbers occasionally crossed through and new numbers scribbled alongside.

"Anything in particular you have in mind?"

The first man had followed the addict through the
wall and was standing just behind him to the left. He
had removed his helmet and was standing with his
weapon propped against his right shoulder.

The addict shook his head, unable to speak.

He breathed in again, closed his eyes, and analyzed
the smell.

It was simply paper, aging paper, and maybe the
sweet underlying waft of metal and oil and wood
and plaster.

But it was more than that to the addict, much more.

The smell was an olfactory amalgam of words and
phrases, knowledge and ideas, dialogue and thoughts.
It was the largest collection of history the addict had
ever seen, larger even than he had ever dreamed
about, dreamed about in the quietest moments of the
loneliest days and nights huddled tightly in his cot.

Here were snippets of stories and articles, sections
of treatises and criticisms, chapters of opinion and belief. Vowels and consonants, prefixes and suffixes,
prepositions and adverbs, nouns and adjectives. . . .

The accumulated smell of the words came at him in
a tumult, soared up his nostrils into his brain in a
flood of imagined images.

The vast emptiness of space . . . the swirling cold
depths of the oceans . . . the ancient monuments long
forgotten to today's diluted version of humankind.

Though he had not yet stepped forward to glance
at even one of the millions—perhaps billions—of
pages torn from the old books, the addict knew it was
all here: Dickens, Homer, Tolstoy, Shakespeare . . .
Melville, Bradbury, Updike, King. The great literary
minds of every century in the planet's history gathered
together under the one roof—he looked up again and
saw that it was a composite of roofs, a cavernous cov-

ering that had, at one time, protected perhaps a whole range of warehouses.

"Wow!" he said, unable to think of anything else.

"Quite a collection," the man ventured.

"Quite a collection," the addict agreed. He pushed his tongue against the back bicuspid on the right and swallowed the fractured enamel. Then he bit down on the tiny microchip button, felt the brief tingle of vibration of the homing signal.

The man stepped forward and looked at him, frowning. "You okay?"

The addict swallowed and smiled, thumped his chest as though he had indigestion, eyebrows raised in apology.

"It always gets people, the first look," said the man, nodding that he understood.

"Hey, I'm fine. Absolutely fine."

"So, what's your poison?" The man smiled and nodded to the walkway straight ahead of them. "That way is mostly twentieth-century literature. Same for the next two tiers down. Most come at twenty credits a page, six for one hundred. You buy more, we can do a deal."

"Right," the addict said. "A deal. We'll definitely have to do a deal."

"The next three tiers up are nonfiction, philosophy, science, religion. The two after that have classical works, including poetry, and sheet music."

"Sheet music?"

The man shrugged. "The words and notes to the old songs? I dunno. Not my bag. Not any of it."

The addict looked puzzled. "You don't . . . you don't use any of this stuff?"

"Nah." The man shook his head vehemently to emphasize the point. "Don't see the attraction. Just words and stuff. Doesn't mean anything."

The addict nodded and smiled. "The daughters of earth."

"Say again?"

" 'I am not so lost in lexicography, as to forget that words are the daughters of earth, and that things are the sons of heaven.' Doctor Johnson said that, almost three hundred years ago."

"Yeah, right." The man frowned momentarily, and then his face lightened. "You like all this stuff, huh?"

He turned back and walked to the rail, leaned on it and looked down. "Yes, I like all this stuff." He scanned the myriad pages before him. "Must've taken a long time," he said, "stripping all these pages out of the original books."

"Sure did. Not many books left after the wars, and a lot of folks who, like you, feel they need to drink it all in." The man moved up alongside the addict and leaned over the rail. "When you have one book and maybe a thousand customers, you gotta think of ways to satisfy the demand."

"Sure," the addict agreed.

"Could have sold the whole book for maybe fifty credits, which is pretty much all anyone can afford. Maybe one hundred for the more popular ones—the ones folks remembered reading—but the supply isn't infinite. The demand is infinite, but not the supply. You know what I mean?"

"I surely do," the addict said.

"So we strip 'em out."

The addict tried not to let the man see him wince.

"That way, six hundred-page book gives three hundred sheets; three hundred sheets at twenty credits apiece gives—"

"Six thou."

"Right. Six thousand credits. Against, what? Against fifty or one hundred."

"It's a case of simple economics," the addict said. "Commerce."

"You got it in one."

"It's not a new concept."

"Say again?"

"They used to do it in the old days, the dealers,

guys like you." He turned around and leaned back against the rail. "They see the demand and feed it. Used to be that way with comic books."

The man frowned. "They the ones with pictures?"

"They're the ones," the addict said, smiling, jabbing a finger at the man. "Superhero stuff, stuff like Superman, Batman, all that stuff. So few of them survived the Second World War, they became collectors' items—we're talking, what? Two hundred years ago? Two fifty?"

The man shrugged. "No idea."

"No, well, folks bought them for crazy prices, squirreled them away in protective bags. Each time one was sold at such and such a price, the dealer whacked it up the next time he got a copy of that mag."

"You know a lot about this stuff."

He shrugged. "It's a hobby."

"Everyone needs a hobby," the man said, pointing to the two bolts fixed into the skin of his temples. He gave a big grin.

The addict returned the grin, and said, "Then it was books. First editions, signed limited editions . . . all that stuff. At first, it was just the signature that made the limiteds special. Then they came with extra chapters, special introductions, special afterwords.

"Then folks got tired of that and turned their attention to the old paperbacks." The addict whistled and waved his hand as though he'd burned his fingers. "Those were crazy days."

"Hey . . . you weren't there? You couldn't have been."

"No, I wasn't there. But I've spoken with people who have spoken with people who knew people who knew people . . . you know what I mean? Time marches on."

The man shuffled side to side impatiently. "Ain't *that* the truth."

The addict ignored him and carried on. "Condition was always a big thing, but then, when all the great condition books and magazines had been bought or had simply deteriorated into a lesser condition, the prices for those went through the roof." He paused, nodding. " 'Course, you have to remember that people had different levels of spending power then. It wasn't governed by the State the way it is now."

"Right," the man said, his voice indicating that he didn't really follow what this guy was going on about.

"Yeah, and then the shit really hit the fan after the wars. Every country—and I mean *every* country—decimated. Billions wiped out over the space of the first eight, nine years, and billions more over the next fifty or so. The new global State didn't want folks looking to the old books and the old ways, didn't want them making themselves dissatisfied . . . questioning the status quo. So they took steps to remedy the situation. They got rid of whatever books they could find."

"That the Blanking?"

"Yes, that was the Blanking." He turned and looked at the piles of pages towering the aisles, a cityscape of white monoliths, and he dreamed of a life which could be long enough to read them all. "Have you ever wondered," the addict said, his voice low, "if it hurts them?"

"What?"

He looked over his shoulder and nodded at the piles. "If tearing out the pages hurts the books."

There was a silence. Then the man said, "Look, I don't know what you're talking about, mister. What say you just tell me which part you're—"

"I'm interested in all of it," the addict said.

"Well, okay, just tell me what you want."

The microchip in his mouth buzzed once and then again.

It was time.

Turning around from the rail, the addict smiled and said, "I want it *all*."

The man frowned, gave a half-smile, not understanding. "You want it—"

The addict kicked out once and sent the man's helmet skittering along the gantry, where it spun and swirled a few times, taking it closer and closer to the edge until it disappeared over the side. The next kick took the man in the crotch, like the next kick and the one after it, each one delivered by the addict in quick succession with alternate feet.

The addict pulled his hand back, flexed the fingers into a right angle, and plunged the hand forward into the man's chest, a single jab. There was a dull crunch and the man coughed. He coughed again, dropped his weapon, and fell to his knees. The next cough brought up what looked like food and some pieces of splintered bone.

Lifting the weapon from the floor, the addict brought the butt down on the top of the man's head. The man was dead even before he fell face forward.

He wiped the blood in a long smear along the man's plastic coveralls and, after a quick inspection, flicked off the safety guard. The barrel hummed quietly.

He turned to the rail and quickly scanned the gantries in front of him. Nobody seemed to have noticed the scuffle. But he was still going to have to move quickly. He backed along the gantry until his back was against the wall. He was a little more sheltered here, safe from a casual glance by one of the people tending the stacks of paper. He crouched down to make his presence still harder to detect and turned to face the wall through which he had stepped just minutes earlier.

It was a simple destabilized molecular sheet. Although the outside had been treated to give the appearance of brickwork, the inside bore no such illusion—just a flat expanse grafted onto the real brickwork at either side. Fixed to the wall at the right was a small panel with four buttons. There was no writing on the panel.

The addict duck-walked to the panel and studied it.

Four buttons. Two red, one green, one black.

He shook his head. What was he thinking about? The color coding could mean anything, and time was already against him.

As if on cue, he heard a metallic voice talking through static.

The addict moved to the side of the rail and cautiously looked over. Just a few feet below, on a protruding stanchion, was the helmet. The voice was coming from inside. The addict knew it was asking about him.

He shuffled back to the panel, took a deep breath and pressed the green button.

Nothing happened.

He pressed one of the red buttons.

He almost dropped the weapon when the siren started. It whooped and wailed, so loud he could feel its vibrations in the metallic gantry beneath his feet. Somewhere behind him he could hear the sound of shouting voices, almost lost beneath the siren.

He pressed the black button.

The wall shimmered and became translucent. He could see shapes standing beyond it, outside on the street.

Then he pressed the other red button.

The siren stopped.

But the voices continued. And now he could feel other vibrations . . . running feet.

He span around as the first shape came through the wall, crouched down, gun at the ready. The shape looked down at him, just a glance, the black visored helmet nodding once, and then it moved forward, further along the gantry.

A second shape appeared, then a third and a fourth, each of them moving quickly to the side, computerized laser rifles primed and already sweeping the tiered gantry system for signs of movement.

A fifth shape handed the addict a telephonic headset.

A sixth dropped a rope and grapple at his feet and then moved forward.

The addict slipped the headset on. Immediately there were voices, voices shouting instructions . . . to get the ones on the ground first; the others had a long way to go. To watch out for anyone moving toward wall panels which could mean self-destruct instructions.

Then one voice said, "You okay, Reader One?"

He nodded, looking up at the shapes. He couldn't tell which one was asking the question.

"Then get down to ground level," the voice said. "Main office must be down there. They'll be aiming to get rid of it all. And when they do that, they'll do it from the ground."

The addict looked at the rail.

"We must preserve the pages," the voice added. "Jesus Christ, I have *never* seen so many as this." There was a pause and, turning back, the addict caught sight of a black shape standing just inside the wall, staring up and down, shaking its head. The figure fitted the grapple onto the rail and tossed the rope over the side; then it turned to face him and waved a hand.

"Go," the voice said.

The addict shouldered the strapped weapon and rolled over the edge, allowing his hands to slide down the rope as it swirled beneath his interlocked legs and feet.

Already the sound of the lasers was deafening, drowning out the voices from the headset. But it wasn't deafening enough to drown out the screams. Or maybe it was just that he knew they were there . . . could imagine what they sounded like.

He allowed himself to slide down.

As he passed each gantry tier, he slowed and stared at the piles.

So many sheets of paper. So many pages. So many millions and billions and trillions of words.

A shot hit the metal alongside him and he braced himself, expecting the man to get a better aim, trying to spin himself around and jam one foot onto the gantry to steady himself enough to be able to train his own weapon.

Halfway around, already swinging the rifle up to let off a few hopeful shots, the addict saw an overalled man burst apart as one of the lasers hit him from behind. The arm that bounced against the gantry to his side still held its weapon.

Through the smoke, covering his face against the smell of burned flesh, the addict saw the black shapes swinging across the gantries up above, ropes attached to the roof by suction pads. It was almost balletic. If it were a TAPped presentation, there would probably be music piped over the top of all the noise . . . the sounds of people shouting, people screaming.

People dying.

He let go of the rifle and felt it swing by his side as he let himself slide down to the floor.

He landed awkwardly, a few feet in front of a man in an overall punching the ammunition clip on his rifle. The man's head raised to look at him and the addict could see the eyes . . . just for a second.

They were filled with fear and with anger.

Then the head dropped down again as he declipped and then pressed it home again.

The addict lifted his weapon and fired. Twice.

The shots sent the man flying back along the corridor, bouncing against the gantry supports before skidding to a halt alongside the rear wall.

The addict crouched and followed.

The place was a maze of metal and smoke.

"How you doing, Reader One?" a tinny voice asked in his headset. It was not the voice he had heard earlier.

"On the ground," the addict shouted into the mouthmike.

"See anything?"

Something touched the top of his head, and he fell forward, spinning, bringing his weapon around. On the floor, his knees bent up against the gantry, he saw a sheet of paper flutter, side to side, until it landed, slithering beneath one of the supports.

When he looked up, he saw the rest of them.

The air was filled with sheets of paper, their surfaces covered in the spidery blackness of type. Some of them were burning, leaving tiny trails of smoke as they descended.

He grabbed at a sheet and shook out the flames, glancing at the words between the blackened edges of the page. It wasn't something he recognized, but the simple commitment of thoughts to paper, of the recording of opinions or beliefs or even complete fiction filled him with awe. The way it always did.

They had always hoped that one day they would find a stash like this one. They had hoped but had never dared believe.

He looked around and saw the black figures swinging down onto the ground level now. As he looked up the tiers, he saw other black figures on the edges of the gantry, their weapons readied but nobody to fire at. Several of these figures were already giving the all-clear.

It took them sixteen days to move all of the pages, filling the cavernous interior holds of the stripped-down water carriers, delivery modules, and old sky-buses before lifting off shakily into the sky to carry the pages to a hundred safe-houses scattered around the city.

Watchers were placed at street corners, upper-story windows and on rooftops for two square miles of the warehouse, each fitted with a mouthmike and a "lights out" implant in a rear tooth to be used in the event of capture. The operation went smoothly thanks to the fact that the warehouse was in a sector that nobody ever visited anymore. During the repeated pick

ups, the addict realized just how much of the city had
fallen into disuse. It was this fact that most depressed
him . . . perhaps even more than the criminalization
of reading: the fact that the city was somehow being
run down beneath their very eyes . . . turned into
something else.

This was why the organization had been necessary.
The People's Literation Society, a middle ground between the authorities which sought to suppress literature and the entrepreneurial pushers who sought to
benefit from the suppression. If asked, the addict
would have found it difficult to say who he despised
the most.

The first drop took place during a busy lunch pe-
riod, from an old delivery module that skirted the mo-
nolithic towers of the business district three times
before its load was dispatched. Then the module
slipped into and amidst the tiered traffic flows until it
was gone. Two Prowlcars arrived minutes later, by
which time the module was safely "home" and already
being dismantled, its telltale livery being replaced or
restructured or redesigned. The addict estimated they
"set free" more than half a million pages of around
three hundred to four hundred words a page.

The sheets released on that first drop fell from the
air onto the dirty streets and walkways of the city
like confetti.

A TAPper propped against a building side outside
a recreation brothel stooped to pick a sheet that had
brushed his bare legs. As he lifted it for a closer look,
another sheet landed to take its place. The sheet contained pages 69 and 70 of *The House at Pooh Corner*.
The TAPper frowned and studied the words, wondering just what, exactly, a "tigger" might be. When he
got to the end, he wanted to know more about Piglet
and about the blue braces of Christopher Robin (whoever *he* was). The boy scratched at the rash around his
cheek-studs and watched another sheet flutter down
toward him. Maybe that one would provide some

answers . . . or maybe he would have to search around—even ask around—until he found other sheets. . . .

A man wearing a banker's sarong picked up a sheet containing pages 175 and 176 of John Steinbeck's *The Acts of King Arthur,* glanced around nervously and then scrumpled the paper into his waist-pouch. Seconds later he was lost in the crowds watching the pages rain down upon the city, heading home where he could read in safety. He felt gloriously excited. A few steps farther along, he stopped and grabbed a fistful of sheets which he thrust after the first one. . . .

An old woman, bald and bearded, watched a sheet flutter through the gloom of the lower levels, watched it waft to and fro, easing itself finally onto a ledge just a few feet away from her. Maintaining her muttered conversation with herself, she abandoned the metal mallcart containing her entire life's belongings and retrieved the sheet—pages 85 and 86 of Jostein Gaarder's *Sophie's World*—and, returning quickly to her possessions, slipped it beneath a makeshift pillow whose stink of urine and sour breath she no longer noticed. The world had come back to her, suddenly, contained on a simple sheet of paper. The streets had been opened.

"What came first?" she asked a passing Hostess, reading from the paper and wagging her finger to the heavens. "The chicken or the 'idea' chicken?" The Hostess pushed her to one side and moved quickly to an elevator platform: she obviously didn't know the answer any more than the old bearded hobo woman. But as she stepped onto the platform and pulled the gate across, the Hostess went over what the old woman had said. . . .

High above the streets, two men leaned on the protective rails outside a middle-level nicotine store, watching.

"Snow," the addict said. "It's snowing."

"It's snowing seeds," the man beside him answered,

nodding. "The seeds will find accommodating soil, and they will be nurtured. They will find warmth and care and they will form roots and grow . . . grow into knowledge and curiosity and emotion." He pointed to a young man walking determinedly through the fluttering sheets without stopping. "Some, like him, will ignore what's happening. They will turn a blind eye—but only at first. Eventually even they will want—*need*—to know more. Those with a two-page sheet from *Moby-Dick* will want other sheets, more story . . . the same with those who have read—*lived*—brief moments from *Dracula* or *Oliver Twist* or *The Wind in the Willows*. They will want to read and to live other moments."

"And what if they can't find them?" the addict asked.

The other man shrugged. "Then they will construct their own stories inspired by the tastes they have received today. Thus has it ever been, thus will it ever be." He stared out across the city, turning his face to the gently wafting pages. "There can be no turning back. Not now."

"God, but I hope you're right," the addict said.

The man beside him smiled and said, in a loud, proud voice:

> " 'Scatter, as from an unextinguished hearth
> Ashes and sparks, my words among mankind.
> Be through my lips to unwakened earth
> The trumpet of a prophecy! O, Wind,
> If Winter comes, can Spring be far behind?' "

"Ah, Shelley," the addict said, nodding as he suddenly remembered the old order of the seasons. "Famous last words?"

His friend shook his head. "Prophetic *first* ones."

The sirens, when they began, did not sound frightening. They sounded afraid.

THEY'RE COMING TO GET YOU. . . .
ANTHOLOGIES FOR NERVOUS TIMES

☐ **FIRST CONTACT**   UE2757—$5.99
   Martin H. Greenberg and Larry Segriff, editors

In the tradition of the hit television show "The X-Files" comes a fascinating collection of original stories by some of the premier writers of the genre, such as Jody Lynn Nye, Kristine Kathryn Rusch, and Jack Haldeman.

☐ **THE UFO FILES**   UE2772—$5.99
   Martin H. Greenberg, editor

Explore close encounters of a thrilling kind in these stories by Gregory Benford, Ed Gorman, Peter Crowther, Alan Dean Foster, and Kristine Kathryn Rusch.

☐ **THE CONSPIRACY FILES**   UE2797—$5.99
   Martin H. Greenberg and Scott Urban, editors

We all know that we never hear the whole truth behind the headlines—let Douglas Clegg, Tom Monteleone, Ed Gorman, Norman Partridge and Yvonne Navarro unmask the conspirators and their plots—if the government lets them. . . .

☐ **BLACK CATS AND BROKEN MIRRORS**   UE2788—$5.99
   Martin H. Greenberg and John Helfers, editors

From the consequences of dark felines crossing your path to the results of carlessly smashed mirrors, authors such as Jane Yolen, Michelle West, Charles de Lint, Nancy Springer and Esther Friesner dare to answer the question, "What happens if some of those long-treasured superstitions are actually true?"

Prices slightly higher in Canada.   **DAW 215X**

Science Fiction Anthologies

☐ **FIRST CONTACT**
   Martin H. Greenberg and Larry Segriff, editors   UE2757—$5.99

In the tradition of the hit television show "The X-Files" comes a fascinating collection of original stories by some of the premier writers of the genre, such as Jody Lynn Nye, Kristine Kathryn Rusch, and Jack Haldeman.

☐ **RETURN OF THE DINOSAURS**
   Mike Resnick and Martin H. Greenberg, editors   UE2753—$5.99

Dinosaurs walk the Earth once again in these all-new tales that dig deep into the past and blaze trails into the possible future. Join Gene Wolfe, Melanie Rawn, David Gerrold, Mike Resnick, and others as they breathe new life into ancient bones.

☐ **BLACK MIST:** and Other Japanese Futures
   Orson Scott Card and Keith Ferrell, editors   UE2767—$5.99

Original novellas by Richard Lupoff, Patric Helmaan, Pat Cadigan, Paul Levinson, and Janeen Webb & Jack Dann envision how the wide-ranging influence of Japanese culture will change the world.

☐ **THE UFO FILES**
   Martin H. Greenberg, editor   UE2772—$5.99

Explore close encounters of a thrilling kind in these stories by Gregory Benford, Ed Gorman, Peter Crowther, Alan Dean Foster, and Kristine Kathryn Rusch.

Prices slightly higher in Canada.   **DAW 104X**

Buy them at your local bookstore or use this convenient coupon for ordering.

PENGUIN USA   P.O. Box 999—Dep. #17109, Bergenfield, New Jersey 07621

Please send me the DAW BOOKS I have checked above, for which I am enclosing $_____ (please add $2.00 to cover postage and handling). Send check or money order (no cash or C.O.D.'s) or charge by Mastercard or VISA (with a $15.00 minimum). Prices and numbers are subject to change without notice.

Card #_____ Exp. Date _____
Signature_____
Name_____
Address_____
City _____ State _____ Zip Code _____

For faster service when ordering by credit card call **1-800-253-6476**

Allow a minimum of 4-6 weeks for delivery. This offer is subject to change without notice.

OTHERLAND

TAD WILLIAMS

In many ways it is humankind's most stunning achievement.
This most exclusive of places is also one of the world's best
kept secrets, created and controlled by The Grail Brotherhood,
a private cartel made up of the world's most powerful and
ruthless individuals. Surrounded by secrecy, it is home to the
wildest of dreams and darkest of nightmares. Incredible
amounts of money have been lavished on it. The best minds
of two generations have labored to build it. And somehow,
bit by bit, it is claming the Earth's most valuable resource—
its children.

THE CATFANTASTIC ANTHOLOGIES
Edited by Andre Norton and Martin H. Greenberg

☐ **CATFANTASTIC** UE2355—$6.99

With fur fluffed and claws unsheathed, they stalk their prey or stand fast against their foes . . . with tails raised and rumbling purrs, they name and welcome their friends . . . with instincts beyond those of mere humans, they ward off unseen dangers, working a magic beyond our ken. . . . they are Cats, and you can meet them here in stories by C.S. Friedman, Mercedes Lackey, Elizabeth Ann Scarborough, and Ardath Mayhar, among others.

☐ **CATFANTASTIC II** UE2461—$6.99

Far more than nine feline lives are portrayed in this delightful romp along the secret ways known only to those incredible cats. With stories by Elizabeth Moon, Susan Shwartz, Nancy Springer, and Andre Norton, among others.

☐ **CATFANTASTIC III** UE2591—$6.99

SKitty, unflappable space traveler, makes a triumphant return, as does Hermione, who gives another detailed report on the serious duties of a respectable familiar. Join them and new feline friends in stories by Charles de Lint, Mercedes Lackey, Lyn McConchie, and Ardath Mayhar, among others.

☐ **CATFANTASTIC IV** UE2711—$5.99

Meet wizard's four-footed helpers, a feline with a most discerning taste in jazz, some Japanese cats talented enough to improvise a Noh play, among other fabulous felines in stories by Mercedes Lackey, Jane Lindskold, Elizabeth Ann Scarborough, and Andre Norton.

☐ **CATFANTASTIC V** UE2847—$6.99

Twenty-four sleek new tales about cats of the past, cats of the future, and cats only too ready to take matters into their own paws! Stories by Mercedes Lackey, David Drake, Barry Longyear, Ardath Mayhar, and others.

Kate Elliott

The Novels of the Jaran:

☐ **JARAN: Book 1**   UE2513—$5.99
Here is the poignant and powerful story of a young woman's coming of age on an alien world, where she is both player and pawn in an interstellar game of intrigue and politics.

☐ **AN EARTHLY CROWN: Book 2**   UE2546—$5.99
The jaran people, led by Ilya Bakhtiian and his Earth-born wife Tess, are sweeping across the planet Rhui on a campaign of conquest. But even more important is the battle between Ilya and Duke Charles, Tess' brother, who is ruler of this sector of space.

☐ **HIS CONQUERING SWORD: Book 3**   UE2551—$5.99
Even as Jaran warlord Ilya continues the conquest of his world, he faces a far more dangerous power struggle with his wife's brother, leader of an underground human rebellion against the alien empire.

☐ **THE LAW OF BECOMING: Book 4**   UE2580—$5.99
On Rhui, Ilya's son inadvertently becomes the catalyst for what could prove a major shift of power. And in the heart of the empire, the most surprising move of all was about to occur as the Emperor added an unexpected new player to the Game of Princes . . .